OUR SONG

KEITH WATERHOUSE

OUR SONG

Hodder & Stoughton
LONDON SYDNEY AUCKLAND TORONTO

Lyric of 'More I Cannot Wish You' from GUYS AND DOLLS by Frank
Loesser reproduced by permission of MPL Communications Limited

British Library Cataloguing in Publication Data
Waterhouse, Keith, *1929–*
   Our song.
   I. Title
   823'.914[F]

   ISBN 0 340 42501 6

Hodder and Stoughton Editorial Office: 47 Bedford Square, London WC1B 3DP.

OUR SONG

ONE

She thinks I'm writing a novel.

What else could I say? One of my abortive letters to you was insufficiently incinerated, the grate's ashes yielding the compromising fragment, *"You could be a right little cow sometimes, Angela."* Dialogue, I explained, at one bound getting out of a tight corner and providing an excuse for sitting at my desk far into the night with my thoughts about you.

Latitudinal thinking, as you would have called it. I miss you, Lady Malaprop.

Do you remember when I first called you that? No, of course you don't. It was our third or fourth visit to the Taverna – Our Restaurant as it should have been, had they brightened their ideas up a bit, or you not been such a fussychops. A bit pissed you were, and that sniffy head waiter, King Constantine of Greece as we'd dubbed him, even more patronising than usual. So when he corrected your order I insisted, haughty as they come, "No, Lady Malaprop asked for Torremolinos. Still, if you haven't heard of it, by all means let's have the taramasalata." You giggled, then asked, "Lady who?" Happy days.

I'm sorry the Taverna, or failing that Luigi's, didn't meet her ladyship's exacting standards. We never had an Our Restaurant, did we? – or, come to that, an Our Pub, an Our Wine Bar, an Our Hotel. We did have an Our Song, though, once, but you didn't know the tune.

Judith calls it a splendid idea, my fictitious novel. It'll be therapy, she said. So it will, but for a different trauma than the one she imagines. She wants me to show it to her agent. Can you imagine Nick Tearle's face as it dawns on him that he's one of my minor characters and his fling with my wife a fragment of sub-plot? But tempting though the prospect is, sooner or later the manuscript will have to go missing – left in a cab perhaps, no carbon copy, silly Roger. Or maybe I'll say I grew disgusted with it and threw it in the bin. And maybe I shall.

I'm not drowning, you know, not even waving – just treading

water after the splashdown from what's beginning to seem, in its retrospective unreality, like a sixteen-month mission to the planet Venus. At my age (fifty-two just a week ago – in the circumstances, I couldn't expect you to remember that now) the experience is shattering, bruising and the ultimate disillusion – but it isn't terminal. I know, I can tell, and not from wishing fears upon myself as you've always said I do but simply by putting our affair on the scales and comparing it with all the lightweight, short-weight, makeweight relationships I've had before, that you'll be with me now until my death. But you won't be the cause of it. Relax. This is the last and the longest letter I'll ever write you, my dear, so make the most of it. And you can take that pained little smile off your face – it's not a Jekyll and Hyde one as I used to call what you used to call my whingeograms. Not unless that's how you care to read it. It's a love letter. Therapy.

You were born, I once said (and you were not amused), with a silver cock in your mouth. My count on your ex-sleeping partners present at Tim's christening stands at half a dozen confirmed and two suspected, and none of them arrived in anything less than a Porsche. You missed your vocation, Angie. You should have been a full-time gold-digger like your friend Belle.

Given that they were all there with their wives or constant companions, your turning up must have created something of a frisson. Certainly it did with me – I'd never known anyone gatecrash a christening party before. And with Judith. I don't think I ever told you how closely I was cross-examined.

"Who's that extraordinary creature dressed all in black?"

"Angela Caxton? Oh, I suppose she's what you might call a freelance factotum."

"Is that what they're known as these days? Who brought her?"

"I don't think anybody did." You'd used a technique I remember from my LSE days, when we impoverished students would gatecrash PR thrashes at the Savoy to stoke up on their canapés. The trick is to saunter up and down for a while as if waiting for someone, wander in with eyes scanning the middle distance for the friend with the invitation who might just be there already, then mingle. Difficult to carry off in the garden of a private house, though less so than had the party been indoors. I wonder how our relationship would have got off the ground had Timothy been born in winter or christened in the pissing rain.

Judith didn't approve at all. "Did you invite her?"

"Certainly not."

"But she can't just have walked up the drive thinking, 'Hello, there's a party, I'll just wiggle in on my stiletto heels and help myself to a glass of champagne'?"

"From what I've heard, it's exactly the kind of thing she would do."

"And you'd find that amusing, would you? What does she think this is – Breakfast at Tiffany's?"

While I've always maintained that this was the afternoon I fell in love with you, the condition didn't immediately make itself known. At the time I shared Judith's irritation and some of her scorn. You know how wary I am of people who set themselves up as characters, hence my rudeness to that stage Irishman I found chatting you up at the Marquis of Granby (not the "absurd jealousy" you diagnosed), and anything approaching the kooky leaves me cold. And so I'm sorry, I had to agree with Judith when she said how absurd you looked on that boiling August day.

"Black dress, black stockings, black gloves, and that ridiculous black veil – do you suppose she meant to gatecrash a funeral and came to the wrong house?"

I didn't know then that the black outfit was your only set of what you called your dressing-up clothes. My heart was to lurch in pity (the first constituent of my love I was ever able to identify, though compassion would have been a politer word for it) when I first saw inside the cupboard that passed for your wardrobe, with its collection of Oxfam cast-offs and that row of dry cleaners' wire coat hangers waiting – not in vain, I'm glad to say – to get lucky. You didn't want me to see in that cupboard, did you, my love? But that was probably less to do with the pathetic scope of its contents, as you insisted, than with the tangle of men's neckties which you hoped I hadn't noticed among your jumble-sale heap of shoes. There must have been a dozen or so, I don't know: they'd gone the next time that cupboard door swung open of its own accord as it eccentrically did from time to time; and then you weren't in such a rush to close it.

I said to Judith, just to ingratiate myself and with no thought of being cruelly perceptive, that when women dress to startle it's usually because they lack confidence. I knew I was giving her a feedline and she didn't fail me. "It's more often because they lack taste. So come on, Roger – what does she want?"

Across the lawn I could see you animatedly chatting up my dandruff-speckled next-door neighbour – I wondered why: the bemused old devil talks about the encounter to this day. His wife marched across from the buffet to reclaim him, deflecting you with her glassy smile. You looked about you with an uncertain confidence, seeking more easy game. Some who had already been easy game turned away.

"I can only imagine she's meeting someone here," I said.

"It's Timothy's christening party, not a place of assignation. How does she come to know you, anyway? Or you her?"

"I hardly know her at all. We were introduced by Hugh Kitchener."

Luigi's. The first what-might-not-have-been of my collection. Charles Peck and I had set off for a quick bite at Sheridan's Oyster Rooms, but after ten minutes hanging around outside the agency for a taxi that wouldn't come, Charles said, "Oh, sod it, let's go across the road." What if a cab had turned up?

There were six of you, all moderately pissed by the time we came in for our late lunch. Hugh had just won that double-glazing account and it was an office celebration. I never was quite sure how you fitted into Kitchener Associates, Angie. Market research, you rather grandiosely claimed, but it seemed to me you were just doing a bit of summer temping. Anyway, it doesn't matter. There you were.

You were sitting between Hugh and that bearded Old Etonian – correction, Young Etonian, sod him – in graphics, who you rather wittily characterised as "Pont Street-wise", and who you told me was trying to touch you up under the tablecloth while you were giving me the eye. Trying? Since you had a cigarette in one hand and a glass in the other, he couldn't have been meeting much opposition unless you were fighting him off with your thigh muscles.

The first thing I noticed about you, of course, was your hair, like everybody else. Then the flattering fact that you were noticing me. Then your chocolate-box prettiness, mitigated by the liveliness of your countenance. Then your pealing laugh – always fractionally ahead of your companions, anxiously high-pitched, eager to please. I noticed that your glass hardly ever touched the table, except to be refilled. You were bringing your cigarette and your wine to your lips in jerky alternating gestures, one hand coming up as the other went down, marionette-fashion. I nodded benignly across at the company in general but you in particular and you smiled quickly, dazzlingly, back, then threw back your head and laughed at something Hugh had said, that was probably not very funny at all. You looked happy but euphorically on edge. The result, very possibly, of being groped under the tablecloth while looking over your next prospect.

You've asked me often enough what Charles made of that first eye-contact encounter and I've always waffled round it, not choosing to remember. In fact what he murmured as he perceived our glances interlocking like rutting deers' antlers was, "Roger, something tells me you're in with a very good chance of making a raging fool of yourself."

He was right as we both know, but prematurely so. He'd read your eye-signal correctly but not mine. Yours said, "You're going to be a notch on my bedpost." Mine said, "Afraid not, ducky, I'm just window-shopping." But I did like what I saw in the window.

Presently Hugh came across to our table to gloat over his double-glazing victory. We could have done with that account ourselves as you know, and had we got it . . . but there's another could-have-been. I can't believe I would never have met you but for that lunch at Luigi's – it was well on the cards that our paths would cross, if only, to be prosaic about it, that you were accessible in my small world. Who's to say, anyway, had the boot been on the other foot, with my own agency having the celebration lunch and Hugh Kitchener treating his associates and you to a consoling pasta, that we wouldn't still have locked glances?

But had we got the account, then Peck & Piper's fortunes might have taken a different turn, and that could have staved off the showdown between Charles and me, which in turn – but there I go again. How does your standing reproach go now? "Darling, why do you always have to look at our relationship in such an abtuse way, if there is such a word?" There isn't. There's abstruse, but you were having a crack at something between abstract and obscure, and you were right. Given the choice between the here-and-now and hypo-thesis, I would always settle for what I didn't have. It was rosier, in a melancholic, masochistic sort of way, to dwell on what life might be like without you than on what it would have to be like with you. I know now.

Though I was itching to ask Hugh Kitchener who you were I could see no way through the thickets of shoptalk and had just about given up when Charles brought you up purely as a diplomatic change of subject. We'd been indulging in some heavy-handed joshing about Hugh consorting with double-glazing cowboys, and tolerantly complacent though he could afford to be over landing his biggest account yet at our expense, I'm afraid it went on just one nose-tap and "Know what I mean, squire?" too many for his sense of dignity. Simply to de-ruffle his feathers Charles said: "By the way, Roger's dying to know who your red-haired little friend is?"

Hugh's reply was a pre-echo of mine to Judith in answer to the same question. "Ah, now Angie's our freelance factotum." But Hugh said it with a smirk, as if the expression were a synonym for office bicycle. Doubtless, to some, it was. They can't have known you'd coined the term yourself. I didn't like that smirk. Already, I was protective.

Introduced by Hugh Kitchener, I was to tell Judith. I hoped we should be. But after a few more minutes' chit-chat he returned to your table. There was a general scraping back of chairs as Hugh Kitchener settled his bill and your party prepared to break up. One or two were already ambling to the door and as you rose I thought you were going with them, but you were only off to the Ladies. I checked my small sigh of relief: probably you'd emerge from the loo and head straight out of the restaurant without a backward glance.

Charles and I addressed ourselves to our lunch. While I couldn't allow myself to keep craning my neck for the sight of you coming out of the Ladies, I did keep a covert eye on your empty place. You were hovering by our table before I realised you were back, the whiff of your perfume deflecting my attention from the forkful of cannelloni I now wished I hadn't been stuffing into my face as I saw you standing there, smiling like a friend.

You said, "As we've been pointed out to one another I thought I'd come over and say hello. I hope you don't mind." Charles and I lumbered to our feet, I eagerly, he reluctantly, suddenly an interloper at his own table. We introduced ourselves and you began to prattle at once. "Is Suzie still with you? Isn't she a love! She's one of my oldest friends so that must make us friends too." I didn't ask why you weren't aware that one of your oldest friends had married three months ago and now lived in Scotland. You took the news in your stride, burbling with a careless show of delight, "Oh, fantastic, I'm really glad, I must send her a present," and for the few seconds Suzie remained in your head you probably meant to.

You made Charles and me sit down, refusing to allow me to engage in a floundering attempt to fit another chair around our knee-to-knee table for two. Instead you knelt unselfconsciously on the tiled floor with your elbows on the edge of the table. "There. I'm your apostle, kneeling at your feet." "Disciple," I said. "I thought they were the same thing," you said.

I considered myself, at turned fifty, a little stiff in the cerebral joints for flirtatious banter. But with a bottle and more of Luigi's house white wine inside you, you prattled and burbled so easily that it was contagious. I tipped up my glass for you to sip from, and you made a comic performance of resting your chin on the table as you gurgled it down. I touched your hair, the colour of Oxford marmalade, and murmured a clumsy compliment you'd heard a thousand times before. "It needs washing," you said. The details I've forgotten from that day wouldn't tip a horizontally-balanced eggtimer.

Charles didn't take to your style at all, especially when the wine dribbled down your face and you said, pretending to sober up from giggling, "Oh dear, Charlie doesn't approve." No-one ever called him Charlie. You'll remember how stiff he was. Anxious to break the ice that was building up between the two of you as spontaneously and intuitively as warmth was generating between the two of us, he asked awkwardly, "Hugh tells us you're a freelance factotum, what does that mean exactly?" He got one of your forced, trilling laughs as you

12

backed off at once. "Oh dear, I often ask myself the same question," and you clambered quickly to your feet. I could tell you were feeling suddenly foolish. "Whatever it is, I really ought to go and do some more of it." Then, with a fleeting, flashing smile and an airy "Bye!", you were gone, instantly regaining your confidence as you followed the straggling rearguard of Hugh Kitchener's celebration party out of the restaurant with the self-assured, self-conscious sway of a woman used to being admired from behind.

And if you want to know what Charles said as you left Luigi's it was "That one's a little handful and no mistake" – and no, we didn't discuss you further, then or ever. Discounting the odd snide throwaway line, you remained indeed so much undiscussed, even when Charles and I parted company, that sometimes I wondered if he knew what was going on under his nose.

Back at the office, though, I did mention to our newish secretary Rosie, knowing she was as great a friend of her predecessor's as you claimed to be, that we'd come across you. "Lucky you," said Rosie drily. I said something about your being a big friend of Suzie's and she said, significantly or so it seemed to me, "I wouldn't say friend. I suppose they used to see one another in the Corkscrew sometimes, but anyone who uses the Corkscrew has to come across Angela sooner or later. She practically lives there." This went into the file I hadn't quite yet realised I'd opened on you.

Rosie, comfortably married with a home to go to in Sydenham or somewhere, didn't approve of the Corkscrew – no-one ever did who didn't call it by its nickname, the Screw. She didn't approve of you either, my love. No woman ever did who called you by your full name, Angela, and those who didn't were few. But with Rosie as with Charles, you were never a subject of discussion – except, for all I knew (or cared), with one another. Even when you were ringing me up three times a day and, should I chance to be engaged or with a client, having long burbling chats with Rosie as if she too were your best friend, she never brought your name up.

By and by I began to notice how this was a common reaction, or lack of reaction rather, from those who knew you. It was unsettling, disturbing, as if there were a conspiracy of silence surrounding you – not protective but wary. It seemed that the more people knew I was involved with you, the less inclined they were to be drawn on the subject of you. I remember once meeting you for a quick drink at the Marquis of Granby before you had to dash off and meet Belle for supper, or so you said. After you'd gone and I was finishing my gin, one of those chaps one knows yet doesn't know, a young copywriter I think, came over and asked, "Wasn't that Angela Caxton?" I gave him his answer, expecting some follow-up, however superficial. He merely nodded his head a number of times, as if assimilating a piece of technical information, and drifted back to his group at the bar, the flashiest and youngest of whom turned imperceptibly and looked me up and down. I've had that type of encounter three or four times and never known what to make of it. By rights, you should have been the kind of woman who gets talked about. Instead, you were the kind of woman everyone shuts up about.

The Corkscrew, well-abbreviated as the Screw, was never one of my haunts. At lunchtime, when it was but one more overcrowded wine bar, it was just about bearable, though having my quiche passed along to me shoulder-high by a chain-gang of junior account executives was not my idea of the good life. Between six and eight it was a hellhole. I would sooner have spent the Happy Hour in a disco.

So when I found myself heading for the Screw that evening, despite having been warned that Nick Tearle was coming for dinner so I'd better present myself at Ealing Church Grove prompt, presentable and reasonably sober, I was entitled to ask myself what I thought I was up to.

My love, I had no idea. You'd been on my mind in a blow-hot-blow-cold sort of way all afternoon. One minute I'd be indulging myself in juvenile lustful fantasies, stoked up to fever point by the near-certain conviction that if I propositioned you I should not get No for an answer; then I'd take a pendulum-swing back into prudery, adapting Groucho Marx's maxim to tell myself that I wouldn't want to sleep with anyone who'd have me as a one-night stand. I asked you once if that's what you had in mind, at that time. You answered, as you answered so many of my questions, "I don't know," adding, "I never used to think as far ahead as tomorrow in those days. I daren't think beyond next week even now." Upon which I was the one to change the subject.

I wasn't, to be honest, thinking very much further than tomorrow myself at the time. Hopefully you'd be in the wine bar and not too embroiled in that seething mass of middle-league media types to deny me the chance to buy you a drink and extend our acquaintanceship a little. I'd already decided to invite you to lunch – again (and this was intuition, not arrogance) I'd absolutely no doubt that you'd accept, and I'd given myself the pleasure of racking my brains for just the right venue. That's right – Le Bistro, yet another candidate for Our Restaurant had you not subsequently thown one of your tantrums there. (Something else I might take on as therapy if this letter doesn't do the trick is to go through Gunby T. Gunby's *Good Living Guide* and put a red cross against all the places I may consider myself barred from because you've made a scene there.) But where lunch would lead to I didn't conjecture, except on a fantasy level when we finished up at a certain flat in Fulham – a location borrowed from my one and only previous liaison in my thirteen years with Judith. But you were so incurious about my brief seven-year-itch fling with Anita, the Merry Widow of McIntyre, Pike & Lipton that I was quite offended. You had very little to be retrospectively jealous about but you might at least have put on a show of prudent interest.

The Screw, halfway through the two-hour Happy Hour, was as usual swilling over with the flotsam and jetsam of the agencies – medallioned creative artists in designer jeans and dark glasses, bearded layout men, scruffbags from the Wardour Street cutting rooms, all with their attendant Debbies and Sandras, a smattering of velvet-collared account executive Hurrah Henries with their Sloanes. I couldn't see you anywhere. I fought for a drink and squeezed myself into a corner with a coat-hook sticking into my neck. As always on the three or four times I'd been lured into the Screw, I felt old and grey and nondescript in my Austin Reed suit and St Michael check shirt. A pre-lunch gin and tonic, a bottle of wine shared with Charles in the ratio of my two glasses to his one, a large Armagnac and the euphoria of meeting you had left me not entirely sober. What might otherwise have been a quick wave of depression refused to lift, and I began to get maudlin.

As well as a Happy Hour for the up-and-comings in the agency game, the Screw would have done well to have had an Unhappy Hour when middle-aged, middle-rung types like myself could brood about being neither successes nor failures. If you can't even fail successfully, I remember chuntering to myself with gin tears prickling my eyeballs, what can you do?

I'm afraid I forgot you completely as I went into one of my whither-Piper spins. I was in for a boring evening at Judith's little dinner party for her pushy literary agent and an assortment of social spare parts: the prospect gave me just the emotional drop I needed to arrive at the conclusion that I was leading a pretty boring life. Obviously, that was what must have led me to the Screw that night; but I didn't make the connection, not just then.

I felt like a dud battery – no spark left, if there'd ever been any. Charles Peck and I and Hugh Kitchener had quit McIntyre, Pike & Lipton on the same day eight years earlier. We'd talked for a year about starting our own agency. At the last moment Hugh pulled out and said he wanted to go solo. He was right. I was forty-two, Charles was forty coming on fifty, while Hugh was barely into his thirties. From wanting our experience and expertise he suddenly switched to not wanting two ageing albatrosses round his neck, and who could blame him? Hugh set up on his own and shot ahead – Charles and I pottered along, trawling the occasional big fish in our small pond but usually catching minnows or worse, grey mullet. On my fiftieth birthday we landed the account for Chambers' Sanitaryware. I got so monumentally staggering pissed that Charles had to drive me home because no cab would take me. He didn't mind in the least: he thought I was celebrating. Poor Charles. Poor me. My mental scenario, which that night I mentally tore up, had had it that by fifty I would be buying up Charles's half of the business, selling out to J. Walter Thompson and joining their board.

And it had had me living in the stockbroker belt with two children by now at private school and Judith giving swish dinner parties to woo potential clients, and writing her cookery stuff as a well-paid hobby. Well, Ealing isn't Tower Hamlets I suppose, but it isn't Virginia Water either. Improved, the place is worth quadruple what we gave for it but it was Judith's cookery articles and books, not the likes of Chambers' Sanitaryware, that paid for the conservatory and all the other frills. It never crossed my mind, when Charles decanted me on the porch to an extremely frosty reception from Judith, that she had as much reason to be disenchanted as I had. Her stuff sold, but it was never going to be in the best-seller class and she knew it. Her column, syndicated to regional newspapers, was never going to be snapped up by Fleet Street or the women's mags. She had a husband who got home half-cut every night and fully-cut when she'd prepared him a special birthday supper. And – the big and – we couldn't make a family between us, or so we thought. But that night of my fiftieth birthday piss-up – it can only have been that night, though God knows how because you know how easily I fall prey to Brewer's Droop – our luck changed.

Had you pressed me, and you never did, I should have had to admit that up to the day that Timothy's imminence was announced I was subconsciously or subliminally half-hankering for an affair. It was an idea slowly forming, like the foetus inside Judith. I had no one in mind and nowhere in mind to go and find whatever I might have been looking for – certainly not the Corkscrew. Perhaps nothing would have happened, perhaps I might have had a brief fling with another Merry Widow and got it over with for another seven years, perhaps I should have found an alternative and more premature way of making a fool of myself in Charles's eyes. But Timothy came along and saved me for my Lady Malaprop. Another might-not-have-been.

I can't remember how much of this Roger Piper This Is Your Life stuff was going through my mind when I came looking for you in the Screw, but I know I was feeling pretty sorry for myself. The two

16

denim-clad types wedged up against me with their glasses of house dry, their eyes darting like those of predatory, swooping birds as they scanned every angle of the wine bar for talent, looked young enough to be my nephews, yet they were comparing notes on location shoots in the Bahamas. The furthest I'd ever been on Peck and Piper was Leeds. You were nowhere to be seen and the place was hot and stinking of cheap scent and expensive aftershave. I decided to have one more gin and tonic and leave.

I suppose I had never properly taken in the Corkscrew scene before. One fuzzy, panoramic glance across the wasps' nest of bobbing heads and waving hands was enough to persuade me that it was not for the likes of me. Now, ploughing towards the bar with the resolve that should I find a place to put my glass down first I would swim for the stairs and head for a quiet one at the Marquis of Granby, I quite suddenly got the place into sharp focus.

It was a sexual inferno I was in, a seduction scene in a hall of mirrors. Every reaching hand touched flesh, every gesture had its secret meaning, every mane of golden hair tossed back was an invitation, every sleeve stroked an acceptance. Eyes met, looks coupled in a visual embrace, fingers brushed then locked in a dovetail grasp, arms encircled shoulders as if on a dance floor. A dance, indeed, was what it was, though nobody could move above six inches on either side. The men, posturing, swayed struttingly, the girls, pouting, swayed sensuously. They were dancing to the music of their own voices. Every word or fragment of conversation I could make out in that orchestrated babble seemed to have its sexual connotation, every laugh was provocative, every smile a tease. I thought I recognised your laughter, the same slightly forced, wanting-to-please laugh I'd heard in Luigi's that lunchtime, though pitched higher; then it was lost in the crashing waves of sound, and then I caught a flash of marmalade-coloured hair, and then I saw you.

You were with the bearded Kitchener Agency graphics type you'd been sitting next to at lunch, the one I christened The Fuzz because I never knew his name and you always professed not to be able to remember it. Little realising that he was the future subject of an amusing anecdote revolving around his clumsy attempts to goose you under the tablecloth, he was confidently steering you towards the stairs, one hand on your shoulder, the other gripping your arm. The gesture was so proprietorial, and you were so compliant, that he might have bought you in a sale – a slave auction perhaps. Twice you turned back to him: once to give him a conspiratorial smile and a look that was a visual sigh of impatience at the slowness of your progress towards his bed or yours – you never told me which – and once when you were brought to a complete stop by a conga line of new arrivals snaking towards the bar. You were very drunk, your face shiny, your flaming hair tumbled. He was sober, calculatingly so it seemed to my jaundiced eye. His thoroughbred though fashionably loose-lipped good looks would have impressed a model agency but to me he looked a public school lout who would pee in your sink. I wondered at your taste in men. The hand on your shoulder travelled to your neck and pulled your laughing face towards his. Your lips met in a fleshy kiss, and then you were laughing again, raucously now, as you pulled away. It fitted very well into the tableau, went with the overall mood of careless degeneracy. It was a moment fixed in the preservative of scent and cigarette smoke and sweat that hung cloyingly in the air like the sweet decaying smell of an Arab souk. You moved on.

You've always fallen asleep during old movies in hotel rooms, so you never saw the end of *Brief Encounter* where Celia Johnson sits at her husband's feet and he pats her like an old sheepdog and tells her she's safely back from a long journey. I hadn't been anywhere at all, only down the alley to the Corkscrew, but quite suddenly as I watched the pair of you threading your way up the stairs, your hand now tugging his as you reached the half-landing, I had a yearning to be home in Ealing, sitting in a chintz armchair with the evening paper and a glass of sherry, and somehow, without confessing that I had really nothing to confess, giving Judith the reassurance that wherever I had been, I was back. I gave you a few minutes and then got out of the Screw, the only man in the place craving for the clean taste of Ovaltine.

When finally we had our first lunch you harked back, as I did, to that day, but neither of us to that evening. You made a funny narrative of how The Fuzz had run after you to the office lift in his eagerness to invite you to the Kitchener celebration lunch, how he had contrived to sit next to you at Luigi's and how you had thwarted his under-the-table explorations with the deflatory remark, "I hadn't realised you were left-handed." The whole point of the story being how his strenuous advances came to nothing, you didn't spoil it by confessing that a few hours later they were to come to a good deal; nor, since you didn't yet know me, was there any reason why you should. But I did wonder why you bothered to tell it. For my part, though I'd already mentioned having been into the Screw looking for you, I said nothing about having seen you there. I'd joined the conspiracy of silence.

For the time being, anyway. The subject did come up, but not until many months later. We were half-watching a soft porn movie on a hotel TV in, I think, Leicester, when you threw off a remark about how offputting you would find it to be kissed by a man with a beard. "What about The Fuzz?" I couldn't help asking. At first you affected not to remember him, then you denied ever having slept with him, then when I confessed to having seen you together at the Screw that night, you became angry and accused me of spying. I was angry too, at myself as much as at you, for allowing myself to be manipulated by your evasions and manoeuvrings into reacting like a jealous adolescent. I hadn't wanted to listen to myself ploddingly question you but my curiosity was aroused now and I had to press on.

"So where were you going that night? His place or yours?"

"I can't remember. I was very pissed."

"But you did sleep with him?"

"It's a year ago, Roger. I was very different then, a different person. You've changed my whole outlook."

"So you did?"

"I don't know. If I did it wasn't important enough to remember."

"But you remember everything else about that day."

"Not all of it. Haven't you ever had alcoholic ambrosia?"

I've had alcoholic amnesia, darling, if that comes to the same thing. But not moral amnesia. Some things you genuinely forgot, but some you forgot on purpose.

"Anyway," you went on, sulky now, "why does it matter, when it was before I met you?"

"But it wasn't quite, it was on the actual day you met me."

"Before I started seeing you, then. Why is it important to you?"

"Well it isn't, except that you made a long comic story out of how you'd rebuffed him, when there was no need for you to bring the subject up at all."

"It was because I didn't want you to have a bad impression of me. I didn't want you to know I'd gone off with him that night."

"But if I hadn't seen you together in the Screw I shouldn't have known anything about it. And given that I *did* see you, then of course your story didn't hold water. So there was no point in telling it either way."

"Can we drop it now, Roger?"

"We can drop it whenever you like, but why did you first say you hadn't slept with him, then that you couldn't remember whether you had or not, then that the only reason for that cock-and-bull story was – "

"Roger, I'm going to have a bath."

I'll never know why I let myself in for those arguments. It was like swimming in glue. Afterwards, my head spinning, and knowing I'd got nowhere nor was I ever likely to, and wondering where it was I wanted to get to anyway, I'd feel like a bullying pedagogue. And it was all so futile. What it came down to was that we'd arrived at one another from different sexual planets. I should have had the sense, at my age, to leave it at that. But my age, compared with your very

19

young twenty-eight, was one of the problems. Or yours was, as I maintained in my more self-defensive moods.

It was on a Tuesday that I first went looking for you in the Screw. I gave it a miss the next evening, and the next. I'd somewhere gone off you, to tell the truth, Angie. It turned out that a couple of our bright young copywriters had spotted me down there – much to my surprise, since I'd imagined myself to be a middle-aged fly on the wall – and they joshed me about it, affecting to disbelieve that I had just gone in for a drink. Surely I must know that the Screw was notorious as the one place thereabouts "where you can score any night of the week", or as one of them alliteratively put it, "where groupies gather"? And so on, their nudges now spawning lurid anecdotes, though none of them featuring, thank God, a girl with red hair.

Common sense told me to leave it at that, but in the restless mood I was in common sense irresistibly personified itself into the priggish Mr Littlechap figure we had dreamed up years ago in a disastrous Fibre Flakes campaign – pinstriped, pipe-smoking, and looking a bit like Charles. I couldn't stop asking myself what I had let myself out of. On the Thursday I lunched alone at Luigi's, in the slender hope you'd be there even if it had to be with The Fuzz. I'd say hello as I passed your table but otherwise I'd leave the first move, if there was to be one, to you, and if none were forthcoming then that would be that.

You weren't there, of course. You'd finished your stint at the Kitchener Agency so I couldn't ring you there (I tried). They weren't going to give out your number to someone who in a fit of blustering panic declined to give his name, and you weren't in the phone book. I could have looked for you in the Screw on Thursday evening but the prospect profoundly depressed me and I went into a Mr Littlechap phase. But when Friday came and the weekend loomed with its vista of Mr Littlechap activities like mending the baby alarm and drinks with the neighbours, I weakened again.

Wives get it wrong. It's supposed to be sex alone that draws men like me into situations like the one I was angling for. It isn't, it's the excitement. And it isn't the excitement of the chase, it's the excitement of having someone to be excited about. They're wrong, too, in waiting complacently for the bloom to fade. It doesn't, or never did with me. In the sixteen months we had, you exasperated, infuriated, offended, disappointed, depressed, alienated, saddened, wounded, even disgusted me, but never bored me for a second. There was never a moment when my heart didn't lift at the thought of you, never a rendezvous when my pulse didn't beat faster the nearer I got to you. Could there be any chance of seeing you now, tonight, after all I've been through with you and however badly you've behaved, I should count the minutes as eagerly as I did towards that hoped-for Friday evening encounter at the Corkscrew.

Bracing myself for the seething hellfire caves I'd stumbled into earlier in the week, I was surprised, not to say relieved, to find the Corkscrew almost empty. I should have realised, and so should you, that Friday is traditionally the day when the advertising profession doesn't come back from lunch. You were quite wistful about the absence of familiar faces when I subsequently touched on it. You said it made you feel as if everyone had gone to a party and left you behind. As I got to know you better I learned that that was how life in general made you feel.

You were sitting by yourself at a corner table, nursing a glass of wine and flipping through a dog-eared copy of *Cosmopolitan*. I can't say you came over as the woman projected by *Cosmo*'s image survey. Your dark glasses were pushed up over your head in the approved style, but they had the air of a prop in a dressing-up game. You wore the same black skirt I'd seen you in at Luigi's on Tuesday, a white lacey blouse far too wispy to support the chunky Covent Garden boutique jewellery that was all you had in those days – the bunch of cherries, I think – and scuffed blue patent leather shoes. The hem of your skirt had come unstitched. I stood at the bar regarding you – you hadn't seen me come in. You looked lonely, waif-like and forlorn. My stomach lurched. I ordered a bottle of house champagne and carried it across to your table.

Waif-like or not, you accepted champagne with the blasé air of one who regularly bathed in it, while being suitably gushing about how marvellous, fantastic and wonderful it was of me to produce it for you, and how marvellous, fantastic and wonderful it was to see me. Your surprise seemed simulated. You so much had the air of having been sitting there waiting for me to turn up that I almost apologised for being late.

I asked you how the freelance factotumising was going on. You said oh, it was so-so at this time of year. I guessed it was so-so at any time of year. The little black jacket slung over your plastic handbag was shiny at the elbows. The copy of *Cosmo*, I saw, had a Kitchener Agency distribution sticker on its cover, and it was last month's.

Then, on the second glass, I asked you what exactly it was you did, expecting the same flip non-answer you had given Charles. Instead you replied very seriously: "I try to remain self-employed – that about sums it up. Apart from working in biscuit factories and things when I was supposedly reading history at York, I've only ever had a job for a year and I hated it. But not having one is a full-time job in itself."

I confess I was only half listening as you launched into what was evidently a well-rehearsed, much-told, anecdotal account of life among the Sloanes at the Chelsea Auction Galleries during that stray working year. Never mind: you were to tell it to me all over again, forgetting you had already done that particular party piece for me; and both times you missed out the not unimportant detail that it was there you met the lover who was to come between us, or as you would have it, between me with my stupid jealousy and my allowing myself to love and be loved.

I was studying you, card-indexing you, or trying to. Downwardly mobile middle-class voice – Daddy may have been a lieutenant-general but your bedsitter accent had him demoted to major. The famous marmalade hair, at close range, looked what I was to describe as slept-in. Joke, darling: I only meant that the tousled effect owed nothing to the hairdressing salon. And also at close range, I thought I could detect a touch of the hard centre in the chocolate-box face (though it didn't stop you exuding soft centre sex). But I couldn't categorise you. There was no-one you reminded me of, no social pigeonhole I could slot you into. You were, as I'd already decided during that brief meeting at Luigi's, a one-off. So there was no standard formula for the chemical reaction I was experiencing. It was not that I fancied redheads, or was drawn to overtly feminine women or very funny ones (I've always found both categories rather tiresome, as a matter of fact). In the words of an old song before your time (no, not Our Song), it had to be you. Cheap music, as well as being potent, makes good points.

You were talking about the various jill-of-all-trades part-time jobs you'd done after your stint at the Galleries: historical research, market research, street-corner consumer questionnaires, classified ads telephonist, a bit of temping. Your career seemed to have followed a downward graph. Acknowledging as much you concluded: "It's an up and down life, though I must admit there've been fewer ups lately. So if you do ever hear of anyone looking for a freelance factotum it'd be lovely if you'd put a word in." I said I'd keep my ears open. You went on, throwing the question away between sips of champagne, "I suppose you're not looking for anyone in that line at Peck & Piper?"

So was that all you wanted me for? I couldn't be absolutely sure then and I can't be absolutely sure now – I'm not talking about what we subsequently became to one another – because I never tested the question. Despite the let-down feeling at the realisation that you were angling for work, I swallowed the bait at once. I heard myself saying recklessly, "Peck & Piper, alas no. But I do need some research doing on a project of my own that might interest you."

My famous survey on the teenage market for that non-existent seminar in Harrogate. I know it remained a sore point with you, my love, but your background material wasn't totally wasted – all right, it was, given that it just went straight into a filing cabinet; but I really did have it in the back of my mind to profile the teenage consumer, and the stuff is presumably still there for anyone at Peck Associates, as the old firm now styles itself, who cares to dig it out. And more importantly, it did get us to Harrogate.

"Mm – *love* to," you said at once (there were a lot of italics in your speech) when I suggested lunch to discuss what I wanted you to do. Confident though I'd been that you'd say yes, I wondered now whether you'd have accepted with such alacrity had there not been a money-earning proposition attached. An unworthy thought, perhaps. And when it came to pinning you down, you couldn't have been more elusive.

No, you couldn't make Monday, you had to see "some people". Tuesday was not good for me, Wednesday was no good for you – your dentist this time. Thursday I had a pencilled-in lunch with I forget who but I was happy to cancel – no, you had an appointment with your bank manager and couldn't change it. You ran a finger down the page of your diary to Friday, which from the corner of my eye I could see was blank except for a scribbled initial.

"No, sorry," you said, "Friday's a complete write-off. I have to have lunch with Cheevers."

That was the first time you ever mentioned his name (and you would have been hard put to have mentioned it much earlier). No forename, no explanation as to who he was or why lunch with him was seemingly compulsory. I didn't ask, wasn't then even curious. I said with a sigh of impatience, "Then that takes us into the following week."

Swirling half an inch of champagne around your glass with what struck me as self-conscious pensiveness, you said: "That's if next weekend is a no-go area so far as you're concerned. I'm free on either day, but I expect you have family and things?"

After the blanks I'd been drawing, I felt absurdly cheered up at the brassy implication – proposition, even – that though I was obviously a married man, weekends would be all right with you if they were all right with me. But of course weekends were not all right, particularly the one you'd suggested. I told you about Timothy's christening, and you burbled a great deal about how super and fantastic and marvellous it was and how terrific and wonderful I must feel on having become a father at fifty. By the time you'd finished congratulating me I felt ninety.

I poured the last of the champagne. It was getting on for seven and Judith had me down for one of the innumerable social engagements she was determinedly keeping up after the birth of the baby.

23

Transferring my briefcase from floor to lap to signal that it was time to drink up and leave, I said, "How about Wednesday week, then?"

Without consulting your diary again you said, "Oh, I can't even begin to think that far ahead. Besides, if you really do want me to do some research for you, I wouldn't mind getting down to it as quickly as poss. Why don't we have a drink one evening early next week and then we can take it from there?"

The bureaucracy involved in starting an affair is incredible. It took another fifteen minutes to arrange a rendezvous on Monday – same time, same place, unless either of us gave backword. Hurriedly we exchanged numbers – my office one, your Banks Place number. Islington: mentally I planned the tube map route back to Ealing. As you said to me in recounting the saga of how you found your way to the house to gatecrash the christening, why do people always live so far away?

Monday came and you didn't turn up. I rang you and got your Answerphone. You never called back. It was puzzling because I'd offered you some work and you'd given me the impression that you needed the money. I went into the Screw once or twice but there was no sign of you. I called your number again but this time you'd forgotten, or omitted, to connect your Answerphone as you so often did. I began to feel foolish at having quite elaborately concocted an assignment – for by now I'd drawn up a briefing that would keep you busy for a good four or five days – that you clearly didn't wish to pursue, just as you clearly didn't wish to pursue me or to be pursued by me. I felt flat. I thought about you, about that effervescent meeting with you when I touched your hair, about the easy intimacy of drinking champagne with you, then about seeing you carried off out of the Screw like so much plunder, then I wrote you off.

It was Charles who noticed you first. He'd left a christening mug for Timothy in his car and as he went down the drive to recover it he saw you coming along Ealing Church Grove like, as he put it, "the Mona Lisa in one of those paintings by Carel Weight." But you don't know Carel Weight. The day I planned to take you to the Summer Exhibition after lunch, you wanted another bottle, and then we had another row, and then you stormed off. He paints leafy suburban scenes which are cosily reassuring in their familiarity until you peer into the dappled foliage when you see a ghost flitting by. I can imagine that glimpse of you through the trees with the sunlight filtering through the leaves to catch your marmalade hair and white skin set all in black.

I've said that although Charles never asked about you, he was not above the odd snide comment. This, in those early days, was one of his more overt asides: "And did you ask your little friend to come as the spectre at the feast, or was that her idea?" I snickered perfunctorily, feeling disloyal to you in my embarrassment. I'd felt a variety of emotions as I saw you teetering round the corner of the house and across the lawn on those absurdly high heels that always reminded me of a little girl dressing up – first, the simple, uncomplicated excitement at seeing you again that I always felt from start to finish; then pleasurable surprise at your initiative in finding out where I lived and the trouble you must have put yourself to in trekking across London on a hot day; then, arising out of that, the instinctive panic, though as yet I had little to feel guilty about, of a married man whose mistress has turned up on the doorstep. Of these, the pleasurable sensations were uppermost but I have to admit that embarrassment and concern were significant ingredients.

You were immediately at home yet not at home. Locating me at once across the lawn but affecting not to, in case whoever the woman was I was chatting to – Charles's wife Lucille I believe – should turn out to be Judith, you gave a neutral little wave as to a none-too-near acquaintance at the vicarage garden party, and tripped across to the buffet, conscious I know that practically every eye was upon you, though I suppose a good half dozen heads – I didn't notice at the time – must have swivelled ever so casually away to avoid meeting your eager, inviting glance.

That trained freeloader Gunby T. Gunby won the scramble to help you to champagne. I could see you responding to his chit-chat vivaciously, gratefully, before he peeled himself away, perhaps put off by your over-friendly, almost kittenish, demeanour. At least I know that's the effect you've often had on women, and Gunby is nothing if not an old woman. He did it the polite way, though, palming you off on my next-door neighbour before waddling off. Then your new admirer, who would surely have had a heart attack if you'd fluttered your eyes at him much longer, was reclaimed by his wife and you were momentarily alone, looking suddenly so much out of it in your unsuitable clothes that you reminded me of an urchin with its nose pressed against a pastrycook's window. You looked again in my direction but Judith had joined me and commenced her grilling. I wanted so much to draw you in. In what must have been plaintive desperation you started to talk to Ingrid, the new Danish au pair girl, who was equally at sea. Sensibly you drew her towards the buffet for more champagne and at once you were lost in a scrum of instant Angela-worshippers.

You would not come over until Judith had gone off to greet some new arrivals, her last word (for the moment) being "Well no-one can say she isn't conspicuous by her presence." One anxious eye on Judith as she retreated towards the drive, I came forward to meet you, only to be left standing in the middle of the lawn as you impetuously tripped across to embrace Charles, flinging your arms around him with a shriek of pleasure and kissing him on both cheeks as if he were a long-lost lover. With a plate of chicken salad in each hand, he had great difficulty in disentangling himself.

Was that how you greeted the half dozen or so present who really had been your lovers? Had I then known who they were I should have taken more notice. Hugh Kitchener, I do recall, smartly side-stepped when he saw you approaching – I thought it was your appearance, rather than your presence, that embarrassed him. I saw you talking animatedly to that PR creep Tom Whiting and his sidekick Jerry Passmore, who I now wish I had thrown out since like you he hadn't been invited (a prurient thought, Angie: did you get a kick out of gossiping to two ex-bedfellows at the same time?) but there was no physical contact. I don't know about the others. It doesn't matter.

Certainly you didn't embrace me. After your performance with Charles, your formal handshake must surely have aroused Judith's suspicions had we been in her field of vision just then. I was quite flattered, choosing to believe that you thought you were being discreet.

"Angela, what a lovely surprise!" The first time I'd ever used your name. I don't think you noticed.

You gave that injured little laugh I came to know so well, the one you always used when I caused you real or imagined or feigned offence. "Surprise or shock? I knew I shouldn't have come. Shall I go?"

I noticed that even as you made the offer you held out your half-empty glass for the roving waiter to dispense more champagne.

"No, of course you shan't go, you've only just arrived."

"But quite obviously uninvited. Some of your friends are looking at me daggers."

"They're admiring you or envying you, according to sex. And of course you're invited – if I'd had your address I should've sent you a card," I lied, adding with a not altogether drummed-up air of grievance, "In fact had you managed to turn up on Monday I'd brought one along for you."

"Oh, I'm *sorry* about that, Roger." The first time you'd ever used *my* name – and I certainly did notice. I experienced an absurd, exaggerated frisson of delight out of all proportion to the moment. "And for not returning your call, but I did want to get as much done as I could on your samovar thing – samovar? seminar – while I had a completely free week." With this you were floundering about in your handbag, shedding keys, cigarette packet, cheque book and a trail of screwed-up tissues as you delved for a sheaf of folded, closely typed A4.

Had I not, when I leafed through it, recognised your prime source as a *Marketing Week* survey which had been published only three weeks before, and which indeed was what had planted the thought of researching teenage buying patterns in the first place, I should have been more impressed than I was. What did impress me, though, was your initiative in preparing the document at all without any briefing, and I said as much.

"That's because I like working for you," you said simply. The afterglow of this seductively unexpected confession was such that I didn't care to question its substance – much less ask myself why enjoyably working for me should have prevented you from meeting me for a drink or at the very least from answering my call.

But I did, like a fool, hark back to the question somewhat later in our relationship, when you at once got on your high horse:

"I thought you were pleased to see me at Timothy's christening party. Are you saying now you were making that up?"

"Angie, it's nothing to do with the christening party. We had an arrangement to meet up in the Screw when I was going to brief you – "

"You mean I didn't do the work properly?"

"We're not talking about the work either, we're talking about you not turning up that evening."

"But I told you, I was busy doing your research. I went all the way out to the British Newspaper Library at Colindale, if you want to know. I wanted to get it done and present it to you so that you'd be pleased with me."

"So busy that you couldn't ring me?"

"My Answerphone wasn't working."

"But you don't make calls with your Answerphone, Angie."

"No, but it wasn't picking up messages, so how could I know you'd rung?"

"You *did* get my message, Angie. You apologised for not replying to it."

"Because I was *busy*. I've told you – I was busy all week."

That must have been the first of those frustrating circular arguments we ever had, where I would feel like a dog chasing its own tail and invariably got so utterly nowhere that I wondered afterwards why I'd started it in the first place.

"Angela, I was very grateful to you for preparing that paper and for fetching it out to me at Ealing, but I do know the sources for that kind

27

of material and it doesn't take all that long to ferret out. You had ample time to meet me that Monday evening and you had ample time to reply to my phone message."

"Make your mind up. If I *had* been able to meet you, I would hardly have needed to ring you, would I? You see, two can play at that game."

"What game, for Christ's sake?"

"Semantics. Trying to prove a point by playing with words."

"If you mean semantics I'm not trying to prove any point. I was just asking, in the mildest possible way, why you stood me up at the Corkscrew at what you must have known was the verge of our relationship, otherwise you would hardly have bothered to traipse out to Tim's christening party."

Arguing with you was like teaching a child the rules of a complex game it doesn't want to play. As I was to do so often, I willed myself to stop it. But as you were to do so often, you unexpectedly willed me to go on.

"Well, perhaps I had to see someone."

As you were entitled to, of course, since you hardly knew me. And as you remained entitled to, come to that, even when you knew me better than anyone ever has, or at least had the opportunity to. "Then why couldn't you just say so? Whom did you have to see?"

"How can I possibly remember?"

"By looking in your diary."

"I don't always put things in my diary. If you really want to know, I think I had to have dinner with Cheevers."

"But the reason we were supposed to have a drink in the first place was because you couldn't make lunch, and one of the days you couldn't make lunch, whichever it was, was because you were having lunch with Cheevers."

"I was, but one of us must have cancelled."

Banging my head against a brick wall, I always allowed myself one more thump.

"All right, but what about the rest of the week, since the subject's come up?"

"I wish it hadn't come up. What about the rest of the week?"

"Why did you never call me?"

"Roger, I was living a different life then. There were other people I had to see – things I wanted to wind up. If I was going to have a long-term relationship with you I wanted these others out of the way."

"But you couldn't know then it was going to be a long-term relationship and if you did, then all the more reason to actually start it, instead of standing me up."

"If you choose to believe that, that's what you'll have to believe."

To think there was a time when I would get into these head-swimming altercations voluntarily. We had them almost from the start. Even at Tim's christening party we had a taste of what was to come, but then I found your convoluted loop-the-loop logic endearing. And I thought I could flick the chips off your shoulder as lightly as dandruff.

"It really is good of you to come all this way, Angela," I said, riffling aimlessly through the report while you held my champagne glass. The incongruousness of the situation must have come home to you at that point, for you said: "Oh, I really shouldn't have barged in on you like this but I have a friend who lives in Richmond which isn't all that far away, so I thought I might as well kill two birds with one stone. I'm sorry."

"Please stop apologising – I'm delighted to see you. Truly. So have you just come from Richmond or are you on your way there?"

"You mean you want me to go?"

"I mean I want you to stay as long as you like and let me pour you champagne."

"I noticed it's Lanson Black Label, the same as you gave me at the Corkscrew that evening."

"And which you liked, so I asked the caterers to be sure to serve Lanson today in case you dropped in." You liked my joshing flattery. It was like feeding you sugar plums.

"Just one more glass to confirm that it's the same high quality, then, and I must be on my way."

"If you're going to Richmond I'm sure someone here could give you a lift."

"No, I'm not going to Richmond, my friend's away."

"Oh, but I thought – "

"Yes, I was, but then I rang her but she was out. So I thought I'd drop in on you anyway. You're sure you don't mind?"

Head swimming slightly I said: "For the tenth time, I don't mind. In fact I'm the opposite of not minding. And thanks again for your notes. Can we have lunch when I've had time to study them?"

"Yes please."

"On Monday?"

"Yes please."

"Le Bistro, one o'clock?"

"Yes please."

You didn't say goodbye – or hello, come to that – to Judith, who had rendered herself unassailable behind a thicket of her relatives, through which she was giving us hard looks. You went off across the lawn as if heading for the drive, but then I saw you seeking out Ingrid, who after a word led you into the house – to powder your nose, I supposed, and doubtless to give the place a quick once over. Later I found the christening present you'd left for Timothy on the hall table. We'd met just twice before this party, our first encounter lasting a few minutes and the second barely an hour. That early Victorian silver rattle must have cost a good eighty pounds. Your overdraft and sundry outstanding final demands, I was to find, totalled over two thousand pounds, and that was apart from what you owed in rent. But even without knowing that I knew you didn't have money to throw about. I was touched and exasperated. It was preposterous. I was coming up to fifty-one years of age and I was falling in love with you, and that was preposterous too.

Two

During all those sixteen months with you I was never entirely sober. Quite what the ratio was of champagne to euphoria I wouldn't care to guess; but now when I get pissed, which I do most days, it still brings soured echoes of being in love – the bouquet turning to a belch, you might say – so I suppose the alcoholic content must have been quite high. Nearly every memory of you has a drink in it or one not far away. Experiencing you was so much bound up with drinking with you that I'm left wondering if it's possible for teetotallers to fall in love. They must be long, those days of Perrier and roses. Joke.

I heard your pealing laugh just then, and your cry of "Hey, that's *fun*-nee!" and cliché or not it was like being stabbed with a skewer. Very quick, in and out, but leaving a dull pain, or rather compounding the dull pain that's always there. I ought to have another quadruple gin to make it go away, but when it does go away it brings you back, and that's unbearable. I loved you, Angie. Past tense, but the past is here and now, otherwise there'd be no point in memory.

But memory is only anticipation in reverse. I should think *plus*, you were always telling me. Think of the good things. I did try to, and I still do. Here's one: if we didn't have an Our Restaurant, my darling, we did have an Our Drink. You hated my counting – how many nights away together, how many lunches, how many rows even – and quite right too: it's a grotty, grey little habit. But I bet we must have drunk a good six hundred bottles of champagne from start to finish of our loving. Seventy-odd Methuselahs. Christ. If they gave you fivepence back on the bottle like they do with Newcastle Brown we could have stayed legless for three days on what we got back on the empties. That last monumental binge could have been triple-monumental. So triple-monumental that we might have drunk our way out of hating. So triple-monumental that you might have fallen into a week-long stupor and never driven out of my life that drizzling November day.

I'm bleeding. Think plus.

I suppose if I hadn't fetched a bottle over to your table that first

31

evening at the Screw we might equally have conducted our affair on gin and tonic, of which even I can only take so much. We might have been more sober, wiser, less loving people. As it was, it seemed altogether fitting and natural to have a bottle of Lanson Black Label all chilled and ready by our table at Le Bistro, where I waited as anxious and expectant as an adolescent at the park gates on his first date. And we drank champagne ever after, except when we wanted to drown our happiness, when we went on to Armagnac.

It can't be more than three hundred yards from the office but I gave myself half an hour to be there on time, incidentally setting the pattern for an ongoing, absurd over-promptitude born of a fear that one Cinderella minute late and you'd be gone. Another counting ritual: the number of hours amounting to days, weeks, whiled away in Hallmark card outlets, souvenir boutiques, record shops, paperback shops, during those long, last-lap ninety-minute hauls between twelve thirty-five and three minutes to one.

You made an impeccable Scenario Five entrance, just as I thought we were on Scenario Four. I'd got through three glasses of champagne and was gloomily resigned to finishing the bottle. Mentally I paid out the odds I'd allowed myself on Scenario Four coming up.

Scenario One was the outsider. You arrived in a flurry of hugs and kisses, knocking back my champagne before even sitting down, whereafter we hit it off so well that we were groping one another under the table before the main course had arrived. We skipped coffee and took a cab to your flat where we sank on the floor and were at it even as you closed the front door with your foot.

Scenario Two, on which I was offering evens, gave us a jolly, pissy lunch with a lot of laughter and more champagne; you reluctantly turned down my suggestion of lurching round to Freddy's Club for positively only one more glass, but made it clear that there would be other times, other opportunities, other possibilities.

Scenario Three, another evens bet, had me cast as the uncle figure, a hand-patting role with me handing out sage advice on whatever problem – job prospects, love life, finances – had prompted you to accept my invitation to lunch. I did a lot of work on this scenario. While we started off on a distinctly platonic note you gradually fell in love with me, taking the hero-worship route, and we consummated the affair some six or seven lunches later.

In Scenario Four, two to one on, you simply didn't turn up. There were several drafts of this one. Scenario Four take two had a message waiting for me on my arrival, pleading unavoidable engagement. Take three had you ringing me at Le Bistro from a simulated emergency dental appointment. In take four, the sweetest version, there was a poignant little note, explaining how on reflection you didn't want to start something you wouldn't know how to finish. In all these versions I sat long at my table, becoming slowly, methodically and melancholically drunk.

I'd dreamed all these options and alternatives in what interminably remained of the weekend after Tim's christening. Scenario Five, the favourite, saw you flurrying in half an hour late, shedding possessions and gushing apologies. I scripted it absolutely right, though I say it myself. (And as *cinéma vérité* goes, the other scenarios proved to be reasonably accurate as one lunch led to another.)

You wore the green dress that Cheevers had given you. What an extraordinary business that was, a lover reclaiming from his wife's pile of Oxfam discards the things he thought his mistress would look good in, and presenting her with them. For a long time after I heard that story I gleaned a good deal of comfort, on a juvenile, snickering level, out of contemplating what a cheapskate he must have been. But you saw it as a touching gesture, and it was. Oafs like me pack their mistresses off on shopping sprees with blank cheques and are despised for it. Rescuing Mrs Cheevers's tossed-out dress had a love-in-the-attic touch about it, a tenderness I couldn't hope to match in the gaucherie of middle age. And you looked delicious in it.

Three waiters danced after you, picking up your scattered files and papers, relieving you of the shabby little jacket you shrugged off like a sable, and clearing a path to the corner table I'd asked for specially.

You didn't like it. Too small, not really a table for two at all, and anyway you wanted to sit next to me rather than opposite so we could go through your research. "What's wrong with that one there?" and you pointed at a table for four, permanently reserved for Saatchi and Saatchi. You did succeed in hijacking the next best table and we got settled in at last, although I'm afraid those few moments of chaos lost you points for being a suspected member of that self-congratulatory sorority who describe themselves as "quite mad". But then you soothed me at once, patting my hand and teasing, "Have I got you in a tizz? Never mind, now you can relax." Reflecting that, but for your being half an hour late, I should have been relaxed in the first place, I realised with benignly bleak resignation that you had it in you to twist me around your little finger.

It must have been going on for two before we even looked at the menu. We polished off the champagne and ordered another bottle. The lunch was already a success, although you lost more points for a rambling account of why you were late – flatmate Belle losing her key on way back from night at boyfriend's, and you having to wait for her return to let her in. Admittedly the story touched on her scatter-brainedness rather than yours, but there is such a thing as guilt by association. It was the first I'd heard of Belle by name to my

33

recollection. I disliked her instantly, not least for sharing a flat with you. (I had been nurturing an outside hope of switching to Scenario One before the meal was over.)

"And what's Belle do?"

"I've never been really sure."

"Oh, I got the impression you were old friends."

"So we are – we were at the Chelsea Auction Galleries together. Didn't I tell you about her?"

I raked back through your anecdotal history of your one and only regular job.

"Was she the one who got fired?"

"For going to bed with one of the porters, yes."

"In the firm's time, on a Louis XVI chaise-longue, in one of the viewing rooms. Yes, you told me." But not that you shared a flat with her. Perhaps you'd prudently suppressed the information because I hadn't been able to help looking a little shocked.

"Then you ought to be able to work out what she does."

"Well, I gather she's fond of bouncing up and down on beds but she doesn't do it for a living, does she?"

"I think so."

"You mean she's a prostitute?"

"I think it's called being an escort, really. She told me she'd stopped doing it but I'm not sure. She's away from the flat quite a lot and she's always leaving hotel bookmatches lying around."

You had, from the start, a knack of tossing shrapnel bombs into the conversation. You'd say something with so many possible implications, that opened up so many avenues and went off at so many tangents, that I would be hard put to decide which wild goose to chase. How did you come to be sharing a flat with someone who was on the game, under whatever euphemistic cloak? Did she bring her clients home with her? Had she embroiled you in her trade? Or tried to? Had you been curious about what she had to do for her money?

"And do you approve?" I asked lamely.

"I don't approve or disapprove. She doesn't talk about it and I don't think about it. It's none of my business. Ooh, big fat juicy olives, yummy!" you exclaimed, as the waiter placed a dish of appetisers before us, and the subject was not so much dismissed as banished. I don't believe we ever had a single conversation that we reached the end of, to my satisfaction at any rate. That's why talking to you always left me vibrating like a tuning fork, in that nerve-jangling condition one arrives at after wrestling none too successfully with a difficult crossword – exhausted, frustrated, yet exhilarated at the prospect of having one more crack at the problem later. Like the quantity of champagne we swigged, this compulsive curiosity –

34

usually about nothing in particular, except to get questions answered, to get sentences finished before you started another one – must have contributed to my general state of permanent high excitement, but unlike the champagne, it was an element I could have done without.

I can't remember what we ate, only that it was a long time coming but neither of us minded. You went off on some other anecdotal tangent, I've forgotten in what direction, remembering only that the mysterious Cheevers, as he was rapidly becoming, came into it somewhere and I couldn't pin you down on who he was. You were not being purposely mysterious, you never were, though you were often evasive: it was as if you were bubbling over with so many things you wanted to say to me that you kept leaving one thing half-said in order to start on another, like an excited child opening Christmas presents. Abandoning the Cheevers story you set off on some other never-to-be-completed excursion. I melted to your effervescence, feeling churlish and ashamed at my sporadic waves of uncharitable irritation when you came over too strongly as a "character" or exuberantly did something that seemed to me, with my settled ways, vaguely gross, like rolling your olive in butter "to make it glisten more".

All the while you'd been shuffling your dropped papers into some sort of order and now you presented them to me – an enormous file augmenting the stuff you'd brought along to the christening thrash with photocopied graphs, tables, analyses, and sheafs of marketing surveys – far more than I should have ever needed even had the Harrogate seminar not been a total fiction. I felt guilty at having put you to so much work to no purpose, if not to no avail – I recklessly offered you getting on for double the going fee but you said, "No, that's generous of you and you're so lovely, but I couldn't. It's twice my usual rate and quadruple what I'm worth." If you owed thirteen weeks' rent when I first got a glimpse of your troubles in October, you must have owed seven weeks' rent then.

"But you've put so much into it, Angela."

"Angie."

"Is that what your friends call you?"

"Only specially selected ones. You're only allowed to call me Angela when you're cross with me."

"It's a hell of a lot of work, Angie."

"I've already told you – I *like* doing things for you."

"Why?"

"Because I do. You're appreciative – a lot of people aren't, you know."

"But as it's the first time you've ever worked for me, how could you tell whether I'd be appreciative or not?"

"Kind eyes."

I wondered if all this very acceptable buttering-up was a standard routine of yours. But I didn't wonder too much, for fear of spoiling it. Nor, even as I scribbled a cheque for the amount I'd suggested – you didn't demur a second time – did I speculate on your motives. Cats don't wonder why they're being stroked, they just purr. I hadn't had much to purr about for a long time.

I riffled through the papers you'd brought me. If I tell you that I was on the verge of confessing that the project was made up, I have to confess also that it wasn't with the object of coming clean, but because I wanted you to know I'd concocted it for the sole purpose of seeing you again, upon which you'd butter me up some more. Then I thought you might have torn my cheque up or been furious at all that effort wasted – as indeed you were, when eventually I did have to come clean – and so I contented myself with thanking you again in extravagant terms (your generosity with compliments was catching) and stuffed the files in my briefcase. My first souvenir of you – some marketing surveys on teenage spending power, tied in blue. As I piled compliment on compliment it was your turn to purr. You looked ridiculously, meltingly pleased with yourself, a cat that's laid out a row of mice on the doorstep, then swallowed the cream.

Over lunch you talked, with selective frankness, about yourself – the dyslexia you were still struggling to conquer (I was relieved now not to have revealed that all that reading you'd done for me had been for nothing), the schools you'd run away from or been expelled from, your father's cruelty, your mother's suicide. You told me far more than I had any right to know on so short an acquaintance (and later far less than I had a right to expect on so close a one) and again I'm afraid I wondered if this was one of your set pieces, aimed to intrigue and impress. If not, you showed a command of the narrative form which appeared to desert you altogether whenever there was something about you which I particularly wanted to know but which you particularly didn't wish to tell me. You hit all the right notes, too: bravely wistful about your mother, sorrowfully understanding about your father, comically rueful about your Madcap of the Fourth school escapades. I was filled with compassion and admiration for your resilience, as I guess I was meant to be (it's a shame your father thrashed your ambition to go to drama school out of you – you would have made a good actress, given the right parts. Adventuresses?). I took your hand where it rested on the table, meaning to give it a sympathetic squeeze. But your fingers folded warmly, naturally over mine and we sat holding hands while the waiter, with an air of speculative amusement, cleared the plates. He gave you an especially knowing look, and me, as I retrospectively came to realise, a pitying one.

I wish you'd said you knew Le Bistro almost as well as I did, Angie – that you'd been taken there so often it was a marvel we hadn't seen one another there. I know you didn't say it was your first visit in so many words, but you did contrive to plant the idea – "what a restful room" etc. – that I was introducing you to the place. Perhaps you wanted to give me that small pleasure. As you so often said, so many of my impressions rested on whether I chose to think the worst of you or the best of you.

On that day I thought only the best – the better for holding hands. And then I saw Gunby T. Gunby regarding us from the window table we'd vacated at your insistence. He nodded sardonically and returned to his midday *Standard*, but not before you'd waved frantically as if seeing off an old friend on the *QE2*. You must have exchanged all of twenty-five words with him at Tim's christening party, before which you'd never clapped eyes on him. At once I was touched: the outwardly brash wave revealed your vulnerability, your yearning to know people and feel part of a set.

Concurrently with the emotion aroused by that pathetic gesture – specifically, a desire to give you things: love, money, new clothes, new friends, that you so often sparked off in me and which I was then feeling for just about the first time – I was also experiencing, and also for the first time, slight twinges of apprehension – gestating guilt, I suppose – at deceiving Judith. Gunby was far more Judith's friend than mine as I've told you more than once: they used to team up on press trips to vineyards and suchlike back in the days when he was still a Fleet Street hack – and yes, my little Miss Noseyparker, I think it highly probable that they *did* sleep together on one or two of those jaunts, human nature being what it is and Gunby T. Gunby being what he is, namely a thrice-married stoat. But why did you want to know? Whenever I asked you if you'd slept with this or that personality encountered or waved at in the places we used, you'd say it was all lost in the mists of time and what did it matter? Double standards, my dear.

Be that as it may: Judith – I know I've told you this too but I've never ceased to be amazed at how little you could retain in your memory if it didn't interest you very much (or if you found it inconvenient) – had been doing bits and pieces for him ever since the first year of his *Good Living Guide*, and they lunched regularly. It struck me as immensely bad luck that our second assignation ever would as likely as not be on the agenda when next they met. Already I was working on my story for Judith – I'd been stood up by a client, you'd got the wrong date for a lunch with, oh, Hugh Kitchener, and we'd joined forces. I would release this improbable cover story before Gunby had a chance to broadcast his own account of our lunching together, thus spiking his guns. I didn't do any such thing, it goes without saying, having learned during that fling with my Merry Widow that the least said, the fewer the supplementary questions: and glad I was that I didn't, since it was so long before Gunby and Judith next lunched that his little Roger-Angela morsel must have been jettisoned in favour of spicier tittle-tattle, for I never heard a word about it.

But it was worrying, on and off, for the next few days: not so much on account of the fear of exposure over what after all could be technically proved to have been an innocuous lunch, as of the realisation, with something of a jolt, that I was already leading a double life. Forever after, so long as it lasted, I should be two people, one going through the motions of domestic and business life, the other involved, on whatever level, with you. It didn't need Gunby's beady little eye savouring our togetherness over his newspaper to tell me that the deception had started.

"Do they know he's Gunby T. Gunby of the *Good Living Guide*?" you asked loudly, with the head waiter only three feet away.

"If they didn't, they do now," I said with a mock frown, more tolerant in those days of your unwavering indiscretion. "You'll notice they've given him our original table. That shows what a good table it was."

"Yes, it's a good table for one, as I said. Why is he lunching alone?"

I said, "I expect he doesn't have a ravishing red-haired lady he'd like to reward with a nice lunch for working her little bum off for him." Creaky, but the best I could do at short notice: I hadn't yet got in the swing of paying you compliments. You seemed pleased enough, though.

"Oh, I hope that doesn't mean I shall always have to sing for my lunch?"

Your shrapnel-bomb way with words had its pleasantly intriguing side too. There were all sorts of implications to savour there – we were at the beginning of something, we were going to lay down ground rules, the curtain had gone up and we were about to act out our play. Tingling with pleasure, I noticed Gunby pushing away his plate and decided to cross over and exchange a word with him before he came across to exchange a word with us, which would inevitably expand to coffee and brandy.

You never bothered to ask what I talked to other people about, only what they'd said about you. In fact I couldn't help noticing from the start that you were practically your sole topic of conversation, unless you were paying lavish compliments, or later on delivering lavish insults, and even then they were usually in relation to how I responded to you. Yet you were never selfish – merely utterly self-absorbed.

When you turned to the astrology column there was always a pause before you read out my horoscope. That was because you were reading your own first.

People talk about people like us rather less than one imagines, you know. All Gunby had to say about you was, "D'you know, Roger, I've been trying to place your stunning companion ever since she introduced herself at your very agreeable party, and it's only now I see her in context that the penny's dropped. She comes in here quite a lot with young Ben Cheevers, doesn't she?"

"How do you come to know Ben Cheevers?" I bluffed, not knowing why I bluffed, not knowing why I was mentally filing Cheever's newly-learned Christian name as well as the description "young", not knowing why the name of Cheevers should mean anything to me anyway, but already feeling that soon-to-be-familiar pang of alarm at the mention of it.

"Oh, he took on my stepdaughter Tilly at the Chelsea Auction Galleries, to her immediate regret. She fell for him as they all do, silly girl. Still, a lesson learned and no lasting harm done but if your charming guest asks why I always cut the little bastard dead, there's the reason."

So you must have known Cheevers for six years or so, always assuming that he was established there when you arrived from York University – and it would be an anti-coincidence to believe that he didn't arrive until you'd left. And you still had lunch with him regularly, and indeed either you'd "had" to have lunch with him only a few days ago when I wanted you to have lunch with me, or to have dinner with him when you were supposed to be having a drink with me. Or both. And you hadn't mentioned that Le Bistro was a regular rendezvous. But then why should you have done, and whose business was it but your own whom you had lunch with? Why was I wrapping a cloak of mystery around your shoulders? Perhaps because premonition told me it was just about your size.

"I must get back to my table and wade through all the bumph Angela's dug out for me," I said, not fooling Gunby for a second, for he tapped his nose roguishly and promised, "I shan't interrupt you, don't worry." The gesture was a welcome – or so it seemed to me in the sensitive state I was getting into with all these minor buffetings – to the company of lechers to which Gunby T. Gunby and this Ben Cheevers, by the sound of him, belonged – a sub-culture of seedy affairs and quick flings that I didn't intend our fledgling relationship to be any part of. Odd how puritan one can be in setting off on a course of adultery. Immoral indignation, you could call it.

How far you yourself belonged, or had belonged, to that world, didn't yet exercise my mind but it did occupy a back cell of it. By way of a test case, after Gunby had made his predictable detour to our table to ologeanously kiss your hand as he took his leave, I recounted the famous story of how he screwed his first wife's sister on the office floor when she came round to warn him that he was on the verge of breaking up his marriage with his philandering. I told it as a funny yarn and you laughed in all the right places – but failed to supply the expected moral coda as to what a shit he must be. And so I asked you, beginning my desultory research into the kind of man you regarded as "your type", whether you could ever fancy someone like Gunby. You said, "God, no, he's too old for one thing," which was not what I wanted to hear, particularly as he happens to be two years my junior. Perhaps noting my peeved reaction you went on quickly, "And he's gross," which was better, though I think you meant his Bunterish proportions rather than his lifestyle; "And he's – brrrrr! – clammy. Like Mr Toad," which was better still. He had his uses though, ultimately, didn't he, my love? Had I known how much we were to be in his debt, I should have proposed a toast to Gunby T. Gunby with that final glass of champagne we had with – was it the crème brûlée and two spoons?

I'm glad, though, that I did nothing so distracting: for it was over that last glass, and possibly influenced by the fact that it was the last glass of seven, not counting the intervening claret or whatever we had which you hardly touched, that without warning you began to write Scenario Six, the opening line being:

"I think I'm in love."

I thought at first it was Scenario Three we were on – I was to be your agony uncle, then, listening to a flippant confessional that would mask whatever torment you were going through and giving the advice you wanted to hear. Gather ye rosebuds but don't get caught in the brambles, or something equally sage. After the first fleeting thud of disappointment, I was surprisingly relieved. I was off the hook.

"I bet he's married," I said.

"Yes, he is, much to my annoyance."

"Are they always?"

"There's no 'they' or 'always' about it. I don't make a practice of falling in love."

Reserving my opinion on that, I prompted with elephantine playfulness, "And are we allowed to know who is the lucky recipient of this exclusive affection?"

You said lightly, as if we were discussing nothing of any consequence, "It would be you, silly, if you weren't being so pompous."

You've always insisted that you meant it, and so you did, in a teasing, superficial way. It was a good lunch we were having, the champagne was flowing, you were relaxed and happy, and you did feel a wave of love towards me. At the time I chose to believe you too little, so disapproving was I of my own silly squiggles of delight, acutely conscious that this was girlish, giggling stuff on a level with passing love notes in the playground. Later I came to believe it too much, convincing myself, because I wanted to, that you were authentically in love with me long before you actually were. At bottom I knew, though, that in real life your love welled up and came in waves, impetuously, and then receded, as I could tell when I found myself beached by the ebb tide.

Feeling half-ashamed of myself, I allowed myself to go along with what seemed to me like a game of mental footsie. With a coyness appropriate to someone a third of my age, and of the opposite sex, I bantered, "I'm not really pompous, am I?"

"You can be. I don't mind, it's quite endearing."

"And how do I unpompously get you to repeat what you just said?"

"That I'm in love?"

"That you think you're in love."

"I am. Madly."

I pedantically noted the discrepancy between the reservation attached to your original declaration and the absolute certainty of its rider, but wary of my new-found reputation for pomposity, left it alone. Instead, quickly converting your confession into its crude worth, I asked thickly:

"So what's to be done about it?"

"That's rather up to you."

Even at that early stage, I didn't quite see it that way. You were the one who was single and as unattached as maybe. You had a flat, shared it was true with this reprehensible Belle but she could presumably be got rid of for a few hours – go on her beat, perhaps. You, when all was said and done, were making the running.

"I wish it were," I said lamely. "But you know my situation."

"Yes, and you have an adorable baby boy with whom I'm even more in love, and I'm talking lots of nonsense. Thank you for a *lovely* lunch. Must dash. *Mmm* – there!" And kissing me briskly on the cheek and sweeping up your things you were out of the door before I'd even taken it in that you'd left your seat.

You hadn't dashed far. It was a good ten minutes before I'd got the bill paid and left, but there you were, pretending to be looking in the window of the pâtisserie next door, and looking so very much as you had at Tim's christening party, all alone in the world and left outside, that I wanted to rush into the shop and buy you a bag of buns.

"Lovely cakes," you said lip-smackingly, with a glancing smile as if you had been waiting there by pre-arrangement while I went to the men's room. "Yum yum. Wish I hadn't had a pudding now."

I pointed to a creamy confection encrusted with strawberries. I was so pleased to see you again, to be lifted out of the little trough of despondency I'd fallen into upon your abrupt leavetaking. The sun was streaming down and I felt good. "They all need nice homes. Why don't you adopt that one?"

"Don't encourage me. I should only make a piglet of myself on the bus."

"Are you sure?" I could sense you happily wavering. "You're not sure, are you?"

"Well, perhaps – *that* one," and you stabbed a finger at the first present I ever gave you, a chocolate éclair costing 85 pence. Buying it was as much a treat for me as it evidently was for you – all the accompanying fuss and dither as you drooled over the display inside the shop and changed your mind then changed it back again, then demanded a cake box to take it home in, then made them cut the box down to size so your éclair wouldn't slide about in it and lose its cream, made me feel like Father Christmas in his grotto. That was one for our snapshot album, one of those euphoric moments that are forever fixed in memory – even one with the sticking power of a used envelope, like yours. I was always glad and grateful that you remembered that little interlude. But it made it all the more disappointing that you couldn't properly remember our first lunch. I was still assuming that everything to do with us was as clear in your mind as in my mind, and I was dismayed to find what a vague and confused image you had of an occasion that to me was as bright and sharp as the first perfect print of a lithograph. You blustered prettily – then not so prettily:

"Darling, I *do* remember – please believe that. How could I *not* remember?"

"By forgetting."

"Don't be plutonic," you said bafflingly. I let that one go. Only now, remembering what you would have forgotten – for that exchange, I'm sure, will have been as blanked out of your mind as was the subject of it at the time, and this reminder of it will be as two mirrors reflecting one another into an infinity of nothingness – does it occur to me that you meant "Don't be laconic." Dry, would have been the adjective I would have chosen personally: there was a certain amount of play-acting in my role too and I was casting myself as your mentor, a waspish Clifton Webb figure who would be your Svengali.

Then you went on, "I haven't forgotten, it's just that I don't have a good memory for dates and places. We had several marvellous lunches that first month and I couldn't be absolutely sure whether the first place you took me to was Le Bistro or one of the other places. What does it matter? We were getting to know one another, we were falling in love – they were *all* firsts."

"But Le Bistro was the *first* first – you remember that now?"

"Yes, I do, and your buying me an éclair and I took it home and kept it in its little box and wouldn't eat it, because that was another first. Your first present."

"I thought you ate it on the bus."

"No, that was another time. *Now* who's forgetting?"

"It was that time, Angie. Our next lunch was at Luigi's and the reason we went there was because you said when I rang to invite you, 'Anywhere except Le Bistro, not that it wasn't absolutely lovely but it's too near temptation, I scoffed my éclair on the bus home and nearly had to get off, I felt so queasy.'"

"Do you tape our telephone conversations, Roger, or just make verboten notes?"

"The only conversations I've ever taped have been one-sided ones into your answering machine when I've known perfectly well you were in but you've omitted to switch the bloody thing off," I retorted, getting a dig in. "And no, I don't keep verbatim notes, I have a verbatim mind."

"Then it's a pity you don't remember things more clearly yourself. It wasn't an éclair I ate on the bus, it was a florentine."

"Which I got you from the Patisserie Valerie in Old Compton Street after we'd been to Wheeler's one day. That was ages after our first lunch."

"All right, so I'm confusing one lunch with another. What on earth does it matter *when* it was?"

And what on earth did it? It was absurd, wasn't it, two adult people – well, one perhaps more adult than the other, but both grown up enough to be in love – arguing like infants in the nursery about a cake? We fell into a smouldering silence, angrily swilling champagne around our glasses – this was in that American Bar in Brook Street, do you remember? No, you don't. We were both so convinced we were right – you in your contention that it didn't matter, I in my belief that it did. I was fully conscious of the absurdity of the stand I wanted to make, that was why I didn't make it. I wanted to say, "Look Angela, the basic point which you are waffling away from is that you really do have no clear impression of our first lunch and that I find hurtful. And you didn't take the éclair home, you ate it on the bus, or so you told me at length, so why are you now pretending otherwise?" But I should have sounded like Captain Queeg going on about the strawberries. So I said instead:

"And why didn't you tell me you used to go to Le Bistro with Cheevers?"

"Who says I did?"

"Gunby. He used to see you there."

"Why were you talking about me to Gunby T. Gunby?"

"I wasn't – he was talking about you to me. At Le Bistro. The first time we went there. Or did we come across him somewhere else?"

"There's no need to be sarcastic."

"Aren't you going to answer the question?"

"If Gunby's already told you he's seen me there with Cheevers then you already have the answer, so why are you asking?"

"That wasn't the question. I asked you why you didn't tell me."

"Why should I? It wasn't important."

"You could have said you'd forgotten."

"I had, almost. And it *isn't* important, darling. Going to places with you makes them seem altogether different from going to them with him."

"What places?"

"You *know* what – Le Bistro."

"What other places?"

"There was nowhere else."

"Then why put them in the plural?"

"Roger, you are not going to put me in the witness box!"

I just couldn't help myself. I didn't even want to know, that was the ridiculous thing. What the hell did it matter where you'd been with him, I asked myself, wretchedly emulating you as I mulled the thing over. Then it came back to me that that wasn't the question I'd asked. What I did want to know was why you were so cagey about telling me that which wasn't important. Going round in circles with you had the effect that I was going round in circles with myself. And with every will-o'-the-wisp evasion, the need to interrogate you, to pin you down like a butterfly, grew stronger. I was pulling our relationship down to see if it had any foundations; and you were wilfully trying to break it to see if it was unbreakable.

I bet you haven't the faintest idea how that evening ended. I'll let you into a secret: neither have I. Not with one of your spectacular flouncing exits – that would certainly have stuck in my mind. We probably calmed down and went on for supper – I know it was one of our when-the-cat's-away evenings, but I don't know where I took you. How sad, to remember only the bickering part.

All right. But I remember our first lunch and our second lunch and our third lunch and our fourth lunch and where they took place – Le Bistro, Luigi's, the Taverna, and the Taverna again, in that order.

44

Luigi's found you in the same happy-go-lucky, Little Miss Scatter-brain mood, or should I say role, as at Le Bistro. With the second bottle you were drunk enough to talk soberly and we had the same serious interval for confessional when you told me a little more about yourself, or rather subtly revised and refined some of what you had already told me. The schools you'd actually been thrown out of narrowed down to one, the others now being down to moving house or some other expediency. Your father taking a stick to you turned out to be a one-off aberration when he was goaded into it by your precociousness, though you still made him sound pretty much a monster. Your mother's overdose now seemed to have a question mark hanging over it, and when I asked you whether the coroner's verdict was accidental death or what, you were evasively amnesic – "You have to realise I was only eight. I didn't even know what an inquest was." "But didn't you ask later?" "I must have done. I just blocked it out of my mind, I suppose." And tears of self-pity, the first gush of a whole lachrymose Niagara Falls of them I've witnessed since, welled in your eyes. Although I sensed even then that they were cheap, self-induced tears I felt that the vulnerability was genuine underneath the pose, and my heart went out to you and I had an urge to do something for you, to kiss it better, to give you a new toy. The pudding trolley was going by and I made you dry your eyes and have the profiteroles.

Our first two visits to the Taverna would be inextricably melded into one by now (happy, giggly, hand-holding times they were, and I don't know whether it was at the first lunch or the second when I christened the head waiter King Constantine – only that it was after the look you got when you asked for more Turkish delight and more Turkish coffee) except that I know it was towards the end of the second lunch, when our ankles were intertwined under the tablecloth, that I blurted out:

"Look – are we having an affair or not?"

I know it was the second time because I'd wanted to ask it the first time, but hadn't the courage. We'd had four lunches by now and I felt we were marking time – pleasurably so, but marking time.

You did a fair imitation of a demure maiden, lowering your eyes and abstractedly fishing the bit of lemon zest out of your Greek, or have it your way, Turkish, coffee.

"It's not for me to say."

I can tell you for whom it was to say, though, and that was Judith, because the previous evening I think it was, she'd asked me for the first time if I was, in her words, "having it off somewhere?" I didn't mention it to you because it was too premature to be telling you things like that, and anyway it turned out to be a not-too-serious enquiry. The slender "evidence" wasn't the feared report on our Le Bistro tryst from Gunby T. Gunby but a smudge of lipstick on my handkerchief that wasn't even yours – the consequence of a peck on the cheek from the Merry Widow who I chanced to run into in the Marquis of Granby. I expect the fact that I had, quote, had it off with the Merry Widow in the past made me ill at ease, since Judith then asked why I was looking so shifty if I'd nothing to hide, whereupon I got very defensive and said, "If I have been having it off, I'd very much like to know when." Judith said lightly, "Well, I don't know what you get up to when you're locked away in your creative sessions, do I? Or who you get up," and off she went to make omelettes. I brooded a bit over supper, not over Judith's flippant accusation but at how to make it come true.

And so I said to you, as I paid the bill at the Taverna, "We seem to have reached a half-way stage, don't we?" I didn't quite know what I meant by that, but it seemed less bald than, "We're not getting anywhere, are we?"

"You can always turn back if you want to," you said.

"Do you want me to?"

"No. I should be very sad if you did."

"Then we are having an affair. Or we're about to."

"We must be."

But you wouldn't say where we were going to have it.

How did we come to reel round to Freddy's Club that day, do you remember? No, it's no use asking you. All I know is that I was supposed to be back at the office for a marketing conference. I called Charles and spun him a yarn about stumbling across a potential client at lunch and taking him for a drink, which he didn't believe for a second. And the first person we saw, in fact the only person we saw apart from his guest as we entered that dark red plush and gilt plaster cavern – "Like getting into a chocolate box and pulling the lid down," you said – was young Graham from the office, the coming man of Peck & Piper. And he really was entertaining a client. What the hell were we doing there, apart from my wanting another hour of your company?

I've got it. I was walking you down to Jermyn Street where I was going to buy you some of the cheese you'd liked at lunch, and you suddenly decided you had to go to the loo. "Now why didn't you go when you were in the restaurant?" I chided, and you giggled and said I sounded exactly like your late Uncle James when he used to take you to the theatre and you invariably wanted to go the moment the curtain went up. I said I was feeling far from avuncular and wheeled you into Freddy's.

I nodded briefly to Graham and murmured to you, "A guy from the office and the apple of Charles's eye. Try to look like a client."

You said naughtily, "Shouldn't *you* be the one looking like a client? He probably thinks I picked you up in Shepherd's Market."

Another first: our first post-lunch bottle of champagne at Freddy's, of God knows how many since. I'm going to leave my liver in a bottle for Freddy to put behind the bar. He came smarming out of his little office to greet us and I was possessively gratified by the fuss he made over you, kissing your hand and paying you extravagant compliments. But I was even more pleased, childishly so, to find that he didn't know you. I was quickly growing used to it transpiring that you'd already been to all the places I took you to, but without ever bothering to mention the fact and even being at pains to let me think you hadn't. The fact that you'd had the air of never having been to Freddy's before and this turning out to be perfectly true impressed me greatly: I reflected idiotically and rosily on how honest and open you were with me. "You're a *very* lucky man," murmured Freddy suggestively before gliding over to Graham to butter him up. I felt it, pathetically so.

Graham and his client departed, both of them giving you speculative, up-and-down glances. We'd obviously been given a mention on their agenda under any other business. I said: "I wouldn't mind our being looked at like that if we'd done something to earn it."

"Perhaps we look as if we have," you said with your mock demureness.

Our hands intertwined and locked. "I wish we had somewhere to go," I said.

"So do I." You said this in a low, wretched, hopeless voice, as if resigned to our woeful condition. I was rather nettled.

"But haven't we?" I persisted.

"Your place or mine?" you asked flippantly.

"No, seriously, Angie."

"You mean a hotel?" Your baffled naïveté was as simulated as your demureness, but less attractive.

"I mean your flat."

"So my place?"

"Is there any reason why not?"

"Why not your place?" Your sparring mood was new to me then and I was slow on the uptake. My defences were not so much down as non-existent.

"Come on, Angie!"

You made a great show of gathering up your things. "To your place? When? Now? Fine! How shall we get there – tube or cab?"

"Don't be silly."

"But you're asking me to come on. I thought we were going to Ealing Church Grove."

By now I was aware that you'd dug your elephant trap and I'd blundered into it. I held up my hands in a comic "Kamerad" gesture. "All right, all right, point taken. Married man wants to seduce single girl very badly but only if it's in her bed, not his. As a matter of fact, Angie, I'd have no objection at all to taking you back to Ealing – "

"Oh, thank you very much." Yes, I shouldn't have put it like that. Especially since it wasn't true.

"It's true. But the house isn't unoccupied by day, as you must perfectly well know."

"Neither is my flat. As *you* perfectly well know."

"You mean Belle?"

"Who else? *I* haven't got a family tucked away, you know."

You did mean Belle. It would seem that she spent most of her day sleeping or idling round the flat and could be relied on to be out only at night. (Or, as I privately reminded myself, when I rang you up and you were out too.) Whether she escorted her escorts back to the flat you didn't say and I didn't ask.

I pestered on. "But she must go out sometimes?"

"Yes, I've told you – at night."

"So if I made myself available in the evening, we could go round to your flat, is that what you're saying?"

"What do you mean, make yourself available? You sound as if you were putting time aside for a blood transfusion."

"Yes, I put that crudely. I'm sorry."

"Besides, she isn't out each and every night of the week. What would you do if you made elaborate arrangements to see me and then Belle wasn't going out?"

"And you couldn't persuade her to? I'd still take you to dinner."

You softened. "I'd like that."

So dinner I took you to, upon Belle proving to be laid up with – what was it again? Flu, I think, but you changed it to a bad attack of the curse when the subject came up again in a reminiscent chat. Or was it the other way round? The remarkable thing is that I believed you both times. And even if I hadn't, and had launched into one of my periodic attacks on you for not knowing where truth ends and lies begin, what was I myself being with Judith but deceptive?

I told her that night I had to have supper with an entirely fictitious potential client called Tipper, the same one I'd pretended to Charles to be seeing that afternoon at Freddy's. I put it out that he was someone who'd been at school with me – as a matter of fact, someone called Tipper was, and in sweating moments I've pictured him turning up out of the blue and ringing me at the office, or worse at home – and who ran a calendars and greetings cards business. Where I got that invention from I don't know. It's awfully easy to lie, as you know, and as you also know there's a compulsive desire to add unnecessary little details. I quite forgot the principle I'd applied during my fling with the Merry Widow – never elaborate, never explain – and told Judith rather more than she needed to know. While she didn't exactly disbelieve me she didn't exactly believe me either – " 'Entertaining a client' is rather a shop-soiled phrase, which is why the Inland Revenue won't let you set it against tax," I recall her saying. "So if you're going to take up wining and dining your clients as well as double Scotching and lunching them, why not invite them back here?"

That's why your next dinner invitation was a long time coming. Besides, that evening at the Peking Experience wasn't entirely a success, was it, my love? I picked it out of Gunby T. Gunby's *Good Living Guide* as being sufficiently off the beaten track to save me feeling ill at ease lest someone I knew should be sitting three tables away, and sufficiently near your flat for us to be able to slip across to it with the minimum of fuss engendered by non-arriving cabs. Belle's indisposition would have got us off to a bad start in itself, but your proving to know the place quite well – naturally – got us off to a worse one, because it was way out of your price range and that led me to wonder who would have taken you there, so near to home, and whether the ever-present Belle had been as much a stumbling-block to others as she was to me.

The beginning of the evening is etched on my mind as a dreadful example of how not to begin an evening. I was nervous, you were tense. I said something about picking up a bottle of wine on the way to your flat and asked oafishly if you had a reliable minicab number to get me back to Ealing. You were non-committal. I bantered, watching you flake the crust off your bread roll as you always did when you were on edge, "Hey, relax! It's not going to be an ordeal, you know!" You said, "I'm all right – really. If I do seem a bit tensed up it's because I'm feeling guilty for having dragged you so far out of your way. I love Chinese but we could just as well have gone to Mr Chow's in Kensington and then you'd have been on your way home."

You had a lot of verbal knacks, and one of them was saying something in such a way that it made a supplementary question necessary before you would get to what you were driving at. Humiliation may not have been the object but it was the end result. And what you were driving at was that we weren't going back to Banks Place that evening. You could have said so, you know, in a less roundabout way. "I would have understood," I was about to write, but of course I wouldn't. I didn't understand anything, and don't understand much now. But it would have been more straightforward.

That evening put us on a downhill course for a while. It was not so much an anti-climax as a false climax: our affair, if you could call it that yet, had been heading for consummation, there had been the tension and the excitement that comes from anticipation – on your part as well as on mine, I believed, and do believe – and then . . . stalemate.

We were by now a good six weeks into our relationship – a long time to tread water. We continued our lunches, indeed they settled into a routine, Tuesdays and Fridays, and on Fridays we would always go on to Freddy's Club, staying longer and longer until I realised, with a twinge of guilt (but only at not feeling in the least guilty) that I had established a pattern of never going back to the office after Friday lunch. On a couple of occasions young Graham was at Freddy's again with different people, so clearly our champagne sessions were getting back to the agency and to Charles. I didn't care. Recklessness in a hitherto cautious nature is one of the classic symptoms of love or infatuation or sexual obsession, and a liberating one it is. I still felt heady in your presence: you still conveyed excitement, it wafted in with you like a perfume. And you were fun. Lunch was fun. A capacity for mockery – of others, of one another, and of ourselves – was one thing we had strongly in common – in fact it was probably the only thing we really did have in common apart from the civilised superficialities like middlebrow music and *Good Living Guide* living. We became something of a double act, mischievously combining against bad service in restaurants, or when the service wasn't bad, speculating about the little dramas that were going on at other tables and inventing imaginary conversations. We were at play. We enjoyed ourselves hugely and kept falling in love with one another, when we would touch hands and rub calves, and if we were on the second bottle you would sometimes whisper, "I wish we were together" but you never made any proposals as to how we could be. In uncharitable moments I began to wonder if you weren't something of a cock-teaser.

Even if you were, I wanted to sleep with you. Not desperately, except when on a second-bottle high – one cannot stay in a state of mental erection for weeks on end with no fulfilment in sight – but as a matter of principle, a point of pride. You were still, I could gather from casual references, seeing other men, and there was absolutely no reason why you shouldn't; but you were presumably sleeping with at least one or two of them and so I was beginning to feel not only left out but positively and deliberately excluded. This sense of rejection so dominated my sexual thinking that the only way I knew I was frustrated was when I found myself lusting after Ingrid, the Danish au pair. In fact, when Judith unexpectedly announced that she was going to be away for a night – much to my surprise, since she'd always refused to do TV even when she had a new cookery book out, she'd agreed to appear on some magazine programme in Manchester – my immediate response was a quickened heartbeat at the prospect of being alone in the house with Ingrid. I got my daydreaming as far as helping her bath the baby but when I saw myself peering down her dress as she reached for the soap I felt like a dirty old man and banished the image from my mind.

I thought of asking you to come to a hotel with me. I would check in with my briefcase standing in for an overnight bag, take you up to the room after supper nearby, then go home to Ealing in case Judith had rung, returning to the hotel early the next morning to check out. Just working out that plan was seedy enough in itself. I abandoned it.

Stupidly, I didn't even tell you until it was too late that Judith was going to be away. I'd now got it into my head that anything pre-planned would be sordid, for all that I was pre-planning like mad. I took you to lunch at a new place for us then, that brasserie we took up for a while. We went on to Freddy's for post-lunch champagne. We'd been happy and silly though you'd noticed I was preoccupied. Now you asked me what was up.

"I think I should have told you this earlier, but Judith's going to be away from home tonight."

You stiffened at once and asked me away where, and I told you what she was doing.

"So you must have known about this for some time?"

"Yes. I didn't want to make a formal announcement because it would have sounded premeditated."

"Premeditated what?"

"That on such and such an ordained evening we would go back to your flat. I know you'd have hated that."

"And my views don't count, I suppose? What if I don't want you to come back?"

"Don't you?"

"Whether I do or not is beside the point, because Belle happens to be in bed with – " With what, or perhaps with whom, I forget. If it wasn't flu the first time it was her accursed curse, and if it wasn't the curse it was her flu. Never mind. "Why couldn't you have told me earlier?"

In my frustration and disappointment I spat back, "Why – would you have had her moved into hospital?"

"I'm asking why did you hug it to yourself, Roger? You criticise me for not being straightforward with you but what do you think *you* were doing?"

"Perhaps I wanted it to be a surprise," I said fatuously.

"Withholding information is a form of lying. That's what you said to me." Had I? It sounds like me.

The afternoon deteriorated. Not only could we not go back to

Banks Place, we were destined not even to have supper together for the second time in our career. You were vague about why. In one breath you had to go back and look after Belle, in the next you were supposed to be perhaps meeting someone about a research job that might come up. It was all very cloudy except in one respect where it was crystal clear – I wasn't going back with you that night.

"I'm sorry. I would have wanted it too," you said with a simple sincerity, taking my hand.

I said, self-consciously deflated and determined to wallow in my wretchedness, "Can I ask you something? Have you taken other people back to your flat?"

The hand stiffened, then withdrew.

"I may have done. What's that to do with us?"

"How did you get rid of Belle?"

"I didn't have to. They weren't married men."

"You mean you had them round in the evening when Belle was out doing her escorting?" Yes, that's what you meant, and it led to a tiresome, accusatory diversion where I wondered sardonically how it chanced that Belle was laid up on just the two evenings when I was able to discard my married mantle, and whether any of your other suitors had been similarly inconvenienced.

At length you said: "I wish you'd stop being so bitter and twisted, Roger. Don't you understand it's because of them I'm so reluctant to have you round?"

Ingenious. "No, I don't."

"You don't understand that you're special?"

"What's so special about being refused your bed? I think I'd prefer to be run-of-the-mill." I could have made a meal of that theme but you placed a gentle finger on my lips, one of your (and my) favourite gestures.

"Now listen to me, darling. Yes, I have had other people round to the flat but they were silly, pointless, aimless flings that didn't mean anything. I'm ashamed of them and I'm ashamed of the flat and that's why I don't want you there."

"At all?"

"At all."

"So it's got nothing to do with Belle always being there?"

"Partly it has. But the main reason is what I've just told you. Why do you want to bring it back to Belle? Why can't you accept that I'm paying you a huge compliment?"

We were well into the second bottle – the second post-prandial bottle, that is – and my head was beginning to spin. I tried to retrieve my corner of the argument.

"Look. You meet all these other characters and they seemingly have no difficulty in getting back to your flat and sleeping with you. I have been battering at your door to no effect for two months now and you tell me it's because I'm special. How do you make that out?"

"Don't you feel you are? Don't you feel that *we're* special?"

Were you cajoling me? "I suppose we are," I conceded weakly.

"You know we are. All relationships are different, Roger. Each one has a different convex."

"Context, Lady Malaprop."

"I *meant* context. I was very happy when you first started taking me out to lunch. I've been happy at all our lunches, when we haven't been squabbling. I'm afraid of moving our relationship off that plane."

"But you said you were in love with me."

"I am, you know I am, but within that relationship."

As you swigged back your champagne with an air of finality I reflected, not for the first time, that I could go off you.

I had an early supper on my own at a Pizza Express that evening, doing the *Times* crossword and feeling sorry for myself. I got home just in time to take a call from Judith in Manchester. At least the evening hadn't been entirely wasted: I had banked a stock of trust which could be drawn upon when next I found myself with a free evening, either with you or somebody else. Ingrid was in her room watching television. I thought about her and you in turns and went to bed lusting after nobody in particular.

Our conversation that day had produced what was effectively a declaration of intent on your part. It was your unilateral policy. Our relationship took something of a small seismic lurch after that. You'd said you were nervous of moving it off the plane it was on, but it did move, arising out of that very nervousness – that's if you were levelling with me.

I became more reserved with you, less curious about you. I'd determined never to ask you to come to bed with me again but I found I didn't need that determination. I'd no real wish to sleep with you. Once or twice, when Tuesday or Friday rolled round, I confess I'd no real wish to lunch with you. For the first time I began to miss my occasional shoptalk lunches with Charles, which had fallen off rather in recent days. In fact looking back I believe our very last one must have been that famous day at Luigi's when you came over to our table. Though Charles was far too reserved to be bosom pals with anybody, they were chummy affairs, those lunches, the only chance he gave himself of relaxing with me. I saw now that I had traded in my friendship with Charles for my friendship with you, and I began to wonder if I'd got the bargain I'd thought I had, now the glitter was tarnishing.

Was I falling out of love with you? Had I ever really been in love with you? I gave serious thought to the question. The answer seemed to be that whatever I felt for you was like a plant that needed water. It had to grow or wither.

A day came when I really and truly couldn't make our Tuesday lunch. I was relieved yet depressed to find that Friday no longer seemed as far off as it once would have done. There was no way I could contemplate not seeing you again but the withering process had begun.

Perhaps you sensed it too. You never said as much, but one lunchtime at the Taverna, when we were winding up King Constantine and having such a nice lunch that I would have said "This is quite like old times" had I ever admitted that we were into new times, you asked, as if we had been discussing it only five minutes ago:

"*When* do you say you have to go to Harrogate?"

I had completely forgotten about my fictitious seminar in Harrogate and the work you had done for me on it. No, not completely; sometimes when I opened my filing cabinet and caught a glimpse of that bulging red folder I would feel sentimental and guilty about it.

"Oh, the twentieth, I think," I said at random.

You said lightly, spearing a stuffed olive, "Would you like me to come with you?"

THREE

You screwed, and that's the word for it, like a promiscuous college girl grimly ploughing her way through *The Joy of Sex*. It was a dismaying experience, but we got it right in the end, didn't we, my love? – just about the only thing we did get right. They were golden, those champagne afternoons. It nearly always was afternoon, or morning, for the unromantic reason that we were usually too far gone by nightfall.

I'd already realised that we came from different sexual cultures, but not how very different they were. I'd never encountered the generation gap in bed before: such partners as I'd had may sometimes have been younger – Judith, after all, is fourteen years my junior – but horizontally speaking we did seem to belong to the same world. Making love to you, at first, was like being a parent at a pop concert, tapping his foot and enjoying himself but being very self-conscious about where he is and the company he is in, and very, very careful not to make a fool of himself.

I didn't appreciate at first that you were self-conscious too. You hid it well, because you were used to hiding it well. It was only after we'd confessed to one another our need to relax that we began to relax, and then we became like partners in a bridge game instead of opponents trying to win tricks. It had yet to dawn on me, I don't know why since practically every lunch with you yielded evidence of it, how thoroughly immature you were, and your experience in sex only served to mask your immaturity. For your part, you didn't know how lacking in self-confidence I was, and my maturity served to mask my lack of confidence.

Taking one thing with another we were twin bundles of nerves as we thrashed around on that bed like a speeded-up amoeba in the throes of separation. It is a wonder we survived, but we did. And how we progressed! The first time my own tears ever wet my cheeks since I was in my narcissistic teens was that day in Portsmouth when you took a gamble on not starting the curse and lost, with the result that we found our loins so smeared in blood that it was as if we had been rolling around on a butcher's block. At first we laughed at the sight of ourselves. But you'd been momentarily so fearful that I would be squeamishly disgusted (which I would have expected myself to be) that you then began to weep, out of relief I suppose. Your tears so moved me that I cried too. Perhaps they were champagne tears. Perhaps it was just to do with my being in my narcissistic fifties. But we felt so close. It was a tender afternoon. We got dressed and went out and got sloshed (at that sailors' pub with the parrot, remember?), our relief and delight at having jumped some kind of hurdle was so great. Then we had a monumental row about I forget what, and went back to bed not speaking. What a great day. What a silly day. What a memorable day, the bits I can remember of it.

We did not get sexually off on the right foot at Harrogate. That in part, or I will concede if you like in whole, was my fault. Put some of it down to routine adulterous fears such as what if anyone saw us at the station, and to my accumulated agitation at the logistics of simply getting there and being there.

Telling Charles and Judith was child's play compared with telling you – that the Harrogate fixture was a figment of my imagination, I mean. Not knowing how you'd take it after all the work you'd done, I put it off and put it off and didn't come out with it until we were actually on the train.

"Oh, one little bonus," I commenced with assumed chirpiness. "You won't be left to your own devices as much as you thought you would. In fact we'll have the whole afternoon and evening together."

"What do you mean?" you asked sharply, somehow making me feel that I was upsetting carefully-laid plans. I came clean about the non-existent seminar, laying it on thick that I'd invented it simply as a ruse for seeing you again, all that long time ago, that eternity of nine and a half weeks.

Your petulance, I could tell, was simulated. You decided to be cross because it suited you to be cross. My deception was ammunition you could store in your locker to fire back at me when next I learned you were deceiving me in some way. My plea that the non-existence of the seminar gave us all that much more time together cut no ice with you at all.

"I might have things to do," you pouted.

"What things? I thought you didn't know Harrogate?"

"No, but I like wandering about new places."

"Don't you want to wander around them with me?"

"Perhaps, but I like to be on my own sometimes."

"You're very often on your own, Angie. Come on – this is a chance for us to spend a whole day and night together for once."

"Yes, well I don't like my arrangements being upset."

"But you don't have arrangements."

"I have arrangements with myself." And so you did. Your arrangements with yourself were often a cryptic barrier between us.

You sulked for a while but a Bloody Mary in the buffet car helped to unruffle your feathers, then you asked me what I'd told Charles and Judith considering it turned out the expedition was bogus.

What indeed. For Charles's benefit I resurrected my old school friend Tipper, the one I'd fictionalised into a greetings card manufacturer whose business I was after. I said I'd been invited up to his firm's dinner.

"Oh, yes, your prospective client," said Charles drily. "Why on earth does he hide himself away in stuffy old Harrogate? I'm sure if I were a successful greetings card manufacturer contemplating a national campaign I'd be living it up in – oh, what's wrong with Brighton?"

I didn't rise to my partner's heavy-handed irony, I'd brought quite a bit of business our way in recent weeks – there were after all, three working days when I wasn't lunching with you – so he couldn't complain.

Judith got the same story, introduced in an oh-by-the-way manner over supper. As it happened, she had her own oh-by-the-way announcement for me – a return match in Manchester, her first TV appearance having been so successful. She was getting the taste for it, so she said. Or, as we know now, the taste for something. Anyway, her trip was going to overlap with mine, so that as I got back she would have just departed. I was glad about that because I could see myself rolling home with guilt all over my face like lipstick. I decided not to mention Judith's arrangements to you: I thought I would need that cushioning time to get readjusted to my humdrum suburban world. But on the journey back from Harrogate I decided I didn't need it after all and impetuously asked you to supper. I could have kicked myself when you said, "Oh, Roger, if only you'd tell me things in advance and give me some notice, instead of hugging them to yourself."

So it was another Pizza Express and *Times* crossword evening, but at least I didn't lust after the au pair girl that night. I lusted after you and wondered where you were. Out to supper with a school chum. A likely story. I rang you intermittently until three a.m. when you still weren't home. You must have had a lot of gossip to catch up with.

But I jump ahead, as ever. Getting into the hotel was no great hurdle. I hadn't thought anything out beyond having no truck with any Mr and Mrs Smith nonsense in case Judith or the au pair or the agency needed to find me, and we certainly couldn't be Mr and Mrs Piper for the same reason. I simply told Rosie at the office to book me a room, and trusted it would be a double one as four-star rooms usually are. I steeled myself for the mini-ordeal of the receptionist saying, "And will this be a single or a double occupancy, Mr Piper?" as of course she did, at the same time letting her eye fall on you for a second as you made a great show of perusing a photo-display of Harrogate's attractions across the lobby. You were very cool, though you later said you were quite nervous. Certainly you didn't give the impression that you'd done it all before. But then you certainly didn't give the impression that you hadn't.

Your first words as I closed the door on the porter who brought up our bags were not all that propitious – "Oo, look, they've left us a contraceptive." This was the after-dinner mint on the pillow. I chose charitably to think that you were trying to be worldly in your waif-like way, and smiled at you fondly. But then you sat on the bed and bounced up and down experimentally. It was all too matter-of-fact for me. It was as if you were testing the equipment in a gymnasium.

Otherwise the room as a room didn't seem to interest you much. You glanced around carelessly at the built-in wardrobe and dressing table with what seemed the practised eye of a seasoned traveller. But you took a childish delight in the little grotto of soaps, shampoos, bath foam and other bathroom paraphernalia, and swept the lot into your suitcase before we left. It was a cheap little suitcase, old, but not much used. By then I had got the picture. It was strange bedrooms you were used to, not hotel rooms.

Your nonchalance perhaps disguised self-consciousness, though I believe any self-consciousness you may have felt radiated from me. Prowling the room you picked up the room service menu and suggested we had champagne and sandwiches instead of going out for the late lunch I'd promised. It was a lovely idea, and one which set a precedent, but a mistake in this particular establishment, since room service didn't materialise until I'd rung down four times, by which time I'd worked myself up into a fury. We started well, perched on the end of the bed and indulging in what used to be known as heavy petting – it was certainly heavy for me, a quantum leap from the hand-holding and thigh-stroking and games of footsie under restaurant tablecloths. But every time we heard a footfall in the corridor you'd tug your dress down and I'd leap to my feet and make for the door, only to return ranting about the inefficiency of provincial hotels. Soon I was too agitated to sit with you and was reduced to pacing the room, fulminating, "Christ, how long does it take to prepare a smoked salmon sandwich?" and so on. You found it hilarious. So do I in retrospect, but also in retrospect I see myself as stupid and gauche. At the time I was aware only of my own fury. Finally, as I picked up the phone and demanded to talk to the manager, you saved the day with another sound idea. "I'm going to have a bath," you announced. "Now don't work yourself up into a tizz."

"I'm in a tizz already."

"Then come out of it. It isn't the end of the world and we're going to have a lovely time. Promise. In any case, my getting into the bath will be like my lighting a cigarette when we're waiting for lunch – the moment I climb in, it'll arrive. You'll see." You were right of course, and I felt a surge of gratitude towards you for being right, and for having the knack of calming me down.

You came out of the bathroom smelling like the perfume and toiletries department of Selfridge's and wearing the blue kimono that had once belonged to Mrs Cheevers as it turned out, but we won't go into that now. You looked very fetching in it. You'd put your red stockings back on and you were very fetching in those too: a bit tarty, yes, but teasingly, comically so – you were making fun of the cliché yet at the same time enjoying looking tarty in the same way as you enjoyed spooning down half the pudding trolley at Le Bistro while sending yourself up for your own self-indulgence.

At last, with a paradoxical premeditated spontaneity, we tumbled across the bed and began to make love in earnest. And I do mean earnest. I wish now that we could have kept it on the jokey level of your deliciously silly red stockings, at least for the first few times. You wanted it to be fun, a lark, I wanted it to be a serious commitment, furrow-browed neurotic that I was. At the same time you were very anxious to please, so anxious that at one stage I gloomily came to the conclusion that you were only sleeping with me as a favour because I'd been banging on about it all that time. You put your mind to what we were doing, you drew on your sexual C.V. to contribute towards what we were doing, but it didn't seem all that important to you for it to be done. Certainly you didn't convey any great impression of your getting any special pleasure from doing it to each other. At one point during our gyrations you murmured, "No, I never like doing it like that," as if I'd made a wrong move on the dance floor. That analogy could be extended: I felt like someone trained to the foxtrot and the quickstep who has been introduced to disco dancing.

Or maybe that's not true. It wasn't as if you were introducing me to very much I hadn't come across before, but I was not used to someone going through her repertoire the first time round, so to speak. It should have been delightful but I was too shocked to be delighted, to be absolutely truthful with you, Angie. It was quite plain to me that this was simply how you had sex, full stop, whether with someone you professed to be or probably were in love with, like me, or with a one-night stand acquired at the Screw, like The Fuzz, if one night he was. There were no gradients. And yet we've another paradox here:

59

since there was no holding back on your part, it made you seem inhibited – and I was right, you were. For subsequently, when I found that you had after all been keeping something back, and that was depth and intensity, then I saw that you'd simply been making love in the only way you'd ever known how to make love, and that we had to learn to do it our own way. And so we did. Quality was to be the magic new ingredient, as we advertising buffs say.

Meanwhile, as you blithely and resolutely went from one man-oeuvre to another, from one position to another, as if ticking them off in your catalogue, I became gloomier and gloomier at the realisation of how little my sexual vocabulary overlapped with yours. I know it was in one of our rest periods, sipping champagne and nibbling a smoked salmon sandwich, that I first reflected, but not aloud, We're the difference between the definite and the indefinite articles. You're having *an* affair, I'm having *the* affair. When this goes, for me it's gone. For you, there's always another.

"What are you thinking?" you asked.

"Whether you've ever done it in the shower."

"Would you like to?" you asked, missing the irony. You cuddled up to me coquettishly, as you thought, but your flirting fingers and darting tongue were endearingly kittenish in their eagerness. In fact I think it was after Harrogate I added kitten to my stock of endear-ments. "I just want to *please* you," you whispered. That I *did* believe.

By far the most luxuriant part of the day was long after the champagne had gone, at around half past five when dusk had come upon the town beyond our cocoon and I lounged in front of the television, half watching some local magazine programme and half watching you dress and get ready to go out, which you did as naturally as if we'd been married for years. It made me feel proudly possessive until I reflected that the act of either dressing or undressing in front of someone of the opposite sex was not one you gave a moment's thought to.

But that was only a glancing pang. I was feeling relaxed, content and if you must know it, not a little smug. It had been, after all, a long time since I last notched up three times in an afternoon. (I do wish I hadn't said as much to you at one point, perhaps at dinner. You said carelessly, "Was it three? I never count." Ouch.) I felt, too, it has to be said, some relief at having got it over with, of having emerged from an ordeal. That sounds terrible. I mean that at the back of my mind I must have been worrying about making it with you, about whether we'd be, to use the overused word, compatible. That we certainly weren't, yet, but at least I didn't turn you off: indeed, I was the likelier candidate for being turned off, by your matter-of-fact sexuality. Now I wanted to bask in you. Sooner or later I would have to call Judith, and the thought was already nagging away at me that to put any warmth in my voice would seem disloyal to you after what we'd just been doing, while to withhold it would seem unkind towards Judith. That was another thought I pushed away. I wanted to enjoy you. Enjoyment is one of the capacities you taught me, did you know? I never did have a proper appetite for enjoyment until I met you, Angie.

We went downstairs and had those bloody great Bloody Marys you had to teach the barman how to mix, making him put in triple of everything except the tomato juice. We were well smashed by the time we rolled round to that Italian joint as recommended by Gunby's *Good Living Guide*. It was frightful enough for us to take a rise out of, but not so frightful as to make us wish we were somewhere else. We were having a lovely time.

I said, "Are we going to do this again?"

You said, "We haven't finished doing it the first time round yet, why wish it away?" I must have looked chastened, despite the crumb of comfort to be got out of the implication in that phrase "the first time round" that there was likely to be a second time round; for you said after a while, "I don't know – how many seminaries can you manage in a year?" When I described the difference between a seminar and a seminary you giggled so much that you had an attack of hiccups. I put my door keys down the back of your dress, we spilled most of the second bottle of Chianti and quite disgraced ourselves. Yes, a lovely time.

You were fast asleep in the time it took me to brush my teeth. As I kissed your face and put my arm around you, you murmured contentedly, " 'Night, darling." I wondered uncharitably if you knew who darling was. The same question forced itself into my consciousness when, at about three, we half-woke and began to make love again. You must have been more asleep than you seemed for as I caressed you, you asked in a sleepy but very distinct murmur, "Who?"

But if I had to encapsulate Harrogate into one of our snapshots, that isn't it. The snapshot would be a real one – a picture postcard of the Pump Room you secretly acquired and posted to me at the office (mercifully sealed in a hotel envelope). Do you remember what you wrote? "I can't think of anyone I'd rather have in my seminary. Hurry back to your loving Lady Malaprop."

You wouldn't be hurried back to, that was the trouble. Oh, we met as usual for lunch on the Friday after our "jaunt" as you called it. I took you to a new restaurant to celebrate our new relationship – that fish

61

place in Covent Garden. You hated it and seemed to hate me. Everything was wrong for you – the table was in a draught, the service was slow, the bread was stale, the soup was cold. You wouldn't laugh it off as we had in some of the far worse places we'd been to, wouldn't let me chaff you out of it. You grew more sullen and sulky as the meal went on. I kept trying to talk about Harrogate which for me had taken on an even rosier hue in the interim, but where you'd been tenderly reminiscent on the phone – for of course I'd rung you half a dozen times since our return – you were now pettishly offhand: "Yes, I loved it, I keep telling you, darling – are they going to bring that salad or not?" Only after I rather sharpishly suggested that as there was utterly nothing about our lunch that pleased you we might as well cut our losses and leave, since the puddings were bound to be awful and the coffee like turpentine, did you put a hand over mine and say, "I'm sorry, am I being hateful? It's only PMT." Perhaps. But that lunch adequately put a buffer between Harrogate and post-Harrogate, so that as we slipped back into our Tuesdays and Fridays routine it was, despite the nostalgic references from you as well as me, almost as if we'd never slept with one another at all.

Any idea I might have nurtured that I now possessed an open sesame to your flat, and therefore to your bed, was dashed from the start. "Oh, do put another record on," you snapped when I was emboldened by Freddy's Bar champagne to bring it up again.

"Don't you want us to make love again?"

"Of course I do, all the time, but you know about the flat situation, I've told you and told you."

"So I'm not just another notch on your bedpost?"

"You're being maudlin. Stop it."

Yes, I was, and why not? I was feeling pretty hard done by if you want to know, so why shouldn't I wallow in it? Looking at my situation with a hard eye, it seemed to me you had me jumping through hoops. I was lavishing lunch on you twice a week, pouring champagne down your throat, bringing you presents, phoning you daily, then panting for a reward that was never forthcoming. Who, I asked myself self-pityingly, did you think you were?

I believed you when you said you wanted me, if only because I was reasonably sure you were not sleeping with anybody else by now, or if you were you were keeping pretty quiet about it, and sheer sexual appetite must have surfaced in the cycle of your moods from time to time. One Friday afternoon, on a whim induced by one of our periodic and half-hearted resolutions to stop drinking so much, we gave Freddy's a miss and went to the cinema. A revival of *Guys and Dolls* with Sinatra and Brando – the only film we ever saw together, or rather didn't see, for we were groping one another in the back row like teenagers. Once, when we were coming up for air, you murmured with that same consummate brinkmanship that had led you to ask if I would like you to come with me to Harrogate, "I think it's time you addressed another seminary." As well as being tremendously excited at being thrown another bone at last, I was touched and glad that you had saved our seminary joke from the oblivion in which it had been lying out of my fear of pestering you for sexual favours.

Our Fridays had been getting longer and longer – it was rarely that we staggered out of Freddy's before eight these days, you to go home to Islington and sleep it off, I to go home to Ealing and grump through supper about having to suck up to clients. ("Don't you have any teetotal ones?" was the nearest Judith got to commenting on my state.) So I had ample time to take you for a drink in that champagne bar behind the Curzon. It was packed, and while we managed to find a couple of stools to perch on, we were practically nose to nose with a media-looking couple across the table, so pleasurable though it would have been, a discussion on seminary plans was not on.

"What did you think of the film?" I asked, with a certain amount of covert facework to indicate that it wasn't the film I was talking about. But the message didn't get through.

"It was all right if you like musicals," you shrugged. "What did you think of it?"

"Nowhere as good as the stage version."

"You've seen that, have you?"

And your message to me – the warning note of your asperity – didn't get through to me either. That couple of hours in the back row must have had a brain-soddening effect on both of us.

"Yes, at the National."

"With Judith, I suppose."

"Well, I didn't go on my own." I was aware that the couple across from us had begun to listen. Your voice rose, almost as if to make sure they didn't miss anything.

"Do you often go to the theatre with Judith?"

"Occasionally. If there's anything worth seeing."

"Isn't that strange!" you said in a high voice, affecting to be speaking to thin air but in fact appearing to address yourself to our intrigued listeners across the table. "The number of times you've asked me where I'm going or where I've been and who I've been with, and not once have you ever told me about your evenings at the theatre with your wife."

"You've never asked."

"Why should I have to ask?"

"What I mean is," I muttered, trying to keep my own voice low, "that you've never shown any interest in my social life. If I thought you wanted to know when we go to the theatre, whom we have dinner with, who comes round for drinks, then of course I should tell you."

"No, I don't want to know."

"Then what are you complaining about?"

"I'm not complaining at all, I'm just wondering why it never crosses your mind that I might like to be taken to the theatre sometimes." At which logical gear shift the couple across the table exchanged a sly, amused glance, and you noticed.

"Have I said something funny?" you asked in your hoity-toity voice. At least you addressed yourself to me and not to them, though they couldn't have looked more confused had you thrown your drink in their faces. Neither, come to that, could I. I hate embarrassing scenes as you know. One more example of my emotional cowardice, you once called this aversion. Probably true.

"Let's go," I said with a heavy sigh, playing to our gallery of two. "We've had enough."

"*I* haven't had enough."

"Everyone else has had enough. Up you get." And to my own shame I put on a show of helping my drunken little girlfriend out of the bar.

Some repair work had to be done. "I didn't like to say anything in there – " I began as we came out into the mews.

"No, in case people stared at you. That would never do, would it?"

" – but," I plodded on, "I do very much take to the idea of addressing another seminary."

"If your engagement book will allow it. I wouldn't like you to have to cancel an evening at the theatre."

I brought you to a halt and gripped your shoulders. "Stop it!"

"What are you worrying about? Afraid someone might hear us?"

In spite of or for all I know because of your taunting I wanted to take you on the spot. "No, in case anyone should see us, because I very much want to continue where we broke off in the cinema." I pulled you into the doorway where we began to behave as couples do in dark doorways – until the amused pair of eavesdroppers in the champagne bar happened by, and we disentangled ourselves, even you for once embarrassed.

That spectacular little row disturbed yet thrilled me. It was the first sign you had given me that you cared about my going home to Judith, the first admittance, however oblique, to that outside-looking-in loneliness I had detected in you when you gatecrashed Tim's christening party, the first time you had me face up to the emptiness you must have felt sometimes when you went off to your cold flat after warming yourself on my hospitality and, I hope, my company. I felt terribly selfish at picking you up and putting you down at whim, demanding your devotion whenever you were picked up, hoping you would in effect put a green baize cloth over it whenever you were put down. But I was frighteningly, thrillingly, aware, again for the first time, certainly so clearly for the first time, of something bubbling away under our frequent childish rows and makings-up – unquenchably bubbling away, and *growing*. It came out in the fumbling urgency of our dark doorway encounter so close on the heels of that bruising little quarrel. Yes, something had to be done.

We had to get away somewhere. Judith wasn't the problem – she was now doing her Manchester run, as she called it, once a month on average and was becoming something of a TV personality up there. It was Charles, with his recently developed habit of glancing at his watch whenever I came in from lunch, who was the stumbling block. I told myself I was a free agent who could come and go as I pleased so long as I fulfilled my responsibilities, but I couldn't quite screw myself up to trying the Harrogate ploy on Charles again. Had you pressed me I would have done, but you didn't press me at all. Nor, when I confessed myself stumped for an excuse to spend the night away from home, did you make any suggestions, except facetious ones like, "Why not say you have to take your mistress to Paris?"

I should have liked to take my mistress to Paris. I should have liked to have a mistress. So far, statistically speaking, you were a one-night stand who behaved sometimes like a mistress, sometimes like a close friend, sometimes like an enemy, but rarely as if these were all facets of the same love.

Eventually I did what I'd previously talked myself out of doing and, taking advantage of one of Judith's absences, booked a room at the Bond Street Hotel. The plan was as before: check in with overnight bag before lunch, whistle you up to the room after lunch, eventually send down for a tête-à-tête supper before departing for our respective beds, checking out on the way to the agency in the morning. My original instincts were right, were they not? What a disaster. Why didn't you tell me you felt you were stepping into a French farce before I'd booked the room, instead of waiting until we were actually in the bloody hotel?

It was a nightmare. I couldn't even get you into the lift until you'd had two stiff brandies in the cocktail lounge, and that was after a Bloody Mary and a bottle of wine at lunch. "Do you need to be completely anaesthetised, darling?" I asked acidly after you demanded your second. You fell into one of your silences.

The room hadn't been ready when I'd checked in and so I had left my bag at the porter's desk where, as I retrieved it, you took it into your head to ask in a loud, slurring voice, "Is there a television in the

room, porter, because we have to watch a programme for our work."
You didn't even notice the look you got as he assured you what you
already knew perfectly well, that all the rooms had television. Your
explanation that you wanted to create the impression that we were
going upstairs for a business meeting was so enragingly ludicrous that
we weren't speaking by the time we reached our floor. Then the key
wouldn't work and I had to find a maid to unlock the door. Then we
found the bed still unmade and towels all over the floor so I had to ring
down for another room. The same porter came up to help us switch
rooms and found you sitting on the bed with stupid tears making
mascara tracks down your cheeks, and you got another look, and
when I eventually got the bill it was for double occupancy anyway.
The new room was dark and overlooked the stairwell. There was a
noise coming from the waterpipes. I sank dejectedly into a chair while
you raided the minibar for miniature brandies. I drank mine in one go.
Since sexual activity was a retreating prospect, I thought I might as
well get smashed and keep up with you.

"I'm sorry for snapping at you," I said, "but it was nothing to cry
about, you know."

"I wasn't crying, I was laughing."

No, you weren't laughing, you were crying, but now that you'd
claimed you were laughing, you decided to find the situation funny.
"Oh, come on, darling," you burbled, lurching over and slumping at
my feet, cradling my knees and sloshing brandy and soda over my
trousers. "It's just one of those days when everything goes wrong.
We've had them before and laughed at them."

So we had, in inefficient restaurants where there was nothing to be
done but resign ourselves to the bad service. Here we did at least have a
working bed – but you showed no inclination to take advantage of it.

I said something to that effect. You countered, "You're not in the
mood," which was the wrong thing to say. I retorted, "You mean
you're not."

"No – you're not."

I said angrily, "Angela, we've been seeing one another for fourteen
weeks — "

"Have we? I never count."

"No, I know you never count, you told me that on the solitary
occasion we've ever been to bed together, but at least you must have
counted up to one. What the bloody hell is wrong with you?"

The third brandy had taken its effect. You stumbled to your feet.
"I feel sick and I want to go home."

"Then I'll take you home."

"No you won't, I don't want you to."

When you staggered out of the bathroom with sweat on your

66

forehead I had my coat on and yours ready. You still tried to argue with me as I helped you into it. "Roger, I don't want you to come back with me and anyway we're in no fit state to go to bed, otherwise I shouldn't be leaving."

"I'm going to take you home. Whether you let me through the door when we get there is entirely a matter for you."

You were too pissed to argue further. You fell asleep in the cab and when we reached Banks Place you made no further protests as I paid off the driver and followed you down those slummy area steps.

"Careful, the railings are loose," you said over your shoulder – automatically, it sounded to me, an oft repeated warning. You seemed drunker. I believe if at that moment Belle had opened the door and asked who I was, you wouldn't have known without turning round.

"Won't your friend Belle be in?" I asked as you rummaged for your key.

"No, she's gone."

"Gone where?"

"*Gone* gone. What does it matter where she's gone. Oh, Christ" – this as you tipped most of the contents of your handbag into the storm drain.

Helping you to retrieve them I found your key. "You can't come in, you know," you insisted as I unlocked the door, noticing the scratch marks around the lock where you must have scrabbled with your key after so many pissy lunches – and other occasions not connected with me.

Aggressively you pushed at my chest. "Go on. Leave. I don't want you here." You were so drunkenly unpleasant by now that I should have needed no second telling but for my burning curiosity to see your flat. And to hear about Belle.

"You've let me bring you home to the middle of nowhere," I said firmly. "At least let me ring for a cab." And I bundled you into the dank little kitchenette that doubled as your hallway.

When I was a student I was forced to take digs for a while in the first floor back of a dingy house in Clerkenwell. It was so bleak and damp that I knew I couldn't settle there and so I lived out of a suitcase while looking for something better, not even bothering to unpack my books. My landlady, to her credit, had tried to cheer the room up with a rug or two and some framed prints to hide the mildew; but when it became plain to her that she had a transient on her hands, these little luxuries began to vanish one by one, to be distributed among more grateful tenants. Then essentials began to go: a chair, a lampshade, the towel rail. By the time I moved out it was as though no-one had ever moved in.

Your flat reminded me of that room. The first thing that struck me was how utterly bare and lacking in belongings it was – no knick-knacks, no pictures on the green distempered walls, not even a pinned-up poster; no more than a dozen scuffed paperbacks in the bookshelves, the rest of the space being taken up by carelessly stacked magazines and newspapers. A portable television set but no record player or records. A cheap desk strewn with coffee-stained documents and unopened bills and bank statements and crumpled carbon paper. A typewriter, tipped up on end to make way for a coffee mug and a plate of half-eaten bran flakes, seemed your only substantial possession. No cushions on the sofa, and had I come by invitation and brought you flowers there was no vase to put them in that I could see. It was the saddest room I have ever come across.

"So now you know," you said.

As I wandered towards the one bedroom, the vibration of the creaking floorboards swung open the nicotine-stained, cream-painted door of your cupboard-cum-wardrobe with its Mother Hubbard collection of threadbare garments, including the black number you wore at the christening party, now hanging forlornly by its collar like a headless rag doll; and all those clanking wire coat hangers. Despite the rift between us I felt so sorry for you that I wanted to stock up your wardrobe like a film star's, with an overspill of hat-boxes and dress rails and shoe racks. Then my eye caught the tangle of men's ties among your higgledy-piggledy shoes and fallen coat hangers. You saw me sizing up this strange collection and drunk as you were, stepped smartly forward and shut the cupboard door, banging it twice to be sure it was firmly closed. Mystery.

The bedroom was even emptier than the main room, indeed it looked uninhabited, with only a stained mattress on a three-quarter size bed and a kitchen chair for furniture. But there were marks on the wall where pictures had been.

"That was Belle's room," you said sluggishly, flopping down on the sofa without taking off your coat. There was a Calor gas heater in the fireplace but you didn't light it, although the day was cold. Perhaps the cylinder was spent. "She took all her things with her."

"When?"

"You keep *asking* that."

"No I don't – what you mean is you keep asking yourself what you're going to tell me when I *do* ask that."

"Oh, clever. So you can read my mind now."

Yes, I could, to some extent. Whenever you were in a corner I could hear your squeaking gears grinding away as you contrived to manoeuvre your way out of it. It was some comfort to me that you couldn't do it smoothly.

"But now that I *have* asked, Angie, what's the answer?"

You took a deep, resigned breath to signpost how tiresome I was being. "You obviously don't approve of Belle or I would have told you. She's fallen madly in love with one of the waiters at one of those night clubs she goes to, Dolly's I think, and moved in with him. Right in the middle of Soho. It's a lovely flat."

"You've been there?"

"Yes, if you must know."

"I don't know why you want to sound so defiant about it."

"Because you're grilling me. Stop *grilling* me."

"I have to grill you, just to get a straight answer to a simple question. I didn't ask why Belle left or where did she go, but quite simply *when* did she go?"

"How do I know? I don't keep a diary! Why do you go on and on and on about everything? What does it matter?"

I could have shaken you, you were so exasperating. I'd begun to recognise by now that the churned-up state you kept getting me into must have been a significant ingredient of whatever chemical formula accounted for the excitement you generated, and I often suspected you of churning me up on purpose to sustain my interest. If you were doing that now I could have just forgiven you, but you weren't, you were just being bovine, sullen and stubborn, not caring, not comprehending even, how infuriating you were.

I said, trying to keep calm, "I go on about everything because it does matter. If everything doesn't matter then nothing matters. Do you comprehend that?"

I couldn't have blamed you if you hadn't. I was drunk too and I barely comprehended it myself, although I did know what I meant which admittedly is not the same thing. I could have gone on: And if nothing matters, why am I here, why do I bother? But I didn't want to ask myself hypothetical questions.

And you wouldn't even answer the question I had asked. You simply sat there on the grubby sofa in your coat, swaying, opening and closing your eyes and sniffling back tears like a reprimanded child. "Angela? I'm asking you a question. Angela!"

As angry now with myself as with you, for allowing myself to get into this hectoring posture, this time I did shake you, or anyway seize your shoulders and pull you to face me.

"Angela!"

You wrenched yourself away. "Stop doing that! Let go of me! Don't you know by now that bullying is the last way to get me to answer your stupid questions?"

Had I stayed I would have slapped you. "Oh, why don't you just go to hell, Angela?" I sighed, and trudged wearily to the door, giving you plenty of chance to call me back if you wanted to. You didn't.

At the doorway I paused and said, "Well, *that* was a question and I don't think I addressed it in a bullying manner. Are you going to answer it or would you like me to put it in writing so you can give it due – "

You cut into this ridiculous, self-demeaning display of irony by turning your head away and sobbing, "*Leave*, will you! Why don't you go? You said you were going so go!"

"If I do I shan't come back."

"I don't want you back. I didn't want you here in the first place."

Tossing up in my mind between slamming the door and closing it with marked gentleness, I opted for what seemed the more dignified course in my utterly undignified situation, and departed so quietly that you might have been left thinking I was still lurking in the kitchenette-cum-hallway. I had the satisfaction of picturing your mortification when you discovered I had really gone.

I charged through the slummy streets like one of those lost souls you see waving their arms about and directing traffic. A passing Asian woman gave me a frightened stare and I realised that my mouth was working convulsively as I rehearsed a tirade that would never be delivered: "You think I don't know what you're bloody up to, don't you? I know exactly what you're up to. You're playing Scheherazade, aren't you? Scheherazade, you little ignoramus!" (for I even had you echoing, in your dyslexic way, "Sherry who?"). "The clever little minx who saved her skin by spinning out her stories over a thousand and one nights. That's just what you're doing, isn't it – feeding me just enough dribs and drabs of information about yourself to whet my curiosity so that I'll come back for more, because you're afraid that if you tell me whatever you have to tell me all at once I'll lose interest in you? That's it, isn't it? And you think you can go on as long as you like, playing me like a fish on a hook, but you're wrong." But you were right. You could and you did play me along for as long as it suited you, whether you were aware of it or not, and whether my Scheherazade theory was correct or not.

I tried hard to slow my emotions down, to get my kaleidoscope of churning thoughts into some kind of order. It was difficult. Logic was always the first victim when I got into this state about you. I determined to blank you out of my mind and go back to the office and steady my nerves with some routine analysis work, but I had no idea how to get out of that dismal neighbourhood, where there were no cabs and the few buses seemed to be going only to outlandish places like Stoke Newington. As I stood on the kerb willing a taxi to come by, the unasked, unanswered questions kept throbbing into my head and multiplying amoeba-like as each one threw off its own little group of tormenting supplementaries. Why had you never told me Belle had

70

gone? When did she go? Was it before or after that afternoon in the cinema when we finished up groping one another in a mews doorway? If it was before, how could you seem to be so frustratedly urgent about wanting to go to bed with me when you had the means of doing so up your sleeve? Why did you let me book a hotel room when we could perfectly well have gone back to your flat? Had anyone else been back with you since Belle went? And so on, and so on, and so on, stones tossed into a silent pool and rippling ever wider. I felt, as I deliberately fed my seething mind, like a George Gissing hero (he was a gloomy novelist, darling) who has fallen in love with a prostitute and torments himself with visions of her sordid life. And talking of prostitutes: why hadn't you owned up to visiting Belle in Soho? What were you hiding?

I could have stood there on the kerb and gone mad with a little more application. What you were hiding, to reduce my interrogation to a single question and that a rhetorical one, was the fact that you could have taken me home with you any time that you chose for the last – how long?

I had to know – this and everything else that you'd hinted at, ducked round, walked away from. But why? That was a question to myself, to which I applied myself as soberly as I could. Retrospective jealousy came into it, to the extent that others had had far easier access to your flat and I wondered what sexual cylinder I must have missing for you to have put such obstruction in my way. But mainly it was a driving, obsessional curiosity, a need to know everything about you. Again, why? Why do we read biography? Or rather why do I, since I never knew you read anything except a menu. I didn't know the answer, but I was seized with biographical lust.

I knew that I had to go back to your flat, if I could find it, and talk to you. If you would talk back to me, I would stay with you all night, all the next day if necessary. Bugger the agency. Bugger Ealing. Judith wouldn't be back until tomorrow lunchtime and I'd think up some yarn about having to meet a client at Heathrow and his flight being delayed. I could ring the au pair girl about midnight and say I was having to spend the night at an airport hotel. The plan seemed so perfect that everything seemed perfect – until it came back to me that what I was looking for was enough time to interrogate you like a secret policeman.

As I retraced my steps as best as I could remember them, it crossed my mind for the first time that I could be in danger of being possessed by an unhealthy, neurotic obsession, that perhaps I already was. Passionate love, so I kept reading in the research crap thrown at us by perfume companies and the like, was simply a chemical change in the brain inducing the equivalent of an amphetamine high. A drug, effectively. With perhaps unpleasant and unwanted side effects.

71

It had been cloudy all day and now it began to rain. Soon it was bucketing down. I had left my umbrella not at the office, not at the restaurant, not at the hotel – yes, I fuzzily remembered now, I had got it as far as your flat. I determined that you could keep the damn thing. I was getting wet through and suddenly I felt grown-up and foolish. There was a bus stop near at hand, and a welcoming doorway to shelter in. I would take any bus that came along to whatever point of civilisation it reached, where I could pick up a cab and take me back to the hotel and a hot bath and a large gin and tonic.

Then as I hurried across the rain-slashed road I re-registered a broken-down off-licence that looked as if it had a clientele of winos, and realised I was crossing towards Banks Place. I was as sodden as the pile of rotting cardboard boxes piled up against the shop wall. I had an excuse for a dignified re-entry – I had come back for my umbrella. You'd light your Calor gas heater and dry my raincoat and we'd have a steaming hot cup of coffee and talk, sensibly. I wouldn't even wonder who'd last used my cup before me, or whether it had been breakfast coffee you'd served.

There was no answer to the last-gasp buzz of your tinny doorbell but perhaps you couldn't hear for the sound of water gushing out of a broken fall pipe and making a pond of the basement area. There was no threshold to your door and the water was lapping over the shallow step and under the door. Your little hallway-kitchenette must have been swamped. I rang again.

The curtains, if you had any, were undrawn. Anxious by now, I squelched across and peered through the imitation net roller blind, finding a gap where the brittle material had split with age. You were exactly where I'd left you, still in your coat, and deep in a sleep-coma, your head lolling back over the arm of the sofa and your mouth slack and wet. You were not, I'm afraid, a pretty sight; but it was a relief to be able to dismiss the lurid picture that had begun to form in my mind of your passing out in the bath or stumbling in your pissed state and knocking yourself out.

I rapped on the window with a coin. You didn't stir, of course. I've never know anyone sleep as you do. Logs were not in it. Sometimes when we've spent the night together I have lain awake raging at your sleep, believing you to have switched yourself off on purpose, like your answering machine, to stop me reaching you.

I trudged back through the rain forests of Islington, looking for a phone box. The usual ratio when I've tried to ring you was three telephones vandalised to one in working order. Here, there didn't seem to be a functioning telephone in the borough. Once, as I crossed to an obviously defunct phone box, a vacant cab came by; I let it go, on the slender chance that appearances might prove deceptive. The box

72

didn't even have a receiver – it had been ripped out. So drenched now that it didn't matter any more, indeed I'd begun to exult in it, I tramped on until I found myself in Dalston, wherever that is, and a telephone box that worked. Your answering machine answered, you didn't. I hung up and took a minicab back to Ealing.

I rang you four times that night and still got the answering machine. I hoped you'd wake up out of your alcoholic trance and call me. The phone rang at eleven and I rushed to answer it before the au pair girl could. It was Judith ringing from Manchester. All right: perhaps you thought I'd gone back to the Bond Street Hotel. I rang the desk for messages. There were none. I called your number once more and this time I left a message: "I love you. Will you call me in the morning, either before nine here or at the office?" You didn't. You claimed later, as you often did, that your faulty machine never picked up the call. Whether it did or not, you might have rung me. I rang you instead, the moment I woke up. Evidently you had awakened at some point, switched the machine off and gone back into a deep sleep, for the phone rang and rang and there was no reply.

How many times I called you in the next few days I won't humiliate myself by recalling. I made up little errands for myself in the hope that there'd be a while-you-were-out note asking me to call you on my return to the office. There never was; and so I would call you again. Sometimes your answering machine was on, sometimes I got the ringing tone and no reply, sometimes the engaged signal for hours on end. That comforted me in a perverse sort of way: if your phone was off the hook then it meant, or could be taken to mean, that you were actively rather than passively avoiding me – which could be interpreted, in my feverish state of mind, as caring.

I held out from going round to your flat for four days. I daren't, that was the truth of it: I was afraid of not finding you there, afraid of finding you there with someone else, afraid of you being there and refusing to let me in. Finally, on the Friday lunchtime – our lunchtime, the first we'd missed for ages – I took a cab up to Banks Place. The stupid cabbie couldn't find it and I got into such a tizz, as you would have put it, at his driving round and round in circles and stubbornly refusing to look in his *A–Z* because he "knew it was round here somewhere" that I started abusing him and he made me get out – luckily, hard by the scruffy wine shop that had become my landmark. Even had he been of a mind to wait, I should have foolishly sent him away, for all that it was beginning to rain again and I knew you wouldn't be in. But severing myself from my means of getting back meant there was a slender chance that you would be. Or so I superstitiously tried to persuade myself. At heart, I knew so positively you wouldn't be there that I nearly didn't bother to descend the basement steps. There was a bus coming by at the end of the street and I could have sprinted for it and remained comparatively dry. Instead, I fruitlessly jangled at the tinny bell, then peered through your torn blind again.

Oddly enough for one who thought so much about sleeping with you and whom you slept with, I hadn't given any thought to where you slept in the flat. The bedroom, I supposed, if I supposed anything, but that had been Belle's, hadn't it? Now I saw that your sofa was a Put-U-Up convertible affair. You'd left it unmade and the room was scattered with your things. Your wardrobe door had swung open, or more likely been left open, its contents given the air of having been swept through as at a jumble sale (and hey presto, that bundle of men's ties was gone. What were they in aid of? I wondered again. Souvenirs?). Make-up paraphernalia, stockings and your secondbest handbag littered the bed. Somehow I got the impression that wherever you'd gone, you'd paid a good deal of attention to your appearance. Friday, one of our lunching days. I wondered whom you were lunching with now.

I became aware that I was being watched. A coarse voice called suspiciously, "Was you wanting something?" and I looked up to see a slatternly woman, presumably "Mrs Scroggins" as you nicknamed your landlady, peering down from the front doorstep. I mumbled something about Miss Caxton asking me to check that she hadn't left her Calor gas heater on. The slattern challenged me sharply: "'Oo's Miss Caxton? There's no Miss Caxton 'ere."

I surmised, wrongly as it turned out, that the flat must be in Belle's name, whatever that might be. I had to say something, the old bat looked as if she were on the verge of calling the police, so I started stammering out something about "the other lady". I was incomprehensible and the woman was stupid anyway. She snapped back, "If you mean Mrs Cheevers, she's out!"

It was as if she had taken one of the loose railings out of the area steps and impaled me on it. But I had no time for mortification, for she was clearly waiting for me to get about my business or she would know the reason why, and so I slunk off, my pace developing into a shambling trot to get me out of the immediate neighbourhood in case she thought to dial 999.

Unexpectedly, the teeming questions failed to form themselves in my mind. Perhaps it was already over-full of unanswered ones. Besides, there seemed little to ask. Mrs Cheevers you were not, unless he was a bigamist: you wore his wife's cast off dresses. The situation as I guessed it, and not too inaccurately as it turned out, was that you and Cheevers had moved in together, as to when didn't matter. He'd either lived there with you for a time or established you there, leading a double life. How long this had gone on I wasn't going to conjecture. Whether it went on still I wasn't going to ask. It was none of my business. You were none of my business. I was sick of painting myself into humiliating corners. I was sick of your brick wall. It was over, or would have been, had not Charles of all people come unknowingly to your rescue and to mine.

FOUR

After we'd settled where to meet for lunch I was going to add, as casual as you like, "Oh, by the way, did I leave my umbrella at your place?" Then when you offered to bring it to the restaurant I meant to say, "No, I'll tell you what, bring it with you to the airport next Thursday. It might just be raining in Venice . . ."

It didn't work out like that, as you know. But it did work out, didn't it, my love? Venice was our saviour and our celebration. And our foundation too. When those four days were over, they were what we had to build on. Even had I never seen you again, I had those days to keep. They became, and remain, part of the furniture of my life. Thank you, Angie. Oh, and thank you, Charles. And sorry, Charles, too. You know, we should both say sorry to Charles – but that too worked out for the best.

He was crazy to let me take on the Venice Luggage Fair. By then he must have had enough feedback from people who'd seen us together for him to suspect that I'd probably take you with me. On the other hand he didn't have much option. Benito Benotti was one of our top three clients and for one or other partner not to have gone would have been tactless to say the least. He was Charles's baby, of course, but then so was Mrs Penn of Penn's Edinburgh Shortcake Products, the biggest fish in our little pond, who was going to be in town at short notice with a year's advertising budget in her handbag.

I think I know what was in Charles's mind when he mused, "On the other hand, if you've too much on we could always send Graham. It'd be good experience for him."

"I don't think so," I said firmly. "Benotti expects the organ-grinder, not the monkey."

"Don't under-estimate Graham, Roger. That young man's going places."

"But not to Venice, Charles."

"Perhaps you're right," he reluctantly conceded.

When I say that Charles must have guessed what I was going to be getting up to in Venice, in fact come to think of it he was probably way ahead of me. My immediate reaction when he asked me to take on Benotti should have been, but wasn't, that I could take you with me. Not surprisingly: I hadn't seen you for days, the Mrs Cheevers bombshell had left me pocked with shrapnel, you'd made no effort to get in touch with me and I didn't like you very much. So when Charles put the proposition up my first thought, and this was my sole reason for resisting the Graham alternative, was what a boost it would be for my ego if I met a dishy American sales rep at the Luggage Fair who was staying at the same hotel and didn't know anyone in Venice. But the fantasy led to you at once: I saw myself cruelly, casually, confessing the escapade to you, or more exquisitely still, having it dragged out of me.

Charles was shuffling paper as he always does when ill at ease. "By the way, none of my business, but in case you contemplate getting up to anything in the way of high jinks under the heady influence of the misty lagoon, do bear in mind that Benotti will be in London a couple of months hence," he went on, and then I knew I was taking you to Venice with me. What he meant was that he and his wife Lucille always gave Benotti a dinner party when he came over; Judith and I would be guests as always, and it wouldn't look too good if he'd seen me trolling round Venice with a half-cut redhead on my arm. Benotti had traded in his philandering Italian soul for a year at the Harvard Business School and he no longer believed in mixing business with pleasure. I would have to be careful.

Careful here as well as there, come to think of it. I had to get you an air ticket, book a hotel room for you (I could hardly risk having you turn up on my company bill as Signora Piper), change flights at the last minute so as to avoid Hugh Kitchener who also had a client at the Fair – Charles and he had always travelled to Venice together. How I would explain your presence when we inevitably bumped into Kitchener on the Lido I would worry about later: I had enough on my plate making the arrangements. It was a monumental exercise but I glowed at the prospect of tackling it. Not for a moment, for all that you'd behaved so badly, did it cross my mind that you would refuse to come. Certainly you'd be prettily contrite and pretend that you didn't deserve to come, but I'd forgive you magnanimously, talk you round, and then we'd make plans. "What a lark!" you'd cry, clapping your hands.

We had a week to get things organised. After my conversation with Charles I went straight out of the building to the post office across the street, heedless of whether any intrigued secretary or colleague chanced to be at the windows overlooking the row of phone booths. I willed you to be in, and to answer the phone, and you were and you did. "What do you want?" you asked in a far-off-sounding voice.

At once, "Did I leave my umbrella at your place?" seemed the most utterly banal question it would be possible to ask. I rejected "Angela, can we meet as soon as possible, it's rather urgent" as unnecessarily alarmist – you'd probably think Judith had found out. "Is your passport up to date, because you're going on a long journey?" was what I wanted to blurt out, but your bleak reception deflated me.

"Oh, we haven't spoken for so long, I was just wondering how you are," I said dejectedly.

"I'm all right." You certainly didn't sound it. You were even flatter than you'd just made me.

"So I was thinking maybe it would be nice to meet up for a drink."

"Why? I thought it was all over between us."

"Don't be silly."

You didn't reply and I knew from experience that you wouldn't speak again until I did. It was a way of making me feel that you didn't want to talk to me without actually hanging up and rendering you unable to whether you wanted to or not. I fell for it every time.

"Would you like to meet for a drink, then?" No reply. "At say six o'clock?" No reply. "Freddy's Club?" No reply. "All right," I said, "I'll be there, and I'll wait till half past six." And no reply again. I waited and waited until I began to feel like a heavy breather, standing there in a phone booth with the receiver to my ear and speaking to nobody. Finally I said, "Between six and half past, then. Try to be there," and was softly hanging up when my call ran out of time. I knew you'd be there although you would be late and it was possible you'd only turn up to give yourself the pleasure of announcing that you couldn't stay. Walking back across the street to the office I reflected on your spoiled-brat streak and on whatever streak it was in me that pandered to it.

You've often accused me of being obsessive or obsessional ("obsessival," you called it) about your past, yet the latest obsession, the Mrs Cheevers strand, was pushed so far back on the burner by the Venice development that I almost forgot about it in the new crop of on the whole rather delicious anxieties as the clock over the bar at Freddy's ticked up to half past six, and I wondered whether you were going to turn up although, as I say, I knew you would, whether you would insist our affair was over although I knew it wasn't, whether you would decline the Venice invitation although I knew you wouldn't – after you'd been persuaded, that is.

It was an uphill task, cosseting and coaxing you, apologising for my bad behaviour on the day you had behaved so badly, promising not to be infuriated at your mute response to my questioning (I was so willing to accept your surrender terms that I made a joke: "Why don't you plead the Fifth Amendment in future, darling, then we'll know where we are"), promising even not to ask questions at all – unless, that is, they touched on our own relationship. That was one condition I did insist on. I told myself privately that it was my escape clause, since everything about you touched on our own relationship. The Mrs Cheevers factor, for instance. But that could wait. Gently, I steered you round to the Venice jaunt, painting tempting vignettes of moonlight serenading on the Grand Canal and a room overlooking the lagoon.

"But won't it be awfully dank and miserable in November?" you objected, or wanted to seem to be objecting. It was the first sign of melting.

Probably it would. The previous year Charles had reported St Mark's Square under three feet of water and so foggy that you could not see from one side to the other.

"That's when Venice is at its best," I improvised. "All swirling mists and red sunsets, and no tourists."

You allowed yourself to be persuaded bit by bit, like a nervous kitten coaxed out of the cold with tit-bits. You wanted the few days of happiness I was offering, but you were wary. Once again that wistful, outside-looking-in air of yours so touched me that I yearned for you to be happy. I put an arm around you and you huddled up to me as if for warmth.

"All right," you deigned to say at last. "But no rows, no scenes, no inquests, no sulks?"

"Is that to be unilateral or mutual?" I might have asked. But I whispered, "Promise" and we drank a champagne toast to Venice. And at last you did clap your hands and you did cry, "What a lark!" And your excitement gave me the simple, wholesome pleasure of watching a child open a Christmas stocking.

"Would you like me to come with you?" you'd asked me out of the blue about my trumped-up seminar in Harrogate. In one pipedream I'd had you asking the same impetuous question about Venice. Perhaps you might have done had we started negotiations on speaking terms, but you didn't, so there we are. Whereas, to my consternation, Judith did, or at least she enquired, "Are wives invited?"

"Afraid not."

My feigned regret must have sounded as unconvincing to her as it did to me. "But they're not specifically non-invited? Didn't Charles take Lucille one year?"

"At their own expense, yes."

"I wasn't suggesting at the agency's expense. If they can afford it I'm sure we can. In fact I can easily pay my own way since I've had a very good year."

I'd already priced the whole enterprise and moved money out of my deposit account to cover the cost of your ticket and hotel room and other expenses. I felt ashamed of myself as I said, "It's not a question of it being affordable, darling, it's whether it's worthwhile, just for four days including travelling." I'd make it up to her. Take her somewhere exotic for a winter break. Except I no longer wanted to go anywhere without you.

"Four days is as long as we had for our honeymoon." True. It was in Paris. Funny you never asked. "And I've never been to Venice."

"Neither have I but it's hardly the time of year for it and anyway it's not really Venice, it's the Lido."

"The Luggage Fair may be on the Lido but you're not going to spend every second of your time looking at suitcases, for goodness sake. If you're all that interested in luggage you can go and watch the carousel going round and round at Heathrow."

"I have to dance attendance on Benotti."

"We could both dance attendance on Benotti. It's not as if I've never met him and I'm as capable of making intelligent noises about the latest trend in matching baggage as you are. Will his wife be there? She'd probably be glad of my company while he's selling suitcases. We could take them for Sunday lunch at – what's the island called? Torcello? The one everyone who's been to Venice raves about."

But I was already taking you for Sunday lunch on Torcello. Now I began to grow self-pityingly angry with Judith for denying me this small pleasure. Or rather for trying to deny me it, for even if it ended in divorce I had absolutely no intention of letting Judith spoil it for us. I began to raise all manner of blustering objections – I'd be worried about leaving the baby with Ingrid, it was a working visit and she'd get in the way, Charles would think it a bit off if it looked as if I were making a holiday jaunt of it, and so on. Finally Judith got the message, or rather conceded, since she couldn't have been in any doubt all along that I didn't want her in Venice.

"All right, forget it. You really do know how to make a wife feel wanted, I must say." With which she swept off to her little den at the back of the kitchen where she wrote her cookery stuff, pausing at the doorway to announce: "By the way, I don't think I mentioned it but I'm invited to Paris in a couple of months on one of those gastronomic weekends. If I decide to accept I'll be going alone."

I hoped she would. Indeed my heart glowed at the prospect, not only of a whole unexpected weekend with you but of a new, free regime where Judith went her way and I went mine, like the civilised people we were cracked up to be. I was fooling myself, of course. While something like that arrangement did ultimately come about as we know, Judith's aim in wanting to go to Venice, as I eventually realised, was to prevent anything of the sort taking root. But that's not yet in our story.

A couple of days later I went over to the Alitalia office and bought your ticket. Having it in my possession – "Miss Angela Caxton," the first time I'd ever seen your name spelt out – put me in a great state of excitement; but also, after that exchange with Judith, in a great state of apprehension. I didn't dare carry it about my person, didn't dare secrete it in my briefcase, and the thought of transferring it to some hidey-hole at home – what, behind the lavatory cistern? – brought me out in a sweat. Couldn't risk keeping it in the office: Charles and I had keys to one another's desks in case of emergencies. I had to find you that day. But you were nowhere to be found. We'd had lunch the previous day and I'd told you I was going to pick up your ticket, had hoped you would be able to come with me to the Alitalia office and take it off my hands. No, you couldn't. What was it that had cropped up again? Oh, yes – bit of temping work, you wanted to earn some pocket money to take to Venice. Fair enough. But you didn't give me a number where you might be reached, though you'd promised you would, and by eight that evening when I really did have to be getting back to Ealing, you still hadn't surfaced at your flat. I'd been up there by then, having rung you and rung you. Running the gauntlet of your Mrs Scroggins I put the ticket through the letter box with an affectionate note, then rang you and rang you again, having found a phone box miraculously in working order nearby, then went back to your flat and found it still in darkness, then posted a PS to my loving note asking, "Where the fuck are you, Angela? We have arrangements to make, all sorts of things to talk about. Couldn't you just have been here?"

I got home seething and was so short-tempered with Judith that she cleared off to her den straight after supper to do some work. The phone rang just before ten and it was you, as I hoped and feared and knew it would be.

I picked up the receiver at once, relying on the probability that Judith wouldn't pick up the kitchen extension – she hated answering the phone when she was writing. Your voice was slurred and high-pitched. "How dare you turn up at my flat uninvited and push filthy obscene filth through my letter box?" and so on. I hung up quietly as soon as you drew breath, gave it a few seconds and then took the phone off the hook, leaving it askew over the cradle so it would look as if I had replaced it carelessly. I called down to Judith:

"I'm just off to the pub for half an hour."

"Do. Take your temper for a walk."

I rang you, as I've done so often, from the box opposite the church, idly wondering as ever how I would explain myself should a neighbour one day remark, "Didn't I see you in a telephone box the other night?" The ringing tone went on for some time and then you responded in a dull puddingy way, correctly identifying your caller,

"Yes, what do you want?" I must have woken you out of a drunken doze.

I said, "Angela, I'm sorry I wrote that note, and for turning up at your flat, but I was very angry. Getting you to Venice isn't easy, you know, and I did hope you'd cooperate by at least being there when I got your ticket. What do you suppose would have happened if I'd hung on to it until you deigned to show up again, and Judith found it in my inside pocket?"

No reply. I ranted on, "Would you like her to have rung you for an explanation? It's not beyond her, you know."

No reply. "Where've you been tonight, as a matter of fact?"

No reply. "Look, do you want to come to bloody Venice or not? Because if you do you're going to have to stop just lying there like some kind of fucking primeval slug and give me some cooperation."

You hung up. I rang back, relieved not to get the engaged tone, gratified when you picked up the receiver. At least you were keeping your lines of communication open. I decided on a bold front. "I'm not going to call you again, Angela. I'll just go on and complete the arrangements without your help. If you want to go, be at the airport half an hour before check-in time. If you decide it's all too much trouble, sell the ticket back to the airline or flush it down the loo for all I care." No reply. In the silence I wavered, adding weakly, "So what are you going to do?"

"I'll think about it."

You meant to turn up. I felt chagrined and self-defeated. I could have kicked myself now for calling you back. I should have let you stew, held out to the eleventh hour, made you call me. But you probably wouldn't have done, would you?

It is odd how love, if that's what you want to call these bouts of self-torment, can deflate the ego while at the same time bolstering it. I knew, logically, that you were bad for me, that you demoralised me, destroyed my peace of mind, deflected me from the things I should have been doing, distorted my sense of perspective; yet at the same time you keyed me up, made me feel alive.

Back in my days with McIntyre, Pike & Lipton we had a chap who suffered a stroke down his left side and then recovered. He said the greatest moment of joy he had ever experienced was when the doctor stuck a pin in his arm and he felt it. No, my dear, I'm not quite going to compare that pinprick with your pain in the arse qualities: but just supposing you'd decided not to go to Venice, as you were quite capriciously capable of doing. Contemplating, with masochistic relish, the desolation I should have felt as I vacillated between the check-in desk and the terminal entrance doors, I know that I would sooner have had the desolation than non-desolation, sooner the pain and the anxiety and yes, the fury, than the deadening experience of nothing very much.

On the other hand I was not in the business of becoming your doormat, not even your welcome mat. I was very keen to establish parameters, a thus-far-and-no-further limit on what I would take from you. The trouble was that the limit would have to be perceived and accepted by you, and you showed no indication of even recognising the danger cones when I hoisted them. I missed my shattered sense of perspective, wished for some calm insight on myself. I badly needed to talk to someone about what I thought I was doing, but whom to turn to? Certainly not you – you would have left me more confused than when I'd started.

It was probably around this time – and if it wasn't, there were to be plenty of other opportunities for self-realisation – that it came home to me with a jolt that here I was, turned fifty, and I had no real friends. Charles, of course, but we ran a business together, and since in business efficiency terms you could only count as a liability, I knew what his advice would have to be. The rest of the people I knew were dinner-circuit chums, golf companions, people to talk about double glazing with. I needed a friend to advise me what to do about the only real friend I had.

As it happened, the next day but one was one of our lunch fixture days. I was determined not to ring you. Probably I would have held out until twelve fifteen or so, but I didn't have to, for you rang me first thing, to ask crossly, "Are we having lunch today or not, because if not I want to do some temping and earn some pocket money to go to Venice?" You wanted to tell me you'd be coming, but in as surly a manner as possible. I felt like telling you to go to hell. Instead, I thought I'd give myself the pleasure of telling you to go to hell to your face, and arrived at – Luigi's, wasn't it? – in an angry mood myself, determined to have it out with you and ask what you thought you were playing at. But you were sulkily contrite. "I *was* cooperating – I was cooperating by earning some money so I could buy you a thank-you lunch in Venice. You didn't have to call me an effing primitive slug or whatever."

"Primeval."

"I *said* 'or whatever', didn't I? What a thing to say to someone you're supposed to be in love with."

"Where did you get pissed?"

"I didn't get pissed, there was a wine bar opposite this PR firm I was temping for, where they all usually go for a drink after work. I had two glasses of wine with them because I didn't want to go home to a cold empty flat. What's wrong with that?"

Having seen the cold empty flat, I could find nothing wrong in that.

And there was no point in arguing the toss with you, it was as futile as clouting a kitten with a rolled-up newspaper for scampering up the curtains. I did want to ask if the wine bar in question was the Screw. Instead, I took your hand. "Have you ever heard of Torcello?" I asked. "Famous for Sunday lunch."

"What is it, a kind of pasta?"

"No, kitten, it's an island." Your endearing little gaffe washed away the wretched guilt I'd been feeling at stealing Torcello from Judith. I laughed, you laughed, and we ordered champagne.

Such as we were, Venice was the making of us. The expedition gave us the time we needed to consolidate ourselves. Had we but world enough and time . . . and now we did. The world was Venice and the time was four days. Or, as you delightfully worked it out, your dyslexia extending apparently to arithmetic, forty-eight hours. "Ninety-six," I corrected you patronisingly. "In fact ninety-six and a half. But it will seem like forty-eight."

The happy side of Venice, and most of it was happy, I see in flashback as a film montage – one of those slow-motion affairs, all light and foliage and spume, where you see the couple running barefoot, hand in hand. It was an idyll for us, and the weather was our friend, compounding my lie about romantic swirling mists and red sunsets with an Indian-summer spell of brilliant freak sunshine, warm enough to eat outdoors most of the time – and for other activities I might just soon remind you of.

We did things we've never done before or since – long walks, window-shopping, pavement cafés, museums even, though here your attention span was strictly limited. In fact Venice as spectacle left you curiously indifferent – the same indifference you felt towards rooms. You annoyed me for a spasm by sulking your way round the Doge's palace because I wouldn't take you to the cinema, of all things to do in this enchanted place. I joshed us both out of our petulance, though, by reminding you, "You've already been to the cinema. Don't you remember *Guys and Dolls*?" "Not very clearly," you said, digging your nails into my hand. "My mind was on other things." "So is mine now," I said, "and the back row of the Great Council Hall is rather public." So we gave short shrift to the Tintorettos and repaired to our room with a chilled bottle of Frascati.

The sex was good. All the ups and downs, the spats, the tiffs, the arguments, the accusations, the sulks, the flare-ups, had without our appreciating it until now endowed us with an easy familiarity in bed. It was incredible to think that in over three months we'd slept with each other only once, that after Harrogate we had resumed an entirely vertical relationship which had continued until this Venetian re-consummation. You still conveyed the impression of working your way through a sexual repertoire but after a few performances, for that's what they were in the beginning, it became our joint repertoire. You brought a chameleon quality to bed that I found quite extraordinary – a willingness, an ability, a talent, to adapt completely to my needs yet at the same time persuading me to respond to yours in just the way you wanted. And you could sense without my consciously giving out signals what I didn't like – your matter-of-factness, for instance, the way you'd say "Oh, I never do it like that" or "I never count." From never counting you switched directly, without a blush, to "Do you realise how many times this is since we got here? We're insatiable!" – because instinct told you I'd like you to talk like that. Certain phrases, certain gestures, certain physical acts were keyed out, certain ones keyed in, as if you had me programmed on a home computer. Yet I didn't feel computerised. I felt, as I certainly hadn't that first time in Harrogate, that our lovemaking was exclusive, stamped "Limited edition". Reason told me it couldn't be: but siren-like you lured me willingly into believing that it had never been like this with anybody else. Which for me, at any rate, it certainly hadn't.

What I couldn't get rid of, no matter how special these special feelings, was a ruminating interest in your sex life in general, Cheevers in particular and, even more in particular, your role as Mrs Cheevers of Banks Place. I've mislaid in my memory now how much I knew about Cheevers at this point – how much you'd told me or rather reluctantly allowed me to drag out of you, monosyllable by monosyllable. The chronology of it is of no consequence. I certainly knew that from being a vague relic of your past who didn't matter to you he had become the only man in your life who had ever mattered to you, bar me, although you said it had all long been over and that it had only lasted – now was it six months, twelve months or eighteen months at that point of revelation? Again, it's of no consequence. I know that whatever I knew about Cheevers was but the tip of the iceberg – and that I suspected as much even before the Mrs Cheevers bombshell. But I kept my promise and didn't touch on it at all in Venice, or on any of the other subjects that got you on edge.

Except your flat. I did bring that up, didn't I, the evening I had to have dinner with Benotti and I picked you up later, that's to say at the earliest possible moment (having skipped coffee on the excuse of expecting a call from Judith, and ducked Benotti's invitation to ring her from his borrowed palazzo apartment on the laboured pretence that she was staying with friends and I didn't know their number), and carried you off to that pizzeria you grew so fond of (Our Pizzeria it might have become, had we been there longer) in the little piazza a five minutes zig-zag from the hotel. The day's wintry sun had no staying power and so the November evening was cold, but not so much that we couldn't sit outside behind a protective wall of glass and with comforting radiators beneath the roof awning. We were nicely cocooned. You looked up at the tall warrens of dark or shuttered but occasionally brightly lit rooms overlooking us and wondered, from the glimpse of a chandelier or piece of furniture, whether they were very grand inside or as slummy as they looked from their exterior flaking stucco. That led naturally to the subject of your flat. It wasn't often our talk led naturally to anything I wanted to ask you about and I made the most of the opportunity.

"You're wondering about these apartments as I was wondering about yours. It was only simple curiosity, you know. I just wanted to visualise you in the place where you lived."

"I hope that isn't all you wanted," you said teasingly – I might have said tauntingly, in a different mood. But a few hours earlier we had been making love with the shutters open to let in a watery sun and a wisp of sea-mist from the lagoon. It was as liberating and exciting as doing it in the open air.

"I mean apart from that. I wanted to see your flat as a flat, just to add to my knowledge of you."

"You make it sound as if you're compiling – I know the word's not dosser, but you're not to correct me because you know perfectly well what I mean."

"I am compiling a dossier, and any day now I'm going to make an arrest," I said flippantly.

"What – have me in handcuffs? How exciting!"

You were still teasing but I had one of those walking-across-one's-grave cold shivers that sometimes went through me when you spoke lightly and I sensed something heavier underneath. I said casually, "You've never asked me what I thought of your flat."

"I don't think I want to know."

"Why is it so bare?"

You shrugged. "Possessions aren't all that important to me."

"Not possessions. Pictures on the wall. Posters. Postcards. Things that make a place looked lived in."

"It isn't lived in, it's existed in." Did you play for sympathy or was I over-eager to provide it? Anyway, you got it. But I was still intrigued by that throwaway line about handcuffs. It was lying there and I had to pick it up, but not at once, or you'd know I was fishing.

"Existed in, yes. It certainly gave that impression – almost as if you *wanted* to give that impression. As if you were wallowing in it."

"I don't wallow."

"You do wallow. If there's reincarnation you'll come back as a hippopotamus and wallow in mud."

You laughed. "If I do, I'll waddle up your drive and haunt you."

I laughed too. "You wouldn't be a ghost, chump, you'd be the real thing. A red-mopped hippo."

I let this nonsense go on for a while and then, having conversationally strolled a sufficient distance away from your meaningful (as it did prove to be) little quip about the handcuffs, said longwindedly, "How did we get on to this track? Oh yes, your flat. It's odd what sticks in the mind. Do you know what I see when I think of your flat, Angie?"

"The blank walls, you said." (Yes, I had.) "I really should put some posters up, I suppose. But they do cost money, you know, darling." It was the first time the subject of your financial straits had come up so baldly. But I ignored that for the time being, in favour of chasing a hare of my own choice.

"No, it was your cupboard door, wardrobe door, whatever you want to call it, swinging open, and seeing that sort of mess of men's ties lying there. What are they, Angie – souvenirs or what?"

"Men's ties? What do you mean, men's ties? I don't know anything about men's ties."

"You do, Angie, a great bunch of them, at the bottom of your wardrobe. And then when I came round a couple of days later, because you wouldn't answer the phone and I was worried about you," – aggrieved self-justification: I must have picked it up from you – "and I looked through the window, they weren't there any more."

You had stiffened, put on a fixed smile, angrily snapped a breadstick. The usual signs. "They weren't there because they weren't there in the first place."

"But they were."

"No they weren't."

"But I saw them."

"If you saw anything, you saw a couple of school-type ties I picked up in the Portobello Road and used to wear with a striped blazer I once had. I don't have a bunch of men's ties – what are you talking about?"

"I'm just asking what they were doing there."

"Why? What does it matter?"

"I don't know, that's what I'm trying to find out. If it doesn't matter, why are you bothering to cover up?"

You were still agitated but now trying not to seem so. "Cover up? Cover up? What are you making such a drama about? Darling, we're in Venice, having a lovely time. And I want to go on having a lovely time. And you did promise there'd be none of these integrations."

"Interrogations."

"Those too," you said, wanting to turn it round into a joke. "Come on, Roger, darling. There's nothing to worry about. Why should I lie to you? You were very pissed and saw something that wasn't there. It can happen, you know. Just be grateful you didn't see a pink elephant."

I conceded: I wasn't going to get anywhere, not without rocking the boat so violently that we'd finish up in the drink. "Or a pink hippopotamus. All right, my love. I'm sorry. I do go on, don't I?"

And I dropped it. But you didn't. You would keep on making ploddingly joshing references to the subject during our Venice stay – "Now where did I put my ties?" you'd pretend to muse as you rummaged through your half of the wardrobe. It was, I came to appreciate, a technique of yours. Leave so much room for doubt that to voice that doubt would be preposterous. I was taken in for a long while.

The pink elephant/pink hippopotamus nonsense had restored good humour, and the veil of Venetian magic, rent for a moment like a tear in the clear, star-dazzling sky, enveloped us again. There were kids playing not too noisily out in the piazza, a strolling accordionist, water gurgling from that old fountain, women calling from their windows and hauling up baskets of groceries, things to look at and savour. The rough wine was good, no longer quarrelling with the smoothly superior vintages at Benotti's table earlier. We both fell silent in the flickering candlelight, you savouring your surroundings for once as you devoured some strawberry confection, I wanting to enjoy myself and trying to, but plagued by these nagging questions, as persistent as mosquitoes, which increased and multiplied with practically every conversation I had with you. I pondered my Scheherazade theory. I could apply it to you with ease but how far could I apply it to myself? How much did I want, did I need, to be kept on tenterhooks, to be left in the air, to be puzzled, to be full of doubts – would I be as intrigued by you if there were no intrigue, as fascinated by you if you were as unfascinatingly straightforward as I wanted you to be? I'd no way of knowing. I didn't even want to know. I didn't want to know anything, if only the mosquitoes would go away. I wanted to be happy. If only you'd had the intellectual capacity to be a bit less bloody infuriating. Instead you kept throwing out smokescreens like a pursued animal emitting offputting secretions – out of fear, panic, and inborn instinct.

"What are you thinking?" you asked.

"About the nature of happiness," I said rather grandly.

"What about it?"

I realised I was thinking nothing in particular – just the same old tired thoughts swilling gently about like the little canal by the piazza sloshing lazily in response to a gondola crossing it from a junction of dark walls. "Oh, just how nice it is here," I responded idly.

"Were you thinking about Judith?"

"No – why do you ask?" Why did I ask why you asked – wasn't that what I always complained of you doing?

"Didn't she want to come to Venice with you?"

"Yes, since you mention it."

"Why didn't she?"

"Because I wanted you to come."

"Was that fair on Judith?"

"I wasn't aiming to be fair on Judith. I wanted to be with you. You come first, I'm afraid."

"Not really." Apart from oblique digs such as the night you took it into your head to start on about how I never took you to the theatre, you'd never touched on my marriage before. I was surprised, slightly alarmed, quite pleased. "I come first in some things but not important things."

"You do. You don't know it but you do."

"Before your wife, your home, your baby, your work? I don't."

Well, you did and you didn't. It was difficult to explain, particularly as I didn't know the explanation myself. Perhaps if I could have made a stream-of-consciousness film of all my movements and all my thoughts and all my preoccupations since our first moment together, you would have been able to work out your place in my scale of priorities, and so should I. Or not: I sometimes pushed you into the background despairingly, sometimes I pulled you forward recklessly. I was silent. So were you for a while. It seemed a tranquil silence between us, filled with the little noises of the piazza. Then abruptly you asked:

"Supposing I'd refused to come, would you have brought Judith then?"

"That's hypothetical. I wouldn't have taken no for an answer."

"And I shan't take that for an answer. Would you have brought her, I'm asking?"

"She could have insisted on coming, if that's what you mean."

"No she couldn't, otherwise she'd be here now. You're not being honest, darling. Then you criticise me. I'm asking you a perfectly straightforward question and you won't answer."

"She might have come, I suppose. She did want to, and had you not been involved it would have been churlish not to have let her come." It wasn't the true answer, it was the one I judged you wanted to hear. I could have said I would have come without Judith and pined for you, but you seemed to be requiring me to have a conscience about Judith.

Then you said, ever so delicately describing a pattern in the bread crumbs on the paper tablecloth, "Had you been here with Judith, would you be sleeping with her?"

You had never before expressed the slightest interest in my sex life with Judith. Any jealousy you might have felt seemed to be of status and possessions – that I had a wife and family to go back to, a home of my own, a grand piano. You'd once made much of Judith's grand piano, which you'd glimpsed at the christening party. "Does she play it in the evenings? What does she play? Can she sing?" you asked, as if trying to build up a picture of tranquil domestic evenings. You certainly built one up for me, for I imagined you outside the lighted window, looking wistfully in. I wanted to buy you a grand piano. You'd told me you used to play when you were a little girl.

I was gratified by your interest, but careful in my reply.

"You mean sexually sleeping? It would have happened, I suppose."

You said with your tight smile, "Yes, it's romantic in Venice, isn't it? Silly me for asking."

"I've never pretended I didn't sleep with Judith. and it would have had nothing to do with how romantic it all is."

"Duty," you suggested, your voice measuring out the appropriate level of dry scorn. You rubbed out the pattern you'd made with the breadcrumbs and began scraping them back into a little heap.

"Not duty. Pattern. Habit."

"And how often does the habit take you?" you asked. A flick from a fingernail, and the breadcrumbs were scattered again.

I experienced a moment of Machiavellian glee at the opportunity you'd handed me to pay you out for all the wretched questions I had been forced to ask you while you played at answering like a kitten playing with a mouse. "Why do you want to know? What good will it do?" I could have asked, but of course I didn't, I wouldn't. Besides, I don't think you really did want to know. The conversation had merely drifted in that direction, like the debris bobbing lazily along the canal.

"As the need takes, I suppose."

"That's not an answer. You're being very effusive this evening."

Elusive I should like to have been, if that's what you meant. I could still have happily given you a taste of your own medicine had I thought you would even notice what a disagreeable taste it had. But at any sign that you wanted to be more closely involved with me I was too pathetically eager to draw you in to bother with such ploys.

If you meant evasive on the other hand, I plead guilty. I waffled as I suppose married men always do on these occasions. I was careful to explain the difference between basic sexual need, appetite if you like, and the need I felt for you. It sounded like guff to me. To you it probably sounded like something you'd heard before. Or so I guessed from the cynical little smile you let slip for a second. Perhaps you'd gone over the same ground with Cheevers.

I wish I'd had notice of that question. Of all the conversations I'd had in my head with you, this was one I had never rehearsed. It had never even occurred to me to wonder whether you felt any curiosity about Judith and me in bed. Odd, when I could be so consumed with sexual jealousy myself. But perhaps jealousy stems from lack of confidence, and you didn't lack confidence in that direction. Yes you did, I know you did. I mean you didn't feel so remarkably fortunate at being sexually involved with me that you couldn't bear the thought of someone perhaps being, to put it crudely, better at it with me than you, for fear of losing your grip on me. That was the difference.

Talking about Judith in that way it was difficult not to sound like a liar and I expect I did lie, by omission or distortion wanting to persuade you that it was a marriage of companionship. Wanting to persuade myself, too. It would have made it easier to enjoy my relationship with you and relax with you had it been true that Judith and I were but a premature Darby and Joan. But we were never Tristan and Isolde, I can assure you of that.

I hardly ever talked, because you hardly ever asked – indeed I don't think you asked at all – about our early life together, how we met and all that. I'm sure you would have accepted that two people thrown together on their flat block's tennis court who play all summer long without it very much occurring to either of them to take it further do not have a passionate love affair within them, at least not with each other. I invited Judith to the theatre (your first jealousy!) because the girl I was seeing at the time was on a skiing holiday with some friends. You see what I mean? If I'd been going out with you for six months and you'd taken yourself off on holiday with two other girls and three men, I should have jumped off a cliff or pushed you off one. But that was the depth of the relationships we had in our little world. And Judith accepted because she wanted to see the play and the chap she was going around with at the time had already seen it with another girl. Such was our well-scrubbed innocuous promiscuity in what for you, still in pigtails if you ever wore them – did you? – was well into the permissive age.

It took three months to get Judith into bed, or rather it took three months for Judith and me to get to bed, for while we visited one another's flats for drinks or dinner, either alone or with others, there was never much more than a bit of hand-holding while watching television. Because we were neighbours in the same block, perhaps. Bed-hopping simply wasn't a convention there. Come holiday needs and we locked ourselves into an arrangement with another couple to rent a villa in the South of France, separate rooms all round but with an unspoken assumption that it would culminate in bed-sharing. Thus began the sleeping relationship which continued up to and through

91

our marriage. If it didn't tail off in frequency or ecstasy as so often in marriage, quite frankly it was because we'd established right from the beginning the level at which we proposed to cohabit – a pleasant, tolerating level, an acceptable mean average between the carnal and the platonic which I should think must account for a good number of successful marriages.

As to sexual need: to get into the difference between needing Judith or Judith needing me for that matter, and me needing you – I can't speak for you needing me – I should have to contrast the South of France with Venice. It was Nice, to narrow it down: the sun beating down through the diesel fumes on white, uncompromising boulevards, as compared with the serendipity of unexpected canal vistas, intriguing dark corners, cool courtyards and sun-lapped piazzas. I won't make too much of this imagery and I wish I hadn't gone into the comparison too closely then, for after I'd finished my stumbling explanation of the difference between one kind of sexual need and another, all you said, rather surprisingly and rather crudely I thought, was:

"All I was asking was how many times a week."

I lied about that too, but only because it was an unexpected question and I was fazed. But as you would have said, what does it matter?

That was the only discussion of a soul-searching nature, if you can call it that, that we had in Venice. I wanted us to talk, about ourselves, about what we meant to one another, about what we thought we were doing, above all about what the hell you were *about*; but the more of that unaccustomed carpet of time I saw stretching before us, the more reckless I was with it, happy to squander it in happy smalltalk, knowing we could always turn to more serious things tomorrow, but knowing we wouldn't. It was a wise investment in lotus eating, that Venice trip. What did we find to talk about, do you remember? I don't, very much. You prattled a lot, as you always did when you were happy. I gave you what I'm afraid must have been rather patronising little lectures about Venice and its history, gobbets instantly passed on from the guide book I mugged up while waiting for you to get ready to go out, or on the vaporetto back from the Lido when I felt I had done my duty to Benotti's new range of suitcases for the day. On my first day back you were standing at our bedroom window, waving frantically to every boat and water-bus that came in on the off-chance that I was on it. I was so touched by that. Did you know that one gesture a day like that, like an apple a day for keeping the doctor away, would have broken down all my doubts and broodings, completely destroying the immunity I tried to build up against you out of self-protection?

The second day I was later back than I'd promised and we had our only real spat of the trip. I was in no mood for it, having blotted my copybook with Benotti who'd been insistent that I met a launch-load of freeloading German travel writers, for all that PR was no part of our contract and he did have his own West German representation supposedly handling the freeloaders. Unfortunately the West German representation had gone down with that mysterious ailment you once diagnosed as lunch-poisoning, and Benotti looked to me to come to the rescue.

I did him his good turn with an ill-grace that can't have been very well concealed, for when I had to have dinner with him on that night I've just been talking about, the night you asked about Judith, he gratuitously and obliquely referred to it, sidling the Harvard Business School into the conversation by way of reaching his text for the evening: "But you know, Roger, the most valuable lesson I ever learned in business was not from books or lectures, but from my father, who by the way owned some vineyards, but at the same time he would buy his olive oil in the town. One day I said to him, 'But father, you grow olives, you could make your own olive oil, why do you buy from Signor Such-a-name?' And you know what my father said? 'It's business, my boy. You see, I want to do him a favour.' " The point of this impertinent parable was that eventually the olive oil character died and, having no relatives, left his operation to Benotti's old man, who turned it into the biggest olive oil plant in the region. So now you know why I shan't inherit Benotti Baggage. Benotti repeated the phrase several times. "It's business, I want to do him a favour. My father was right, Roger, may I say? You see, do someone a favour and it is business, because he will always remember it." I wouldn't have minded, but the patronising little twerp was a good fifteen years my junior. And as we know, he didn't do me any favours, the reverse in fact. But we'll come to that. Meanwhile, now you know what he meant when I introduced you at the Cipriano on Torcello, hoping to pass you off as someone encountered at the Luggage Fair, and he looked you up and down and said roguishly, "Now I understand, my friend – you do *yourself* a favour."

Detaching myself from Benotti's Germans with all possible speed, I took a water taxi back to the hotel only to find you'd tired of waiting for me and gone for a walk. You left a loving little note which I still have: "Arms aching from waving, and aching for you. Not gone far. Look for me. Love you." I read it eight or nine times like a schoolboy reading the print off his first Valentine, then set off to look for you in the maze of alleys and little piazzas behind the hotel.

Of course you'd got hopelessly lost and finished up somewhere on the wrong side of the Rialto bridge. With that amazing resourcefulness you always displayed when you'd got yourself in a spot no resourceful person would have got into in the first place, you somehow managed to establish where you were, make sense of the Italian telephone system and get through to the hotel and leave a message to say where I could find you. You could just as resourcefully have found your way back to the hotel and been waiting for me when I trudged back to see if you'd done just that, but never mind. In all we'd lost a precious two and a half hours by the time I found you in that expensive café by the Grand Canal where you'd established yourself with a simpering corps of Italian waiters.

Can delight go hand in hand with annoyance? Yes. Espying you from the bridge I was pleased enough to see you, yet irritated and depressed by the attention you were getting, and enjoying – it was a reminder to me that if I ever dropped you, or you dropped me, the timespan between your saying goodbye to me and hello to someone else would be about five and a half minutes. You were well on the way to getting smashed and that irritated me too, as did your insistence on introducing your bunch of Guiseppes and Luigis as your minders. If looks could speak, theirs would have said suggestively, "You have a right little bundle of fun here, Signor." You were irritated in turn by my insistence on wheeling you away to a quieter place where I could enjoy a much-needed drink with you without having to swat admiring waiters away like flies.

Our contagious pique so manifestly impended a row that it was almost visible above our heads, like a raincloud. I thought we might as well get it over with, and said as much.

"I'm the one that should be annoyed," you said, after denying that we had anything to row about. "First you stand me up for two and a half hours, then you drag me away from a nice café right on the Grand Canal where I was enjoying myself and dump me down in this dingy little square."

"An hour, not two and a half, my love. The last one and a half has been taken up by my meandering around Venice looking for you because you got yourself stupidly lost."

"How can you call me your love and stupid in the same breath? You're such a hypocrite."

And so on. We were like Punch and Judy, having a row just for the sake of it to relieve the random tensions that had built up like static. For my own part, I had a good selection of anxieties to choose from – about skimping the buttering-up job I was supposed to be doing on Benotti, about our being spotted by Hugh Kitchener as miraculously we hadn't been yet, about my cavortings getting back to Judith, to name but three. But the truth is that I didn't give any of these real fears a second thought. My anxiety was the retrospective one of having lost you for all that time, and the prospective one of losing you for ever which any stray little incident – a blown kiss from you to one

94

particular waiter as we departed the café where I'd found you – might jog into active gear.

Your own tensions, I think, sprang from the simple fact of our living together – only for a precious four days, true, but living together as distinct from sleeping together in that we were exposed to one another's domestic foibles for the first time. There was something of a temperament clash here. You found my fussiness over towels in the bath and undisposed-of disposable razors in the sink dreary and middle-aged. I found your lack of consideration sluttish. Neither of us voiced our criticism. In your defence, I would have said that I'd had the practice at living with someone and you hadn't. In my own defence, I would have said that it's not middle age but marriage that creates the finickiness I could see jarring on you. Married people slowly build up a catalogue of resentments against one another simply out of the fact of being cooped up together for any length of time, and these resentments are bound to be projected onto the next person in their lives who leaves the cap off the toothpaste. Not me, dear, the system. I would reflect on this when wondering what life might be like with you if we were married or living together for real. I simply couldn't visualise it happening. It would be then I'd wonder why I was so hopelessly involved with you when I knew I had to wake up sooner or later from what could only be a mad dream.

I explained to you about being saddled with Benotti's Germans and you tiresomely persisted, if not in getting hold of the wrong end of the stick then in failing to grasp the right one. I sometimes wondered about your IQ, you know, kitten.

"But you look after his *advertising*, Roger. What are these German travel writers to you?"

"Nothing at all, but as I say this German PR guy was down with lunch-poisoning."

"Having another lunch with his girlfriend, more likely, the same as you should have been doing. Why do you let yourself be put upon, darling? And what about me? Don't I matter?"

"Not to Benotti, my dear. He's a client. We have to look after clients. That's what we're doing in Venice."

"It may be what you're doing in Venice but all I do is wait for you, for hours on end. I've never been so bored."

"Don't be so childish." Like you, I'd only been stoking up the row to let off steam but now I was genuinely, impotently angry. You just couldn't or wouldn't understand that I'd gone so far out of my way to do what you accused me of not doing – namely, making time to spend with you – that I had seriously upset one of our most important clients and put his account in jeopardy. It was infuriatingly frustrating to perceive that you simply didn't comprehend, couldn't appreciate, the corners I was cutting to be sitting here in not the nicest café in Venice in rather an insalubrious piazza, arguing the toss with you.

But after all, the row was only a raincloud. We walked back over the Rialto bridge in a sulk but finally our hands touched and by the time we got back to the hotel the sun was out for us again.

I stopped at the desk to order champagne and sandwiches in our room: we'd been in too much of a pet to have lunch. There was a message awaiting me from Benotti, asking me to join him at a cocktail party back at the Lido if I could make it.

"Bugger," I can remember saying. Slighting him twice in the same day would be pushing my luck.

"You could swear blind you never got the message," you sirened in my ear, seductively nestling up to me in the lift.

"Is that what you'd do?" I asked, my mind made up. And as we let ourselves into the room and began to get undressed, unheeding of the room service waiter who would be along soon, I answered my own rhetorical question. "Yes, of course it is."

The tail end of that afternoon, and the evening, were so different from the bad start to it that it was as if we were different people at a different time and in a different place. Sometimes, when you were in one of your black moods, I would wonder if you were mildly schizophrenic. This was one of those occasions when it seemed as if the day was, with the clock segmented into Dr Jekyll and Mr Hyde components.

So that day was, after all, a snapshot for our album. And then you loved Torcello, didn't you? Everything was so right that it seemed as if there were a conspiracy to make our last day happy. A pity that Benotti and Hugh Kitchener were not a party to it, but there we are. The weather was perfect with the pale November sun having its last fling, the sky white and dazzling, the shimmering lagoon a Lorelei, the beckoning horizon full of promise. We were consciously loving and on our best behaviour with one another so as not to spoil our last day with a careless word. Though I have complained that having a relationship with you was like walking on eggshells, the truth is that we *could* walk on eggshells when we wanted to, and that day I felt as though we could have walked upon the water.

We reached the island far too early for lunch and we ambled about the place, wandering in and out of the church and the little museum, you with your usual lack of curiosity but anyway radiating a feeling that you were doing something companionable, were content to be doing it because we were doing it together. We strolled on through the vineyards and found ourselves in a remote area of long grass overlooking the lagoon. The ground was hard after a rainless month and the grass dry: we sat down. I'd bought a couple of cold beers at that little place on the canal path on the walk up from the boat and we drank them straight from the can. The beer trickled down your chin and I licked it off and kissed you. The Indian-autumn day was doing its best to be drowsy with the watery sun filtering down and not a ripple on the looking-glass water.

"What are those buzzing things?" you asked lazily.

"Late-flowering insects." We were neither of us al fresco types, or as you put it, "We're neither of us al dente types, are we?"

"You're thinking of yesterday's spaghetti."

"Well?" with a mock pout, knowing a mistake had been made somewhere. "That was out of doors, wasn't it?"

"That's right – spaghetti al fresco," I teased. "You like eating out of doors, don't you, kitten?"

"I *love* eating out of doors. It makes me want to make love out of doors. I never have. Have you?"

A little stab there, at the implication that you'd made love everywhere else but. But I constructively shunted round my train of thought to accommodate the fancy that there was something we might do that would be a first time for you. "Not since I was a panting teenager," I said.

You were lying back in the grass by now, chewing a none-too-clean piece of straw. I leaned over and took it from your mouth with some nonsense about catching rabies. "Will I really?" you said wide-eyed, half-believing. You were so silly that I hugged you, wanting to cocoon you against intrusive knowledge. In an instant we were making love and in another instant, or so it seemed, we had made love. Despite what you'd said about wanting to do it out of doors, which I might easily have construed as a broad hint, neither of us had it in mind to make love there and then. As you said with pretended primness, "Doing it *before* lunch is immoral." And delightful. Spontaneity of this order was something new for us – it was, I only properly realised then, as if we'd always (if you can classify four days in Venice and one in Harrogate as "always") had an agenda, where going to bed was pre-planned. That did continue, with golden exceptions like the present, to be the pattern. When we talked about this once you said it added the dimension of anticipation to going to bed with one another. It did. It also added the dimension of a bottle of champagne or two and perhaps a couple of Bloody Marys. It worried me sometimes that we never made love entirely sober. So while I was pleased that being had out of doors was a first for you, I was even more pleased at another first, which was having you on no more than a couple of beers between us.

We wandered back across the island feeling very much in love, you with your hand on my shoulder in a pleasingly proprietorial way. The restaurant was just as it should have been – open-air ("al dente" as we would evermore say), with the tables arranged to soak up the last of the year's sunshine under cool vine-hung colonnades. As the waiter escorted us to our table I noticed for the first time the grass stains on the back of your white dress. Since I was carrying my jacket, it was easy enough to slip it over your shoulders, but not so easy to communicate to you why I was doing it. "Thank you, darling, I'm not cold," you said, trying to shrug it away. "Yes you are, green with cold," I said over-cryptically. You didn't understand and, stubborn creature that you were, insisted on divesting yourself of the jacket as we sat down.

The result of this little fuss was that the attention of Benito Benotti, who might not have noticed the state of your dress although he certainly would have noticed us, was drawn to our table as if by a spotlight. He was with a party of a dozen or so buyers and trade magazine people. It could have been worse: I might have been invited to his lunch and declined. Though perhaps, not that it matters now, it couldn't have been any worse at all, in that had I not neglected my work so recklessly it would have been very odd indeed if I hadn't been invited. But there we were.

I might have known Benotti would be at that fashionable Sunday lunching resort. I didn't care. I was light-headed with irresponsibility. We nodded with feigned amiability and I put him at the back of my mind. "You've got grass stains on the back of your dress, my love," I said, to explain the jacket business. "Never mind, it'll have to go to the cleaners when we get back anyway," you said carelessly. I've never known anyone with such an under-developed sense of embarrassment as you. "Or perhaps," you whispered, leaning over and nibbling my ear, "I'll keep it in my wardrobe as a souvenir. Along with my collection of ties that I'm supposed to have."

I let that one pass. You giggled as you used to when you had a good half a bottle of champagne inside you, although there was no wine on the table yet. "Do you mind everyone knowing what we've been up to?"

"I suppose I should mind Benotti knowing," I said, "but I don't." I had pointed him out to you and at this you flashed him a huge, knowing smile, and for a moment I thought you were going to wave. I wouldn't have cared about that either. I felt as if I'd downed not half a bottle but a whole one. I was drunk with recklessness.

It wasn't until we'd ordered our ravioli and langoustines and were sipping our Campari sodas that I noticed Hugh Kitchener sitting three tables away with presumably his clients and their hangers-on. While I'd known all along that we were bound to bump into him, and had

98

concocted an implausible story about you being coincidentally in Venice on a trade mag freebie which he could believe or not as he chose, I had begun to hope we might get through the trip without his seeing you. I'd come across him briefly at the Luggage Fair and we'd talked indecisively and insincerely about getting together for a meal when we could manage it, but since he was staying over at the Lido where I was sure he had already eyed up a more congenial companion for his leisure hours (you'd know more about that possibility than I) it had seemed we were in with a good chance of not clapping eyes on him again until we were back in London. But of course he had to be at the Cipriani on Torcello that Sunday. Everybody was there. And still I didn't care, I was so much under your influence and as high on euphoria as if I'd been pumped up with laughing gas.

"Don't look now but Hugh Kitchener's over there," I said.

"Yes, I know," you said in that chilling way of yours, signifying that what you were really saying was, "Yes, I know, I was hoping you wouldn't see one another because as soon as your eyes meet you'll know I had an affair with him." And at that moment Kitchener's amused eye met mine, he raised his glass, and his look was the one which all men recognise that says, "Very nice, cock, very nice indeed, but never forget I had her first."

Although it was the last thing I wanted I couldn't prevent myself from starting one of those plodding interrogations.

"Why didn't you say?" ("Does it matter?" or "Is it important?" she'll say, I told myself.)

"I didn't want to spoil your lunch."

"Why should it spoil my lunch?" ("Oh, being seen with me here.")

"Oh, being seen with me here."

"By someone we know or him in particular?" ("What do you mean?")

"What do you mean?" I was scoring well.

"Forget it, darling. We were sure to run into him and he *isn't* going to spoil our lunch."

Nor did he. But oh, Angie, why couldn't you ever bring yourself to say, "If you think he looked at me in a funny way, or you in a funny way, it's because I once had a fling with him," and you could have added your mantra "It wasn't important" if you liked, because it wasn't important, you were perfectly entitled to have slept with Hugh Kitchener before you saw me coming, indeed you showed good taste since he's such a handsome bugger and successful with it: but what I detested was the feeling of being excluded. Every affair, however brief, is a conspiracy that continues long, long after it's over in anxious eye-messages, those coded signals winking, "Does he know?" – "No, and you're not to let him suspect." – "Don't worry."

"I don't suppose he'll believe I'm here as your research assistant?" you said.

"I don't suppose he will." Then remembering you'd been Hugh Kitchener's assistant for a spell I added with a bitchiness worthy of you, "Anyway, research assistants are almost as much a vocational euphemism as models."

"What's euphemism? Is that when you feel absurdly pleased about nothing in particular?"

"No, my love, that's euphoria, and I've got it. Euphemism is substituting blandness for harsh reality. Like saying someone's passed over when they're dead."

"Or like saying, 'Shall we lie down for a while?' when I want you to fuck me?"

"Not quite, but I prefer your example to mine." I can't have said that without a tremor. A thrill like an electric charge went through me at your first use of the word. And you sensed it. Heretofore it had always been "make love". Hereafter it was always "fuck". It went into your word processor. And I didn't even ask myself, not then anyway, if you'd got it out of your retrieval system. Watched over by Kitchener who was going to have it all over London, and by Benotti who was going to give Charles a blow-by-blow account of my indolence and indifference to his affairs, we were having a marvellous day.

Benotti eventually came over to our table on his way out, and after making that remark about understanding now that I was doing myself a favour, murmured in an aside that he would quite understand if I missed the farewell cocktail party that evening. He probably guessed that I had not the slightest intention of being there. It would have been more civilised had he said he hoped I would bring you along, and it was somewhat surprising that he hadn't, and perhaps I should have been worried by this portent of the way the wind was blowing. I didn't give a sod. We ordered wild strawberries, sloshed the last of our wine over them and called for champagne to give Hugh Kitchener something else to talk about. I was having a wonderful time. So were you. You kept touching my shoulder and I could feel love. If ever I could choose a day to have over and over again, I should have that one. We finished our meal and took a launch back in preference to the chugging water-bus.

"Shall we fuck for a while?" you said, opening the shutters. Everything else about Venice is a haze of lights and music and sunshine and water and wine and food and touching.

FIVE

You told me that my jealousy of Cheevers had more than once nearly finished us. That was before it did finish us. What I never told you in return was that had I known about Cheevers to begin with we would never have even started. It would have been like raising the stakes in a card game in the full knowledge that one's opponent held all the aces.

Or maybe that's not true. Had you been candid about Cheevers from, and at, the beginning, then perhaps I might have been able to handle the situation. But it would probably have been a very different relationship from the one we had. Indeed, it would have had to have been, since coming clean about Cheevers would have made you a different person. And me a less stupid one. All along you said that your affair with Ben Cheevers didn't matter, and I didn't twig for months that what you meant was that it didn't matter to him.

The afterglow of Venice found us very close. I'd expected to be slapped in the face by the cold water of reality upon our return, but apart from severe withdrawal symptoms from not seeing you every second of the day it didn't feel like getting back at all – rather that Venice had set us off on a journey and we were still travelling. I expected, too, to be in a state of tension over readjusting to life with Judith. Instead I was in a kind of angry fever, resentful at being dragged back into family life and domestic life when all I wanted to do was moon about you and our four days together. It was the same at the office: I found it difficult to talk to Charles about Venice in terms of luggage and clients and contacts when Venice meant walking hand in hand, fountains playing in piazzas, and bed.

I missed you. Not only in the conventional sense but I missed having all that time with you. Now we were back in the straitjacket of lunch and early evening drinks. It meant conversations had to be curtailed in order to get on to the next topic, that we – or anyway, I – had to have an agenda almost, that talking to you became an editing process again. Wanting to ask you questions, I now regretted having squandered so much of our Venice time on chatter, when the hours ahead seemed endless and I didn't want to ask you questions.

We met for lunch two days after our return. It would have been the very next day but you couldn't manage it (and soon I was to know why you couldn't manage it). We chose Luigi's, remember? Italian food to remind us of Venice and, so far as I was concerned, a sporting chance of running into Hugh Kitchener. Not caring about gossip, indeed actively soliciting gossip with a view to brazening it out was not mere recklessness, it was the survival instinct converted into an apparent suicidal impulse, like the urge of a vertigo sufferer to stand on the brink. Not that it mattered a damn one way or another by now, since if he'd published the news of our Venice jaunt in *Marketing Week* he couldn't have given it a wider circulation, but I thought if he saw us together in Luigi's there was an outside chance of his supposing that with so much smoke there couldn't be much of a fire. Anyway, he wasn't there.

You were, though – the first time I'd ever walked into a restaurant and found you waiting: the first time, in fact, you hadn't kept *me* waiting so long that I began to wonder whether you'd ever turn up. You stood up as I always did for you and threw your arms around me, kissing me on both cheeks as I always did to you. I said earlier that lovers are a conspiracy. Now we were. We were fuddled on one another's company before the champagne hit the table and we got alcoholically fuddled very quickly, like someone topping up after an all-night party, and monumentally fuddled before the day was over. You were so gay and happy, I was reminded of our first lunch ever and would have gone into maudlin reminiscence about it, except that you'd probably fondly remember the wrong restaurant and spoil it. And it didn't need you to spoil it, my love: I could do that very efficiently myself.

You gave me a jokey postcard with an affectionate thank-you-for-Venice note scribbled on the back. "I wanted to bring you a present, but I didn't have any money," you explained. It was this engaging candour, and the love you were radiating, and the expansive warmth of Venice we were basking in, that encouraged me on the second bottle to plunge in and ask you about Cheevers.

"If I ask you something, Angie, will you promise not to ask why I want to know or what does it matter or why is it important?"

"The answer to your question is yes, Roger. There, you see – you asked me a direct question and I gave you a direct answer. You seem to think I resent talking to you, darling. I don't. It's just that what seems to be important to you isn't important to me, and a lot of things I've forgotten probably because I don't want to remember them."

That was encouraging enough. "I want you to tell me about your friend Cheevers."

"He's not my friend, and I don't carry his C.V. about with me, darling. I said I'd answer your questions, if there's anything that's bothering you, but I don't have a set speech I'm going to launch into – you can't expect a blow by blow account of life with Cheevers, such as it was. And I've already told you as much as you need to know."

"Or as much as you want to tell me."

"Now don't start, darling. Take a deep breath, have some champagne, and tell me what you want to know."

Well, what did I want to know? Why you called yourself Mrs Cheevers for one thing, or at least why you were known to your Mrs Scroggins by that name. But I was saving that, even savouring it I have to admit. If I had got through Venice without asking it I could get through lunch without asking it. There were other things I needed to know first. A background briefing, you might say, before going into battle.

Why did you always refer to him by his surname – had I already asked you that? I can't remember. Anyway, the answer was a mundane one – simply that everyone called him Cheevers, always had done apparently, because he didn't like his Christian name. I didn't like his surname – mention of it always gave me a shudder of dislike. Men who are known by their second names, especially to women, are usually shits or they're dynamic or possibly both. I was jealous of your having been mixed up with a dynamic shit, if such he was.

And such he was. I never told you this, Angie: I once went to see Cheevers, I'd become so consumed with curiosity about him. He – but no, I'd better come back to this, or I shall lose my thread.

What else did I want to know? It would be fruitless asking for chapter and verse on exactly when it started and exactly when it stopped, there were so many versions; though in fairness to you, it was admittedly all a matter of interpretation. First, it seemed I was wrong in my assumption that since you'd worked at the Chelsea Auction Galleries six or so years ago when you came down from York, you'd met Cheevers there and known him since then. "I didn't meet him then. I never said I met him then. How could I have met him then?" How could I know how, when you hadn't told me? I thought you'd met him at the Galleries and maybe you'd started going out to lunch together or having a glass of wine after work as you did with me, and it had taken off from there. No, no, he hadn't worked there then. The truth, if it was the truth, depressed me. It was two years or two and a half years or three years ago, you couldn't remember which or wouldn't remember which. You'd met him at a party and you'd finished up in bed with him. Your own bed, that is – he was married.

And was that a usual pattern with you? Not really. What did you mean by not really? Well, if you'd given me the impression that you hadn't met him until that night, that wasn't strictly true: because while you'd said he wasn't at the Galleries when you used to work there, that wasn't strictly true either. Then what was strictly true? Well, though he wasn't working in the Galleries himself at that time, he sometimes called in to see his father, who owned the place. What did he do at that time, then? Oh, he was on a business course or something. Yes, go on. Well, you supposed you went out with him for a while. You "supposed", did you – and did that involve sleeping with him for a while? It may have done. Oh, come on: did it or didn't it? All right, then, it did: you weren't keeping anything from me, it was just that you didn't think I'd be interested in delving into your past as far back as that. You'd only just come down from university, after all – for heaven's sake, did I want to know about the first spotty schoolboy you ever held hands with?

All right, so your affair with Cheevers started all that time ago. So what happened then? What did I mean, your affair? – it wasn't an affair, you were just seeing each other from time to time. Whatever you wanted to call it, then – what happened? Well, he was swept off his feet by this very attractive American girl in the antiques game who walked into the Galleries one day, and they were married three months later. And were you jealous? How could you be – she was young, successful, intelligent, rich, beautiful (you'd seen them at a party: I could imagine how you'd looked, with your nose pressed up to the sweetshop window) and she had good taste (you got to wear her clothes). Yes, you were jealous.

But while the marriage didn't exactly break down, it didn't work out, Mrs Cheevers spent more and more of her time in New York and Cheevers was once again to be seen on what, curiously and disturbingly, you called the flesh market. The flesh market: what was that? Oh, just an expression you'd picked up from the set he mixed with. What sort of set? Oh, sort of clubby people. What sort of clubs? Oh, just noisy drinking places for people who didn't know what else to do with themselves. Like the Screw, did you mean – pick-up joints? Something on those lines, if I wanted to use quaint old-fashioned expressions. And it was on this flesh market, was it, that you met him again? Yes. Not at a party? No, a club. A place called Prune's in Fulham Road, it had closed down now (Good: that saved me going and looking for it). Then why had you said a moment ago you'd met him at a party? It *was* a sort of party, only one paid at the door. You'd gone there with Belle. Why? Boredom, you supposed.

The pool ripples were widening all the time, the questions multiplying. I had to dam them, contain the interrogation to its essentials. Get back to Cheevers: so he took you home (what happened to Belle? Never mind) and you re-started, or as you would have it started from the beginning, the affair that had commenced or not commenced three years earlier. You met him twice or was it three times or four times a week for about six months or about nine months or about a year and what did it matter? You hoped he was going to leave his wife or that she'd leave him, but it didn't happen. He brought you her cast-offs, though. And every time you persuaded yourself that he was just taking you for a ride or stringing you along or whatever the phrase for that kind of thing is among clubby people these days, he would arrive with a dress or a handbag or a blouse rescued from Oxfam and you would accept it as a token of his serious intent. Weird. You tried to explain it, to yourself I think as much as to me. "It was evidence of kindness. So few people had ever been kind to me. All right, so he never bought me presents but he didn't have to bring me those things either. It was thoughtful, it showed that he cared for me." Not, I snidely thought of asking, that he was a cheapskate wanting to ingratiate himself into bed? No. He didn't have to do that, the bed was always available.

After this six-month or nine-month or twelve-month adulterous honeymoon, he seems to have cut down on the lunches and the occasional dinners, then the evening drinks, until practically the only times you saw him were when he would come round to your flat when you'd give him supper and take him to bed. Sometimes you'd make the supper and he wouldn't turn up. Sometimes he would turn up out of the blue without so much as a bottle of wine or a cast-off frock, to no other purpose than to enjoy a quick screw before going home to his wife. And what about when his wife was on one of her trips to New York – didn't he ever spend the night, or even a few nights with you? That, I thought, would explain why he'd set you up as Mrs Cheevers at Banks Place. But no, he never took advantage of her absences to move in – who would want to, you asked ruefully, in a place like that? Then couldn't you have made it more inhabitable? No, there was no point – he had another woman – still did, in fact: you'd heard they were going to marry when his divorce came through. Besides, he didn't want you for your company and he didn't care about your flat so long as it had a bed in it and he could come round when he pleased.

So that in turn became the pattern: and now I understood that when you said the affair had lasted only a few months you meant before it settled down into this bleak screwing arrangement. He would arrive on your doorstep every three or four weeks or so, late at night after a business dinner usually (or perhaps having failed to get a better offer on the flesh market?), and you would repair to bed for a couple of hours. If Belle chanced not to be out on the town, she would retire discreetly to her room. Thankfully she doesn't appear to have joined in. It all sounded sad and sordid and your explanation was simple and heartrending: "I was lonely and I didn't have any proper relationships with men, I never have had, not real ones. It was something to cling on to; however threadbare and shabby, it was some continuance in my life." Continuity, my Lady Malaprop. I loved you, I love you. I could have given you continuity, if nothing else, continuity by the bucketful.

And so there you were in your cold flat with its blank and cheerless walls, huddled in somebody else's cast-offs and waiting for a lover who would turn up when he felt like it. (Not strictly true, of course – there were the one-night stands and short-term affairs which you always hoped would lead to something but never did – either you ran away or they did. Did Cheevers never roll up and find you in bed with somebody else? I wanted to ask. But I didn't, it might have proved the cue for a Rabelaisian anecdote that wouldn't have amused me.) Should he arrive unusually late, or unusually drunk, or if he left it six or seven weeks instead of three or four between visits, you might send him away with a flea in his ear as you put it. Came the day, or night, when he had left it just that little bit too long and arrived that little bit too late and that little bit too drunk, and couldn't even achieve what he'd specifically come for. There was a row – whether about his previous non-appearance or his present non-performance I didn't care to ask – whereupon, coincidental with my turning up on your horizon, the bastard got his marching orders at last.

Well, not totally, and not immediately – because according to Gunby T. Gunby you used to be seen at Le Bistro with him, while early on in our affair there had been a couple of occasions when you'd been meeting him, somewhat secretively it seemed to me, for lunch or dinner, wasn't that right? Yes, you wouldn't deny that. So what were those meetings in aid of? I wouldn't understand. Try me. Well, for one thing you'd hoped he might be able to put some work your way at a time when you desperately needed to earn some money because you were six weeks (or was it seven weeks or eight weeks?) behind with the rent; and the other thing, this being the thing you didn't think I'd understand, was that you wanted his friendship, you craved the experience of his taking you out to lunch or dinner with no prospect in view except the pleasure of your company.

As a matter of fact, I could and do understand why you should want, albeit retrospectively, to persuade yourself that you'd been something more than an easy lay whom he kept on file, why you should want to jettison some of the uniqueness of that role. How many women can there be, after all, on whom a man can rely for a good screw whenever he feels that way, with the minimum of social niceties and no obligation to pay for it?

If the question "Or *did* he pay for it?" entered my mind at that time, I quickly suppressed it. Another question was just as deeply buried, this one in quicklime. Notwithstanding his marching orders, it was a fair bet that Cheevers had rolled round to your flat at least once after I arrived on the scene, if only to test that you meant what you said and that his free mattress ticket had at last been withdrawn. Had there been one last round of whatever it was the pair of you used to get up to with that bundle of men's ties for old times' sake before you showed him the door? I didn't ask and I didn't want to know.

Then was there anything else I did want to know? Only everything. Was there any point in asking why you were so obsessed with Cheevers? Perhaps not: you didn't even know you were. And perhaps by now you weren't. But when I first knew you his name would come up, even if you had to dredge it up, every time we met. Unless I happened to mention him first, when you would be evasive and change the subject as quickly as possible, there always came that moment when his name fell naturally or otherwise into the conversation. Only fleetingly, perhaps – "I think I might have once gone there with Cheevers" you might say of a restaurant (though scrupulously never of the restaurant we happened to be sitting in, unless I asked how you came to know where the Ladies was or why the waiter should greet you effusively) – and sometimes pointlessly, but always as if responding to a need to keep his name alive to yourself. We had a tiff about it once, when I asked if it were not possible to spend half an hour in your company without your dragging up the subject of Cheevers. You were icily insistent that you did no such thing, but after that you stopped.

But did you still think about him? No, I didn't want to ask that and precipitate another row, particularly as your voice was getting shriller and shriller in resentful self-justification with every answer you gave and every sip of champagne you took, much to the amusement of the waiters and remaining diners in the by now emptying restaurant. Which left me very little I did want to ask at that particular time. But I'd said I wanted you to tell me about the man and so I said on casual impulse, "By the way, are you still seeing him?", expecting an affectionately indignant "Of course not" or "What do you take me for?" Anyway, an emphatic "No" in some form or another; whereupon I would be so relieved that I'd allow you to push Cheevers back in the cupboard with your other skeletons, and we'd order more champagne and talk about Venice and our pledge to go back there one day. Or Paris. Or New York. Or Harrogate. As for the Mrs Cheevers puzzle, that could wait. Whatever the answer to that one was, it was all in the past.

"Yes, and no," you said.

Had I been able to anticipate that reply I would have anticipated my prospective reaction as the familiar flutter of panic accompanied by that swirling in the head I usually experienced when trying to marshal unmarshallable thoughts and impressions. Instead I felt a dull sensation in my chest, a depression, an ache not of pain but of resignation at the hopeless realisation that once again you had landed me back around square one; and that those four days in Venice had been for nothing.

"Go on," I said wearily.

"Don't be angry, darling."

"I'm not angry, I'm bloody astounded. When did you see him last?"

"Don't swear at me."

"When did you see him last?"

"And don't shout. If you shout I shan't tell you."

It was between walking out of the restaurant and counting ten. I counted three. "When. Did. You see him. Last?"

"Yesterday lunchtime."

I would give you up, cut my losses, retrieve my sanity, my dignity too while I was about it. Not make a scene: just finish the meal quietly, thank you nicely for coming and walk away without ever turning back.

"When you were unable to meet me for lunch. Did you have lunch with Cheevers?" No, cancel that question, Angela. Just get on with it. But of course, you wouldn't.

"I didn't mean to have lunch with him, Roger, truly. We were just meeting for a quick drink but the pub was so crowded he suggested it might be quieter at this place down the street. The Chelsea Bunfight is it? Just off the Kings Road, nearly at Worlds End."

"I don't know, I'd have to look it up in Gunby's *Good Living Guide*. What did you have?"

"Why do you want to know that?" Sarcasm was lost on you.

"I don't want to know, Angela," I said in a tired voice. "I don't want to know anything – except what the bloody hell it is you think you're playing at, if you could possibly explain that in the space it takes me to drink my coffee and pay the bill."

You wouldn't be drawn into a quarrel. You put your hand on my arm. "Come on, darling, don't get into a state, not so soon after Venice."

"What about you seeing Cheevers so soon after Venice?"

"I haven't been seeing him and you know it." Baffling, that, until I remembered our separate sexual cultures. Seeing meant screwing in your vocabulary. Sorry.

"Meeting, then."

"That's better. Don't you want to know why?"

"I don't think so, no. Besides, I can answer that question myself by now. Because you can't keep away from him."

"Don't be ridiculous. Until yesterday I've met him exactly twice since we've been together and I've already tried to tell you what that was about."

Your voice was rising again. In a minute you'd be asking what was the mortal difference, by which you meant the moral difference, between my having a meal out with Judith and your having a meal out with whomsoever you pleased: that's if you were going to pursue the same line of attack as the last time the subject had come up.

I felt very tired. I didn't want to argue with you, I didn't have the energy or the spirit for it. I wanted to get back to the office and drown myself in work. But first I wanted to know. I was only trying to fool myself in saying I didn't want to know anything. I wanted to know everything, however fragmented and in whatever order. I wanted to carry the whole broken-up mosaic of your life with Cheevers away in a sack and put it together by myself without your help or hindrance. And I wanted there to be no missing pieces so I'd never have to come back to you.

One more try, and then I'd leave it alone. But I knew I wouldn't. I was addicted. Hooked on extracting words out of you that could only mortify.

"Angela, you said you didn't see Cheevers any more, using 'see' in the generally accepted sense of meeting, socialising with, having contact with – "

"Yes, all right, get on with it!"

This could go either way now. I didn't care. If you flounced out it would be your last flounce ever so far as I was concerned. I ploughed on. "Whether you still see Cheevers or not is of course your own business but you said you no longer did. You've said that several times. Now I ask if you've been seeing him and it turns out that you have."

"I didn't say that, Roger. I said yes and no. I'm trying to be *truthful*."

"Saying yes and no isn't being truthful, it's keeping your options open. Now look, Angie, I know you don't like making statements, set speeches as you call them, but it so happens that I don't like asking questions, whatever impression you may have gained to the contrary. So without my drawing it out of you like a dentist pulling teeth, just tell me what this is about."

"I mean no I don't meet him any more but yes I did yesterday."

"Why?"

"To tell him it was all over."

Did you ever see a TV act called Burns and Allen? I expect not – too young. They might have done some re-runs on Channel 4 but you only watched junk television. You've heard of George Burns, anyway. Gracie Allen was his featherbrained partner who gave such dizzy answers to his questions that they got further and further away from ever understanding anything. He was very patient with her, that was the act. But they were married in real life and I used to wonder if she really behaved like that why he hadn't strangled her long ago.

"But I thought it had been over for months. Or as you've told me at various times, for a year, or fifteen months, or eighteen months, discounting the fact that he was still allowed to come round and fuck you whenever he chose."

"Don't talk like that, Roger, and don't ever use that word again except in our own concept. Promise."

"Context, for Christ's sake. All right – go on."

"Not if you snarl at me."

"Then bloody don't go on."

A token silence as token punishment, and you resumed. "It *is* all over. It *has* been all over, for a long time. But I never told him as much in so many words, until finally I did have to tell him."

"Why?"

"Because he wouldn't take no for an answer. He's kept on and on ringing me."

"You never told me that."

"Only because you go through the roof every time I mention his name, you know you do. I never told you he didn't ring. I didn't lie to you."

Well, we gradually pieced it together, didn't we? How he'd been ringing you every three weeks or so and asking if he could come over, and naturally you said he couldn't. Did you tell him to piss off? No, you didn't, not your style. Did you ever not answer, knowing it must be him so late at night? I didn't ask that one but I thought of all the times I'd called your number and you'd let the phone ring and ring, either asleep or drunk or, as I pictured you, staring at the ceiling, waiting for me to go away.

And so the moment you're back from Venice, you call him. Why? He'd left a message on your Answerphone, which naturally you had to respond to at once, probably before you'd even got your coat off. And you arranged lunch – all right, not lunch, a drink, but it became lunch. And you told him – what?

You looked at me steadily and said:

"That I was sorry not to have returned his call earlier but I'd been away with someone, someone I was very much in love with, whom I was very much involved with and didn't want to lose, so would he please accept the situation and not ring me any more."

You melted me like the unregarded chocolate mint in the saucer of your coffee cup; but at once I threw a hard coating around my soft centre.

110

And what did he say to that? I wasn't going to ask. Why should I care what he said?

"And what did he say to that?"

"He wished me luck."

I felt better. But I wasn't going to say anything. Really I wasn't going to say anything. And after a moment you added in a small voice:

"I told him I'd once been in love with him."

I felt worse. The chill in the stomach, like after too much bad cold wine. I ask you to talk, Angie, but then you don't know where to stop.

"Why did you want to tell him that?"

"Not for a very nice reason, I'm afraid. To gloat, if you must know, Roger. I wanted him to know why I didn't need him any more, insofar as I ever did. That I had someone else now, someone who loved me back instead of just taking what love I had to give. Who cared about me and respected me and wanted to look after me."

Thank you, my dear. The best reference I've ever had. You know, you could be a brilliant ambassadress for yourself when you put your mind to it. I ought to have been furious with you for your continuing deception about Cheevers, because that's what it was in black and white terms; but instead I was grateful to you for taking yourself off on this mission and cutting yourself clean from what I thought you'd cut yourself clean from months ago. I left the bubbling questions to stew and bought more bubbling champagne. We toasted Venice. And if we'd had any sense we would have left it at that, but we had to go on to Freddy's Bar, didn't we?

I should have warned Charles I was taking a long lunch. Or better still, not taken a long lunch. I still feel guilty about that. We were up to our necks in the Christmas advertising schedules and there was a hell of a lot to be done around the office. Having just got back from the Venice swan, the least that could be expected of me was that I'd have sandwiches at my desk. Charles and I had words about it, did I tell you? Not that it matters now, except as one more milestone on my downward path. (That was a joke. I never felt, even in my blackest moments, that I was going anywhere but up with you.) Early the next morning he came into my office and said, "Just to help me in drawing up some kind of game plan for the work we've got to get through, could you let Rosie know at some point whether you intend to be at your desk this afternoon?" Ouch.

So. Freddy's Club. I hadn't meant to bring it up just then but we had champagne coming out of our ears by now and you were becoming genially cantankerous as you so often did at that stage (sometimes not so genially), so I thought, what the hell? Did we need these rows, do you suppose? Could we have survived without them? Not that we did survive, but you know what I mean.

It was unusual for you to bring up a contentious subject voluntarily, or regurgitate it as in this case. You usually preferred not to trouble trouble until it troubled you. But, under the influence of far too much champagne, you said or rather slurred, "So can we put Mister Cheevers behind us now? No more inquests, investigations, no, not investigations – "

"Interrogations."

"Those. You'd make a good lawyer, darling, do you know that? Roger of the Bailey. I can just see you in your little wig. Witness at the bar, do you deny that on the fourteenth – ?"

"Yes, all right, darling, I've got the message. Keep your voice down a bit."

Freddy's was quite full that day. A big race meeting on television. That was another reason Charles was put out. We had a client who sponsored one of the races and Charles liked to go down and join him in his box, but this year, thanks largely to his partner not pulling his weight, he couldn't make it. I really should have gone straight back after lunch. For more than one reason.

"So there's nothing else you want me to tell you?" you persisted. You were asking for it, my dear, weren't you?

"Not really."

"Oh, come on, darling, what kind of an answer's that?"

"Well let's say not at the moment."

"Oh, I see, so you want to keep something in reserve? Something you can drag up to pull the rug from under my feet when I think we're getting on with being happy at last."

"Now don't start, Angie. Drink your champagne."

"I won't start if you will. I mean I *will* start if you won't. There's something else you want to know so start now and let's get it over with."

Deep breath. "All right. Why do you call yourself Mrs Cheevers?"

You tossed your marmalade hair back slightly with a wounded little smile curling your lip, informing our fellow drinkers of your martyred state. "And that's what you've been storing up, is it?"

Though you were right, of course, I said, "I haven't been storing it up, I've been putting it off."

"Since when?"

Why were you suddenly the one asking the questions? I told you anyway, and you put on the hurt smile again and slowly nodded your head several times as at the confirmation of worst fears predictably realised. "So all the time we were in Venice you were harbouring this nasty little secret."

"I've not been harbouring it, Angie – you have."

You swept on, as if I hadn't spoken, "And whenever we'd just made

112

love and I asked you what you were thinking, there it was festering in your petty little mind and everything you said to me was a lie."

That I wasn't going to have. "Angela, there is only one liar around here, and as for nasty little secrets festering in petty little minds – "

Which was as far as I got, for as you will well remember it was at this point that you calmly threw the dregs of your champagne in my face, unhurriedly gathered up your things, looked around you for anything you might have left behind, and walked out of the bar, remarkably steadily for one who had consumed just about her own cubic capacity in champagne.

The racing was on TV and so although the place was crowded not many people really witnessed this diverting little episode. Freddy did, from his vantage point at the end of the bar. Sucking in his cheeks in mock pain and raising his eyes ceilingwards, he waggled his hand like a schoolboy who has been caned. One or two others caught it out of the corner of their eyes but didn't seem sure what they had seen. It wasn't like some of those later occasions where the whole bar or hotel lobby or restaurant had a grandstand view, like that time in Leicester when it was red wine you threw and I happened to be wearing a white lightweight jacket. Every time it happened I warned you that if you ever did anything of that sort again I would ditch you, but you could never break yourself of the habit, could you, my love? As for me, I cried wolf so many times that my "And this time I really mean it!" eventually became a standing joke. I wonder how we might have fared if right from the start I had resolved never to chase after you when you flounced off or hung up on me or went into a three-day sulk? I always sensed when you walked away that you were mentally glancing back to reassure yourself that I was following, but I never had the nerve to sit tight and stare you out. No, that's not true: I did have the nerve, and the resolution sometimes, but what I didn't have was the patience. Days without you seemed so endless, bleak Saharas of time stretching to so distant a horizon, that swallowing my pride seemed a small price to pay for seeing you again, however foul a reception I was in for.

That night I wrote the first of what you came to call my whingeograms. I told Judith I had a market analysis to do and came up to my study and bashed furiously away at my typewriter for an hour, filling three and a half pages of A4, single spacing. You never got it. A market analysis, in fact, was exactly what it was – of the state of our relationship as I saw it. It was, or so it seemed in my drunken state, a sober, sensible assessment of where we were going wrong, or anyway where you were going wrong. There had to be, I magnanimously conceded, limitations to our affair. I was a married man and at this stage, what with the responsibilities of fatherhood and all, was not contemplating becoming an unmarried man. (Dangerous ground here, as well as hypocritical ground. That's why I never posted the letter.) So you were entitled to call the shots, to determine how close or how casual a relationship it was going to be. You had every right to see other men, even using "see" in your sexual sense, and to tell me about them or not as you chose. What you were not entitled to do was to play one type of relationship by the rules of another. If you were allowing yourself to be in love with me, then you couldn't behave as if you hadn't taken that step whenever it suited you. Love was a commitment: we had to be able to trust one another, and we – by which I meant you – had to be honest and open and straightforward. If you wanted, or needed, to be devious and secretive, then I couldn't see where love came into it; certainly I would have difficulty in believing you were in love with me when I couldn't believe anything else you said. And another thing: I was beginning to see how utterly futile it was to be spending a good twelve hours a week in the company of someone so manifestly incapable of telling the truth. If I wanted a diet of fiction I might as well stay at home and read a novel.

It was a pompous, even prattish letter, but at least it had the effect of sobering me up. I tore it into small pieces and put them in my pocket to dispose of on the walk to the pub I now told myself I needed.

I had no intention of ringing you. I had written myself into a calm and rational frame of mind. You were in the wrong and you knew you were in the wrong. You had thrown wine in my face in front of other people, knowing perfectly well how that kind of behaviour gets buzzed around in the gossip-mill atmosphere of the advertising world (and the fact that it didn't was no thanks to you: we could have finished up in *Private Eye* for all the discretion you showed). And I wasn't going to budge on the Mrs Cheevers issue. I was entitled to know what it was all about and you knew I was. So I would await your apology for making that absurd scene in Freddy's Club, and then I would listen to your explanation. And on that note I stepped into the phone box opposite the church and rang you.

I got a long continuous note that meant your phone was out of order. The operator tested the line then came back to say your number was unobtainable, his tone so pronouncedly guarded he might just as well have come right out with it and announced that you'd been cut off for not paying your bill.

I was gleefully triumphant, despite the passing disappointment at not being able to hear your voice. Even as I dialled, I had been mentally chastising myself for my weakness in ringing you when I had resolved not to; now I couldn't ring you however flabby my willpower. Unless I traipsed up to Banks Place, which I was in no position to at this hour and which I was buggered if I would tomorrow or the day after the way I was feeling, the ball was in your court.

Instinct told me you'd be in touch soon enough. A slightly more cynical instinct told me why you'd be in touch. Did I want to start paying your phone bills and other final demands? I'd give that my attention when it came up. Meanwhile, if you held out for a day or two as I supposed you would, I could take advantage of the absence of your company by going off to have a look at your Master Cheevers.

You never believed for a second – I told you often enough, but I don't think it even registered – that I wanted you to have had happy times and good relationships, and that had I been able to give you fond memories, even of Cheevers, instead of empty ones, they would have been yours wrapped up in ribbon. It was heartrending to think of you all the while having to radiate that desperate, attention-grabbing gaiety of yours out of the knowledge that if you didn't float your own balloon, no-one was going to do it for you. You once told me that Belle had said you were the loneliest person she'd ever met – and considering her vocation she must have come across one or two contenders. I wouldn't argue with her. I carry a sad mental picture of something else you told me: how, some weekends when we couldn't see one another and you had no-one else to see, you would go to that ratty wine shop at the end of Banks Place and buy a half bottle of warm champagne which you drank all alone, out of a tumbler, as a reminder of the times we'd had and would have together. Loneliness, or rather your lack of the resources to cope with it, made you over-eager for company, and that's probably why you were on the whole a bad picker of men, from the evidence of the ones known to me who passed through your life. (I count myself the exception. I would, wouldn't I?) They weren't necessarily bastards, they hadn't necessarily "used" you in the traditional cast-off glove sense: they were simply not the type of personality from whom you could expect very much back. Without getting too psychological I guess anyone who craves involvement yet fears it is going to go for the shallow water.

While it was only human nature for me to hope that Cheevers would prove a colourless, owl-spectacled, hollow-chested runt in a dandruff-speckled cardigan, I did want him to look as if he'd been someone worthwhile for you, to detect sparks of decency and humour and generosity. I should never have gone.

It was a curious experience, wandering into the Chelsea Auction Galleries like that. Though I chose one of their viewing days and there were enough people pottering about, I felt like an interloper, an intruder, a spy. But then I was a spy, wasn't I? That was why I'd walked past the place three times before going in – not out of

115

trepidation, but out of shame. But I was here now, and I was going to go through with it.

Something of a vicarious *déjà vu* sensation came over me as I picked up my catalogue and shuffled into that galleried cavern with its ordered ranks of mahogany and polished leather. That smell of Antiquax and brass polish must have been so familiar to you once, the office behind the frosted glass partition where two Sloaney-looking girls were lounging in the open doorway sipping coffee would have been where you and Belle worked. (Was Belle a Sloane, I wondered idly, or had the place gone upmarket, and she downmarket, since those days?)

One of the girls caught my eye as I meandered uncertainly forward, and asked if she could help me. Six years previously I might have been having this small encounter with you. You were twenty-two then, I would have been just double your age. We might have got a head start on ourselves. I wonder how much of that subsequent water under the bridge we would have dammed or diverted.

Getting to see Cheevers was more difficult than I'd anticipated. Which one, the girl wanted to know? I remembered your having told me his father owned the business. Junior, then. And could I say what it was about? I gave her my not very well prepared story of having an art deco desk I wanted to put up for auction – I knew they sold a lot of that kind of stuff.

"Then you want Mr Cheevers Senior – Mr Cheevers Junior handles eighteenth century mainly." Damn. I would have thought it was the other way round. "But I'm afraid he's not here at present." Thank goodness for small mercies.

Instead of cutting my losses and clearing off, I ploughed on: "In fact Mr Cheevers Junior's a friend of my partner who I believe has already mentioned this piece to him, so he is probably half-expecting me." It was a terrible stew I could be cooking for myself. Supposing this girl picked up a telephone and gave Cheevers the gist of what I'd just said? I could hardly run for it: my cock and bull story could easily take on the patina of a minor mystery, material for a passing anecdote which he might relate to you in the event of your having just one more lunch or just one more drink with him on whatever pretext. He might describe his mysterious visitor and you might recognise the description; and not even my fury at your still seeing Cheevers behind my back would stem your own fury at my seeing him behind yours.

I could see that these were childish fears arising out of a childish escapade; but behind them was a real fear, of this very childishness insinuating itself into the fabric of my life. I was in my fifty-first year and I was playing hookey from my office and weaving a web of stupid lies in order to catch a glimpse of the man who used to be my mistress's lover. What next? Putting a private detective on your trail to see whom else you consorted with? Donning a false moustache and keeping a night watch on your flat? It had to stop – but not until I'd seen Cheevers.

I was directed to the upper gallery where I was told he was around somewhere cataloguing some pieces. Eliminating the overalled porters – which, I wondered in passing, was the one who had laid Belle on the Louis XVI desk? – and prospective buyers, there were four youngish men hovering about, any of whom could have been Cheevers – conceivably enough, anyway, for me to experience four separate stabs of jealousy. Then I spotted an absurdly youthful-looking character, far too young to be anything more than a junior clerk, sitting in his shirt-sleeves at an escritoire bearing the label LOT 191, where he was annotating some typewritten notes. I went up to him.

"Could you point out Ben Cheevers?"

"Senior or Junior?"

"Junior."

He raised his gold pen and pointed to himself, deadpan.

We're going back a year, Angie. He was only twenty-three years old, wasn't he? and don't try to persuade me I'm mistaken because I checked up – no, not with Somerset House, though I might well have done just that had I not run into Gunby T. Gunby in the Gay Hussar on one of those increasingly rare days when I had a genuine business lunch. "You once called him a young bastard," I said, having brought up Cheevers' name in the pretence of having to recommend him to an important client. "Just how young a bastard is he?" He worked it out. Cheevers was a year older than Gunby's stepdaughter with whom he'd had a brief fling, so that made him twenty-three and a bit. Married at barely twenty, apparently – against his father's wishes, and in consequence not yet a director of the family firm but a mere wage-earner, with a lot of gambling debts. The more I heard about Cheevers the more he seemed to have the makings of what used to be called a rotter. Just your type.

You'd told me only that Cheevers had married very young. You didn't say how young and I didn't think to ask at the time – a missed trick. When I did ultimately ask you to tell me what by now I already knew, you wouldn't. "I never ask people's ages, they're not revelant." – "Relevant." – "Relevant, then. I didn't ask yours, Roger – remember?" – "Anyway, how old is he?" – "I've told you, I don't know." – "Older than you, younger than you?" – "I don't *know*. A bit younger, I think. What does it matter?"

Twenty-three and a bit. Just about what I'd figured him out to be as I faced him across LOT 191 in the Chelsea Auction Galleries. My mind clicked into instant calculator mode. Over six years ago since you'd met him and started sleeping with him, right? He must have been around sixteen or seventeen. On a business course, you said. Bugger off, Angie, he was still at school. Did he give you his school tie to start off your collection?

The discovery told me far more about you than you'd ever told me yourself. At twenty-eight you were a young twenty in most of your intellectual responses, largely out of fear of facing up to the adult world I would say. Although I often called you immature, it was to an extent a self-induced immaturity – you helped stunt your own growth. At twenty-two, coming more or less straight out of York University into the Chelsea Auction Galleries, you would have been the same age as Cheevers emotionally. Very likely he was the older of the two in that respect. Who seduced whom? As you would say, what does it matter? It was probably six of one climbing into bed with half a dozen of the other. He seduced you after your fluttering eyelids said "Seduce me."

What was the attraction? I didn't have to ask. His status as the boss's son may have helped him on the way, since you were always flattered by the attention of the well-connected or the well-heeled or the successful; but you would have gone for Cheevers, as I gathered most of the female population of London did, even had he been a barrow boy. Especially had he been a barrow boy. He was everything I didn't wish him to be. The young sod could have been a film star if he'd put his mind to it. The hard blue eyes, the gaunt bone structure with only his loose lips fleshy, the designer stubble, the close-cropped straw-coloured hair – it needed only the addition of a laurel wreath to complete the impression of a degenerate Greek god. Or, in his Asser and Turnbull stripes and double-breasted waistcoat, a professional snooker player. Less than half my age and not much more than half my weight, he exuded swagger and scorn and the arrogant confidence of the sexual spider.

I could see myself reflected in his hard, predatory stare – a paunchy middle-aged no-hoper in a crumpled suit, long past his sell-by date. If I'd told Cheevers I was your latest lover he would have laughed with incredulity. Which should have given me a smug feeling of posses-siveness, but it didn't. The contest was so unequal that I should have raised the white flag there and then.

He was waiting for me to say something, with what seemed paranoiacally to me like a mocking half-smile on his thick lips. I gave him my art deco desk story.

"Have you brought a Polaroid of it?" Irrelevantly, or perhaps not so irrelevantly, I tried to hear that minor public school simulated off-cockney voice coaxing you into bed. As if you'd needed coaxing.

"I'm afraid not."

"Then there's not a lot I can say about it. In any case you really want to talk to my father about that sort of piece."

"So I've been told, but he's out and I didn't want to waste my journey."

Did he go in for insolent shrugs, or was that my warped imagination? Certainly his whole demeanour was of dealing with a nitwit. I let the conversation run itself down and was just about to slink off when he said something very strange. Or rather, that was to lead up to something very strange.

"And who did you say sent you?"

I thought I'd better stick to the same story I'd given to the Sloane downstairs. I lied glibly enough, dredging up the name of yet someone else I'd been at school with. "My partner actually. Eric Gregory. We're architects. I think you know each other." God knows what I was going to say if you and I ever bumped into the sod and you introduced us. Claim to have a double, I suppose.

"Probably," Cheevers said non-committally – carefully so, I thought. "So you did want me, rather than my father?"

"Well, Eric said I'd find you helpful," I waffled.

"Sorry I haven't been more so." Then after a pause, as if judging whether to say what he was about to say or not, he went on with just a touch of significance, "Is there anything else I can do for you?"

So many facetious answers, such as "Yes, get off my back" flashed through my mind that I didn't give myself a chance to wonder what the hell he meant. I wondered later, of course, and came up with some intriguing theories, but I still don't know for sure.

"I don't think there is, many thanks. I'll bring in that Polaroid."

And now I did slink out, so profoundly depressed at my encounter with your ever-present ex-lover that I went straight to that pub across the road where doubtless you've passed many an evening, and sank four double gins within twenty minutes. Your phone was still out of order.

It took you four days to call me, which rather made nonsense of your reason for doing so – "Can I see you for a few minutes, Roger? It's rather urgent."

A familiar phrase to philanderers the world over, I would guess, and one which I'll now admit to having heard from the lips of the Merry Widow seven years earlier. If I never told you, it was only because you weren't curious. I had to produce a hundred and fifty pounds and she organised everything else, as calmly as if arranging an appointment at the dentist's. Had your call been for the same reason – and looking back, I'm not at all sure that you didn't mean me to think it was, in case I was at all reluctant to meet you after having champagne chucked in my face – I doubt if it would have gone so smoothly. Certainly I should have had to fix up the whole thing and then you would have got smashed and not turned up or something equally stupid.

Yet what would my own reaction have been? I did muse on that in passing after you rang off. With the Merry Widow I confess to feeling nothing very much except routine apprehension in case anything went wrong. She was a mature and capable woman who had been through the experience before and knew what she was doing. You hadn't, so far as I knew, and didn't. You once or twice, when maudlin drunk, touched on wanting children, but within the context of impossible dreams. I couldn't imagine you looking after a child, you were such a child yourself. But would I have wanted you to have my child? I just couldn't get the question within "all things being equal" sightlines, couldn't get my own status quo out of the picture. Here was I, a married man with a son already: there I would be in Ealing with one child while there you would be in Islington or wherever with the other; I should be leading an absolute double life with the future strewn with landmines. It was so crazy it didn't bear thinking about, which was why I thought about it.

Put it another way, then. Did I wish, being safely hypothetical now, that the child I did have was yours? Through the gauze that now separated my real, unreal life in Ealing from my unreal, real life with you, I could discern, like some gadabout Edwardian papa peeping into the nursery between engagements, the slumbering form of Tim who in proper circumstances would have had me for a proper father. My self-questioning seemed shallow and tawdry. As for you, I didn't dare bring myself to ruminate on what you might want for yourself, for us, and how it might be accommodated. At times like this I realised how immature I was myself. My maturity was confined to the practicalities of life, it didn't run to impossible dreams, only small and possible ones. I could mend a fuse but I was still afraid of the dark.

And in any case, I knew perfectly well that it was only about your unpaid phone bill that you'd at last decided to ring me. I decided to play it cruel. After all, you did deserve it.

"Angie, I'll see you on two conditions. One is that you apologise and the other is that you answer my question."

"Apologise for what?" You sounded as if you genuinely didn't know.

"For throwing drink in my face."

"Oh, come on, darling, it was only a little drop and you know I didn't mean it." You had exasperation down to a fine art. It was one of those times when I wanted to hug you and slap you simultaneously.

"Whether you meant it or not, you did it and made me look very silly and I want an apology."

"Oh, we mustn't have Roger looking silly, must we? Very well, then, I'm sorry." And I accepted your taunt as an apology.

"And I shall want to know why you call yourself Mrs Cheevers."

"Anything else?"

"Not for the moment. I'll see you in the Marquis of Granby at six."

"Not Freddy's?"

"The Marquis of Granby." I was buggered if you were getting club champagne.

But we should have gone to Freddy's. Half the agency people in London were in the Marquis of Granby. I couldn't help but be buttonholed by a bunch of them, including – now I know that the names of your lovers should be engraved on my heart, but I can't remember what that radish-faced type from Creative Consultants calls himself. Yes I can. Roy Hadath. A sprig of the Hadath Foods family. Another silver spoon.

He turned imperceptibly away, affecting not to see you, as you entered the pub, but there were plenty of appraising glances to make up for the lack of one from him. You wouldn't come over. I reached you at the other end of the bar just as one of the more junior associates of the Kitchener Agency, last seen at that lunch in Luigi's on the day we met, was about to peel away from his group with the idea of buying you a drink and seeing what the evening might hold in store. You had a lot of friends, Angie. I decided on a bottle of champagne after all.

"Why wouldn't you join me?" I asked.

"I did tell you I didn't want to come here."

"You said why not Freddy's, but you didn't specifically say not the Marquis of Granby. You've never said you didn't like it here."

"We've never been here on a Friday. It's always too crowded on Fridays."

"You could still have come over."

"I didn't particularly want to talk to Roy Hadath."

"Why not?"

"I just didn't, that's all." You might as well have said, "Because I once slept with him and I should have felt awkward." I didn't push it. Not in that direction, anyway.

"How do you come to know him? Have you worked with Creative Consultants?"

"No, he was going to get me some work but it never transposed."

Transpired, my Lady Malaprop. Oh dear – you just would fall for the casting-couch ploy, wouldn't you, my love? Another piece of the jigsaw, as I thought, slotted in.

We carried our bottle of champagne through to that back area that passes for the Marquis's dining room at lunchtime but which is little used in the evening. There was room to talk, but for a good while we didn't. For my part, I was holding to the view that since you had asked to see me – urgently – it was up to you to get on with it. For yours, you were simply being more childish than I was.

But I won. After a longish silence you said, "You'll have gathered they've cut my phone off."

I could have done a lot with that. "Oh, have they?" I could have said with well-feigned surprise. "When was that? I haven't rung you since you stormed out of Freddy's, so I wouldn't know."

"Yes," I said.

"I *have* paid the bill, I *know* I've paid the bill, but I never fill in my cheque stubs so how can I prove it?" Your bluster was so childishly transparent that I melted. But I quickly froze myself again.

"You can prove it very easily by getting your cleared cheque back from the bank."

"They won't return my cheques."

"Then it'll be on your statement."

"They never send me a statement."

You could happily, or unhappily, have gone on all night in this ridiculous strain. Since you wouldn't admit to owing the money, you could hardly ask me to lend it to you. Diplomatically, I got you to agree at last that the bill you were absolutely certain you had paid could just conceivably have been for the previous quarter, so the quickest way to get your phone reconnected might be to pay the contested bill immediately, then you could always get a refund in the event of it being a tiresome mistake on their part, as doubtless it was.

After poking with affected aimlessness around your bag for a while, you produced the final demand, as if in triumph. I do believe you wanted me to suppose that you were mistaking the bill for a receipt. I quickly disabused you. I was astonished by its total. A hundred and ninety-five pounds something, I recall – unlike you, I could look it up in my cheque stubs. Even my phone bill wasn't as high as that and both Judith and I lived on the telephone. But you still wouldn't ask for the money.

"Luckily there's no problem about paying it," you said defiantly. "It's just that I have to work out with Belle how much of it is hers, and now that she's moved I can't get in touch with her."

"Why not?"

"Because my phone's been cut off, silly."

Burns and Allen again. But if I felt like the straight man in a comedy sketch, I didn't let on. If you want to know, Angie, I didn't feel like any such thing. Your lack of organisation, your refusal to face facts, your manipulation of logic to explain your own flaws, irritated me greatly. So did my growing realisation that you were going to flounder on in this vein until I offered to pay your phone bill, sooner than put yourself to the humiliation of asking me to.

I brought the charade to an abrupt end by discreetly writing a cheque while you were in the Ladies. I hoped there would be no more waffle and there was very little. After the minimum of "Oh, Roger, I didn't mean you to – " and "Darling, I couldn't" you put the cheque away with not undue haste, then kissed me on the cheek and said simply, "You're a love", spoiling it just a little with the rider, "And you will get it back, I promise, as soon as I've sorted things out with Belle."

We both knew we'd entered a new stage in our relationship. I was ever so faintly irritated by the hollowness of your promise but predominantly I felt protective towards you, wanting to help you and experiencing a glow of privilege at being allowed to do so. With an insane irrationality I told myself that picking up the bills for your flat while still being denied access to it put me in a morally superior position to all the others who had passed across your threshold. I could believe such things while at the same time recognising them for the tosh they were. Love is not so much blind as suffering from double vision.

I could also be soft-headed and hard-hearted at one and the same time. Or so I tried to be. I wasn't going to let you get away with ducking out of your side of the bargain. It was nettling enough even having to remind you of it.

"So was that all you wanted to see me about?" I asked, heavily humorous or humorously heavy.

"You know it wasn't, silly! You couldn't get in touch with me and I knew you'd be worried and I wanted to see you."

Yes, after four days. "You do remember my two conditions?" Somehow you were suggesting that you were bestowing a favour on me by deigning to turn up to touch me for nearly two hundred quid.

"If you mean apologising for that stupid Punch and Judy row in Freddy's Club, I thought I already had, don't you remember? We were both very pissed and we behaved like idiots and I've said I'm sorry and so should you be." And that was all I was getting on that front.

"And what about the other condition?"

"What do you mean?"

You were going to drag it out of me. "Something you were going to tell me."

You gave one of your little sighs and looked to the ceiling for sympathy. "Oh, don't start, Roger. You'll have to be going home soon so why can't we be nice to one another and enjoy our champagne? Talk about where you're going to take me for lunch on Tuesday."

Tired suddenly, I mentally tossed a coin between making a scene and not making one. No-one who knew me was within earshot. I decided on the scene. I picked up my briefcase and rose heavily.

"I'm not taking you anywhere on Tuesday, chum. I don't like people who don't keep their word."

"What word? What are you talking about? Sit down, darling. Don't be silly."

"Then keep your side of our agreement. I've kept mine. I turned up because you wanted to see me." Possibly because I was semi-subconsciously routing myself homeward I suddenly and irrelevantly wondered what Judith would make of it could she hear me going on in this banal way. I had an uneasy vision of her jack-knifed in laughter.

You reached up and tugged at my elbow. "I hope you turned up because you wanted to see *me*. And what agreement? I truly don't know what you mean. Come on, Roger, you're getting into one of your states. Sit down for a while, you don't have to leave yet."

I sat down with a heavier version of your own martyred sigh earlier. I sipped champagne, tossing another mental coin on whether to be conciliatory or not. You seemed so genuinely puzzled that I was on the verge of believing that you really didn't know what I was driving at. But then, after it sank in with you that I wasn't going to change the subject or indeed say anything at all until you did, you said in coaxing, soothing tones, taking my hand:

"You're really making something out of nothing, darling. I've never ever called myself Mrs Cheevers, why should I want to? The flat was in his name only because these people usually want references and Mrs Scroggins wouldn't have got a very good one either from my previous landlord or my bank. Cheevers said if he gave her a cheque for the first three months' rent she wouldn't bother about references and he was right, she didn't. And that's all there is to it. He didn't ever live with me, if that's what you're driving at. I wasn't even seeing him very often by this time, only once every three weeks or so as I've already told you. And if you don't believe me, ask yourself why I invited Belle to share the flat with me when she broke up with the guy she was living with. It was a convenience, Roger, but then I was saddled with the name so far as my landlady was concerned. But I've never called myself that to anybody else, I promise."

I didn't bother to ask you, though I did myself, why the hell you couldn't have said all that in the first place. Perhaps you needed time to think up your story. Nor did I ask why Cheevers bothered to set you up in a flat he was only going to visit every three weeks. It made a kind of sordid sense.

I did ask, "So he used to pay the rent?"

You treated me to one of your short, mirthless laughs, then took the opportunity to slip in a blatant piece of buttering-up. "Darling, don't ever make the mistake of thinking other people in my life were as kind and generous as you." That meant I would be paying your rent before long. I quite looked forward to it. "He never paid for anything."

"What about those first three months?"

"I paid that back. Or at least he used to deduct it from my earnings."

"What earnings?"

"I was doing some work for him at the time."

"What, at the Chelsea Auction Galleries?"

"No, he has other interests."

"What other interests?" I didn't notice whether you were flustered or not. My mind was back with Cheevers and his careful, exploratory question, "Is there anything else I can do for you?" You'd just mentioned Belle: now I wanted to know if she had any connection with Cheevers, beyond having worked at the Galleries alongside you. Had he set you both up in the flat together, and if so, with what ulterior motive? But I was getting feverish in the brain now and in any case there was no point in coming to questions of that sort. You wouldn't even answer the one I'd already asked.

Jesus, I must have bored you sometimes. I bored myself even. I bore myself now. Why did I try to chase ten hares at once?

Because they were there.

If not flustered, you were certainly peeved. "Oh, Roger, won't you *please* stop cross-examining me? I try to be truthful with you but you will go on and on and on asking all these pointless questions. *Business* interests. What does it matter, what interests? You wanted to know why my flat is in Cheevers' name and now I've given you an explanation and if it's not exciting or intriguing enough for you then I'm very sorry, but now can we drop it?" And we did.

There was always something else, wasn't there, Angie? Whenever I persuaded you to open a door, it always led to another one, closed.

Six

I once tried unsuccessfully to interest you in a science fiction story I'd read about a man who did not possess the gift of forgetting. The consequence was that he was a walking jelly of pain, recalling every slight and humiliation, unable to shed his memories. Melodramatically, I wanted to persuade you that I was that man. I'm not, thank God: I remember far too much, but I forget what I need to. Or, like you, what I choose to.

For your birthday you wore the yellow silk dress I sent you off to buy, with new purple shoes and, after I'd pinned it on for you, the enamelled bluebird brooch you were wearing the last time I ever saw you. We went to Langan's. You were seven minutes late and had three champagne cocktails before we moved to our table, where you ordered – No, I won't recite it, though I could, and what we had to drink too, there and at Freddy's Club. We talked gaily, banteringly, and paid one another extravagant compliments. It was a lovely day.

Of Christmas Eve a fortnight later, or rather what we termed our official Christmas Eve, it being December 23rd and a Friday, my last day for accepting lunch engagements, I remember little except that I wanted to take you to the Savoy Grill but couldn't get a table, and so we went to that place in Covent Garden, I forget what it's called. I can't remember what you wore or what you ate or even quite what I gave you as a Christmas present. It was either the watch or the Filofax: I do know that whichever occasion was which, I accompanied both gifts with a joshing little lecture on the need to get yourself organised, turn up for appointments on time etc. What a sanctimonious sod you must have thought me.

I know too that I didn't get a Christmas present from you. You explained prettily how you'd had your heart set on buying me a Mont Blanc pen costing the earth, but that seeing me so often had left you with no time to look for temping work and earn some money.

As I wrote in my whingeogram, a packet of cigarettes would have done, my darling. I still feel a complete shit about sending that letter, and a worse one about the scene I made when you did find a couple of days' work just after Christmas, with Kitchener Associates. I pretended that I didn't want you embarrassed should Kitchener make any veiled or for that matter unveiled reference to our relationship. The truth was that I didn't want you being ogled at by The Fuzz among others, or to be reminded of going off with him that night I came looking for you in the Screw. Quite rightly, you said you'd work where you pleased and that anyway you needed the money. The next time I saw you for lunch you produced my Mont Blanc pen which must have cost you just about every penny you got for those two or three days' work. When you asked me, as you did from time to time, how I could love you when I found you so exasperating, there was your answer.

End of testimonial. I'm rambling. It's late at night as I write these pages and I'm tired and not a little pissed. Our official Christmas Eve. Yes. Not a happy time. It was a low-key lunch. You were going off with Belle to stay with her family in Manchester, so while I didn't approve of your choice of company at least you weren't spending Christmas alone in your cold flat. That prospect didn't bear thinking about: I simply wouldn't have known what to do about it, since we always go down to Judith's mother's deep in the country, which would have ruled out even a quick dash across town to drink a Christmas toast with you. So I was relieved about Belle.

And so were you. You said ruefully over lunch, "The saddest sight on Christmas Eve is watching a man tie his shoelaces." The image was so poignant that I refrained from bitterly wondering why you weren't watching me tie my shoelaces this official Christmas Eve, or who it was you had watched tying his shoelaces. It was going to be a good while before we saw one another again, Charles having insisted on closing down the agency until after the New Year. While I was determined to invent an office crisis that would give me a snatched hour or two with you in the interim, we were both morose, already missing one another, although we didn't dwell on it, I don't think. Christmas was a time to be got over. It's not the season for extra-marital affairs, is it? Those that survive must have something going for them. Ours did, and for nearly a year at that.

But as I say, I have no clear memory of that day. Yet I always rushed to blame you for not remembering the things you wished not to remember. Your birthday is fresh in my mind because it was a happy time, our official Christmas stale in my mind because it wasn't. As simple as that. As simple as you. Why did I try to make you more complex than you were?

Selective total recall, I suppose I have. There are whole swaths of time that are either a blank or a blur. It wasn't all alcoholic amnesia. Sometimes I wouldn't be able to remember what you'd said to me five minutes ago, even when it was important to have understood what you'd told me – by which was usually meant, what I'd got you to tell me. Eventually, slowly, I began to see that you spoke in fragments, from a mind that was as disorganised as your handbag, and from a truth-base that shifted according to your mood. It wasn't that you lied to me all that much, not by your own lights anyway: it was just that your idea of the truth was orbital. That was why so much of what you had to say simply drifted off into the atmosphere – there was nothing to hold it down.

So while we hardly ever stopped talking about who you were and what you were about, a lot of it has gone. Sometimes you'd say something that was so obviously untrue that it wasn't worth retaining, but then weeks or months later you'd casually drop some observation or crumb of information that linked with it in some way – not that made it true but that showed me your justification for having said it, if only I could remember what it was you'd said.

Much of what you told me about Belle, for instance, is in that swirling mist of half-memory. I was interested in Belle only insofar as she threw any light on you. Only when I belatedly came to realise what a powerful beam she did throw on you did I come to appreciate how much I'd let drift by that I should have netted.

To take an example within that example: one day you told me an inconsequential tale about Belle getting locked in an office overnight, having gone back there with someone she'd picked up at the Screw. It was anecdotal prattle and I disregarded it. Then weeks later, in the course of having one of my whinges about your never admitting me to your flat, I asked you how come the likes of Hugh Kitchener *et al* had been welcome there if you were so ashamed of the place. You said that in most cases they hadn't – you'd either been to their flats if that was convenient (ie, if they weren't married), or sometimes you would have discreetly gone back to somebody's office. So vivid a picture of you screwing on an account executive's desk flashed through my head that I barely took in what you volunteered next, which was that you'd once got locked in some graphic design consultant's studio with him and to your embarrassment had to remain there until released by the cleaner. You made a self-pitying little speech about how disillusioning and dispiriting it was to spend all night with someone you'd nothing really in common with, but to whom you had a sexual commitment because in the situation you had got yourself into he had the right to expect it. (One of these days I really must see if I can make a coherent summary of your peculiar moral code.) But I was hardly listening to that either, for it had slowly dawned on me that a story you had once told me about Belle you were now re-telling about yourself. I reminded you of the coincidence, but you were insistent that that was just what it was, and that the circumstances were entirely different. Whether they were or not I hadn't taken enough in to be able to judge. But I did make a note to listen more carefully in future should Belle and her escapades come up again. As of course they did – we'll come back to Belle.

Memory was never more hazy than at Ealing Church Grove, and here alcohol really did play its part. If ever I chanced to get home remotely sober it would be to become positively unsober very quickly indeed. My large ones were either euphoric after a good experience with you or compensatory after a bad one – or worse, no experience with you at all. The humdrum domestic tasks somehow got done but as often as not I could not remember doing them. I would come across a final demand for the electricity bill and sit down to write a cheque, only to find from a spidery entry on the previous stub that I'd paid it the night before but omitted to throw the reminder away. Often, now, I would find blank stubs in my cheque book – did I pick up the habit from you? – and have no idea what they were for until my statement came in (when they would prove, as likely as not, to have some connection with you. We'll come back to that too). I would forget engagements. Frequently my first intimation that dinner guests were expected was when Judith prodded me awake and begged me to have my wits about me when they arrived. Fortunately I didn't need my wits much – they were usually her guests nowadays, not mine. Nick Tearle was increasingly among them, I did begin to notice. But if it crossed my mind to wonder how many times a year a cookery writer needed to ask her agent to dinner, the thought was soon lost in the alcoholic twilight in which I endured those evenings.

You never knew Nick except by reputation. He might easily have become another notch on your bedpost had you ever come across him in your chequered past. He was a good agent for a certain class of book, the kind that gets written on word processors, but a complete philistine and cynic who cheerfully admitted to never reading anything except with a view to selling it. Against that he was presentable, wore his success lightly and had a good sense of the absurd, which I guess was what endeared him to Judith. He was still unmarried in his late thirties and Judith had once hinted that he could be bisexual; but when I idly repeated the conjecture after he had started to become our frequent dinner guest, having noticed that the women he turned up with tended to be professional rather than passionate attachments, she said crossly, "Oh, honestly, Roger, just because a man's still single it's not necessarily because he can't find a husband!" With hindsight I might have seen the significance of this volte-face. The plain fact was that Nick had an eye for the main chance in every field, and Judith, reasonably available without threatening to become an encumbrance, had become his main chance in one particular pasture. But to switch agricultural clichés, I couldn't see the wood for the trees then. You were the trees.

I do remember one conversation with Nick. This was at his flat at the Barbican, when he was reciprocating Judith's hospitality by taking us to the theatre. The party was to assemble at his place for a pre-curtain drink, and I was the first to arrive, having arranged to meet Judith there straight from the office, with dire warnings to arrive neither late nor drunk. I should certainly have been both had I been seeing you beforehand but you had taken it into your head to be otherwise engaged. You didn't mind my going off home to Ealing so much but whenever I was meeting Judith to go out to dinner or to a party or the theatre it got your back up. For what it's worth I never enjoyed those evenings much, even when I needed a rest from you: I could always see a tilted nose pressed up against the window.

Nick poured me a gin and tonic – I declined champagne, I'll have you know, for unashamedly sentimental reasons – and after making a few polite noises about my work and the agency, and cheerfully confessing that if he had landed us with a terrible play (he had) it was solely because the author of it was writing some book or other he was interested in, he began to talk about Judith.

"She's going from strength to strength, Roger. You must be pleased as Punch."

"I am." I was. I was glad for Judith's sake that she was doing well at what she enjoyed doing most; glad for mine that it kept her occupied, and that between her cookery writing and looking after Tim she had little time to squander on me. Besides, it got her out of the house – which was what Nick wanted to talk about.

"You know there's a good chance of her getting her own programme in Manchester?"

"Yes, she showed me the video of the pilot. It looks very promising."

"I hope they take it up, because then there'd be every chance of getting it networked and then her book sales and journalism really would take off." And then I could be the neglected husband, left to his own devices. Great. "But meanwhile, what I wanted to ask, Roger – you don't mind Judith trolling off to Manchester from time to time?"

"Of course not, why on earth should I?"

"You'd be surprised at how even the most liberated of husbands can take against having a career wife when she shows signs of getting to the top. Especially – "

Especially when the husband's career shows signs of plummeting to the bottom.

"Especially when there's a baby to consider," amended Nick after only a moment's hesitation. "You know, Roger, she feels guilty at leaving you to fend for yourself."

"Then she mustn't and you must tell her she mustn't," I said hotly, meaning it. I was not going to have Judith feeling guilty at giving me the opportunity to be with you. I didn't even feel particularly guilty about it myself, none of those occasional evenings with you having yet led to anything. If anyone should have felt guilty it should have been you, Angie. Out of a good half dozen evenings we'd had the opportunity to spend together so far, you'd wrecked all but one with your tantrums. The source of the row was always the same – your refusal to have me in that damned flat of yours – but it was a theme with many variations. Once you affected to be put out because I never took you to meet my friends. What friends? You were my friend. Enemies, as the old saying has it, I didn't need.

Nick had something else to say before his other guests arrived. He approached the subject with well-judged diffidence.

"You're going to tell me to mind my own damn business, but Judith's rather worried about you, mate, did you know that?"

"Did she tell you that?"

"After much prompting from me, because I could see that something was troubling her. Do you mind my playing father confessor?"

"Not at all, though you're a bit young for the role." More to the point was when the confessing had gone on. Although Nick Tearle had been our frequent dinner guest I wasn't aware of Judith ever drawing him on one side, and so far as I knew they hadn't had lunch recently. Maybe they had long tête-à-têtes on the telephone.

"It's all part of the service, mate, as any agent will tell you. The fact is she thinks something's bothering you."

"Does she? Why?" Apart from my getting home half-cut every night, that is, and then sitting up here in my study far into the night, brooding over what I now preferred to call a zonko brandy to disguise the fact that I was drinking in quadruples these days.

"She says you've seemed abstracted for the past few months. I must say I've had the same impression myself sometimes when I've come round for dinner."

Any number of reasons for that, old pal. I could be thinking of where my mistress is while we're all sitting round the table yakking about AIDS or the SDP or violence on television; or how much more profitably I could be spending my time; or what she and Cheevers used to get up to with that bundle of ties in the wardrobe; or how soon I dare get up another "seminary" in the resort of her choice; or whether, as claimed, she really did lie in her bed wanting me, and if so, why then

131

wouldn't she let me anywhere near it? Or any manner of things, but all touching on my Lady Malaprop.

"Well, I do tend to take my work problems home, I suppose."

"Don't we all," said Nick, who quite obviously didn't. "It's a good idea to try and leave them locked up in the office, I always find. They can get out of all proportion. Switch off completely, that's what I try to do."

I was damned if I was going to be lectured on my lifestyle by one a good fifteen years my junior. I noticed he hadn't refilled my glass. In a moment he would be advising me to cut down on my drinking.

"Has Judith put you up to saying all this, Nick?" I asked with a touch of curtness.

"Good heavens no, of course not. I'm just speaking as a mate. You don't mind, do you?"

"Since you put the question, actually I do mind."

"Subject dropped, then. But please don't think any of this comes from Judith. She's very loyal to you, you know, Roger." Loyal, of course, not being the same as faithful. At this point the doorbell rang, just in time to save us the embarrassment of ponderously changing track.

While I desultorily thought about checking up on the pair of them after this conversation, it wasn't for another three months or so, when Judith's TV series had got under way and she was travelling to Manchester regularly, that I got round to it. One morning after she had set off with her little suitcase I rang his office on a whim.

"Could I speak to Nick Tearle, please?"

"I'm afraid Mr Tearle won't be in today, he's had to go to Manchester. Who's speaking, please?"

"Oh dear, I've just been told I'm ringing completely the wrong agents. Sorry to have bothered you."

Analysing my emotions, I guess relief was uppermost. I could stop feeling so damned guilty at not being a proper husband – insofar as I ever did feel all that damned guilty, that is: I have to confess to inducing guilt from time to time as a form of self-flagellation, because I felt I deserved it. I won't pretend that jealousy wasn't an element: not of Judith having an affair as such, but of her preferring someone sexually to me, if that's what she was doing. You see, I was pretty sure that she hadn't turned to Nick Tearle merely in consequence of being neglected by me. It was more than possible that he excited her, full stop, in a way I never had. Coupled with my missing-cylinder self-doubts when contemplating my sexual status with you, this did not make me feel like the proverbial million dollars. Yet I hoped my reading of the situation was right. I should have felt a terrible shit otherwise. And after all, she had wanted to come to Venice. My last call, I suppose that was, before she seriously took up with Nick. So I'd had my chance.

I told you she never asked about you. As a matter of fact she once did, after a lunch with that notorious gossip Gunby T. Gunby. Judith asked out of the blue, "Do you ever see that Angela girl who gatecrashed Timothy's christening party?"

"Occasionally," I thought I'd better say. "She's always on the look-out for research work or whatever and I sometimes use her or am able to put her on to other people wanting somebody."

"Why do you bother?"

"I feel rather sorry for her," I said truthfully. "She's led rather an odd life."

"She's still leading it, apparently. You know she's slept her way through the advertising world, don't you? Including a good half dozen who were at the christening do, by all accounts."

"By Gunby's account, you mean."

She left it at that. She was probably trying to warn me off – I'm pretty sure that if she thought an affair with you was already in progress she would have asked outright. Or perhaps she thought I was getting a fling out of my system. It didn't concern me much. My preoccupation was with trying to identify your half dozen representatives at the christening party.

But we won't go into that again. I just thought you might be interested to know who my informant was.

And I'm digressing. Judith's affair with Nick – should I do anything about it? The answer, a prompt one, was no. The only reason for confrontation would be if I wanted either to break up our marriage or come clean about you and go for a reconciliation. I didn't want either. By this time, jumping ahead to changed circumstances, you and I were seeing one another and sleeping together quite often. Insofar as anything between us was ever satisfactory, we had a satisfactory arrangement. It was our status quo. I had never ever seriously contemplated living with you, moving in with you – I knew we should squabble like cats and it couldn't last five minutes. Despite what you said when pissed and maudlin, you were not the living-with kind. That, I told myself, was why you'd always gone for married men.

Yet when taking advantage of Judith's absence in Manchester to have supper with you that evening, I found I was bracing myself for a contingency that wasn't going to happen – the likelihood of your either asking me to leave her or expecting me to break the news that such was my intention. In fact you were remarkably uninterested in my reaction to my wife having an affair. All you wanted to know was what it would mean pragmatically (you said dogmatically) to us. Would it mean we could spend more time together, that I could stop looking at my watch whenever I met you for an evening drink? Would I be able to start seeing you at weekends? Would she stand for my going off on holiday without her (ie, with you)? Not once did you touch on the possibility of my marriage breaking up. I think that was because you feared that it might. It would get you into deeper water than you wanted to swim in.

And so, perversely, I now did, and for the first time, begin to think about leaving Judith. I surprised myself at the conventionality of my reaction. Instead of indulging myself in daydreams about living with you – perhaps because they were so unattainable – I dwelt instead on the most mundane practicalities of ending a marriage. It wasn't about starting a new life, it was about wondering what to tell the neighbours. It was about getting change-of-address cards printed. It was about getting my laundry done. And yes, it was about what kind of a fool I should look if I moved in with you and a week later you moved out.

Nevertheless, I did plunge in and ask straight out if you wanted me to leave Judith. Can you remember anything of that night, by the way? We were at that steak joint off the Haymarket we took up for a while. We had met up at Freddy's Club where I had made my Judith and Nick revelation the occasion for a two-bottle apéritif, and so we were by now well plastered, I even more than you.

"You wouldn't, so why ask?" you said.

"Why wouldn't I?"

"What about Timmy?" You were the only person in the world who called my son that. It was somehow proprietorial and it irritated me.

"I should still see him."

"But you wouldn't like him growing up to call someone else Daddy, would you?"

"Perhaps not." You were right, of course. You often were, where intuition had anything to do with it.

"Then as I say, why do you bother to ask?"

"Why don't you bother to answer?"

"Because as the politicians say, I don't answer hypocritical questions."

I gave you a patronising smile. "Hypothetical."

"Just for once, darling, I happen to have chosen the right word. I said hypocritical and I meant hypocritical. Supposing I said all right, Roger, yes I do want you to leave Judith, what would you say then?"

"That I'd think about it."

"And what should I be doing while you thought about it?"

"Looking for somewhere for us to live," I said recklessly.

"And how do you know I want to live with you, when you've never asked?"

134

"I'm asking now."

"No you're not, you're playing games."

You were right again. I was smashed out of my brains and should never have set off along this road. Yet if you'd said Yes, you wanted me to leave Judith and live with you, I should probably have done something about it. As the philosopher said, all permanent decisions are made in a temporary frame of mind. Indeed I should have had to make a move, for to have opened up that can of peas (I won't call it a can of worms) and then closed it again must have forced you to end our relationship, with the tatters of pride you passionately clung on to.

I said, "Angie, I know I'm pissed and perhaps I am playing games as you say, but if so it's only because the whole of my bloody life has become a game since I met you. Let me ask you another hypothetical stroke hypocritical question. Leave Judith and Tim out of it. Supposing I weren't married any more – supposing, nothing to do with you, I turned up one day a divorced man and asked you to marry me. What would you say?"

You said, soberly, unhappily, "I'm not going to answer that, Roger. If I did, you'd take it the wrong way, knowing you. The plain fact is that I don't see myself marrying anybody. I did once upon a time, but I don't now. I'm not the type."

"Then you *have* answered the question."

"All right, I've answered it, so I might as well answer your other one as well. No, I don't want to live with you. I've never lived with anyone, as you know, I wouldn't know how to live with a man. If you and Judith ever did split up and you took a flat or whatever I don't say I wouldn't come round and spend nights or even weekends with you but it'd be your place, not mine. I'm not a homemaker as you also know."

There were going to be tears before bedtime, I knew it. "You mean you'd prefer to peer into the sweetshop window than to come into the sweetshop?"

"I mean I've always been happy with the bags of sweets you brought out to me and I've never expected more." You were ever ready to bang an analogy into the ground, I thought irrelevantly and with seeming cynicism. Better that brittle reaction than dwelling on the pathetic implications of what you'd just said. It hurt too much.

"I've never given you very much," I said.

"More than anyone else ever has. Much, much more."

And then the tears did roll, mine as well as yours. But they were champagne tears, and I was left uncomfortably aware that our relationship was built on sand.

★

But back to that evening at the Barbican. If I was getting a reputation for being abstracted and anti-social, I couldn't have been any less companionable than Judith as we sat through that terrible play. I, of course, had drifted back to you, so as we passed the evening in stony silence. Nick's other guests must have thought we'd quarrelled. We hadn't – yet. Judith saved it until we got home when, unusually for her, she joined me in a nightcap.

"Why aren't we invited to the Pecks on Wednesday?" she asked baldly the moment she came into the room after seeing that Timothy was safe and snug. No wonder her nose was out of joint – Judith hated missing out on the social swim. I noticed it was a stiff one she poured herself.

I said, "But I'm going to be in Edinburgh on Wednesday – Penn's Shortcake Products, remember?" That was what I'd spent most of the evening daydreaming about. It had been the day before that Charles had asked me to go in his place to sell Mrs Penn on our spring shortbread offensive. I can't remember now why he said he couldn't handle the chore himself – I probably didn't even take it in, being already on the Edinburgh shuttle with you. In any case, he was lying through his teeth, as I was about to learn.

"Besides," I added, "Charles and I don't live in one another's pockets. We don't necessarily go to all his do's."

"We go to this one, Roger. It's his annual dinner party for Benito Benotti."

And I didn't even know Benotti was going to be in London. Of course I knew he always came for a few days at this time of year on his way to some big exhibition in Birmingham, but Charles had said nothing at all about his visit being imminent. And certainly nothing about the annual sucking-up dinner.

"Oh, that," I said, making a fair shot at sounding as if I'd known about it all along. "Well, for one thing I've already done my quota of arse-licking in Venice last November, and for another, even Benotti can't expect me to be in two places at once."

"Perhaps not, but he can expect you to be at Charles's dinner table. Surely Edinburgh can wait."

"It can't actually. It was the only white space Old Mother Penn could find in her diary."

"What – height of the Scottish season, is it?"

I gave her the grimace her little dig demanded. "How did you come to hear about the Benotti dinner anyway?"

"By the most humiliating means possible. I came across Lucille Peck with that stupid MP's wife who's always there, Barbara Stranton, having coffee at Harrods. I showed them the new dress I've bought to wear on the box the week after next and Barbara asked if I meant to try it out on Benotti on Wednesday. Lucille went bright red and changed the subject. Why on earth couldn't you have at least warned me, Roger?"

"I forgot, darling." (Yes, darling, I call Judith darling too. It's an all- purpose term in marriage, you know – often even a term of abuse.) "It's not the star event of the social calendar, you know. You're not missing out on having your name in Jennifer's Diary."

My tit-for-tat sarcasm was misplaced. "I'm missing out on the bloody dinner party, Roger!" cried Judith with unaccustomed vehemence, slamming down her glass. "We don't have such a wide circle of friends that it isn't going to be telegraphed to each and every one how we've been snubbed. I want you to go back to Charles and insist that you change Edinburgh and we go to his dinner party."

"No, I can't do that, Judith."

"Why not?"

Because I've told Angie she's going to Edinburgh on Wednesday and she's probably already got her shabby little suitcase half packed and if I change the date Charles will probably find himself able to go after all.

"Because I've already told Charles it doesn't matter," I lied. "You're making far too much out of this, darling. Our not being there is no big deal at all. Frankly, I was glad to have got out of it. Benotti's an opinionated bore."

"While you are invariably the life and soul of the party. Has it crossed your mind to wonder why Charles wants you out of the way?"

Oh, yes. Benotti's had something to say about my trip to Venice. Not a favourable notice, I would guess.

"Judith, please get it into your head that we have not been snubbed and Charles does not want me out of the way. We're partners, remember."

"For how long?" asked Judith prophetically, draining her glass, and reeled off to bed, leaving me for once not automatically switching my thoughts to you but musing uneasily on this turn of events.

I would have to have it out with Charles, that went without saying. But on Monday when I returned to the office after an uneasy weekend he was not there to have it out with, having gone to meet Benotti at the airport and accompany him to Birmingham. Like much else that happened at the agency these days, this came as news to me. I told myself I didn't give a sod. I at once got on the phone and invited you to a bonus lunch. "*I* see. When the cat's away . . . ." you said archly after I explained why I was unexpectedly available. My uneasy feeling returned for a while. If Charles was the cat, that made me the mouse. Our partnership hadn't started out on that basis. We had been equals, neither one dominating the agency. Now Charles was carrying me – because I was carrying you.

But whatever self-doubts and misgivings I was beginning to entertain were drowned in champagne, gin and single malt whisky up in Edinburgh. It was the perfect jaunt, not quite as memorable as Venice perhaps, but unmarred by rows. Unmarred, too, by over-involvement in work while you twiddled your thumbs.

Unfortunately for me, I completely misjudged Ma Penn, a cookie as tough as her own oatcakes. She presented herself as a twinkling but canny widow-woman, much given to homely aphorisms and coyly susceptible to flattery. Believing her to be eating out of my hand I joshed and joked through my business with her and her henchmen in ninety minutes flat, whereupon, switching from roguish charm and smarm to big-city slickness, I shot off on the pretext of having some hustling to do back in London. I know I should have invited the old bat to dinner, but having declined her buffet lunch at least it couldn't be said against me that I was failing to reciprocate hospitality. I didn't think she was offended. If anything, as she saw me off with the whimsical observation, "Well, I must say you don't let the grass grow under your feet!" I took her to be impressed by my decisiveness and bustle. I wasn't to know that when she cocked her blue-rinsed head pertly to one side, it made contact with a chip on her shoulder even bigger than the one on Benotti's.

Anyway, I had other egos to massage. We had champagne and smoked salmon sandwiches in that nice room with the big double bed overlooking the Castle – a curtain-raiser for the hotel odyssey we were soon to embark on. We made love as easily and effortlessly as if we had been meeting like this twice or three times a week for a year. Hard to believe there had only been Harrogate and Venice in well over half a year. As we lay back in pleasant exhaustion in the early afternoon dusk you read me a smug little lecture: "There, you see! Don't ever say I don't want you enough. I want you all the time, but the time has to be right, like this." It was a contradiction but I knew what you meant – not at your flat.

We had a bath together like honeymooners, sank a couple of Bloody Marys downstairs, then sauntered along Princes Street to the Café Royal, your hand lightly resting on my shoulder in that delightfully proprietorial way you had taken up, as if to announce to the passing, unglancing Edinburgh lassies that this middle-aged greying man was spoken for. There was a full moon and the evening was clear and frosty – another snapshot. The restaurant was pleasantly bustling – not so much a snapshot this time as a post-Impressionist painting, all lights and gleaming white tablecloths and plush and marble. You took my hand across the table and said, "Now we're going to have a nice evening" – a warning that contentious matter was to be avoided. You needn't have worried: when I caught you in loving mood like this I was as loath to shake you out of it as you were to be shaken.

We talked about this and that. Your family came up somehow. Now your father was no longer the cruel despot, more of a crotchety old dear. Your mother's suicide was no more than a dark rumour put out by a malicious aunt, long dead. Your childhood now seemed almost normal, almost happy. While your immediate past was still out of bounds, you were unknowingly shedding some light on it. It was that orbital truth again. You weren't re-revising your parents saga, you were simply reflecting a different facet of it appropriate to the current segment of your mood-cycle, as the moon goes through its phases. But there was never to be a full moon: I could see, more clearly than I had ever done, that you were simply not programmed to tell the complete truth about anything, only to reveal the shards of light that illuminated you at any particular time. I said, "Thank you for talking about yourself." You said, smug again, "You see, darling, I *will* tell you about myself if you let me and don't harass me." I held my peace.

We dallied too long over next morning's breakfast in our room, and it wasn't until well into the lunch hour that I made it back to the office, getting the same kind of looks from young Graham and Co that I used to get on returning from one of my long lunches with you, back in the days when I was still bothering to return from them. Charles came back at three, passing my open door without a glance. I got up and followed him into his office.

"Will it keep, Roger?" asked Charles, making a great show of running a finger down his afternoon's appointments, and adding pointedly, "I know there's much to say but I did hold lunchtime open for you."

"Yes, I'm sorry I couldn't get back sooner, Charles – I wanted to go over some of the small print with Mother Penn's chief exec – Buchan, is it?"

"Buchanan," said Charles, looking studiously at his David Hockney print across the room. "And Graham, in my absence, was fielding a furious phone call from him within ten minutes of your leaving Penn House yesterday, when you refused lunch on the grounds that you had to catch the shuttle back to London. Now just what the hell is going on, Roger?"

And that young bastard Graham hadn't warned me. I had no possible explanation. All I could do was go on the offensive.

"All right, Charles, I'm not going to piss you about. Yes, I'll admit to giving Mrs Penn short shrift. No, it wasn't for the nudge-and-wink reason you think. I needed some time on my own to work out how I stand after the shitty trick you've just pulled on me, if you really want to know."

"By which you mean keeping you away from Benotti, presumably."

And then the pair of us were at it hammer and tongs like the stars of a TV drama series about these two partners in the cut-throat world of advertising. Benotti, it emerged, had politely but positively declined to dine with the Pecks if I was to be among those present. I had slighted him and snubbed him in Venice blah blah blah and he had seriously thought of taking his account away from us. The same went for Ma Penn and her shortbread blah blah blah. It had taken all young Graham's diplomacy, blah blah blah. Then there'd been rumbles from some of the other clients about my cutting meetings short or turning up for them late and pissed – tired and emotional, in Charles's purloined phrase. Not to mention, not that Charles wished to intrude into my private life, that I was getting talked about in the business generally. I was in trouble.

I'd always looked on Charles as my friend. A friend would have asked was there anything I wanted to talk over, anything he could do to help. I might even have taken him up on the offer. It was only now I could see myself as others saw me, and I was not a pretty sight. I was in bad shape. If Charles had said something about red lights and warning bells then I might have tried to get my act together – not ditched you, that was utterly out of the question, but tried to regain some sense of proportion and get our relationship in perspective as a very nice thing that had happened in my life but not one that I could allow to ruin it.

But being Charles he didn't say anything like that. What he did say was, "I'd meant to take you somewhere quiet for lunch to talk this through, but now we've started we might as well finish." And he did mean finish. I was being fired from my own agency. And my very first thought, even while dully comprehending what I had brought myself to, was how would this affect my seeing you? Reflex action, I suppose. Pavlov's poodle.

"I think you're saying you want to dissolve the partnership," I said, after a deep breath.

"I'm afraid so, Roger."

Having gained points for dignity by pre-empting him on that, I promptly lost them again by continuing, "And there's no point in talking about new leaves, pulling socks up and all that?"

"I wouldn't think so, would you? As I say, your personal life's your own, but it probably goes beyond that, doesn't it?"

"Identity crisis?" I hazarded drily.

"You said it, chum."

"Perhaps I'm going through the change of life?"

Ask a flippant question and Charles would always give you a serious answer. "That's not for me to say either, Roger. You've certainly undergone some kind of personality change that I'm afraid makes us incompatible, businesswise. Shall we talk?" He locked the door, told Rosie to field his appointments to Graham and accept no more calls for either of us, and we got down to the nitty-gritty.

I barely listened. We were carving up everything I'd put into the agency – and by the way, that meant poundweight for poundweight of effort and inspiration with Charles before you came along – and all I could think of was whether I'd be left with means enough to take you to lunch two or three times a week. Somehow, I've never been able to pinpoint exactly when it happened, I'd gone topsy-turvy on myself. The real world of work and family had become an unreal, dream world, the dream world of you had become my only real world.

Charles didn't have the capital to buy me out outright. That meant either splitting down the middle and each setting up independently with such clients as decided to stay with one or other of us, or working out a formula which would make me a sleeping partner with a declining stake in the business as the years went on. I won't bore you with the details, which without being patronising you wouldn't understand anyway. You had the archetypal mistress-figure's attitude to business: you didn't exactly suppose that money grew on trees but when I pretended it did you had great difficulty in accepting that the trees needed to be cultivated.

I considered, or affected to consider, the alternatives. Setting up on my own would mean I could hire you as my assistant. In response to that gleeful thought, common sense sounded a rare warning: that if this should be a true reflection of my priorities, I would be bankrupt within six months. The sleeping partner idea, with young Graham taking over my clients, would assure me an income come what may, so that financing my future with you would be underwritten. An attractive proposition. And that, dear Angie, is how I planned my way out of the agency that Charles and I had built up brick by brick over eight struggling years. Looking back, I think I should have been made a ward of court or something. But I was never in any doubt, once Charles had put his cards on the table, that I was doing the wisest thing. Wisdom must be comparative: nobody ever told me that.

"Well – I hope it's for the best," said Charles, when we'd ironed out as much as we could without lawyers present.

"What if it's for the worst?" I said light-heartedly. Light-headedly, rather. I was about to say that I couldn't take in the implications of what was going on, but in truth there weren't any implications. It was all spelt out.

"I hope it won't be for the worst, for either of us," said Charles solemnly, meaning he hoped it wouldn't be for the worst for me. If he thought he could kickstart me into pondering the uncertain future, he was mistaken. The farthest I could project myself was telephoning you with the news and a commiserating or celebratory drink at Freddy's.

Everything related to you. Reflecting on how I should break the news to Judith I found my musings converting, before my eyes, into a rehearsal of how I might set about telling her that I was in love with you. The ordeal of taking my leave of the office equated with informing friends and neighbours that I was leaving home. If I could do one, what passed for my reason insinuated, then I could do the other.

In the event, wrenching myself free of Peck & Piper was no great trauma, thanks to the good offices of Charles who gently pumped out the rumour that I had decided to develop "other interests", which was truer than he knew. Judith, it turned out, had been primed by Charles's wife Lucille who had called to apologise for her clumsy handling of the Harrods gaffe over the Benotti party. The way Lucille told it with belated tact, Charles and I couldn't see eye to eye on structuring the company's future. Something else I won't bother you with: so long as I still got my cut out of the agency it was good enough for Judith, who'd never had a high opinion of my business acumen anyway. Her main concern was that I mustn't be perceived as a failure by our circle of successful friends. No, that's unfair: she didn't want me to be perceived as a failure by myself. I could see what bothered Judith: the suburban spectre of my running to seed while she went from strength to strength. The successful wife with the husband she had to make excuses for. The prospect should have bothered me too. All that concerned me was how many days a week I could reasonably sneak off to spend with you on the pretext of "looking around".

"Looking around" was what Judith earnestly didn't want me to put out that I was doing: "It always rings so hollow, like 'considering one or two offers'."

"All right, then until something turns up why not tell whoever wants to know that I'm working as a consultant?"

"That's even worse, Roger. It's what executives call themselves when they've become unemployable. What *do* you want to do with yourself?"

I want to start leading a double life full time. Keep my old office hours but go round to Angie's place every morning. We'll make that grotty flat really nice, get some pictures on the walls, a bit more furniture, flowers, make it look lived in. Sometimes we'll go out to lunch, maybe to the cinema, other times we'll stay in and make love, or not. Talk, if she wants to. Watch television. Drink champagne.

"Roger? Or don't you know?"

I switched off my pictures in the fire. "I don't, actually. Do you mind? You see, until this afternoon I thought I was in the advertising line."

"But you've seen this bust-up with Charles coming. You must have some plan in mind, however vague."

"No, I haven't."

"Will you stay in advertising?"

"I can't, if I keep on my connection with Peck & Piper." Besides, who'd take me on? "Piper?" I could hear the likes of Hugh Kitchener saying. "I haven't seen him sober for six months, with or without his floozie." Suddenly I felt a wave of resentment against you for letting me get to this stage. When had you ever urged me to take myself back to work instead of going on to Freddy's Club? Why had you got into such a sulk in Venice over the time I had to spend with Benotti? Why hadn't you made me have lunch with Mrs Penn in Edinburgh? This upsurge of self-pity had been festering ever since I'd rung you to give you my news, only to find that you'd gone out without switching on your answering machine again. Where were you, as they say, when I needed you?

I came out of this reverie of blame and bitterness to hear Judith asking if I would like to go away somewhere while I considered what I wanted to do.

"Away where?" I asked guardedly. Away from you, that's where. It would serve you right.

"Wherever you like. So long as you wouldn't be too much on your own, brooding."

"Wouldn't you be coming?"

"I'd love to but I've got so much on, what with my being a famous TV star and everything. Besides which, it's your problem, Roger. I think you're better solving it alone."

Even retrospectively, knowing what I know now about her carryings-on with Nick Tearle, I don't think this was entirely self-interest on Judith's part. She really did think it would do me good to go off and re-charge my batteries or whatever is the end product of taking long walks on clifftops. I felt a warm surge of gratitude towards her.

I would take you to New York. I had only ever spent four days there myself but I would show you the place as if I owned it. We'd stay at the Waldorf Astoria, dine at the Russian Tea Rooms, watch the ice skaters at Rockefeller Plaza. It would be like Venice with skyscrapers. And no clients to bother us.

"I wouldn't mind getting away, it might restore my sense of perspective," I said. How long? A week? I could lose my sense of perspective irredeemably in a week. "I'll give it some thought."

So that was Judith settled. Which left you. Not having been able to contact you at once, I now thought I'd leave telling you about my break with Charles until we met, just in case you took it into your head to blame yourself for having precipitated the split-up by persuading me to linger in bed and take the later shuttle back from Edinburgh. I should have known that you have never blamed yourself for anything in your young life. Never mind. I also wanted to be with you in person, sharing a bottle of Freddy's house champagne, when I followed the bad news with the good news that we'd be going away together.

You were rather stupid about the whole thing, I'm afraid. So much so that I never got round to mentioning New York, and by the time I saw you again the whole idea had been overtaken by events. Sorry you never had cocktails in the Rainbow Room, my love. Even you might have been impressed by the view.

"But how *can* he get rid of you? I thought you were supposed to be partners?" you kept saying dully when I'd unfolded the story. Or perhaps not so dully, since that was precisely the truth of it.

"We are partners, but partnerships are like marriages," I said, condescendingly I'm afraid. "And Charles isn't getting rid of me, we've decided on a legal separation."

"Just because you've got back late from lunch a few times?" You were genuinely wide-eyed and disbelieving. "There must be more to it than that."

"There is more to it, kitten. Ever since you and I came together I've been neglecting the business in order to spend every available minute with you, and now Charles, quite rightly, has had enough of it."

Too late, as you folded your arms and tapped your fingers against your sleeve, I could see that this was going the way of one of our three-times-round-the-lighthouse conversations. "I see. So you've put all the blame on me?"

"You weren't even mentioned, Angie."

"But *you* blame me, don't you? *I* didn't know you were neglecting things. I don't know anything about your business."

"No, I know you don't. You've never wanted to." Below the belt, that. When did I want you to? The last thing on my mind when you came sweeping in through a restaurant doorway with your marmalade hair tumbling about your face was the advertising game or any other game except the one we played ourselves.

"Besides," you chuntered on, getting the bit between your teeth now, "don't you think I've had to neglect my work to be with you? You're not the only one."

"What work?"

"The work I have to get in order to live. You just don't know how many jobs I've turned down so as to be with you."

"Such as when?" I asked cynically.

"Such as before we went up to Edinburgh."

"Which job did you turn down?"

"I didn't say I turned anything down," you amended scrupulously. "But if we hadn't gone to Edinburgh I could have been out looking for work, making phone calls and so on. How can I find work when I'm with you all the time?"

We'd already reached that frequently-arrived-at point where I've wished I had a tape recorder with me so I could play our conversation back and make you see how bizarre it was, how unreasonable you were. Here was I, spilling it all out about my career collapsing in ruins thanks to our continuing relationship – not that I had a moment's regret – and within minutes you had switched it round to a whinge about what came down to your own inability to get off your bottom and find a bit of temping when you had a need to.

But there was more.

I said, as a lead-up to New York, "Well, I'm afraid you're likely to have even less time in future, now I'm no longer in gainful employment. To start the ball rolling, how are you fixed for a nice long lunch tomorrow, because we've got some planning to do?"

A spasm of irritation at my arch tones crossed your face, as well it might have done, then you looked doubtful. "Surely that's got to stop now, Roger? How can you afford to take me out to lunch when you're out of work?"

I explained kindly, and I expect patronisingly, how in this unequal life of ours, not having any work did not necessarily equate with not having any money. Now you began to look thoughtful – even, although I may have later imagined this in the light of what you were about to hint at, a bit foxy.

You said, eyes downcast and swirling your champagne about in your glass as you did when you had anything significant to say, "I still think we ought to see one another less during the day, not more. I really do have to find work and earn some money."

"Why wait until now to tell me?"

"Is there a right time to tell you? It's been on my mind for a while now – am I supposed to keep it cooped up?" No, my love, but yes, there is such a thing as picking the right moment. Get on with it, now you've started. "I've got to live, like everyone else. I've got the rent to pay and all sorts of other expenses, and though I'm very grateful for what you've been giving me, you know I am, it doesn't go very far."

I'd been slipping you the odd tenner or twenty whenever I sensed you needed money, sometimes more. I'd paid one or two bills for you when you'd insinuated them into the conversation. Until now I'd resisted formally keeping you or half-keeping you or even partly keeping you. I didn't want you to feel that kind of obligation to me, and to tell the truth, I didn't want to feel an obligation to you. I wanted us to meet because we wanted to see one another, not to hand over your housekeeping money. But I was being selfish. I worried about you not taking care of yourself but I didn't give much thought to how you were supposed to set about it.

I said, "All right, Angie, I hear what you're saying, but look at it this way. For who knows how long – three months, six months, however long it takes for me to find something suitable for my fantastic talents – I'm going to have time on my hands, time I couldn't put to better use than spending with you. Instead of choosing today of all days to decide you've got to get out and earn some money, why don't you let me give you so much a week? We can work out how much you need, and set it against my need for your company. What do you say to that?"

You shook your head most prettily. "I can't take charity."

"It isn't charity, kitten. It's what I'm prepared to invest in order to see you. Just as I invest in lunch for the return of two or three pleasurable hours with you."

You strayed from the point as usual, even though the point was one of your own making in a roundabout way.

"You don't have to take me to lunch, Roger."

No, of course not. I could take you for walks in the park, couldn't I? We could meet at bus stops or in museums, or wherever couples do meet who don't have flats to go to. I didn't deign to reply, except with a heavy sigh. Your move, Angela.

"Besides," you went on, again with the downcast eye and the swirling of champagne (I wonder what you did for a gesture before you had the opportunity to drink it), "it's not only the rent and day-to-day expenses." And then it all gushed out about your debts, while concurrently the overdraft statement, the long overdue Barclaycard account, the absolutely final notices, the threatening letter from the finance company who had already re-possessed your secondhand car (it was news to me that you'd ever owned one) and now wanted the two hundred pounds they'd been unable to raise on it, came tumbling out of your handbag.

I was dismayed – but for you, not at you: appalled at what you'd been hiding away in your house of secrets. As usual I overdramatised the situation. What to me was an intolerable burden must have been to you little more than a nuisance, a bewilderment. Not caring about money meant not understanding money which meant not appreciating the trouble you were in.

I riffled through the sheaf of bills and demands, mentally totting them up. "Why on earth didn't you tell me you've had these hanging over you all the time I've known you?"

146

With your sad little smile, and in your best little girl voice, you said, "I hoped they'd go away."

And they did, didn't they? What an extraordinary evening that was. I'd arrived at Freddy's in search of sympathy for being heaved out of my own agency, and I ended writing a cheque for two thousand two hundred pounds to clear your debts. My own troubles were forgotten. But Angie, did they have to be forgotten by you too? I was half way home before it came to me that you'd uttered not a word of sympathy or concern, only a few words of thanks for helping you shrug a weight off your shoulders.

I've talked about my missing cylinder: did you know you had one too? With your lack of human curiosity you found it impossible to conceptualise circumstances you weren't involved in, thus sympathy with any predicament not your own direct concern came hard to you. As, come to think of it, it also did where you were or ought to have been involved. But that's the way you were, my love, and there was no changing you.

An extraordinary evening, did I say? It was the night our lives changed. I got home to find Gunby T. Gunby sprawled across my sofa, knocking back my whisky. Judith, noting my look of amnesic panic as I shook his flabby hand, said hurriedly, "Don't be alarmed, you haven't forgotten a dinner party, darling. Gunby's just dropped in off the M4 after inspecting a clutch of motorway restaurants. Since I didn't know when you'd be back I gave him an omelette for his stomach's sake."

"I thought you took on all the plums like the Ritz and Le Gavroche and left the routine caffs to the troops," I said to Gunby, after allowing him to ladle out a dollop of syrupy praise for Judith's way with eggs.

"I do, indeed I do, being of sound mind and body, but I have one of my inspectors off ill."

"Ptomaine poisoning?"

"Worse. Having most of his guts removed. He'll be away for six months, if not longer. That's why I dropped in – to offer Judith my hand in gastronomy."

"It would have been fun," sighed Judith. "Lording it in all the best hotels – "

"The worst hotels, my dear. I get the best hotels."

"But what with Tim and my programme in Manchester and one thing and another, I simply couldn't think of it."

"Turned me down flat," mock-mourned Gunby.

Judith said carefully, topping up Gunby's glass, "I did suggest another candidate, though."

"Yes," said Gunby, rather glumly I thought.

147

"Might you be interested, darling?" pursued Judith. "All other things being equal?"

It didn't cross my mind that things possibly could be equal, that Gunby would even dream of offering me the job. So it was merely in the spirit of making polite noises that I asked, "What does it entail, exactly?" I was most surprised to hear Gunby's reply, as he raised his re-charged glass, "It entails having lunch with me at the Savoy Grill tomorrow."

So we did. I've never been sure of Judith's motives in recommending me – whether she genuinely wanted to help her lame-duck husband over a stile, or was looking for time and space enough to develop her affair with Nick. Or both. Or maybe the second motive arose out of the first – an egg and chicken situation.

Gunby's motives in seizing on my unlikely candidature turned out to be straightforwardly, or if you like deviously, mercenary. Having pronounced his smoked salmon up to scratch and complemented it with a forkful or two of my potted shrimps, he said, "As Judith was saying before you got home last night, it's ideal for someone in your position who's looking around, because it doesn't lock you up in a full-time job. You'd be expected to visit three hotels in a fortnight, plus restaurants within their particular areas. But the question is whether the pay's at all a crucial factor."

"It needn't be," I said promptly. I would have paid him for the privilege had he known it (and he probably did). Three hotels every fortnight! Three rooms, three beds, three nights, three golden afternoons – there are people married and living together who spend less time with one another! You know, it was a funny thing about our relationship, Angie. Every time it looked as if it could be on the verge of foundering – usually over the running battle about your flat – something turned up to keep us going. In that respect if no other, we led charmed lives. Windfalls of luck.

"Reasonable expenses of course," continued Gunby with uncharacteristic magnanimity. That was because he didn't have to pay them, the bills being picked up by the *Good Living Guide*'s sponsors. Salaries, however, came out of his own fixed-budget running costs, which was why, dabbing lemon juice off his gleaming chin, he went on to say, "But frankly there's very little in it apart from the opportunity to live it up a little. To tell you the truth, it's a job that very much suits a bachelor. He can soften up his girl with a few slap-up meals in Town, then if she gives him the green light and he wants to take her away somewhere, well, no-one looks too closely at whether the bill's for single occupancy or double."

He was on to me. He all but winked as he drained his glass of hock and signalled the sommelier to open the claret.

I said, "As a husband and father, I don't think I qualify."

Now Gunby positively did wink. "We all qualify, my friend. You qualify and I qualify. Enjoy life, that's what it's for."

I felt a little nauseated, then hypocritical for being so. But the only doubt in my mind was as to whether I ought to ring you now, between courses, on the pretext of going to the lavatory, or wait until after the meal.

"All right," I said. "Then if you think I'm up to it . . ."

There was no further mention of pay, and Gunby T. Gunby let me settle the bill.

Seven

So began the mad hotel odyssey that was to be the last phase but one of our mad affair. (Mad as in our hotel saga means bizarre, mad as in us means insane.)

It is all by now a jumble of champagne buckets and room service sandwiches, of king-sized beds and queen-sized beds and disappointing twin beds and dwarf-sized double beds and good-night mints on the pillow and coffee-making "facilities" or futilities as you called them; of quilted bars and carpeted corridors and Musak-tinkling lifts and buffet breakfasts; of Do Not Disturb signs and Please Make Up Room signs (and our fury and frustration at arriving back from an amorous lunch to find the bed-linen stripped and the blankets on the floor, the towels gone, a vacuum cleaner in the middle of the room and no sign of the maid); of lilliputian cakes of wrapped soap and miniature phials of shampoo and bath foam which you always swept into your handbag, and bookmatches that always went into my pocket so that lighting your cigarette in Leicester with matches picked up in Nottingham I could never be absolutely sure where we were.

One town is superimposed upon another: I have Cardiff with a view across Morecambe Bay, that hospital-like brick box in Swindon transplanted to the edge of the New Forest, the swimming pool at the Blackburn Confotel installed in the basement Balmoral Suite of the Newcastle Confotel, the hotel where we first stayed in Harrogate on that blissful "seminary" cannibalised with the hotel across the Stray where we played a silly game of secret agents on one of our earliest undercover missions for Gunby T. Gunby's *Good Living Guide*.

Not all my snapshots are double exposures. A treasured one is of you walking barefoot on the sands at Lytham St Anne's with the tide far out, and perching you on a groyne to bathe your toe where the cuttlefish shell cut it, and you looked so young and fresh and freckled and innocent with the sea breeze blowing back your marmalade hair that I wanted either to take you there and then or buy you a bucket and spade and make sandcastles. I see us in Lancaster where we did our Bonnie and Clyde act in the preposterous restaurant I was supposed to

150

be reviewing, behaving so badly that we were asked to leave and finished up eating fish and chips in a car park, swigging warm off-licence champagne out of the bottle like a couple of winos. I have a dream sequence in the middle of Birmingham where you were waving at me from the other side of a road it was impossible to cross for the barriers, until we signposted one another to the pedestrian underpass that turned out to be a warren of inter-connecting tunnels, and we ran around in confused circles trying to find one another until finally we chanced to come out simultaneously into an open-air arena of rubble where one of these days they mean to build a garden of rest, and you fell into my arms and clung to me and wept in fright and love and exhaustion.

Some of these scenes I sometimes see in slow motion, as in an art house film: like your running towards me in the New Forest, arms outstretched, the sun dappling your hair as it must have done when Charles spotted you flitting up Ealing Church Grove to gatecrash my life. And in Brighton where you insisted on swimming in the sea, I have a still moment of you perched on a rock like the mermaid sculpture in Copenhagen harbour (where I wanted one day to take you but never did, along with New York and Paris) and looking every bit as immutable and permanent as you let my love lap against you like waves while you gazed out to sea, never moving. (Yet there were other, flitting, images where you were never still, but came and went and never said where you'd been, when you were as elusive and enigmatic as a dancing shadow.)

Few of our Punch and Judy squabbles stand out in such isolation. Some do, but I cannot often match the scene to the scenery. It was in Leicester that you threw the red wine in my face but was that the result or the cause of my haranguing you for having no capacity for embarrassment? Where was the cobbled market square we were crossing on our way back to the hotel after dinner when you burst out, "Fucking, fucking, fucking, that's all you ever think about!" because you were tired and I'd made the mistake of wondering aloud whether you'd like me to let you sleep and wake you later. I was never so desolate: sex was our bonding glue and if we didn't have that we would fall apart. I had already mapped out the stiff goodbyes on the platform at Paddington or wherever, and a future of roaming these hotels on my own and picking up the occasional middle-aged adventuress over a late-night brandy, when – though not until we were back in our room and you were making a great sniffling show of packing your little evacuee suitcase – you coaxed, "Come on, darling" as you always did when you wanted conciliation talks, and it proved you were suffering from time-of-the-month stomach cramps. They passed off at once. Perhaps we just needed a crisis after a couple of days' unendurable calm.

Was it in Norwich or Nottingham that we got on to the massed band of your ex-lovers who had been at Tim's christening party with you? I don't know how it came up – yes I do: we were in that pretentious converted lead mill or smoke factory or whatever it was supposed to have been, that dreadful nouvelle cuisine rip-off joint where we made the chef-owner come out and explain how he justified his two thousand per cent mark-up on one fanned-out sliced carrot and a bit of raw cauliflower. You casually remembered Hugh Kitchener taking you to lunch in Covent Garden when he'd made a similar fuss, and I not quite so casually enquired, your anecdote told, "How did you come to know Hugh, by the way?"

The benign mood our Bonnie and Clyde interlude with the restaurant boss had put you in began to evaporate. With a getting-on-for-glacial smile: "I thought we weren't going to have any more interpolations."

"Or interrogations, even. You're quite right, my love, though it was only an idle question," I said, not very convincingly I fear. To get myself off the subject I went on, "But can I ask you something else, if it's not of an interrogative nature?"

"If you must."

You were positively freezing up now. You thought I was going to press you about Kitchener. Deciding to be in a huff myself I asked coldly, "Why are you being so huffy, Angela?"

"You wanted to know something, Roger. Come on, what is it?"

I decided not to be in a huff after all – it would have got me nowhere, the mood you were getting into. "Darling Lady Malaprop, I was only going to ask about your funny way with words. Have you ever talked to anyone about it?"

"Only with you," you said, ready to be mollified. We were on safeish ground here. This was fine, this was: it was about you directly, not about you and someone else.

"Well, not really. We've joked about it," I half-conceded.

"I've told you about my dyslexia."

"But not what anyone might have told you was the cause of it. Not that I know about such things."

"My disturbed childhood, I suppose."

But my love, I don't think you did have a disturbed childhood. It sounded as if you had the first time you told me about it, but the more you filled in the picture the less disturbed your childhood seemed. Yet why did you want to give me that impression in the first place? Maybe that was a sign of a disturbed childhood.

I put it as carefully as I could. "You say that, darling, but looking back and detaching yourself from whatever's happened to you since, was it really as disturbed as all that?"

You sat in what I think I was supposed to interpret as stunned silence for a moment, then rose stiffly and took yourself off to the cloakroom. When you came back, after a good ten minutes, you had been crying. You sat down again with a melting display of dignity, like a minor princess who has just heard that the bailiffs are in but who has got to keep up appearances at the state banquet.

Unprompted, you said quietly, "You're quite right. Compared with some of the things one reads about I suppose my childhood was positively idealistic." I didn't correct your dyslexic English for once. It did cross my mind, surprisingly for the first time, that perhaps you were simply not properly educated. I should always have looked for the simple explanation first. There were whole areas of your personality where there turned out to be less about you than met the eye.

You dabbed at your nose and permitted yourself a little sniffle. "How did we get into this, anyway?"

These exchanges had left me with the familiar feeling of drifting gently out to sea in an open boat. I reached for my oar.

"I've no idea," I said truthfully. "I seem to remember I was asking about Hugh Kitchener."

And I couldn't, or so it seemed for a while, have asked at a better time. You were so eager to get off the topic of the unhappiness or otherwise of your childhood that you became the soul of co-operation.

"What do you want to know about him?"

"Just how you met him."

"You mean how I came to sleep with him?"

"I suppose so."

"It was at a party. I was pissed and lonely and I didn't want to go home. He has a little flat he sometimes borrows when he stops up in Town and we went there."

"Oh, I see."

"What do you mean, Oh, you see? You mean, Oh, you dis-approve."

No, I mean Oh, I seem to have a knife in my chest. "It's not for me to approve or disapprove. It's just that I've always assumed you met him through work. I thought he'd taken you on to do a research project or a temping stint and it had developed from there."

"No."

"So it was the other way round. You slept with him and that led to his giving you work."

"If that's how you want to put it." The danger cones were well hoisted now. You had pushed away your plate of veal congealing on a blob of what looked like strawberry jam and now you were puffing

153

furiously on an unlit cigarette, this being a no-smoking establishment as it just would have been.

"And is that how you usually got yourself work?"

"Roger, can we be clear about one thing? I never slept with men to get work. I slept with them because I felt like it."

Oh. "But it did lead to work?"

"Sometimes, yes."

"And all these other agency people you went around with, did you meet them at parties too?"

"Which other agency people?"

I named the half dozen christening party guests whom Judith had named to me. We now went into a diversion where you first denied having slept with them, then couldn't remember whether you'd slept with them or not, demanded to know who'd told me about them, and finally asked why I was always raking up the past.

The waiter was unlucky enough to be clearing our plates at this point. Brandishing your unlit cigarette you called for a match. With a grimace of sympathy he said, "I'm sorry, madame, we have a no-smoking rule. I know it's nice to light up after a good meal but the chef says it spoils it for the other diners."

"Oh, really? Actually I was about to light up after a very bad meal and as for spoiling it for the other diners, I would have thought the chef was doing that very well without any help from me."

Oh dear. But I'm afraid that for once I wasn't going to play Clyde to your Bonnie. I pressed on, as the waiter fled, "Let's not get into deep water on this, Angie. All I'm doing is trying to get impressions sorted out in my mind. I'd always had the idea you'd met these people professionally but now it seems you met them all at parties, is that right?"

"Most of them, yes."

"Which parties? Whose parties?"

"Mainly those clubs I've told you about."

"Where you met Cheevers?"

"Yes."

I was surprised you didn't ask why I had to drag Cheevers' name up again. I would have replied that I didn't, he dragged himself up at every opportunity. "And did he introduce them to you, as a general rule?"

"He might have done in some cases, I can't remember. As a general rule, no. They weren't the kind of places where you need introductions."

"Informal," I said ironically.

"Roger, you're asking and I'm telling you."

So I was and so, for once, you were. I asked something else that had mildly puzzled me. "All the people you've had these flings with, the ones I know about anyway, seem to have been quite well off. Is that a coincidence or do you like well-off people?"

"I've never been a gold digger if that's what you mean. I like being taken to nice places, why shouldn't I? *You* take me to nice places. And what's wrong with liking successful men?"

Nothing at all, dear, so long as I'm the exception that proves the rule. "They're supposed to be sexier," I said.

"They are."

It was then, perhaps goaded by such uncharacteristic and untoward frankness, that I made my famously unwise remark about your having been born with a silver cock in your mouth. Had there been any wine left in the bottle you would have carefully poured youself a glass and thrown it in my face: I could see you were itching to. By way of a substitute gesture you got up, unhurriedly as always, and before walking serenely out of the restaurant fetched me such a blow across the head with your handbag that it flew open, and the waiter had to bound after you practically on all fours, retrieving cigarette packet, cheque book, keys and other portable bric-à-brac.

A cathedral-like hush fell over the restaurant, the only sound being that of cutlery being studiously applied to near-empty plates. I signalled for the bill, treating the waiter to a wry facial shrug to indicate that you were the cross I had to bear but that it was worth it taking one thing with another. After a moment the chef-owner, who I seem to remember was called Nigel, made his second appearance of the evening.

"Good evening, Mr Piper. As I gather your companion didn't enjoy her meal, normally I shouldn't dream of charging for it, but I wouldn't want Mr Gunby to think I was trying to bribe one of his inspectors."

I stared at the insolent bugger in surprise – alarm, even. It was as if our cover had been blown. "Now how on earth did you know where I was from?"

He produced the sheaf of notes I had made on one of the hotels we'd stayed at and given you to type up. I'd recommended, solely on the basis that we'd had to wait forty-five minutes for them to send up a bottle of champagne and when it did arrive it wasn't chilled, that they should lose Gunby's distinctive coronet award. There was the giveaway.

"The lady dropped these on the way out. I must say I wish I'd known you were coming, Mr Piper. We have a little kitchen crisis this evening – I would have asked you to come when things are nearer to normal."

"We all have our little crises," I said. "It was a good meal. Thank you."

And I gave the place such a terrific write-up that Gunby called for a second opinion from someone who liked that kind of gunge and it finished up with one of his coveted coronets. Thereafter whenever we made a scene in a restaurant I always gave it top marks. It became our private joke, and the fact that we could joke about our rows made them more endurable. But I still can't remember the name of that dump. I expect it'll come back to me when the new *Good Living Guide* comes out at Christmas. Or would if I could bear to read it. It would be too painful.

And was it in Halifax or Huddersfield or where that we had that set-to about Cheevers and the bundle of ties? It was one of the few recorded cases of our ever having a row in bed – not that we always went to bed the best of friends but we were usually so legless that we were both asleep the moment our heads touched the pillow. But tonight we were both feeling so queasy after an indifferent Chinese meal that we lay awake stuffed with monosodium glutamate and both radiating diffused bad temper just aching for a target. A pity for the Chinese joint that we didn't have the row there – it would have got a glowing recommendation.

I'd bought you a new suitcase for our travels and this was its first outing. You hadn't quite finished unpacking and as you did so you said, "Thank you for my new suitcase, darling. It's very handsome."

"What have you done with your old one?"

"Sent it to the jumble sale."

"Pity. I had quite a sentimental regard for your evacuee's case."

"My what?"

"Evacuees. Little kids who were trundled off out of harm's way during the war. You've always reminded me of one on these little jaunts of ours, with your little cardboard suitcase."

"That's because you keep me out of harm's way."

You went off to do whatever you had to do in the bathroom. I switched off the light and lay there thinking nothing in particular. I felt a wave of nausea at the aftertaste of glutinous spare ribs. A ball of fried rice seemed wedged in my upper chest. A thought, one of the stray questions I'd always wanted to ask, or rather had asked more than once but without a satisfactory reply, drifted into my head and lodged itself there like the undigested Chinese food in my stomach. I would probably have chased it away again had I not been feeling so disagreeable.

You got into bed and we lay there in the dark, unable to sleep. I put my arm around you. It occurred to me vaguely that we could be more constructively occupied than simply lying there suffering.

"I don't suppose you've got any Rennies?" you said.

"No, I haven't."

"Why are you snapping?"

"Sorry. We weren't on the same thought plane. It didn't seem a very romantic thing to say, that's all."

"Indigestion's not a very romantic thing to have."

"No."

You detached yourself from my embrace, patting my arm to indicate that you were not doing this in any hostile spirit. You turned over on to your side. Out of the blue, or out of the blue so far as you were concerned, I blurted out:

"Is that what you did with your bundle of ties – send them to the jumble sale?"

"What?"

"Like your old suitcase."

You didn't answer at first. I thought you weren't going to answer at all. It wasn't beyond you to feign sleep when there was something you didn't want to get into – one of the reasons we had so few rows in bed. Then in a small voice you said, "No, I put them in the bin."

"So they weren't a figment of my imagination after all?"

You turned back to face me in the dark.

"But they were, darling. After I threw them away they didn't exist. That part of my life didn't exist. Don't you see?"

Oh, that kind of figment. There was no point in arguing the toss with you. I once skimmed an article in a magazine called *Parents* which Judith had started taking, about the difficulties of applying intelligence tests to bright five-year-olds. One of them had been asked why she thought a pint of water was bigger than a pint of milk. She replied, "Because when the milk has been drunk it's not there any more but the water doesn't get drunk." That was you – a bright five-year-old. Not a cunning twenty-nine-year-old, I never thought that.

"Whose were those ties? Cheevers'?"

"You know they were."

"What were they doing in your wardrobe?"

I believed your answer, though I'm not sure I believed his. It was when he'd brought you over one of his wife's cast-off dresses intended for Oxfam. She'd thrown out some of his old ties and they were in the same bag. Or so he said. And since they were on the premises, he decided he wanted to play games with them.

"What kind of games?"

I was grateful for the dark. You would never have answered me otherwise. Your voice was getting smaller and smaller but clearer and clearer.

"Oh – you know. Bondage games."

"No, I don't know. Did you play these games with other people, or just him?"

"Just him."

"Can I ask why?"

"Because he wanted to."

"Didn't you want to?"

"Not particularly."

How non-particular was not particularly? No – I couldn't chase every hare.

I raised myself up on one elbow. "But are you saying you'd do anything he wanted just because he wanted to do it? Supposing he'd wanted – oh, I don't know: supposing he'd wanted to tie you up and whip you?"

"He did."

"Did what? Want to or whip you?"

"Oh, Roger!" You reached out and massaged my shoulder, as if to soothe the anxieties out of me. "Why will you ask all these questions about a very unimportant part of my life? I've told you, they were only *games*. It was like doctors and nurses."

"Doctors and nurses don't tie one another up."

"We didn't tie one another up. He just tied me up, that's all."

Oh, well, so long as that's all. "What did you do then?"

"I couldn't do very much, if I was bound hand and foot, could I?"

Once again you demonstrated your knack of conjuring up clear and vivid images, a peepshow illuminated by cold harsh light. I don't think the bile rising in my throat was entirely the result of our Chinese experience.

"You know what I mean, Angie. What did he do?"

"I can't remember."

"Don't be ridiculous."

"I *can't* remember, Roger. He did all sorts of things at different times. How do I know what he did on this one night? It was all so long ago."

Why did I ask you questions when I didn't want to know the answers? But I did want to know. What I didn't want was the kind of answers I was getting.

"What sort of things?" I asked heavily.

"Oh, you know."

"But I don't know, Angela, that's why I'm asking you."

"You don't want a catalogue, surely? We didn't have orgies or anything – he was just showing me the different things that men like doing, or having done. You *must* know – the kind of things their wives won't do for them."

"'Showing' you. You sound as if it was a demonstration."

"That's exactly what it was."

"And what was the point of it?"

158

I sensed you shrugging in the dark. "Curiosity, I suppose."

"On your part? You mean you asked him to do all these things?"

"Oh, do stop it, Roger! You're asking and asking but all you do is get hold of the wrong end of the stick."

"Then show me the right end."

"There's nothing to worry about."

"Isn't there? I think I'll be the judge of that."

"Roger, I was there and you weren't. I've said I'm ashamed of a lot of the things I did in my past, but they weren't all that shocking, you know. I'm not going to go through life wearing sackcloth and ashes because of a few childish games."

We lapsed into silence. I lay there in a fog of depressed confusion. I asked for information and I didn't know what to do with it when I'd got it. Even if you gave me the complete picture, what was I supposed to do then? Come to some conclusion, I expect – either to accept that all this stuff was in the past, or to go on fearing that it would continue to throw a shadow over the future, in which case the only course was to give you up. That was probably what you were afraid of, or would have been afraid of if you ever troubled to review your situation with me. There was often a note of panic in your voice during these interrogations which suggested not only that I was digging too deeply for your intellect to be able to cope with, requiring you to rationalise and explain what remained inexplicable even to yourself, but also that you feared being cornered into telling me too much, waking up sleeping dogs.

I had to leave it alone. I told myself, willed myself, to leave it alone.

I reached out and touched your hand. You fluttered your fingers across my palm.

"Angie?"

Just one question more. These childish games as you called them. How adult were your responses?

"Angie?"

You weren't feigning sleep, you had simply gone dumb on me. I could sense that you were lying there with your eyes open, staring into the darkness.

"Angela? Come on, darling, we can't leave it like this. I want to ask you something."

You wouldn't reply. I kept prompting you, coaxing you, willing you to speak. At last, as you silently turned over with an air of finality, I fell into a dyspeptic rage and pulled the eiderdown away just as you were tucking it up around your shoulders.

"Look, you are not going to sleep on me, Angela, I want to bloody talk!"

Pettishly, you tugged the eiderdown back. I pulled it away again. "You're not going to sleep! Make your mind up to it!"

159

We were both angry now, but you were in control of your anger where I was not. You clicked on your bedside light and picked up the telephone, imperiously and ostentatiously waiting for the operator.

"Hello, could you get me the night porter, please? There's a man in my room annoying me."

You were so absurd that had I not been so furious I would have burst out laughing and hugged you. Instead I said wearily, "Oh, do leave off, Angela. What's the point of this stupid charade? You can't get the operator without punching zero and if you want the night porter the number is five two."

Your face set in an I'll-show-him scowl, you punched out the two digits. I grabbed the phone from you and banged it back on its cradle. Then I tried to pin you down by your shoulders.

"Grow up. Do you hear me? You may have played childish games with Cheevers but you're not going to play them with me."

You misunderstood, as ever. "No, I'm not, so don't ever ask me to." You wrenched yourself free and slammed into the bathroom.

I sat up in bed, fuming and fidgeting, and reached out for something to read – anything to dispel those swirling images in which, as through a fish-eye lens, Cheevers' saturnine features loomed up and receded and loomed up again, like some carved creature on a carousel. I wished now I had never gone to see him, that I couldn't put a face to the name: it would have helped me to keep my thoughts on an abstract plane.

Did you know what you were doing, Angie? I mean by being so evasive and elusive? When you weaved and dodged like that were you consciously trying to prevent me from ever reaching a conclusion about you? Did you think that once I did reach a conclusion it would all be over – not because I was shocked or didn't think you worth knowing any more, but simply because there would be nothing else to tell, nothing for me to drag out of you, nothing there, the onion finally peeled, Salome's last veil, Scheherazade's last tale?

I had picked up the padded folder of hotel hokum. I read it mindlessly. Excellent conference facilities . . . sauna . . . health club . . . private rooms available for banquets or meetings . . .

You were a long time. Probably like me you were suffering from the effects of that Chinese meal. I wondered whether I should call out to reassure myself that you were all right. Then I saw that the pencil line of light was no longer visible below the bathroom door. I got up and listened at the door. Silence. I pushed the door open a crack and then, meeting darkness, opened it fully. You had made a bed of towels in the bath and were either fast asleep or pretending to be. A great wave of tenderness washed over me. I wanted to pick you up and carry you back to bed and watch over you without your waking up. But then came another wave, of resentment, which left me hoping malevolently that you'd wake up with a terrible crick in your neck.

I closed the door gently, turned off my light and got into bed. I lay awake long into the night thinking about you but getting nowhere, the same sequence of thoughts ratcheting round and round like a roulette wheel. Or a treadmill. Wearying of it all, I deliberately turned my thoughts homeward, to my son Timothy, getting on for a year now, to my marriage drifting like a becalmed yacht towards its still distant end, to my junked career, to my ridiculous role as one of Gunby T. Gunby's inspectors of bed-linen, vegetables and fine wine, and all for the sake of what? But I was coming dangerously close to getting myself, and us, in perspective. I drifted into sleep, waking up only momentarily at whatever hour it was when the bathroom door creaked open and you crept into bed. I put my arm around you as if in sleep and you took my hand. In the morning we agreed that it must have been the Chinese meal that had made us so spiky with each other, and another monumental row was behind us. But you did have a terrible crick in your neck, I'm happy to say.

I didn't deliberately set up these inquisitions, you know. If their frequency increased during our hotel odyssey it was because we had more time together, and because some of that time was inevitably less euphoric than hitherto – no-one can fizz for twenty four hours a day. There being no need any more for an agenda of selected topics to cram into our few precious hours together, it was only natural that some of the things I wanted to ask about and talk about would fall into the conversation, almost unbidden. You always resented it. Digging up graves, you called it. But contrary to your fixed belief, my love, the past doesn't exist in a vacuum, it's connected as much to the present as the present is to the future, and it was impossible to live an entirely present-day life with you, except on the most superficial level (to which, I suspect, you wouldn't have objected one bit) without our being a party, even if a third party, to one another's past life.

Our journey to that place in Bristol is an example of how what ought to have been an enlightening conversation, and which with anyone else would have been an enlightening conversation, would escalate into a smouldering row, simply because of the brick wall effect of my persistence in asking questions meeting your reluctance to answer them.

It was the first time we'd ever driven anywhere together. Although I charged mileage to Gunby – he drew the line at first class rail fares – I would never take the car on any of our jaunts because of the strong likelihood of finding myself driving when pissed, and the even stronger likelihood of you driving when pissed (as I warned you against more than once, and a fat lot of good it did when you took up driving again). I don't know whether you had any idea what that hotel odyssey was costing me. The petrol allowance covered only a fraction of our fares, then there were cabs I couldn't charge for, champagne in our room, endless Bloody Marys. You never asked, although I'm pretty sure you must have known I couldn't swing it all on Gunby. You were remarkably incurious about money.

But that's by the way. Because this country house hotel, the name of which has left me, was a good way outside Bristol and we didn't want to be stuck there that night if the menu looked unspeakable, I picked up a hire car at Temple Meads station. It was a lovely day in early summer and the roads were quiet. Once we were clear of Bristol you started begging me to let you drive. You nagged away in your pretty-please way, like a child wanting a ride on the helter-skelter, until finally, as we turned off into a B-road, I let you take the wheel, for all that I hadn't registered your name as an alternative driver, and that the likelihood of your having a licence about was remote.

You turned out to be a surprisingly good driver. That sounds patronising: surprising, I mean, for someone who hadn't driven for so long.

"I used to love driving," you prattled on. "When I was at the Chelsea Auction Galleries I used to drive one of their vans sometimes. Then Belle and I bought this beaten-up Renault between us and I drove everywhere, even down the street to the paper shop. I used to park on the pavement like the French do and flutter my eyelids at the traffic wardens. I loved it."

I loved you. In this effervescent mood you were back as you were when you first bubbled into my life at Luigi's, so many months ago now. I could just imagine you tootling around in your own little car, breaking all the regulations and getting away with it.

We had the sun roof open and your marmalade hair was streaming back from your face. You were wearing sun glasses. You looked adorable and happy. I was happy too. So now what could I do to ruin it?

"And how many tickets did you get for speeding?" I asked.

"None at all, believe it or not. I charmed my way out of them."

"Of course you did."

"But I had enough parking tickets to paper a wall. I never paid them, of course. I thought they were supposed to catch up with you in the end."

"You're better than most at not being caught up with. Except by

162

the finance companies. Was this beat-up Renault the one they grabbed when you didn't keep up the instalments?"

"That's right."

"But it was owned jointly by you and Belle?"

"Yes, though she hardly ever drove it, except on one famous occasion when she picked up a hitch-hiker on the way to Brighton and got herself seduced on the Downs. Then she came into some money and went to live on one of the Greek Islands for a while, so she said I could have her share of the car. But I couldn't keep up the payments."

"She 'came into some money'. You mean she met somebody rich who took her for a prolonged holiday?"

"Something like that. You're not going to start asking questions, are you? I'm having such a lovely time driving, don't spoil it, darling."

But I had to spoil it, darling. Second nature. "I'm not asking questions, kitten, we're just chatting. It's inevitable that some of my chat ends with a question mark. And I was curious about your car-driving days. Until you showed me that letter from the finance company I'd no idea you had ever driven."

We were deep into the country now. An alley of trees arched across the winding road and we were driving through shadow. A shadow, too, fell across the vista of my pleasant, rambling thoughts. I didn't want to ask you but I felt compelled to:

"By the way, you did pay the finance people out of the cheque I gave you?"

"Not yet, why?"

Because it was bloody weeks ago, that's why. "You realise they'll charge you interest? Why haven't you paid them?"

"If you must know – "(Yes, I must, since it was my money) "I've got a query on the amount they say I owe and I want to go in and see them."

"Then why don't you?"

"Because I'm always out with you somewhere," you said plaintively. "I always drop everything to be with you, you know that, you must realise how things mount up."

"You never tell me about them."

"They're such mundane things, like laundry and filling forms in and changing electric light bulbs. I'll make an appointment and go and pay what I owe next week. The money's waiting in the bank, I haven't touched it. Promise. Now can we forget it and enjoy our drive?"

That "I haven't touched it" meant you had touched it, I knew it. But I said nothing, not on that topic anyway.

"But your overdraft and those other bits and pieces – you've paid those off?"

"Yes, I have, and thank you very much for giving me the money."

I hesitated. It was unlikely that the subject was going to come up in as natural a way for some time, and it was one of those aspects of your life that intrigued me.

"Those debts I cleared up for you, and don't get me wrong, I was very happy to do so . . ." I was, too. Absurdly so. "But one thing puzzles me."

"Where all that money went?"

"Yes. Or rather what it went on. Forgive me, darling, but you don't have much to show for it."

"No, I know."

And then you fell into your customary silence, waiting for me to prompt you. I decided for once to let you prompt yourself. You accelerated angrily.

"Steady. You took that bend far too fast."

"Sorry, darling. Tensed up."

"Don't be. If there's something bothering you we'll talk about it when we reach the hotel."

"No, it's not bothering me but it might bother you. I knew you'd ask me about all the money I've got through sooner or later."

"Do I take it that Cheevers comes into this?"

"Well, I didn't give money to all and sundry!" you snapped defensively, defiantly, your foot again pushing hard on the accelerator. Resentment boiled within you, you had steam coming out of your head almost. You thought I was baiting you into a corner again. What a nice day, let's taunt Angie. Wrong, my love. Shall I tell you what I'd been mainly thinking on that drive, up until then? What a marvellous wheeze it would be to present you with a car of your own. Just do what in fact I subsequently did – give you the ignition key in a gift-wrapped box, then feast off your delight and wonder before leading you out into the street where you'd find your own little car all polished and waiting. Tied in ribbon I'd meant it to be, but I quickly went off that, it smacked rather of those insecure show-offs who hire aeroplanes to spell out I LOVE YOU in sky-writing.

As you screeched round another bend at seventy, I nearly went off the idea altogether. You were a good driver but an impetuous one. You drove in character. And why didn't I listen to that clear warning to myself?

"So you gave Cheevers money?"

"Sometimes. That's why it was so laughable when you asked if he'd been paying my rent. He never had any money, not for long anyway. He's an impulsive gambler."

"Compulsive. Yes, so I've heard. How much did you give him?"

"I didn't give it him, he borrowed it."

"They always call it borrowing. Did he ever pay it back?"

"No. That was one reason why I used to go on seeing him when you didn't want me to, in the hope that he might."

"And how much was it?"

"I don't know, I never counted it up." No, you wouldn't have done. Silly question. "It was all done so casually – ten pounds here, twenty pounds there, cheques for fifty pounds if I didn't have any cash about me. Then when the bank wouldn't let me draw any more, if I wasn't earning anything I had to start selling things."

"Had to?"

"Did, then. That flat's so grotty that buying anything nice for it was always a waste of money anyway. I used to buy things I didn't even need on my credit card, knowing he would take them and sell them."

"So he did the selling. It sounds as if running up your credit card debt was his idea, then, to raise money for him."

"I can't remember. I don't think it was initially. It was just that if I didn't have any money to give him he'd go on and on about why had I bought new cushions, why did I need my pretty desk lamp, what did I want with all those records when I'd already sold the record player? It was just the easiest way out to let him take the stuff and sell it."

"Well, at least when he sold off your things he brought you his wife's cast-offs." For once the irony was not lost on you. You nodded ruefully and concentrated fiercely on your driving, your pleasure in it now marred with sadness as a mascara-weighted tear trickled down below your sun glasses. Sad at what, my love? The waste of your time with Cheevers, I hope. Did he make you give up your little car? I wondered, but didn't ask.

I would buy you new cushions, a pretty desk lamp, replacement records, a new record player, pictures for your bare walls. And a replacement for your beaten-up Renault. The plot for that, despite my reservations, was already forming beautifully on the back burner of my mind.

I loved buying things for you, just as you loved having things bought for you. You said no-one before I came along had ever bought you presents. I don't know how true that was – certainly there was no evidence of anyone ever having arrived bearing gifts. Perhaps Cheevers had made away with them. But nothing, in my new life of semi-leisure, gave me greater pleasure than roaming about the antique supermarkets and such places buying you little bits of jewellery and other trinkets. Nothing very valuable because I could never persuade you to treat your possessions with care, but you were as delighted by a few new pages for your Filofax as by your string of cultured pearls. When you lost the jade earrings I gave you, or rather when you stupidly left them behind on the bathroom shelf of some hotel or other and then blamed me for letting you forget them, I spent hours every week trying to track down their replicas, until finally I found them and you were suitably and gratifyingly touched. I wished, without turning it into a whinge, I could have let you know just how much time I'd spent on looking for those earrings, how many antique markets I'd scoured, how I'd made journeys to Camden Lock and Islington and Chelsea; and not because I wanted to present myself as a martyr but because I wanted you to know how much love and affection the things came packaged in.

What the hell was that Bristol hotel called? The something Manor. A nice enough place but far too far away at the back of beyond. You had to keep an eye open for a telephone box and turn left, then right just past a white farm gate, and so on for several more turnings. "Darling, I'm relying on you to navigate," you said, and I wished we'd still been on the main road where we might have finished our discussion.

Cheevers must have had a hell of a hold over you, Angie, however much you protested otherwise. I wouldn't allow myself to think that it was only sex or rather simply sex. Perhaps an overbearing sexual manner might have appealed to your lazy nature – I would describe your lovemaking style as actively passive. But your overall personality must have had a need of him. Seeing you with a detached eye I could judge that you needed a dominant person in your life, someone in the role of that martinet or non-martinet father of yours. Not a straightforward father figure, because what you'd done was to assign the father role to me and the dominating role to Cheevers. That seemed as good an answer as any.

But what was the question?

"Roger, are you watching the road? I'm sure we should have reached that turn by now."

"No, we're here."

A signboard signalled the hotel drive and the question was shelved without ever being framed.

We were living a life of sorts together then, in a twilight, dreaming way. This odyssey of ours accounted, plus our regular lunches, for most of what passed for the working week. I would see Gunby once a fortnight, put in my reports and expenses, and get my next batch of assignments. I wasn't bad at the job, such as it was, being reasonably conscientious and objective except for lavishly over-praising the dish of the day where you'd all but thrown it at me in some ill-starred four star establishment. Gunby had no complaints – I was working for nothing, after all – and Judith had no complaints. I was out from under her feet, she could now give her dinner parties without necessarily inviting her piss-artist husband, and if they were dinner parties for two that was all right by me too. Life in Ealing Church Grove was never more agreeable, as a matter of fact. My relations with Judith were what I would term cordial and considerate. We would discuss domestic and family affairs, often touching on Judith's burgeoning career (less often on my own languishing one) but never getting more personal than that. I never asked about Nick Tearle, though she would often mention him in the context of his being her agent. She never asked about you. I think now she probably regarded you as a possible passing fling which had ended when I left the agency. She must have guessed I was not leading a celibate life on these hotel jaunts – for I was by now certainly not leading an uncelibate life at home – but she didn't probe. Her trips to Manchester continued and she went off, presumably with Nick in attendance, on the freebie gourmet outing to Paris with which she'd once threatened me. The subject of holidays was skirted round. Neither of us could fit one in and Tim was too young to need a holiday anyway. Next year perhaps . . . Unspoken was the mutual thought that by this time next year everything might be different.

It was unspoken so far as you were concerned too. We were drifting pleasantly, conscious that our odyssey was a journey to nowhere in particular. It would end sooner or later and then another phase would set in, but meanwhile it was something to be experienced, not tested or talked about, except in the most pragmatic way such as deciding whether to meet on the platform or the train. Most of our lunches in London now seemed to be taken up with making elaborate travel arrangements which you promptly forgot. I made you write them down in your Filofax but you forgot that too. I would have palpitations every time I went to meet you at Euston or Kings Cross, fearful that you'd gone to Paddington or Waterloo. And each time you turned up, always with only seconds to spare, and spilling trashy magazines behind you as you minnied across the station concourse, my churning irritation would be washed away by relief and my heart would lurch at the sight of you. Once you did miss the train and I stormed off to Leeds without you, there to lie fuming on a hotel bed for two hours – I looked at my watch every fifteen minutes – when the next train would be in and I would hear you timidly knock on the door, which you did. And you would be so contrite, which you were, that my anger would evaporate at once, which it did. And so, with such foresight, I had the champagne and the smoked salmon sandwiches waiting, and we did not descend to the bar until dinner time.

You were always available. You always had been almost from the start. If you ever had any arrangements you would cancel them – for me, for me, I would tell myself as you agreed without demur to get out of your two days' temping and accompany me to some God-forsaken provincial town. Soon you had few arrangements to cancel. Your meagre social life – a drink with Belle, perhaps, a snack lunch with one of the handful of shadowy girlfriends whom you tended to stumble across in the street rather than keep up any kind of regular contact with – was always subservient to your life with me. Meeting so often now, it became intolerable not to see one another at weekends and so we began our pattern of meeting at halfway-house pubs in Kew or Hammersmith on Saturdays and Sundays, when I was reckoned at home to be round at the local or playing golf. I was touched that you would travel across London for a quick couple of drinks, but concerned on your behalf that you had so little to do with your time that you didn't mind taking the trouble. And when you said more than once that you would always drop everything to be with me, yes, my love, I believed that, and yes, you would, but the truth is that you didn't have very much to drop.

So while we drifted along on our hotel odyssey I worried, not about the possibility – the certainty, I should say – of it ending, but the desirability of it doing so from your point of view. I couldn't see any future for you: the blank screen ahead alarmed me. My own future didn't concern me – I was a spent force professionally, I'd lost any desire to do any proper work and was content to potter along. My marriage, I was beginning to see, was almost certainly coasting to an end, but I couldn't pair that eventuality with any kind of permanent life with you. I puzzled about that a lot, concluding simply that you were just not a permanent person. You might be for someone, in due course, but you couldn't be for me, we'd cast ourselves in the wrong mould. And so I worried about what was to become of you. With romantic masochism I concocted a scenario where I would have to give you the time and the opportunity to meet someone else. I think I gave myself the power of veto should he prove to be just another of the well-heeled ratbags to whom you seem to have been attracted. You would marry him and set up home and I would fade into the background, meeting you occasionally for lunch perhaps but only on a platonic basis. Which come to think of it is where we came in.

I tried to tell you something of this vision for you but you only giggled and prattled about knights on dashing white chargers, refusing to take me seriously. There was a song I wanted to quote to you from *Guys and Dolls* – not the film version we saw together all that time ago, but the National Theatre production I saw with Judith and which you got so shirty about. "Mansions I can wish you –" but no, I couldn't remember it.

"I don't want mansions," you said. "Hotel rooms will do. I'm living a life of luxury already, don't you realise that?"

"You're living off sugar plums," I said.

You pulled a face. "I think you'd rather I lived off prunes."

The sugar plum supply dried up rather abruptly, didn't it? My predecessor on Gunby's *Good Living Guide* had one operation too many and quietly expired. Gunby called me into his cramped little office over an Indian restaurant in Charlotte Street. The conglomerate that subsidised his publication insisted on his having a full-time team, and now that the chap whose place I had been keeping warm had gone to the great Ritz in the sky, he was expected to fill the vacancy. He was sorry to say I didn't quite fit the bill to become a permanent fixture.

"Still, you've been doing it for six months now and one hotel bed's much like another, don't you find? You must be getting fed up of it by now."

"Well no, I'm not as a matter of fact," I said hopefully.

"Well let's say one or two establishments have been a bit fed up of you."

A panorama of scenes and rows, sometimes Bonnie and Clyde attacks on the restaurant itself, sometimes Punch and Judy fights between ourselves, flitted through my head. The places you'd stalked out of in the middle of dinner, the wine you'd flung, the times you'd sat at tables with tears streaming down your face and plopping into your food even as the waiter served it. It was all so preposterous, it was so unbelievable that I should have put up with you, that it seemed unreal, like a film.

"But how would they know I was from the *Guide*?" I asked. "I've never announced myself."

"Someone's been announcing you," said Gunby pointedly.

And just how many times had you booked tables at restaurants telling them I was from the *Good Living Guide*. You couldn't remember. Only three or four times, and only when they'd said the place was full – I wouldn't have wanted not to be able to get in, would I? No, and that would never have been a problem if you'd booked the bloody tables when you were asked, instead of at the last minute. Oh, yes, and how could you, when you were always out with me? Did I want you to go straight home and book tables the moment I told you to, and if so why did I always cart you off to Freddy's Club and get you so legless that you weren't capable of phoning anybody? Yes, all right, but it was a bloody stupid thing to do, when I'd particularly dinned into you never to mention that we were from the *Guide*. Oh, but you never had, you'd just hinted that Mr Piper was somebody very important from London and that they'd better give him a good table and a nice meal because he was very particular and might write to the *Good Living Guide* about them. Oh, Christ, Angie, you could be so embarrassing. Why did I find it an endearing quality? Because when you did something like that you were trying so hard to please, to be efficient, to do what I wanted you to do, but it was all so much beyond you that you were as unconvincing as a little girl dressing up in her mother's clothes and smearing her face with lipstick to look grown up. I berated you for a while and then forgave you, as always.

We had one more hotel in hand. York. In fact I have a secret: we didn't have York in hand at all, it was my treat. I wanted to tell you, because I would have liked you to know that I was doing this for us, but then you would have regarded it as an option and dithered and altered our arrangements and wanted to go somewhere else, so I let you think we were going on a last Gunby T. Gunby fling. I chose York because you took your degree there (God knows how), but you were quite unsentimental about the place, could remember little about it and had no favourite spots you wanted to revisit. We walked around the city wall and you talked, quite freely for you, about your student days. You were, of course, seduced by your tutor. I have news for you, my dear – I already had that down in your C.V. Then with just about the entire male population of the campus to choose from you had an affair with a clerk from the chocolate factory you met in a pub. He was "nice" and made the only marriage proposal you ever had, but you thought that once outside the university you'd outgrow him. You said you felt intellectually inferior to your fellow-undergraduates but intellectually superior to him. It was the only time I've ever known you have a stab at psychoanalysing yourself. Was it only for my benefit that you smothered this gift of self-insight? I wish you could have talked as freely and openly about your life after your student days. I still don't comprehend why you cocooned it in mystery so.

York is another of our snapshots. Curiously, since it was our last encounter with a hotel bed, we didn't make love. I took you to that nice restaurant on the river and then we walked about and did a bit of pub-crawling and went out to eat again and finished the night roaringly but pleasantly pissed. Then we overslept and had to scramble for the train because I had to be back in Town to see my dentist. But it was a memorable day, with the old buildings throwing cool shadows and the narrow streets bubbling with tourists, and you looking so fetching in your sun hat and dark glasses and crisp white dress. In that restaurant on the river when I ordered more champagne to go with our strawberries, I proposed a toast to our hotel odyssey and you responded very prettily, saying what a wonderful period it had been in your life.

"Don't put it so much in the past tense," I chided.

"But it is over, darling. No-one else is going to pay us to romp around hotel bedrooms."

"You know our luck, Angie. As one door shuts another one opens."

"I hope so," you said, not sounding at all hopeful.

I wanted to ask what your Piper policy was going to be henceforth. Were we to revert to a lunching relationship, with your flat still out of bounds? Would I be expected to think up the equivalent of our "seminaries", taking you off to distant places though not of course with the frequency of our hotel odyssey? That, I surmised, would be the answer. It would be something for me to resent I knew, but for the moment I was prepared to bask in the prospect. It was such a beautiful summer's day, tinged into autumn by our sweet regrets at leaving our odyssey behind, and I wasn't going to spoil it.

Nor, it was to transpire, had I reason to. When we got back to London there had been a flash rainstorm and your flat was ankle deep in water, even more unhabitable than it had been already. Characteristically, you said nothing to me until I dragged it out of you two days later, after wondering what the hell I had done wrong. I couldn't reach you. Your phone gave out a long continuous hoot which I angrily but wrongly assumed meant you had been cut off again. I remember slamming the receiver down and pacing up and down Ealing Common fuming to myself, having jumped to the conclusion that the money I'd given you for the phone bill hadn't been paid in. For once the facts were against the unwavering accuracy of my instinct regarding you. When I calmed down and checked with the engineer, it proved that your phone was out of order but that nobody had reported it. What could that mean? What was going on? I had no way of knowing. We were completely cut off from one another, incommunicado. I fumed and fretted again. How the hell could you do this to me? Reply, of course, came there none, for we had no system of replying. I had to wait, patiently, until we met routinely, as it had become in a thoroughly unroutine way, for lunch. I always made a point of metaphorically pinning to your lapel, like one of those name tags that the conference addicts who infested most of our hotels used to wear, the name and address of the restaurant where we would next be meeting, and the time and date. But while I always confirmed by phone I could never entirely trust you not to have forgotten.

So after you had been on the missing list for forty-eight hours it was not exactly in a hopeful frame of mind that I headed for the Soho Brasserie where we were supposed to be having lunch, only to see you, to my considerable surprise as I turned into Old Compton Street, letting yourself out of one of those narrow doors with eight or nine light-up doorbells with names like "Dawn, Model" on them. I'm glad

I didn't play a game of cat and mouse with you, as I was tempted to, pretending not to have seen you and then trapping you into lying about where you'd come from, because when I crossed the street to greet you, you were not in the least flustered, only very sorry for yourself. You turned out to be staying with Belle, her "bloke" as she appeared to call him being away at the moment, because your flat had been declared uninhabitable by the health inspector after the flooding.

And couldn't you have called me? No, you didn't want to bother me. Never mind bothering me, what about my having been worried sick about you? Oh dear, you hadn't thought of that. No, you never did.

"I'm sorry," you said, all contrite after you'd been coaxed out of your sulks by a glass or two of champagne. "I wanted to get it sorted out on my own."

"Sort what out on your own?"

"Give Mrs Scroggins the rent I owe her so I can get my belongings out of the flat, and then find a new place."

And you were going to do that on your own, were you? You might as well have tried to climb Mount Everest on your own, my love. As usual, I felt waves of pity for you. I couldn't even be angry that you'd got behind with your rent again after I'd settled your arrears more than once and you'd sworn you were paying it religiously each week out of the money I was now giving you. As to how much at home you felt in that rabbit warren of hookers, and what you did with yourself when Belle's illuminated doorbell rang, I didn't like to ask. I was quite prepared to accept, because I wanted to, that her flat was somehow hermetically sealed off from the other activities in the building, but you would have been hard put to have explained how architecturally.

But I wanted you out of the place, and quickly. "Have you started looking for somewhere yet?"

"How can I? I haven't any money."

"I'll take care of the rent and the expenses, Angie, you know that."

"Why should I expect you to do that?"

So that you could have a nice place, reasonably handy for me, where I could come and see you and take you to bed and drink champagne. No. So that you'd have a nice place to go home to, unlike that rat-trap you've been living in, and hopefully will invite me back to. And another reason:

"Because I love you."

You didn't put up much argument, being in a state of shell shock after your experience. The only problem was shaking you out of the inertia that was your inevitable reaction to any crisis. I tried to prod you into looking around for a place straight after lunch, picking some area like Earls Court or Notting Hill and blitzing the estate agents.

172

No, you wanted to think about it. Thinking about it involved buying a *Standard*, heading for Freddy's Club and getting steadily pie-eyed while flipping aimlessly through the property pages. You promised faithfully that you'd get up in the morning and spend the whole day looking for somewhere to live, but naturally, by the time you came to meet me for a drink as arranged at five thirty, you hadn't been anywhere at all. Nor the next day. I tried to insist on tagging along with you to see that you really were looking for a place in earnest, but you wouldn't let me. I may be paying the rent but it was to be your flat and you were going to choose it yourself. Quite right, except that you wouldn't do a bloody thing about it.

But I'm not going to go into all that again. You drifted on, in typical Angie fashion, until Belle appears to have told you that her "bloke" was returning from wherever he'd been – prison, I shouldn't wonder – and you would have to move out. And you had found the flat in Cromwell Villas before the day was out, and we were coming up to the beginning of the end.

EIGHT

Those last four months were the happiest of our short life together. From the day you moved in and I arrived with flowers, uninvited but welcome, it was clear that we had taken another lurch forward. Towards the brink as it happened, though we weren't to know that, or if we sensed it we put it out of our minds. Except once, when you'd been happily established at Cromwell Villas for a month or so, and you were sitting at my feet one rainy afternoon, gazing at the pictures in the dancing gas fire. Suddenly and seriously you said, "It's our anniversary soon."

Yes. Tim's christening party being the landmark, we'd decided. I was surprised you still remembered. I'd had to remind you of it a good half dozen times and a week had passed since I'd last mentioned it.

"What would you like as a present?" you asked. I already knew what you were getting and hugged myself at the surprise in store for you. That was the only important thing.

"Just a token," I said. "I don't want you to go mad." If you had any money you were quite capable of buying me gold cufflinks.

"So long as you don't expect a pair of slippers," you said unexpectedly.

In the event I didn't get anything. It was to have been an expensive Liberty's silk dressing gown that I was to keep at your flat – a sweet, extravagant thought. But as it happened you didn't have enough to pay for it just then, and somehow telling me about it seemed to replace the gift in your mind, so I never got it. And the idea of something cheaper never swam into your mind.

"Why slippers?" I asked.

"Oh, because sitting there in the armchair with your paper you look as if you ought to be wearing them, but I don't want you to go regarding yourself as a fixture here."

We had rather got into the habit of cosy afternoons, hadn't we? By this time I'd fed Judith that cock-and-bull yarn about thinking of going into the antiques business, so I was free to spend my days supposedly pricing stuff, boning up in the museums or lunching contacts. She either believed me or affected to – I think her main concern was that I'd actually take the plunge and make a hash of it. Perhaps, if our new set-up had gone on much longer, I should have had to go into it willy-nilly, to maintain my alibi.

So we had a pattern. If I wasn't taking you out to lunch I'd arrive about noon with a bottle of wine and we'd have a picnicky sort of meal, then we'd open a bottle of champagne and go to bed for the afternoon. Sometimes you'd surprise me, like the day after you gave me my own latch-key and I let myself in to find you lying on the sofa wearing only black stay-up stockings. I never did dare ask where you'd got the practice to be so delightfully tarty when you felt like it.

If we were lunching out, we would always come back to your flat and tumble into bed. The notion of not doing so never arose, nor was it ever discussed why, on moving flats, you'd abruptly revised your Piper policy. Perhaps it was true, after all, you were simply ashamed of the old place. As I've said, I never looked for simple explanations.

They were good days, but they couldn't be lasting days. It was an unreal life and that was what you were talking about.

Even so I was a bit hurt at being told I mustn't regard myself as a fixture. "I never did have it in mind to become part of the furniture," I said. "What's brought this on?"

You shuddered. It was a cold day for late summer and the gas fire didn't throw out much heat. I meant to get you something more efficient before winter set in. "I get frightened sometimes. I've become so dependent on you."

It was true. It frightened me sometimes too. What if I were carted off to hospital or run over by a bus? You couldn't have survived financially for a week. What if there were some crisis, say a run of bad luck at Peck Associates and my income began to dry up? I was already quite alarmed at what I was spending – your flat, though I never liked to tell you, was costing me twice what I'd figured on paying, and then there were our lunches and booze and your upkeep and one thing and another. I didn't begrudge any of it, indeed I took a kind of masochistic delight in spending money on you, but as my deposit account got lower and lower I worried about running out of funds.

"I like you to be dependent on me," I said. I half did, half didn't, half wanted to keep you in a cage, half wanted you to fly away.

"And I want to be. You're my security blanket."

"Then what frightens you, kitten? I'm not going to go away."

"You could do. I could say or do something stupid and you'd go and this time you wouldn't come back."

I could see what was bothering you. It was a house of cards I had built for you there at Cromwell Villas. One flick and it would all come tumbling down.

175

"You're being hypocritical," I teased, remembering how you'd confused the word with "hypothetical" more than once. But you took me literally, as you so often did when the joke wasn't signalled or shared.

"Am I? You mean because I said I didn't want you to become a fixture, yet at the same time I'm terrified of losing you?"

Terrified of losing me? Gratifying if true, but I thought I was estimating that admission at its proper weight when I said, "I wish I could offer you more security, Angie. If I had your rent and everything paid by banker's order would that make you happier?"

That wasn't what you meant, though. You shook your head. "I shouldn't *have* to depend on you, Roger, that's what I'm trying to say. I should be able to stand on my own two feet, pay my own way. But how can I? My whole life revolves round you now."

It did, and it was odd, looking back, how it had happened, when every time I had tried to draw you nearer you had always pulled back, yet all the while you were being sucked closer and closer towards me as by a whirlpool. Was it something to do with the passivity of your nature, that even when you did pull back it was never in any positive way, just a deadweight resistance against being more involved than you wanted to be? I don't know. We were closer than we'd ever been yet we were not close. I still knew so little about you, you wanted to know so little about me. It was a relationship that was getting wider instead of deeper. Yet it brought us both a lot of real happiness. It was real, wasn't it, Angie?

What a nice little flat that was – you were lucky to find it, and luckier that Mr Hakim was perfectly happy to accept six months' rent in advance in lieu of references. You didn't even have to call yourself Mrs Piper. For once a garden flat really did look out on a garden – you loved your view across the square; even though you couldn't get out into it, you could press your nose against the window, as you'd been used to doing all your life.

The furniture was adequate but sparse, the things that make a place look lived-in such as pictures and bric-à-brac more or less non-existent – much on a par with Banks Place though without the bleakness. And so there I had my mission to refurbish. Each time I came to you it was bearing gifts – framed posters, vases, knick-knacks, your Chinese jug, the joke alarm clock that had no perceptible effect on your punctuality, champagne glasses, ashtrays, napkins, egg-cups, proper coat hangers to replace your melancholic clanking wire ones, table lamps, your radio, bathroom scales, kitchen jars – all the ordinary accoutrements of life you'd either never acquired, let Cheevers dispose of, or discarded along the way. It became my hobby. I would scour London looking for just the right butter dish or

176

breakfast cup to suit your personality (once a neighbour reported back to Judith that she had seen me roaming the antique supermarket in the Kings Road, which handily supported my alibi). But of course it wasn't your personality I was expressing, but my own. Left to yourself you would have kept your flat empty, ready to move on, everything you possessed compressible into one suitcase.

Indeed you gently reproved me about it once, saying that the flat was beginning to look cluttered and that you liked to have space around you.

"You're an Oliver Twist in reverse. You ask for less," I said, quite hurt (I had just come in from a long trek round Camden Market to replace the shade to that converted oil lamp which you'd broken). But you were right. It was for my own pleasure that I came laden down with presents – the pleasure I got from seeing your delight, or simulated delight as I suppose it must often have been. Occasionally I wondered if the urge to give you things was simply an obsessional trait, along with the urge to ring you up or the urge to write you letters. I feared I was spinning an obsessional web around myself and around you. You felt the same sometimes, I know. Once I arrived to find you grizzling quietly to yourself, sitting on the floor huddled over the coffee table and clutching a duster. You had been cleaning the flat and it had never looked nicer. "I feel trapped," you sobbed. "I know I'm ungrateful but sometimes I feel as if you're bricking me in."

Another time you were so claustrophobic that you made a pitch to free yourself. It was after I'd had your push-button phone installed – do you remember the fun we had when we found it could play tunes? I'd think of a tune and you would punch it out and see who we got. The first seven notes of "Twinkle Twinkle Little Star" got us a service station in Kilburn or somewhere, and "Mary Had a Little Lamb" connected us with the Ministry of Defence. You recklessly started to play the whole of "Three Blind Mice" and got someone in Portugal. We were having a wonderfully silly time and who cared about the phone bill? Then we played "Guess the Tune." "See if you know what this is," I said, and played the first few notes of "Mansions I can wish you." You didn't know it, I don't have to say, and I had to remind you that I'd nominated it as Our Song. We both thought it highly appropriate that it got us through to a wine shop.

But then your new toy started playing up, getting wrong numbers, crossed lines and a variety of bleeps and buzzes, and that led to one of our rows. After the engineers had tried to clear the line a few times they concluded that the fault was in the instrument itself and wanted to come round and fix it, but you were never there when they called. One day when I had been trying vainly to get in touch with you rather urgently – urgently in our terms, that is: I only wanted to let you know

177

I'd be a bit late since Judith was away and I had to babysit while the au pair girl went to the doctor's – I exploded with exasperation and demanded to know why you couldn't just be bloody in when the engineer called.

"Because I was bloody out," you flared back, immediately on your high horse. "You don't know what it's like being cooped up here day in, day out."

"You're not cooped up, what are you talking about? You can come and go as you please."

"Except when I'm expecting you, which nowadays is every single day except Sunday."

My turn on the high horse. "And you object to that, do you?"

"I'm not saying that, but I don't see why you should start making a scene because I want to go out now and again."

"Darling, I do not object to your going out."

"Oh, thank you very much."

"But if the telephone engineer says he's coming round on such and such a morning, why can't you just stay in until he gets here?"

"I did stay in, but then I wanted to get something nice for your lunch. You say you like me making lunch for you but you never seem to realise that I have to go out shopping to provide it."

And so on, and so on. We both fell into a sulk at one another's unreasonableness. You'd prepared a very nice cold collation which we ate in silence. At the end of it you very pointedly picked up your glass of wine and went over and sat in an armchair, a signal that my chances of getting you into the bedroom were zero. I smouldered at your ingratitude. I'd worked hard and spent a lot of time and money getting your flat looking just so, and now all you wanted was to get out of it. I was trying to find some way of conveying my case to you without it sounding like a whinge or whine when you abruptly said, demonstrating that I might as well save my breath:

"I'm sorry, Roger, you're suffocating me."

"So you've said," I responded dully. "Bricking you in."

When I say it was a row, it wasn't really, more of a discussion, one of our rare ones. You wanted to sound reasonable. You came over and sat on the sofa where I was and put your hand on my shoulder in that familiar and very pleasing proprietorial way. But it was proprietorship you were objecting to. "Bricked in, walled up – I more and more have this feeling of everything pressing in on me. You're not to think I don't know how much you've done for me, how much you do – there's love all around me, but – " You finished the sentence with a despairing shrug.

You'd rehearsed this, perhaps even the shrug. You'd planned to make this speech, perhaps not knowing when you were going to deliver it, but you'd gone over it several times in your mind, I could tell.

"What do you want to do about it?" I asked, knowing this was the prompt line you needed.

You took a breath and started circling your wine glass with your finger. "I think we should see less of one another."

I knew how to deal with proposals like that, didn't I, Angie? Corner you with logic. "All right, how much less? Do you want to meet four times a week in future? Three times a week? Twice? Once?"

True to form, though, you wouldn't reply directly, wouldn't be trapped. "I don't only mean less in that sense, darling, I meant it's all got too intense, and has been for some time."

"Yes, because we go to bed more often. It's an intense experience."

"I'm not talking about that part, I love our fucking, you know I do. What I mean is that I've come to feel possessed by you. But you don't possess me, you can't possess me, you've got your own life, you've got Judith and baby Timmy, so what's wrong with my wanting my own life?"

Nothing, when you put it like that. "Nothing, but you keep saying that in different ways, Angie – how you don't want to be dependent on me and so on. But you don't do anything about it."

"You won't let me."

"Yes I will. You must do what you want to do."

"Then let me go, Roger."

Go where? You didn't want to go anywhere. It wasn't claustrophobia you were suffering from, it was agoraphobia. Taking comfort from this piece of self-assurance I asked the question aloud. "Go where?"

"Where I can meet other people and have a life of my own," you fantasised. "Why shouldn't I have friends? Why shouldn't I be friends with you, for one? It doesn't have to stop us being lovers."

"And what will the status of these other friends be?" I asked, unable to keep the jealousy out of my voice.

"You see, there you go, Roger. You say you want me to have friends, to meet nice people, but as soon as I want to do anything about it you're madly jealous. All I want is to get out more, to lead a normal life. I thought that's what you wanted for me."

"It is." It was. Mansions I could wish you.

It all blew over, of course. We finished up in bed and afterwards you were extravagantly self-reproachful about how silly and ungrateful you were. It was just a mood, you'd been feeling cooped up, it was probably just the weather, and so on. But that day determined me to do something that had been tinkering away in my head ever since that drive out into the country from Bristol.

For some time now Judith had been talking of trading in her four-year-old Volkswagen Polo for something bigger and flashier, though that wasn't how she put it. She'd earned it, anyway. Now she had her eye on a BMW. I went home that evening and told her I had found a buyer for the Volkswagen. One of my new contacts, an antique dealer I knew called . . . yes, I'm afraid that to be really childish, I did call him Cheevers. It was basically his idea, after all. If he could give you his wife's cast-off clothes, why shouldn't I give you my wife's cast-off car?

"He can't be a very successful antique dealer," said Judith. "I thought they all had station wagons."

"It's for his girlfriend," I said. That covered me in case you were seen by Gunby T. Gunby or whoever getting out of Judith's former car on a double yellow line in Soho.

"Hm." She didn't seem at all keen on the sale, though I'd quoted her a good price. I felt the same irritation as when she'd wanted to accompany me to Venice. She was getting in my way, spoiling my fun.

"It's her birthday quite soon," I pressed. It was our anniversary quite soon. "So he must have a quick yea or nay."

"He hasn't seen it yet."

"Perhaps not, but I've given him a very hard sell on it. He's keen."

"Hm," said Judith again. "I hope you're not contemplating a future as a second-hand car dealer?"

"Don't be a snob, it's a one-off. I already have a future as an antique dealer." My fictitious career was coming along quite well: I'd told Judith that I was by now going in for what I believe is called running – buying from one dealer and selling immediately to another, so no actual late Georgian firescreens or early Victorian glass paperweights need ever turn up at Ealing Church Grove. I made up little anecdotes to support my story, sometimes quite sickening myself with my trite inventiveness. It was all for us. You talked about your life revolving around me – did you ever realise how completely mine revolved around you? We revolved around one another. Two moons, going nowhere.

"Are you all right, Roger? You're happy the way things are?" She asked that question periodically. It was a compendium enquiry, meant to dredge in, I guess, whatever knowledge or suspicion I might have about her and Nick, as well as providing an indicator as to what I thought I was doing with my own beachcombing life.

"I'm fine," I said. "I'm still winding down after those hectic years with the agency. I'm enjoying myself." Or something on those lines – it was a conversation we had several times and I always got out of it as quickly as possible. Judith never pursued it further.

I had the Volkswagen Polo serviced, cleaned and waxed, then drove it round to Cromwell Villas where I found an illegal space on a resident's parking bay a few doors from you. It needed three days to go to our anniversary and you must have passed by it half a dozen times without ever dreaming you were the new owner. Twice you walked past it with me and I could barely resist dropping a hint about the surprise in store for you, especially when I saw that it had got the first of what in the fullness of your first few weeks of ownership was to become a substantial collection of parking tickets. Just so long as they didn't clamp it.

And so our day came, when I arrived promptly at noon and you imagined the plan was to have a glass of champagne and then whisk you off to a special lunch at the Savoy Grill, and you were disappointed because I had no visible tributes in the way of flowers or presents (neither had you, but let it pass). And when I handed over the ignition key in its little Paperchase gift box you were so slow-witted you couldn't make out what game I was playing, not until I took you out into the street and showed you the car, and even then you thought I'd just borrowed it or hired it for us to drive somewhere special for the day, and I had to formally present you with the log book before it dawned on you that I'd bought you a car. Quite disappointing, when I looked back on the delicious medley of toe-curling, finger-tingling responses I'd anticipated.

You made up for it, though. We were indeed to drive somewhere special – the Old Orchard near Epping (Gunby T. Gunby recommended) where I'd booked a table. That's to say you were to drive: your treat. I made you promise that you'd never ever get behind the wheel after more than two, all right three, glasses of wine, and you were very good and would only have a sip of champagne at lunch, just to celebrate our anniversary. "Fancy putting up with me for a year," you said, but that was as far as you would go in the reminiscing vein. Your memory of gatecrashing the christening party was woundingly vague. Through a champagne glass darkly, I told myself; another explanation being that there was so much in your life you wanted to forget you kept your memory in permanent neutral gear. But for all that, it was a wonderful golden day, one to remember – or forget, as the case may be. On the way back we stopped in Epping Forest and wandered out among the trees and made love on a grassy mound, reminding me of that day in Venice. And that you did remember.

I've never known you so happy as you were with your new toy. It gave you another dimension. You drove everywhere you could. In bad weather you'd often meet me at Earls Court tube station, wheedling the policemen not to move you on, just to drive me the few hundred yards to Cromwell Villas. You loved driving me back home as far as the end of the street, though I was nervous of the car being seen in the vicinity of Ealing Church Grove. Sometimes we'd meet at that pub we used in Kew and you'd drive us out into the "country" as you called places like Richmond Park and Ham Common, either for a picnic or as the weather got colder to some cosy little pub. And I'm afraid your two-to-three-glass minimum crept up to four and sometimes more. I was very weak with you but you were a good driver who did all the right things, or nearly all the right things, and somehow the fact that you only had a drink when you were driving me, or so you said and I did and do believe you, made it all right. You were so happy, that was the point. It affected your whole being – we didn't row for weeks, perhaps in part because I chose not to raise the issues that might have led to a row, but also because the car gave you freedom and confidence, made you less reliant on me, so that you could enjoy more the little we had and see how much it really was by now.

And do you know what my favourite snapshot of all is? This will surprise you. At the beginning of November on a clear raw day I approached your flat in Cromwell Villas to find the door wide open and no Angie to be seen. I went back up the area steps to look for you, peeved in case you'd popped up to one of the neighbours or even gone to the shops leaving a welcome mat for the burglars; then I saw you across the street, sporting yellow plastic gloves and your Rupert Bear scarf and washing the Volkswagen. You were completely absorbed and singing to yourself. When you looked up and saw me you squealed with delight and came tripping across the road, still carrying your dripping sponge and wash leather, and threw your arms around me, something you hadn't done for quite a while when we greeted one another. We were to have lunch at the flat which was already arranged, our usual cold collation. You'd bought some chestnuts which we roasted, not very successfully, on your gas fire. It was our last golden day.

The end, when it did come, came very quickly and almost casually, with a number of unrelated strands suddenly being jerked together (while other strands remained loose, slack and unattached, as they do to this day).

The first was Belle. You hadn't told me she was coming over and I was annoyed about that, though glad to have my curiosity satisfied as to what she looked like. I'd already spent my allotted time with you and was on my way to the tube, but then I suddenly remembered I hadn't booked a table for next day's lunch at wherever it was you wanted to go – I don't know, we never got there. All the Earls Court phone boxes were either out of order or occupied and so I thought I might as well nip back to Cromwell Villas and make the call from there, giving you a little surprise into the bargain. The little surprise, though, was mine: for there was Belle, sitting in what I'd always regarded as my chair and making inroads into one of our bottles of champagne. No reason at all why you shouldn't have invited your friends home, don't get me wrong, but I wonder why you didn't tell me you were expecting her, why, as I was to recollect, you'd kept edgily reminding me of the time when I'd not been in too much of a hurry to climb out of your bed earlier. Of course, you knew I didn't approve of Belle or your association with her, so you wouldn't have been too keen on bringing us together, but I don't know why you had to be so secretive. Perhaps because you wanted something to be secretive about.

As a matter of fact, Belle impressed me quite favourably, considering the picture you'd painted of her with all those stories about her casual pick-ups and couplings in the oddest places such as the back of a furniture van with one of the removal men when she was moving flats once. I had nursed a slinky image of a femme fatale in a skintight, low-cut and generally overdone satin gown. Instead here was this quite plain, square-jawed young woman in a rather dowdy black suit and buttoned-up white blouse, only her crossed, black-stockinged legs, one foot gently swinging towards me in a mildly but probably unintentionally provocative way, giving any indication that there was a scarlet woman lurking there within.

You hid your embarrassment or discomfiture at my return in banter – "Oh, he can't keep away, you know", and it was on that level, as I accepted a glass of my own champagne and made my phone call, that we engaged in our brief three-way social chit-chat, both Belle and I taking our cue from you. Or was it that you took your cue from her – lock, stock and barrel? Her manner towards me, lightly mocking yet flattering, was the very model of your first light-hearted, light-headed chaff with me when we first began to have our lunches. Now, it was easy to see what men saw in Belle. How much of her, I wonder, rubbed off on you? Did you study her? Certainly when she burbled, "You look awfully wise, I hope you're not too wise," it could have been you prattling away on one of your good days, and her way of putting a cigarette to her mouth in the expectation that I would get up and light it for her was you down to the steadying touch on my hand when I did so. No matter: whoever owned those characteristics first, they were captivating ones.

Well, now: Belle had some news, did she not, my love? Not news to you, because you plainly knew all about it already, but news to me, because you hadn't bothered to pass it on. Belle was about to get married. Not to her "bloke" but to some fellow she had met not a fortnight ago (that sounded more like the Belle you'd etched in for me) in a West End hotel bar. Dowdy or not, I could now readily see her making these effortless fly-by-night acquaintanceships, of which I had little doubt that this was but another one, whether she meant to marry the man or not. Curiously, and disturbingly, I could just as readily see you in the same situation. The fact is that you were a pair, not a double act but clones almost, with you clearly, though not consciously, drawing many of your traits and mannerisms from her. Couldn't you sense that Belle's moth-like existence masked a weak and insecure character? Yet you took her as your model. Perhaps that's why you kept her away from me – you knew I'd lecture you.

Anyway, it seemed that the wedding was to be in Manchester, Belle's home town, and you were to be the maid of honour. And yes, of course you'd meant to tell me, in fact Belle had wanted to invite me too for all that it was a quiet wedding with just family, but you knew I wouldn't be keen on going in case it fell on one of Judith's days in Manchester, but you really had been on the verge of telling me, really really, promise. And all this you babbled out in front of Belle with no hint of reticence. While you'd kept her secret from me, there were clearly few secrets between the two of you.

My champagne finished, and you and Belle manifestly itching to get your teeth into the wedding arrangements, I was just rising to take my leave when Belle said something curious. Putting up her face to be pecked as if we'd been friends for years, she said lightly, "And don't worry, Roger, I'll see that she doesn't run off with the best man this time, you do know that story?"

"Yes," was all I could say, trying not very successfully to put a roguish laugh into my voice. I had my back to you just at that moment, but in Belle's darting eyes I could see the reflection of the shut-up-you-fool warning look you'd just given her. She gave a trilling laugh and blustered, "No, she didn't really, and it was all a long time before she met you, wasn't it, Angie?"

"Why don't you come to the wedding and keep us *both* out of mischief?" you quipped heavily with a nervous laugh.

"I might just do that," I said, and left.

I did know that story, didn't I, Angie? How you and Belle had gone to a wedding in Chelsea, someone you hardly knew but you'd been swept into the registry office by a carousing mob in the pub you both used to go into. And at the reception, back in the upper room of the same pub, the best man was discovered to have gone missing, as was one of the two uninvited or not-particularly-invited guests. But it wasn't you in that version, was it, Angie? It was Belle who was

184

supposed to have whisked the best man round to her place, returning him just in time to propose a belated toast, which was received with ironic cheers.

So which of you really was it who was mixed up in that little escapade? Perhaps it was both of you, on different occasions, as in those entirely separate and coincidental cases of your finding yourselves locked in different offices all night. No, Angie, I'm not going to be sarcastic, and I'm not about to suggest that everything you claimed happened to Belle, all those harebrained yet let's face it ultimately sordid adventures, in reality happened to you. But I think some of them did or quite did or nearly did or might have done had you known how to handle them as your heroine Belle did, and that you wished now you could wish it all back on Belle, that she had become one of the many masks you hid behind.

But I was not to get a chance to go into all that. Everything began to move so fast now that Belle had to take her turn in a lengthening queue of puzzles and enigmas.

On to the next day. I arrived at the flat irritated. In the first place, in the confusion of stumbling across Belle when I came back to Cromwell Villas, I wasn't entirely sure whether we'd agreed to meet at the restaurant or that I'd pick you up. Trying to ring you from a booth at Ealing Common tube station I got the by now habitual crossed line – you still hadn't bothered to get in the telephone engineers. Then when I decided to pick you up anyway, just for the pleasure of it since it was highly unlikely you would have set off by the time I got there, I espied a traffic warden shoving a cling-film bundle of trouble under your windscreen wiper. You still hadn't bothered to apply for a parking permit, had you?

Not only were you nowhere near ready, it was plain that you had only just got up. So it was in something of a sparring mood that I followed you into your bedroom. "Now look, Angie, I don't mind picking up your bills as you know, but I do object to paying a completely unnecessary parking fine because you're too bone idle to fill in a form."

"No-one's asked you to pay it," you said petulantly, viciously brushing your hair. You were always more prickly when you knew you were in the wrong than when you truly couldn't understand what all the fuss was about.

"No, but if I don't, nobody else will. Do you know how much I've forked out in fines since I bought you the car?"

"Oh, Roger, you're always going on about what you've paid for this and what you've paid for that. You're obsessed with money, do you know that?"

Was I? I was probably getting that way, the more my credit balance shrank. It wasn't that I resented spending so much on you, what I resented was your not appreciating it very much. You truly didn't care about money at all, but I couldn't regard that as a virtue, I'm afraid. It was, let's face it, my money that you were not caring about.

Perhaps you read what was going through my mind. You squeezed my arm in a gesture of conciliation. "I shouldn't have said that, darling. I *will* fill in the wretched form, it's just that I don't understand half of it. Why do they make these things so complicated?"

"In the hope of spoiling our lunch, kitten." I gave you a reassuring peck, the last kiss you ever got from me as it turned out. "Where is the form anyway? I'll look it over while you're getting ready."

"Oh, somewhere," you said vaguely. The subject was already passing out of your mind as you threw open the doors of your wardrobe and surveyed your array of dresses. No forlornly clanking coat hangers these days. "What do you think I should wear to Belle's wedding? I certainly can't afford anything new."

That couldn't possibly have been a hint, surely, coming so hard on that jibe about my being obsessed with money? If it was I decided to ignore it – the more so because it was only three or four weeks earlier, upon an unexpected income tax rebate coinciding with an unusually long spell of sunny behaviour on your part, that I had impetuously thrust a cheque for two hundred pounds into your hands to spend on clothes. Usually you delighted in showing me the spoils of these little windfalls. This time you hadn't. I assumed either that you hadn't got round to your shopping spree yet or that you were looking out for something boringly utilitarian like a new winter coat.

I wandered into the living room and across to your desk, where I riffled through the chromium-plated art deco toast rack I'd given you which you used as a letter rack. I suppose if I'd given you a letter rack you would have used it as a toast rack. Just as I located the parking permit form you appeared in the bedroom doorway, half in and half out of your yellow dress and the light of panic in your eyes. "No, it's not in there, Roger – leave it, I'll find it," you said sharply.

"It is, I've got it." Too late, Angie. As I extracted the form from the rack it exposed what you didn't want me to see – a typewritten envelope, forwarded from Banks Place, with a recorded delivery stamp. "But what's this?"

"It's nothing, leave it there."

"It looks very official for nothing."

You'd crossed the room by now, your dress still hanging absurdly around your upper torso. "Give it to me, Roger, and please stop sprying into my private things."

In your dyslexic confusion you spliced "spying" and "prying" into a compendium word I could see us adding to our private vocabulary.

186

Teasingly, to stop you tipping over the edge into anger, I held the letter out of your reach and said mock-reprovingly, "If I didn't spry through your things occasionally you'd be in one mess after another, now wouldn't you?"

"Give me that letter, Roger."

"When you've told me what's in it."

Not a letter from Cheevers after all. Just an ultimatum from the finance company to the effect that if they didn't have what you owed on your repossessed Renault by whatever the date was, they'd see you in court.

"For Christ's sake, Angie, I thought you'd paid this bloody months ago!"

"You don't have to swear at me. I thought I *had* paid it."

"But you must know you haven't! It's not just a few pounds, Angela, it's two hundred. I gave you the money."

"I know you did, and I'm very grateful. But you gave me such a lot of money to pay so many bills I don't know which I've paid and which I haven't. I know I should have kept proper accounts and filled in my cheque stubs but I didn't. I'm sorry, but we can't all be as efficient as you."

It was one of those times when I could have shaken you until your teeth rattled. Despite everything, I still wish I had.

"Angela. You showed me the bills you owed. I added them up. They came to over two thousand pounds. I gave you a cheque for that amount. I want to know which of them hasn't been paid."

"Only this one." You looked up into my eyes, challenging me to disbelieve you. You could see that I did. You averted your gaze again and switched to your small voice. "And part of my overdraft. I paid off three hundred pounds and they stopped bothering me."

"Yes, I suppose they did, considering there's now money going through your account regularly and they're lopping off the interest. All right, Angela, if there's nothing else you're not telling me about, that's five hundred pounds in all unaccounted for. What have you done with it?"

You gave a distasteful little shake of the head, a gesture that almost persuaded me it was common and vulgar to be bandying figures with you. I'm sure that's what you thought but you could think what you liked, I wasn't going to give way.

"I'm waiting."

"If I'd known you wanted me to account for every penny, I'd have written it all down. I'm sorry, darling, I said I was grateful to you and I thought that was enough. I didn't know you were going to be so meticular about how I spent it."

Particular or meticulous, was that? I didn't bother to correct you.

Your malapropisms didn't amuse me when they sprang out of bluster. "I'm not asking you to account for every penny. I'm asking you to account for five hundred pounds."

By now you had tugged your dress down but left it unbuttoned. "Do you want me to get ready or not, Roger? I thought we were going out to lunch."

"We'll go out for lunch when you've told me what's happened to that five hundred pounds."

You sighed a martyred sigh and commenced buttoning your dress, confident that I would accept your explanation as utterly reasonable and whisk you off for champagne and a Dover sole.

"I didn't spend it on myself, you know, if that's what you're thinking. There were other bills to pay. Some that I didn't bother to tell you about."

"What other bills?"

"Oh, the newsagent and that sort of thing." You added, catching my pull-the-other-one expression, "And then I still owed some rent to Mrs Scroggins."

"But I paid off your arrears." Three times over, I sometimes suspected.

"Not all of them."

"Well let's put it this way. I paid off everything you admitted to owing. Why should you want to tell me you owed less than you did?"

There were self-pitying tears in your voice now. "Because you'd been so generous to me and I didn't want to impose on you." Then, with no sense of self-contradiction, "*I* don't know where the money went, darling. It just went. I can't handle money, you know I can't. At least I didn't sell any of the nice things you bought me. I would have done at one time, you know. So I am improving, really I am." Brave smile through the tears.

I believe now you were telling the truth. You did just fritter the money away. Before you got the car you'd never taken a bus when there was a cab in sight, you'd buy big fat glossy magazines and toss them aside after browsing through a few pages. Some people who have had to live frugally at one time remain frugal all their lives. You abandoned frugality with gaiety when I started to help you out, as we euphemistically put it. You would throw tubes of toothpaste away half used, stockpile supplies of scented soaps and jars of make-up, toss a pair of stockings in the wastepaper bin when only one was laddered. I found it rather touching, to tell the truth – the little girl let loose in the sweetshop at last. Five hundred pounds soon goes.

I didn't think that then. I just couldn't see how you could have got through the money. A nasty suspicion entered my mind, prompted I should think by your having the monumental impudence to give yourself credit for not having sold the things I'd bought you, as you'd once had to sell the things you'd bought for yourself.

"I want you to tell me something, truthfully, Angie. Did you give any of that money to Cheevers?"

You solemnly took both my hands and fixed me steadily with your trust-me expression. "Of course I didn't, silly, and I wouldn't. I haven't seen Cheevers for months, so set your mind at rest."

Sorry, my love, that was asking the impossible. And I'd set the hare racing now, hadn't I?

"All right. What about the two hundred pounds I gave you three weeks ago to spend on clothes?"

"That wasn't for paying bills, it was for personal spending, wasn't it? You said I could buy what I liked with it."

"What you liked in the way of clothes."

"You didn't say that, darling."

"I'm sure I did but let it pass. Have you still got that money?"

"No."

"Then what did you spend it on?"

You assumed a mulish expression, slumping down on the sofa with your shoulders hunched, looking like a mutinous teenager refusing to say where she's been all night. Although I know I induced these lightning changes of mood with my persistent questioning – you would take so much of it and then make a snarling retreat, like a goaded little animal – they never failed to infuriate me.

"I'm not going to tell you," you said woodenly. "You never believe anything I say so I'm not going to tell you."

"Have you anything to show for it? Assuming you did spend it on yourself, that's fine, I don't care what you bought with it but you have to say what you did buy."

"I'm not going to tell you."

"But you didn't give any of it to anybody else?"

"If that's what you want to think you'll just have to go on thinking it." You rose with the air of one having granted an interview that has just ended. "Goodbye, Roger."

"What do you mean, goodbye? You don't think I'm leaving it like this, do you?"

"No, but I am. I've no food in the flat and I want my lunch." You picked up the coat you had thrown over the armchair the last time you came in and put it on. You picked up your bag and then hesitated, your courage evaporating. You probably only had about fifty pence in your purse. Certainly whatever you did have wouldn't run to Dover sole and champagne. I almost relented.

"Well, are you coming or not?"

"You just said goodbye, didn't you? You've squandered – what –

seven hundred quid of mine altogether, Angela. Do you seriously think after that I'm going to lash out another fifty or sixty pounds on lunch?"

"No, I'd be a poor investiture, wouldn't I?"

"Investment, you moron!" I flung after you, but you'd already slammed the door. I heard your footsteps ascending briskly to the street, then clacking away decisively. I waited for the sound of them returning, or at least faltering while you waited for me to catch up with you, but they didn't. I do hope you had some money about you. I never got round to asking whether you got any lunch that day.

It was the first time I'd ever been left alone in your flat. My first instinct of course was to go through it with a fine-tooth comb for letters, photographs, phone numbers, anything that you might have been holding back from me. But I knew that even in one of your flouncing-off moods you wouldn't have left me there had there been anything you didn't want me to see. My next instinct was to wreck the place. I realised that I was very angry, perhaps angrier than I had ever been with you. I couldn't quite make out why: whatever I may have said, I didn't give a damn about that money really. Your stupidity in getting through cash that was supposed to have settled your debts upset me, naturally, but no more than your stupid behaviour in all sorts of other ways upset me. I sat down at your typewriter to write you a whingeogram. Only on the fourth draft (I wonder if you read the other three, screwed up in your wastepaper bin? I would suppose not – no curiosity) did I understand what I was so angry about. I can still quote it verbatim:

My dear Angela,
Your stupidity I can swallow. I never wanted to be your accountant anyway. The only point of trying to clear your debts was to give you peace of mind. I should have realised that you could sleep quite easily in your bed even if you owed money all over London. You're so snugly secure in your insecurity, aren't you? – dependent on me, never trusting me, yet relying on me to bail you out. But you'll never get out of debt because it's in your nature to be in debt, just as it's in your nature to be late and forgetful and thoughtless and disorganised. I just hope you realise these traits are luxuries you can only afford so long as someone else is there to straighten you out from time to time. In other words, without me, or someone like me, to support you, you'd go to the wall within a month.

If you think that's a warning, it is. Forget the money I gave you for the finance company and to pay off your overdraft – if you want to be harassed by bailiffs and bank managers, that's your affair. The money I gave you to buy clothes is in a different category. It was a present, given to you with love, and it's as if I've just heard that you've pawned the watch I gave you or swapped your bluebird brooch for a windmill on a stick.

I don't know what the hell you've done with that two hundred pounds, Angie, but I want you to get it back. I don't care how you raise it but I don't want to see you until you've got that money together, when I'll consider taking *you* back. Don't bank on that, though.

Then I added my PS telling you how to get in touch, put the letter on your pillow where it would be sure to catch your eye, and let myself out of the flat, wondering when I'd see it and you again.

Feeling thoroughly depressed, I slouched off to that pub around the corner we went into once or twice, the Duke of Something, hoping to find you in it, but relieved to find you not. All I had to say to you was what I'd already put in my whingeogram, and you would almost certainly have flared up and walked out on me again, either that or goaded me to fury by woodenly misinterpreting what I had to say and refusing to understand that this semi-final to our last championship row had nothing really to do with money, any more than – oh, than the First World War was really very much to do with the assassination of the Archduke Ferdinand.

It had been a long time since I'd gone through that cat on hot bricks experience of waiting for days on end for you to get in touch with me. To prepare myself for the ordeal I got very quickly smashed – so smashed that I lurched back to your flat to have it out with you. It's a good thing you were out, for I was of a mood to call you names, something I've never ever done. I had to throw up in your basement area – sorry about that, couldn't find my key in time; but I don't suppose it's the first time it's happened in your life, considering the life you've had.

191

NINE

And so into limbo, mooning about the house, doing odd jobs, playing with Timothy, going for walks but not too far in case you were trying to contact me (discounting the two expeditions I made to Earls Court where I walked aimlessly around in the hope of accidentally bumping into you).

Judith thought I was behaving oddly. She didn't want me hanging about the house, that was obvious enough – going down to the kitchen for coffee one day I overheard her on the phone in her den murmuring something about "not awfully convenient at the moment" (sorry, Nick, but my need was greater) – but it was clear, too, that she was mildly worried about me. She brought it up at the first weekday lunch we'd had together in ages. Was I depressed? There was little point in denying that I was – even the baby had noticed it, the poor little sod cried whenever he saw me coming. Was there anything she could do? No, not a lot. What about my new-found interest in the antiques lark – had it waned? Not really, I said vaguely, I was just feeling a bit tired these days. Which was true enough: tired of not being able to go in any direction with you without ending up in a corner, tired of rows, tired of our relationship and itching for it to start up again. This was after two days.

Judith said seriously, "I'm no psychiatrist, but it has occurred to me that you might be suffering from delayed shock. After all, your whole life's been churned up."

"Yes, I know." But I didn't mean what she meant.

"Doing that stint for Gunby was the best thing that could have happened to you after your split with Charles, because it kept you on the go and occupied. But now that's gone I think it's all beginning to hit you."

"Very possibly."

"You don't think you should talk to someone about it?"

"It'll pass." I told myself the same thing, being in one of those black moods where I was convinced I would never hear from you again, or at least not for the fortnight or so it would probably take you to raise the money, and that seemed even longer.

192

I rang you, of course, three or four times, firmly telling myself in my weakness that I would just neutrally ask how you were getting on; but all I got were wrong numbers and crossed lines. That was good for me: your indolence in not having the phone repaired sustained me in a sufficient state of irritation to keep missing you at bay. I did miss you, but only because I wanted to sit you down and rant at you. Wanting someone to be angry with can't possibly be healthy, though it may be therapeutic. But I miss our angry scenes along with everything else.

Five days and nine hours and then came the signal I'd instructed you to give me when you'd got that money together – three rings on my telephone, hang up, and wait for me to call you back. Unfortunately we were in the middle of one of Judith's dinner parties with Nick and a spare part he'd wheeled along for appearance's sake. Judith had got the idea that it would soothe my nerves to play bridge after dinner and so, nerves jangling, it was half past eleven before I was able to make the excuse that I needed to walk off a headache. I left them drinking their coffee and doubtless discussing the edgy state I was in, and walked down to the box near the church from which I'd so often called you, or tried to.

I told you and told you to get that telephone seen to, didn't I? Had you not been so bovinely lethargic I should never have got that crossed line and overheard that conversation. We should still have had our monumental row, since that was by no means the only ingredient of it, but we might have survived – just.

When I say crossed line, I don't know whether technically that's what it was. Sometimes when I tried to call you I'd get wrong numbers, other times I'd find myself listening in to two complete strangers, but it had never before happened that I'd dialled myself into one of your own telephone conversations. Whether it was a freak or not I couldn't say. Maybe it could have happened any time that I chanced to ring you just as you chanced to be talking to Belle or one of your shadowy girlfriends or the laundry or whoever. But it had to be this particular call, didn't it?

I recognised that minor public school off-cockney disc-jockey voice in one, and instantly had an image of you both – he in shirt sleeves with his tie loosened, receiver crooked on his shoulder and a tinkling glass in his hand, you sprawled on your stomach across your bed, your raised heels swinging coquettishly, the telephone receiver cushioned in your pillow. I saw it so vividly that I might have been spying simultaneously through your respective windows.

It was an odd, vicarious thrill, listening to you talking to Cheevers. There was no sense of shock or betrayal – that would come later – simply excitement at finding you out at last, the excitement of the chase I suppose. It was a cheap sensation and I was ashamed of it after

193

I'd hung up and calmed down and it had sunk in that nothing would ever be the same with us again.

As lovers' or ex-lovers' tête-à-têtes go, it had little in it for the eavesdropper, as a matter of fact. I gathered that he'd rung you or you'd rung him – I still can't be absolutely sure which – simply for a chat. A regular chat by the sound of it, though just how regular it was difficult to judge. You seemed to be catching up on one another's news.

Petulance flickered into my swirl of emotion as, once I'd established beyond doubt whom you were talking to, I heard you, in response to my dialling which had presumably interrupted your conversation, explain that your phone had been playing up lately. "The trouble is," you were saying, "the engineer has to have abscess to the flat."

"Access," corrected Cheevers, and you said, "I meant access" and you both tittered, and I was stabbed with jealousy. For no good reason now that I came to think of it, I'd always assumed your verbal dyslexia was a private joke only to us. Perhaps because you'd said it was.

"And I'm never in," you added.

"Out on the toot, are we?" chaffed Cheevers. I wished I'd had a tape recorder with me. I wanted to go over these exchanges again and again, sifting each nuance and inflection. Was he being flirtatious or merely familiar? Knowing? Teasing? Jealous? Avuncular? No, not avuncular, at five or six years your junior.

"Let's say I'm out a good deal more than I used to be," you said. Another stab, a deeper one this time, at the insinuation that you were harking back to times when you never went anywhere, but waited for Cheevers to come round and lay you whenever he felt like it. Was your tone wistful? Spiteful? Triumphant? Regretful? Smug?

I had to stop this, it was crazy. Far better hang up and go home and take it out on the brandy decanter than stand here in a windy, smelly phone box, lacerating myself. Or supposing I interrupted the call? Now that could have changed the course of history, couldn't it, my love?

"Oh, I'm quite a traveller since I got the car," you were saying. Since you got the car. Not since Roger got you the car. "For instance, I have to go up to Manchester on Thursday. Belle's getting married, did you know?"

"So you said."

So you said when? Just a few moments ago, or in some recent conversation? Could be either. I was monitoring that call with the zeal of a foreign agent under the floorboards but I lacked the impartiality and levelheadedness to be able to draw any real conclusions as to how often you spoke to one another these days, why you spoke, whether you still saw one another.

Your talk didn't seem to have any particular point to it, that I had to concede, although that was a dismaying factor in itself. You weren't declaring that you missed him, weren't trying to edge him into inviting you out to lunch or dinner or coming round to your flat. You sounded like two friends – the situation you once confessed you'd very much wanted with him.

You went on talking about Belle. He said he couldn't imagine her settling down and you said neither could you but she'd reached the conclusion that she was getting a bit long in the tooth for playing the field. Had she said that or had you thought it for her, with that curious doppelgänger knack you had of putting your feelings and words and actions into Belle's persona, that self-induced vicariousness that freed you to observe with detachment how someone might react to the kind of person you were if they knew you were that kind of person? I don't know. Other mutual friends were mentioned, none of whom I'd heard of. I was willing you to give something away, to incriminate yourself, but you wouldn't.

In fact, aside from you having this chit-chat at all, the only thing I could really pin on you was what you said when you were about to ring off – "I'd better hang up now, I'm expecting Belle to ring about the wedding arrangements." No you weren't, you were expecting me to ring. Why couldn't you have told him that? You said you'd already told him you were in love – why didn't your lover get a mention, not necessarily by name, during the whole conversation?

Yes, and why did Cheevers say "Hope to see you soon?" even if you did reply, "Well, I'm a bit busy these days"? If you'd told him firmly that you weren't ever going to see him again, as you claimed to have done when you met him after our return from Venice, why did he still entertain hopes of seeing you soon? That one would certainly go on the agenda.

You finally hung up. One thing I hadn't done was to time your call, but you were on the phone a hell of a time, and when I dialled your number again and got through without difficulty, I had hardly opened my mouth before you chastised me for ringing you so late. Your tone was cold. I contrasted it, probably exaggeratedly, with the warmth in your voice when you were speaking to Cheevers. I chilled my own voice in response.

"I rang you as soon as I could. First we had people to dinner and then when I did manage to get out your phone was permanently engaged."

"Yes, I'm sorry, I was talking to Belle about the wedding arrangements."

The words "You fucking liar" were on my lips but I deleted them. If we had the row now I should run out of coins before I had said a quarter of what I had to say to you. Unless you would accept an abusive transfer call? It was tempting to find out.

"Why am I ringing you, anyway?"

"You told me to contact you when I'd got that money together. What do you want me to do with it?"

I'd expected contrition or something like it, but no, you were defiant and sulky. Another phrase formed: "Stick it up your bum." Instead I told you I'd be round the next afternoon after having lunch with my bank manager (who, I might tell you, though it is utterly irrelevant by now, read me the Riot Act about my spending), and rang off before I said anything I might regret. Anything I might regret I wanted to say in comfort over a bottle of champagne.

And how many bottles did we get through? Five, was it? Certainly all you had in the flat, and I usually saw to it that you had half a dozen in hand, because we finished up on brandy. That was a mistake. It was all a mistake. You were a mistake.

Your mood was still cold and belligerent, your welcome cautious coming on hostile. Yet you had dressed up for me, and put on your bluebird brooch, and you had on high-heeled shoes instead of the mules you usually wore around the flat, because you knew they made your legs look good. Maybe your unfriendly demeanour indicated nervousness. Or maybe it was simply an instant reflection of mine, which was sullen and brooding. Anyway, it didn't stop us laying into the first bottle of champagne.

As I opened it, you rummaged in your bag and produced a bulging white envelope. Instead of handing it to me you went and placed it on your desk, distancing yourself from its contents. You really did find money sordid.

"You needn't count it," you said, as to a blackmailer. "Was it two hundred or two hundred and fifty?"

"You mean you don't know?" I bridled unnecessarily. Start as you mean to go on, that was my motto.

"There's two hundred and fifty there, anyway," you said.

"As a matter of fact it was only two hundred."

"Then I'll take fifty back."

"You can take it all back. I don't want the money – I just want to see it used for its intended purpose."

You gave a mirthless laugh that wouldn't have shamed a good rep actress. "You seriously think I could go out and enjoy spending your money on clothes after everything you've said to me about it?"

I raked my memory for what I had said. To the best of my recollection, very little. In fact I was surprised at my own restraint.

We were now well on our collision course, both drinking far too quickly in fast nervous gulps. What a pity we should have put champagne to such use when it had accompanied so much pleasure.

"Please yourself," I shrugged. "But it's your money after all. You earned it."

"How do you know I earned it?" you asked sharply.

"Well didn't you?"

The familiar answer. "I'm not going to tell you." You swirled your champagne angrily, drained the glass, and poured another for us both. This small courtesy, on your part and mine, continued all through the biggest blazing quarrel we have ever had.

I guessed you were just being provoking. "Well, I assume you didn't steal it and I hope you didn't borrow it, so how did you get the money together?"

"I'm not going to tell you." That was the second time, and there was a third one, following my sharp "Angela! I'm asking you!" That really did mean you weren't going to tell me, if I pestered you all night. You didn't so much close your mind as seal it.

"You didn't get it from Cheevers, by any chance?"

You seemed genuinely incredulous. "Are you insane?" I think perhaps I was a little by now. Obviously you hadn't got it from Cheevers – nothing in last night's phone conversation with him even remotely suggested that you could have done any such thing. I was only trawling to see what I could dredge up.

"First you ask me if I gave the money to Cheevers, then when I get it back you ask if he gave it to me! You've got Cheevers on the brain, Roger!"

Yes, of course I had. "All right," I plunged on with the same reckless disregard for the first-hand evidence I had, "did he procure the money for you?" Silence. "Do you know what I mean by procure, Angela?"

"I'm not a child."

"You are a child."

"I'm not going to answer insulting questions."

"Then answer this one. If you didn't get it from him or through him, how did you get it? I mean, if you earned the money temping for instance, why can't you just come out and say so?"

You looked triumphantly amused – "Roger, you wrote in that offensive letter you left on my pillow, thank you very much, that you didn't care how I raised the money so long as I got it back – when, so you wrote, you'd consider taking *me* back. You can ask till you're blue in the face but I'm not going to tell you what you said you didn't want to know, and as for taking me back, perhaps the question is whether I'm prepared to take *you* back."

And I still don't know how you got that two hundred and fifty together, or why you wouldn't tell me. Stubbornness, was it? If you

197

wanted me to think you had followed Belle into the escort game for an evening or two you couldn't have been more explicit except with a Polaroid snap. Had you, Angie? And hadn't you dabbled in it before, telling me about Belle's involvement only to test the water as to my attitude to that sort of thing? Your experiences with Cheevers, to drag his name in again, with that bundle of ties and so on, suggested that you had. Common sense tells me that you had. Wanting you not to have had anything to do with that kind of life tells me that you didn't. You might have been able to distort the truth, my girl, but I could twist it round corners when I had to.

All right, then, on to the next round.

"When did you last see Cheevers, as a matter of fact?"

"You know when, I've told you when."

The trap. "When did you last speak to him?"

"What do you mean? The same time, of course." You sounded so genuinely bewildered that the possibility crossed my mind that I could conceivably be mistaken. There'd been other men in your life besides Cheevers, and that assumed prole accent was by no means unique to him.

But I stared you out. "I'm not going to play cat and mouse with you, Angela. You spoke to him last night, at length. I rang you and somehow got plugged into your conversation. Don't blame me for eavesdropping, blame yourself for being too lackadaisical to get your phone repaired."

This last sentence was simply makeweight while you flickered between outright denial and defiant admission. Momentarily the needle hovered between the two.

"Who says it was Cheevers?"

I couldn't tell you I recognised his voice. Double standards, was that? I demanded straightforwardness from you but I could be pretty devious in return.

"Wasn't it?" I hedged.

Almost audibly, you sighed off your cloak of evasion. Now you were stripped for action. "So what if it was? Why can't you come straight out and admit you've been tapping my telephone?"

And we were into our marathon last bout, round after endless round of it, lunging, lurching, prodding, poking, and usually below the belt. Like your conversation with Cheevers, it was crucial but not all that enlightening. Everything we had to say to one another we'd said before, that was the truth of it, though not at such length and never with such bald cruelty. One of your guerilla tactics was simply to agree with a proposition, to confirm suspicions, to prove me right. It was unbearable. As for example when I accused you of not having got over Cheevers, even if you weren't in love with him any more.

"All right, I haven't, what's wrong with that?"

"But you've pretended you had."

"All right, I was pretending."

"So you're still in love with him?"

"All right, I'm still in love with him."

And you'd leave it there, leave me there, beached, not knowing absolutely whether you were telling the truth at last or, as seemed more likely, simply playing mental ju-jitsu because you couldn't secure a good enough hold to put you on the offensive. When you did feel confident of your position, as on the subject of my possessiveness, my paranoia, my hypocrisy, you gave it all you'd got. As when I tried to get out of you whether you'd rung Cheevers or he'd rung you:

"That's for you to find out, isn't it? You're very good at knowing what I'm thinking, what I'm doing, surely you can work it out for yourself."

"OK, then I'll assume you rang him."

"All right, then I did. Don't you ever ring Judith?"

"Not simply for a chat, no."

"And she never rings you – say from Manchester?"

"You know she does, but if you're trying to draw parallels we're not talking about Cheevers ringing you for a chat, we're talking about you ringing him for a chat."

"What's the difference?"

"Well, if he'd happened to ring you, I could understand you having a polite social conversation with him."

"How very nice of you. But you can't bear the thought of my ringing him because I was lonely, because I had no one to talk to, because I hadn't seen you for a week, because when I do see you you're no sooner here than it's time for you to go home to your fucking wife and your fucking family and leave me on my own again. Why don't you lock me in a box when you've had enough of my company, then you could be quite sure I wasn't doing anything you didn't approve of?"

Your round, I fancy. Scowling, I poured champagne, and like two pugilists swigging from their water bottles we soothed our parched throats before battling on. Or sometimes we'd simply sip and sulk for a while before dredging up another grievance. We had tacitly agreed topics that were picked off one by one. Money, your irresponsibility with. Money, my obsession with. Truth, your disregard for. Truth, my double standards concerning. They were full-scale debates, one of us leading in attack, the other defending, then each summing up before reversing our positions. The past: your determination to bury it. The past: my determination to disinter it. My sexual insecurity, your sexual ambivalence. Another winning round for you, that.

"Roger, in the last however many months it's been since we met – "
"Sixteen." "Thank you, I might have known you'd count them. In the last sixteen months I've never slept with anybody else or wanted to sleep with anybody else, which is more than you can say. Isn't that good enough for you?" No. I wanted to know if it was the longest period you'd ever been sexually faithful to anyone, and if it was I would want to know why you had formerly been so promiscuous and if it wasn't I would want to know why not and whether Cheevers held that particular record. I just wanted the row to fester on, and so did you. We were bloodletting. We racked our brains to think up more grudges and grievances, more scabs to pick.

But no glass was thrown, and the night did have its mildly farcical elements. As if recognising that we ought to pace ourselves, we allowed proper intervals. In the middle of one of my dissertations on your former flat and my exclusion from it, you rose and went into the bathroom where I heard the taps running. I sat there continuing my angry monologue in my head while you had your bath – you emerged thirty minutes later, fully dressed again, and all guns blazing with a comeback you'd thought up while soaping yourself, and so devastating that I've forgotten it. Then there'd be sudden and ostentatious fits of newspaper reading, visits to the lavatory, watching television even. How ridiculous that was – there we were in the middle of a re-run of our famous long-running set piece about your lack of organisation and other such quirks when you suddenly got up and switched on the ten o'clock news. We both sat there staring at the screen, from time to time making pertinent observations about this or that news item as one might to a casual fellow-viewer in a hotel lounge; then as the news ended you switched off the set and before you had reached your chair again you were back in the fray with a sarcastic suggestion that I might like to make out a timetable to account for your every waking minute. Don't think I've never thought of that. An hour or so later we had an exchange that went something like this:

"You know what your trouble is, Angela, don't you?"

"Are you hungry?"

"Pardon?"

"I'm going to make some sandwiches."

And off you trotted into your little kitchenette, reappearing a few moments later to ask, "What *is* my trouble, then?"

I'd been about to say, "Permanent PMT" but you were holding the breadknife. "Never mind," I said with only half-assumed weariness.

You brought in two plates of cheese and tomato sandwiches and we sat there and munched them and chuntered on, spitting crumbs when the going got vehement.

It would have been around five o'clock when I'd arrived at the flat. It was well after midnight before the supply of champagne ran out and with it, the argument. Punchdrunk, heads lolling crazily, we slumped among the debris of empty bottles and sandwich crusts like a couple of winos. We must have been a disgusting sight but we hadn't finished yet.

"Come here," I slurred, too far gone in drink to curb the insane impulse that had stirred unbidden in my weary body, and far, far too gone to suppress it.

"What? Why?"

"Come here."

I said we never kissed again after the little peck I gave you when we were having that spat about the parking permit form – the springwell for the great Niagara of hate and bitterness that had come pouring out tonight. What we did do was quite shameful really. You rose as in a trance and staggered towards me. I lurched to meet you. We threw our arms around one another and, each a dead weight upon the other, sank to the ground where we groped and fumbled clumsily, as uncoordinated in our drunken state as a pair of teenagers. It became a kind of mutual rape. I pinned you down on the floor among the champagne empties and we made love lovelessly but urgently, both taking, neither giving. We both needed it, got nothing from it, and afterwards sank into a drink-sodden sleep, not touching.

It was after three when we stirred. The room was cold, and neither of us had matches to light the gas fire. Guilty and embarrassed we re-arranged our dishevelled clothing.

It was time I was off – I'd done all the damage I could here and Judith might wake up to attend to the baby and wonder where the hell I was at this hour. Time you were in bed too – I remembered it was Belle's wedding the next day, or rather this day.

"I'm going to have a brandy. Do you want one?" you asked in a flat, unconciliatory voice.

"You have to be up early."

"I know that." You poured brandy into our sticky champagne glasses, filling them to the brim.

"Do you think you should drive up to Manchester? Why don't you go on the train?"

"Yes, I will."

"Shall I help you with the fare? Take it from that two hundred and fifty you've got and I'll pay you back later."

In that same level, uncompromising, frighteningly unhysterical drone you said, "I don't want anything from you, Roger, and there isn't going to be any later."

There would have been, though. I should have come round, as indeed I did come round but you weren't there, and we might have

201

patched things up or not patched things up but we had entered another of our new phases now and there was no going back on it.

We drank in silence. We had nothing left to say. It had not been very fruitful. We didn't know anything about ourselves that we hadn't known already, except that we'd pulled our relationship to bits like some exotic and sinister and mysterious bloom, petal by petal, to see how it worked, and now it lay in pieces on the floor among the empty champagne bottles and the crumpled knickers you were now suddenly too bashful to retrieve and put on again.

I knocked back my brandy and winced, my throat rubbed raw with alcohol and spleen. I couldn't think of any parting shot, not even an appropriate way to say goodbye. I rose and put on my coat.

"Well, enjoy the wedding," I said.

You didn't get up as you usually did when I was leaving, even if you were in bed. Swirling the brandy in your glass as you did with champagne sometimes, you said, "I don't regret anything, you know, Roger."

I couldn't handle poignancy just now. I would put it in store, to deal with later. "Thank you for that," I said.

You added quickly, seeing how I'd misunderstood, "I mean this evening, about the things I said. I meant them all. No regrets."

"Oh, I see." There was no need to say that, Angie, particularly since it couldn't possibly be true. It was just a last twist of the knife. And now, in a moment of alcoholic lucidity, I did think of something to say. "I doubt whether you've ever regretted anything in your life, Angela. If you had, you'd be a much nicer person." Famous last words. I don't know whether you heard me. You'd closed your eyes, and sleep with you was instant. I left, closing the door very quietly behind me.

I was round first thing in the morning, of course. I was sure you'd oversleep and either you weren't answering your phone or I was getting wrong numbers and they weren't answering. I had no idea what kind of reception I'd get from you or for that matter what kind of reception you'd get from me. I certainly had no intention of either re-opening the inquest or resuscitating the corpse – I meant only to see that you were up, make you a cup of tea maybe, and leave. But you'd gone. Your bed hadn't been slept in so you must have spent what remained of the night in your chair. The flat stank of booze. It was just as I'd left it a few hours ago, the bottles still littering the floor, the brandy bottle on the coffee table along with our champagne glasses, mine empty, yours half full. There were clothes strewn about the place, the residue of your hurried packing. The railway timetable, dog-eared from frequent reference during our hotel odyssey, lay open at the Manchester pages on your desk. It gave me a pang, that did – so much of a pang that I had the sudden wild notion of hurrying to Euston and seeing you off. I thought better of it at once, having no idea what train you might have been on, and anyway I didn't want you thinking I'd come running after you. As if you would.

But the sight of that well-thumbed timetable had done its work. I felt a melancholy glow at the remembrance of things past and regretted now that our goodbyes had been such bitter ones. (And did you regret having no regrets?) I resolved to write you a last letter, not a whingeogram, wishing you well. I tidied up the flat, or anyway cleared away the debris and hung up your clothes, and let myself out. I did think of leaving the key you'd given me on your desk, but that would have been cruelly final. A letter could be sweetly final.

I was going to take myself home to write it, up here in my study where instead I'm now writing this. But as I reached Earls Court tube station the idea struck me that everything I had to say to you now was in that song I'd tried to remember, "Mansions I can wish you", if only I could find it. On an impulse I took a tube to Leicester Square and went to a sheet music shop in Charing Cross Road. They didn't have it. At a push, I thought, I could get hold of the cast album and copy it down but then Judith might be around and want to know what I was up to and I wanted it to be there waiting for you when you got back from Manchester. So I tried three or four more music shops, then on the recommendation of one of them went to the drama department at Foyle's to see if they had the printed score. I wanted you to know all this, Angie, though I couldn't figure out any way of telling you, I wanted you to know the trouble I was going to, to find that song for you, to find Our Song. It took me two hours to track it down, would you believe that? Foyle's didn't have it, but they put me on to Chappell's the music publishers, just off Oxford Street, and there at last I found the score of *Guys and Dolls*, and it was as I was coming out of Chappell's clutching my prize with an absurd sense of triumph at my last mission for you accomplished, that I bumped into my old flame Anita, aka the Merry Widow.

You never showed the smallest interest in the Merry Widow, my sole extra-marital fling before you came upon the scene. No reason why you should – it was a good six years ago. You probably couldn't have remembered who you were sleeping with yourself six years ago, Cheevers always excepted of course. She was a plump, jolly personality of about my own age with the brassy looks of a barmaid. You would never have guessed that she was one of the smartest copywriters in the business when we were at McIntyre, Pike & Lipton together. It was one of those situations where a couple of people work together for years, then one of them moves on, then they meet up again and see one another in an altogether fresh light. She'd recently been divorced, so I suppose that helped, while I was simply going through a bored patch. We took to lunching casually together, having casual after-work drinks together, then after a while we just as casually found ourselves back at her flat in Fulham, and after a few quite pleasant weeks of that there was the smooth abortion I think I've already mentioned, then soon after she told me she'd met someone who wanted to marry her so that was that. Fun while it lasted, no hard feelings. I came across her in the Marquis of Granby every so often and we had the status of old friends. I wondered, greeting her there in Oxford Street, whether I would ever be old friends with you.

She hadn't really been a widow when we'd first known one another, it was a nickname she went by because she often dressed in black to tone down the natural brassiness that oozed out of her. But now she was. She'd married her man and they'd had a very happy life together but now he was dead, six months ago. But she was as merry a widow as ever. Impulsively I invited her to lunch, choosing a modest Italian place near at hand where I've never been with you. It was, as I expected, a jolly lunch, we chatted easily about all manner of topics that wouldn't interest you at all, while never touching on our old affair, not that that would have held your interest either. We had two bottles of wine, champagne not being offered I'd like you to know. Anita lived in Notting Hill now, in a pretty little pink-washed doll's house behind the Gate Cinema. How do I know this? Because I went there, Angie. I want to tell you.

She had rather a lot of shopping so at the end of the meal I suggested we pick up a cab and I'd drop her off and take the cab on to Hammersmith to get the tube. That's what I meant to do. That's what I would have done had we not had that dreadful scene the night before – that's in the event that I would have asked her to lunch in the first place.

"You can get the tube from Notting Hill Gate," said Anita. I realised she was quite tipsy, having sunk a couple of large gins before we started on the wine and brandy. "It's a long time since you came back for coffee."

"Too long," I said. And it was only then it crossed my mind to sleep with her, I swear.

In the event my anticipation was premature, because when we reached her place she really did start to make coffee.

I'm going to go on telling you this. I said boldly, "Are we going to take it upstairs, then?"

Anita gave me a good-humoured look. "Coffee, I said."

"Ah, but did you mean coffee?" To tell you the truth, I hoped by now that she did. No face would be lost. I would drink my coffee and go.

"If we do go to bed, dear," said the Merry Widow evenly, as if we were discussing whether to go to the cinema or not, "it'll be because there's not been a man over that threshold for six months, and because I'd rather come out of purdah with an old friend than a new one. In other words, we're not starting up where we left off, agreed?"

And so we went to bed and made love, I responding with mechanical animation to the animated mechanics of someone deprived of sex for six months. I remembered nothing of her body, the plumpness gone to fat now; I compared it unfavourably with yours but otherwise thought of you hardly at all, except to wonder if your own method of dealing with our situation would be to make a casual liaison at Belle's wedding party before your return to London. The best man again? No, I wasn't going to think about you.

She went downstairs and brought up a jug of coffee, a bottle of brandy and the *Standard* which had come through the door. I leafed through the paper idly, more to hide my post-coital nakedness than because I was interested in what was going on in the world. It was not your day, Angie. Normally you should have been on the front page but a big fire in Covent Garden claimed that. You were on page three, and I can just hear you joking, "Coo! I'm a page three girl!" A jack-knifing articulated lorry on the M62 outside Huddersfield, West Yorkshire. Five dead including one London woman, Miss Angela Caxton of Banks Place, Islington (for of course you hadn't bothered to change your address in your Filofax), pitched through the windscreen of her white Volkswagen Polo. How many times have I told you to wear your seatbelt?

And what in God's name were you doing on the M62? You must have stuck with the M1 all the way up past Wakefield instead of turning on to the M6 near Birmingham, you cuckoo.

The pile-up was at ten fifteen a.m. To have got that far on that route you can't have set off later than half past six. Christ, allowing time to pack and doll yourself up and your usual faffing around, you can only have had about two and a half hours' sleep. And on top of all that booze. If I was still pissed when I woke at eight, you must have been reeling when you went out to your car.

I'd worried about you driving back from the wedding drunk. I'd never thought of you driving to it drunk.

Ten fifteen. I must have been in your flat at that time, tidying up the empties. The railway timetable – you must at least have toyed with the idea of doing something sensible for once in your young life and going by train. I was so sure you had I didn't even bother to check whether your precious Volkswagen was parked on its accustomed yellow line.

I gave the Merry Widow no sign that anything was wrong, apart, that is, from heading groggily across her tiny landing to the lavatory where I was noisily sick. She put it down to too much red wine at lunch, gave me a glass of brandy to settle my stomach, and sent me on my way. I was a shipwreck that had passed in the night. Sorry and all that, Angie, but as you would have said, it wasn't important, it didn't matter.

Sorry, too, that I left the score of *Guys and Dolls* back at the Merry Widow's, in all the confusion of your dying. But I did look up the lyric of Our Song in the shop and the bit I was trying to remember for you goes like this:

> Mansions I can wish you, seven
> Footmen all in red
> And calling cards upon a silver tray.
> But more I cannot wish you
> Than to wish you find your love,
> Your own true love, this day.

I suppose in the circumstances I needn't have taken the trouble to hunt it down, but I'm still glad I did.

Between leaving the Merry Widow's and arriving at Ealing Church Grove around dinner time I couldn't give you any coherent account of my movements. I walked about a good deal, I do know. I think I walked down from Notting Hill as far as Shepherds Bush tube station, then the next thing I'm aware of is tramping across Ealing Common. I'm trying to remember my feelings, after the gut-churning impact of your news. My first recognisable reaction was one of acute anxiety. Would I be involved in all this? Would the police be round? How much would Judith have to be told? That's not as God-awful selfish as it looks. Unfocused panic is a common immediate response to the death of a loved one. I want you to believe that I concentrated my panic on considerations of myself as a way of preventing myself from thinking of you dead on a motorway hard shoulder. I want myself to believe that too.

Then there was anger and frustration. Anger at your stupidity, your lack of consideration for yourself, never mind anyone else, your final act of self-destruction. Frustration at what you'd left me with. I was trying to unlock you, Angie – why did you go off with the key? All the things I longed to know about you that now I'll never know. But then you wouldn't have told me anyway. You didn't have the intellectual machinery to see how one set of circumstances in your life could possibly link up with and throw its shadow or its reflection upon another, how your life with Cheevers, for example, could have any bearing on your life with me. It was as incomprehensible to you as the suggestion that your overdraft had anything to do with your being short of the rent. Or that our getting through five bottles of champagne and a hefty slug of brandy in one night had any connection with your hurtling into an articulated lorry the next morning.

I'd known you sixteen months, I should have had something to go on by now. I've tried to put the jigsaw together but all I'm left with is most of the edges done and a jumble of pieces, some of them interlocking, most of them not, and some quite obviously forced into the wrong position. I don't know what to do with this infuriating puzzle. I can't go on shuffling those pieces aimlessly about like an old man with his dominoes. Mysteries are supposed to have solutions.

I went straight to bed when I got home, telling Judith I had a headache. She told me later that I looked in a terrible way and she thought I was steering my way round a nervous breakdown. Very likely. During our marathon row you told me I was insane and as I said I think there might be something in that too, it could just prove that I am a little mad by now. Meanwhile I was exhausted. I'd like to tell you I lay awake all night thinking about you but I didn't. I slept like a log.

You didn't make much of a splash in the morning papers either, my love – upstaged by an air crash this time. I thought Judith might perhaps spot your name in the small print of the report in the *Daily Telegraph* but she was in a hurry to get to her word-processor and barely glanced at the paper. Then I wondered if Belle might be trying to contact me. If she was, she didn't succeed – more probably she waltzed off on honeymoon with no idea why you'd missed her wedding. The police didn't come round, of course – no reason why they should, I realised in calmer mood: my name and phone number were in your Filofax but so were those of scores of other men, many of them I suspect former lovers whose names you had rather pathetically copied out of your old address book as "contacts." Nobody got in touch with me, in short nothing happened. It was, compatible with your will o' the wisp personality, as if you'd never existed.

I wept once. I was mooching about on Ealing Common that same morning, fretting obsessively over what to do about your flat. Mr Hakim still had two months' rent in hand but sooner or later he'd have to be located and given notice that you weren't coming back. Then there were all the possessions I'd accumulated around you there. I'd just abandon them, I guessed, bequeath them to the next tenant. There was nothing there I wanted to claim as a memento of you – all your lately-acquired bits and pieces were mementoes of me, of my compulsive desire to do things for you, of my superimposing my personality upon yours. How weird and sad it was, I thought, that you didn't have a single relative in the world to come and take all that stuff away and give your clothes to Oxfam where many of them were supposed to have been sent in the first place, and tidy up after you; and that led me into coming face to face with the image I'd been desperately trying to avoid with all this pragmatic fussing over straightening up your affairs – my Angie lying there in her coffin, with no-one to mourn her. It was unbearable. I sat on a park bench and buried my face in my hands and sobbed uncontrollably. And then I felt worse.

I would have come to your funeral, my love, whenever and wherever it was (not the inquest, though – I don't want to know any more about how you died). I got back to Ealing Church Grove towards lunchtime and collapsed, literally and melodramatically, sprawling full length across the hall and banging my head, so I'm told, against the claw foot of the marble console table. Total emotional exhaustion, that's all, but enough to get me whisked off by ambulance for a thorough going over by a heart specialist – you don't want to know about all that. I was kept under sedation for a week. The nurse reported that I kept crying out "Tell Cheevers!" Judith, remembering this to be the name of the chap I was supposed to have sold her Volkswagen to, asked later, "What did you want to tell him – something about the car?" "Yes," I said, "but it doesn't matter now." I wanted to tell him to go to your funeral. Perhaps he did.

I'll find you, kitten. I'll come to see you and bring you flowers.

Was it love? How do I know, when I've never been along that way before? But if it wasn't, I'd like to know what the hell it was I caught from you. I told myself often enough that it was sexual obsession, but does that have to exclude love? Can't it be an ingredient of it? Why was every emotion heightened if it wasn't love, negative as well as positive – my anger was never angrier, my frustration more frustrating, my curiosity sharper. And I was never more alive, and never happier, and never unhappier.

She thinks I'm writing a novel. I am. I'm trying to transmute you into fiction, make you as unreal in remembrance as you were in unreal life. You'll be easier to live with that way, my love. I'll manage it. It'll take time of course, but who cares, eternity doesn't last forever.